The
Cama-i Book

Fairbanks

Yukon River

KUSKOKWIM MOUNTAINS

Kuskokwim River

USSR
UNITED STATES

CANADA
UNITED STATES

Emmonak
Alakanuk
Kotik

Mountain Village
St Mary's

Chevak

Hooper Bay

Nunapitchuk Akiachak Aniak
Tuluksak
Bethel Akiak
Kwethluk

NUNIVAK
ISLAND

Kuskokwim Bay

Goodnews Bay

Togiak Aleknagik
Iliamna Lake
Iliamna

Anchorage

GULF of ALASKA

Naknek

Togiak Bay

Clark's Point

Kvichak Bay
Egegik

KATMAI NATIONAL MONUMENT

KATMAI
VOL

AFOGNAK ISLAND

Port Lions

Kodiak

KODIAK ISLAND

Karluk

Larsen Bay

Old Harbor

BERING
SEA

PACIFIC OCEAN

Alaska Peninsula

ALEUT

Shelikof Strait

RANGE

Perryville

ALASKA

MILES
0 25 50 100

N

Hueber

The
Cama-i Book

Kayaks, dogsleds, bear hunting, bush pilots,
smoked fish, mukluks, and other
traditions of Southwestern Alaska

Edited with an Introduction by ANN VICK

Anchor Books
Anchor Press / Doubleday
Garden City, New York
1983

THE CAMA-I BOOK Editors: Ann Vick
James Chaliak
Kurt Jaehning
David Kubiak
Michael Murray
Debra Vanasse

ANN VICK continued her work with Cama-i and Foxfire while Director of Education Programs for the Alaska Native Foundation and is currently a partner with Richard Lee in the Education and Resources Group (ERG), an Alaskan firm working with rural education and economic development programs.

Library of Congress Cataloging in Publication Data
Main entry under title:

The Cama-i book.

1. Alaska—Social life and customs—Addresses, essays, lectures. 2. Handicraft—Alaska—Addresses, essays, lectures. 3. Country life—Alaska—Addresses, essays, lectures. I. Vick, Ann.
F910.C35 979.8
AACR2
ISBN 0-385-15522-0 Hardcover
ISBN 0-385-15212-4 Paperbound
Library of Congress Catalog Card Number 82–45127

Portions of this book first appeared in *Kalikaq Yugnek, Kwikpagmiut, Tundra Marsh, Uutuqtwa,* and *Elwani.*

Printed in the United States of America
The Anchor Press edition is the first publication of THE CAMA-I BOOK in book form. It is published simultaneously in cloth and paper covers.
Anchor Press edition: 1983
First Edition

This book is dedicated to the generations—
to those elders who speak
and to those young people who listen

Contents

YUKON-KUSKOKWIM REGION

Foreword

I can't think of a single state more fascinating than Alaska. The whole development of Foxfire/Cama-i has been so rich and so important and so much more difficult in Alaska because of weather, travel, and cost that it makes an amazing story.

During one of my earliest trips to Alaska, I met an Eskimo woman named Emily Ivanoff Brown who told me of an event I've never forgotten. Determined to educate Natives to white ways, the federal government shipped thousands of Eskimo, Indian, and Aleut children—Emily among them—from their villages to boarding schools where they were punished if caught speaking their Native dialects, and where they were taught to turn their backs on nearly every aspect of their former lives. All that they had learned from their parents and grandparents was to be forgotten.

The job was done well. When I met Emily, she had already retired from one career and was, in her seventies, part of a team at the University of Alaska in Fairbanks working through the Alaska Native Language Center to record and reclaim those Native dialects that were left and to reteach them to new generations of Native young people, many of whom labored over the strange words and pronunciations in the same way I once labored over Latin.

Later, I spent enough time in villages with Ann Vick to witness firsthand the enormity of some of the other changes taking place. The rapidity and scope of that change make efforts of the kind that produced this book remarkably important. Alaskans are now moving on many fronts to have more say over their own futures. The Alaska Native Land Claims Settlement Act is only one example. Control of the schools is another. The young people who, with the help of Ann and some fine teachers, put this book together will have a voice in what happens to their state, and the most enlightened guidance always comes from those who have an intimate understanding of their own culture and can choose the most appropriate future directions for it out of that understanding. At the same time, these students are producing for the rest of us documents that allow us to share with them experiences that most of us will never have firsthand.

Of all the states that have Foxfire-type projects (some thirty-three at last count), Alaska, in my opinion, is the one that has had the most spectacular results. Something fine, and important, is happening in the schools that have these projects, and I can think of nothing that gives me more pleasure than that knowledge. I congratulate the students and teachers involved in this book—and wish them well as they prepare for the enormously confusing, complex future they face. They all must be very proud of what they've done. and what they're doing.

Eliot Wigginton

Introduction

Alaska has been getting a lot of attention lately, particularly from writers. Perhaps Alaska attracts writers because its scale is so grand—more than twice the size of Texas, four time zones, a coastline longer than that of the contiguous forty-eight states, the tallest mountain in North America, a glacier larger in area than Rhode Island. And in all of that, 400,000 people in a handful of large cities and 250 small villages and towns, and few roads connecting them.

Alaska has a wild mixture of lifestyles, of personal philosophies, of racial and ethnic backgrounds. What drew me to it in the first place were the contrasts—and the respect a great many Alaskans have for people different from themselves. On our first trip to the state in 1972, Eliot Wigginton and I flew from Seattle direct to Bethel on the Kuskokwim River in western Alaska. We found Bethel in the midst of a flood caused by the thawing river's ice jams. Rowboats replaced cars on the streets closest to the riverbank and our hosts had had a foot of water in their living room the day before. On our first morning we were given the chore of fixing breakfast for everyone—we had been guests long enough! From Bethel we went to Anchorage and walked into a fancy hotel complete with high chandeliered ceilings and plush carpeting. Going upstairs to a rooftop bar we found ourselves—in jeans and muddy boots—warmly welcomed and seated next to a couple dressed for a formal dance, and no one thought anything of it.

There is a tremendous openness and warmth in Alaska, particularly in its rural areas. While we were beginning the Foxfire/Cama-i programs, funding was meager, and for more than eighteen months I traveled among eight communities while leaving most of my household goods and clothes packed in an attic in Kodiak. Each of the communities became in some measure "home," with friends in each place welcoming me back regularly to their houses and families as I circled through. Alaska Natives—Eskimos, Indians, and Aleuts —have extended families within the state; most other Alaskans have their parents, brothers, sisters, and cousins living "outside." Because of this, neighbors become family, people who provide the same assistance and caring as blood relatives. I remember several Thanksgivings in Kodiak with twenty to thirty people getting together for dinner, contributing special dishes for the feast, and finishing up the day with songs around the piano.

There's also an everyday caring that seems commonplace up here. On one of my first trips to Alaska I found I had to make an unexpected trip to Nome, 500 miles northwest of Anchorage and just south of the Arctic Circle. A bellhop at the Anchorage Westward Hotel gave me his parka with the directions to hang it back up in the bellman's closet whenever I got back—he'd be off duty and would pick it up on the next shift. Another time I checked in for a flight to Barrow and discovered that a friend at Wien Airlines' downtown Anchorage ticket office had relayed the information that it was my birthday to the agents at the airport, who had in turn told the flight crew. I had a birthday party courtesy of Wien for the 800 miles north to Barrow.

I don't wish to paint an entirely one-sided picture of Alaska. We have problems. The very size of the state, the fact that we pride ourselves on individuality, the reliance on neighbors caused by distance and isolation, the constant contrasts in the land, in the weather, in the mixture of people—all this makes for a complexity that is not easily interpreted by writers visiting the state. Alaska's history adds other factors. Until the Second World War when the territory's proximity to Japan and Russia made it of strategic importance, Alaska's population was primarily Native—as it had been for thousands of years. Explorers, trappers, and miners came and went but large numbers of non-Natives did not begin to settle permanently in the state until the 1950s. Alaska has been a state for only twenty-four years. Oil discovery has brought income to the state government, along with the problems of how to manage the wealth now and in twenty years when the Prudhoe Bay field is depleted. Change has come rapidly and pervasively and has brought a sense of dislocation to both individuals and communities.

The Cama-i Book offers an Alaskan perspective on Alaska. It was written by 800 Alaskans with an average age of fifteen. With no roads connecting their communities, it was written after interviewing contacts reached by fishing boat, by small plane, by dory, by three-wheeler, on foot, by snow machine and sled, and by telephone from satellite earth stations. Many of the tapes were transcribed from interviews conducted in the Yup'ik Eskimo language. The oldest of the contacts recall seeing the first white men enter their villages.

For the purposes of this book, Southwestern Alaska is that area of the state from the mouth of the Yukon River south to Kodiak Island excluding the Aleutian Chain. The primary occupation is fishing—both commercial and subsistence. It was the site of the first permanent Russian settlement in Alaska yet it remains a part of the state which has been least impacted by mining, whaling, and urbanization. The city of Kodiak is the largest town in the region, but most of its growth has taken place since 1939, when the approach of the Second World War prompted construction of military bases, and when, after the war, king crab became an industry. Because of this isolation, in Southwestern Alaska much of the southern Eskimo language has survived, intact, as have skills and traditions as well as the heritage of Russians,

Scandinavians, and others who came. The isolation has also fostered self-sufficiency and a pride and self-identity that may appear to outsiders as insular.

Cama-i (pronounced "chameye") is a traditional greeting throughout Southwestern Alaska. It is more of a blessing—"Cama-i this house!"—than a salutation. While the staffs contributing to this collection each have their own names for their individual magazines, Cama-i was chosen as a word representative of the entire region.

What started all this? It began with a trip Eliot Wigginton and I made to Bethel, Sitka, and Craig in 1972. Foxfire, through IDEAS in Washington, D.C., had just received a grant from the Ford Foundation to see if the idea warranted growth beyond its Appalachian base and the singular competence and dedication of Wig. One of the people working with another of IDEAS' programs, the Indian Legal Information Development Service, was Jim Thomas, a Tlingit from Yakutat, in Southeastern Alaska. Jim encouraged us to work in Alaska. In June of 1972 we had a workshop in Rabun Gap, Georgia, and four Alaskans attended. For the next few years we worked with students and teachers on the Flathead Reservation in Montana, the Outer Banks of North Carolina, the South Carolina Sea Islands, the Pine Ridge Reservation in South Dakota, the southern coast of Maine, the Eastern Shore of Maryland, the Ramah Navajo Reservation, among the Mississippi Choctaw, in inner city D.C., and at Craig, Alaska.

In 1974 I moved to Alaska and began, through a contract with the Alaska State Department of Education, to work with other Alaskan communities to initiate or strengthen programs involving junior high and high school students in interviewing, writing, and publishing about the past and present of their people. Southwestern Alaska became the center of this activity. Experienced students from Maine and Mississippi Choctaw came to Bethel to assist Bill Mailer, Kirk Meade, and their already operating *Kalikaq Yugnek* program through a week-long workshop on techniques. *Kalikaq Yugnek* students later went with me to conduct similar workshops in Emmonak, Alakanuk, and Mountain Village on the Lower Yukon. Emmonak's *Kwikpagmiut* staff traveled with me to Hooper Bay to work with students there. Appalachian and Washington, D.C., students and teachers held a training session for 125 Kodiak High School students. Kodiak students later conducted a workshop in Eagle near the Yukon Territory-Alaska border and hosted students and teachers from three Kenai Peninsula villages in Kodiak. By 1979, more than 4,000 pages had been published in student magazines in Southwestern Alaska.

In June 1978 Doubleday approached us about developing our work into a book. We sent them additional copies of the magazines and watched as the idea was reviewed at different levels in the publishing house. When a contract was offered, I visited Nunapitchuk, Naknek, and Kodiak to talk it over with the staffs, the advisers, and the school boards. Nunapitchuk, a village thirty miles from Bethel with a high school of about twenty students, agreed to take responsibility for the selection and editing of the material on the

Yukon-Kuskokwim delta, which had, since 1974, been published by six schools and gathered in more than thirty villages. The students throughout Southwestern Alaska proved very sophisticated in their dealings with Doubleday. Hard questions were asked about protection of contacts, about copyrights, about distribution of royalties.

The staffs selected and polished the material during the 1979–80 school year. A big first step was identifying what topics had to be included to reflect their area most accurately. All three staffs—Kodiak Island, Bristol Bay, and Yukon-Kuskokwim—felt strongly that each area within the region was so distinctive that three separate sections were needed for the final book. To mix the articles would, they felt, only serve to confuse the reader and give a false picture of Southwest Alaska. In actuality, villages *six* miles apart can be very different from one another.

This book, then, is an anthology of what Cama-i has published. It does not begin to tell the complete story of Cama-i. The students writing *Kwikpagmiut* magazine were located in four schools as much as 100 miles apart on the Yukon River delta, connected only by light plane, snow machine, and radio. For most of the year, while determining formats and discussing each location's articles in progress, the staffs worked independently, with periodic visits from me, and then in the spring representatives from each school flew to a central location and students and teachers spent several days—and nights—assembling the pieces into a single publication. In that final session we selected the cover, wrote the introduction, designed the table of contents, and proofed and corrected errors. The final camera-ready copy was then sent out to a printer 500 miles away.

One of the finest aspects of Cama-i is watching experienced students become teachers of other students. I recall one trip a group of Emmonak students and I made to Mountain Village, fifty miles up the Yukon, to conduct a workshop. We arrived in Mountain with the wind blowing so hard that the pilot had to sit with his feet on the pedals and the engine going to keep the plane stationary for us to unload. Arriving at the high school, we discovered the power and most of the heating system off and the students dismissed for the day. While we were offered hospitality in the village, the Emmonak students chose to camp in the school. We boiled hot dogs over a Bunsen burner in the chemistry lab for dinner and breakfast, conducted the workshop, and flew back to Emmonak in high spirits, hoping we wouldn't be welcomed with hot dogs for dinner! Every time students have taught workshops with me in Alaskan communities I have seen them, without exception, demand the best of themselves (even while battling severe stage fright), show sensitivity and skills in working with other students, and exhibit a spirit and sense of humor when things didn't work right. In the Yukon-Kuskokwim area students often taught in their Yup'ik Eskimo language, while writing on the board or making notes in English so I could follow what was going on.

Since 1974, Cama-i has brought moments of elation, of pride, of laughter to all of us involved. It has also brought moments of drudgery, of writing and rewriting, of knowing that any error would be repeated 1,000 times in the final publication. We have had elders tell us we had their entire lives on tape, and we have had individuals die before we could even begin listening to them.

Within a school's curriculum, Cama-i is a way of teaching language arts and social studies. But outside of specific skills and course goals, the major principle underlying Cama-i is that heritage belongs in the classroom, that its recognition and use enhances the very process of learning, and that denial of this heritage can impede acquisition of basic education. If a student is hearing, however subtly, conflicting assessments of his or her community and people at home and at school—or hearing no reference to his heritage during the hours he spends in the classroom—a sense of dislocation results and often a loss of confidence. Academic skills do not have to be altered, but in every possible instance a teacher ought to involve heritage and community in his or her efforts to deliver and develop those skills.

What is Cama-i? It is a school board meeting in Kodiak where a sophomore's response to a question about running out of people to interview was, "The knowledge of the people of Kodiak Island is infinite and when they run out of people to talk to, I'll be a grandfather and they can interview me!" It's kids going back again and again until they convince a potential contact that they think what he has to say is important. It's students in Bethel watching a kayak being re-covered with sealskins in the main lobby of the school—a lobby that the next night was to be the scene of the junior-senior prom. It's experienced students from Bethel and Emmonak conducting a workshop session in Mountain Village and, with no adults present, the whole group staying a half-hour after the bell had rung because they were involved in the discussion of whether or not to begin a magazine. And it is students writing article drafts or painstakingly preparing camera-ready copy over and over again, willing to do whatever is necessary, however time-consuming, to get it "right."

Cama-i, like Foxfire, is not magic. The kids get into slow periods. They can't always come up with ideas of who to interview, or, once they've completed the interview, get the tapes transcribed or the article drafted. Everyone loses a bit of enthusiasm during the long winter stretch. For some teachers a Cama-i approach will never work. It will not work with adults who are uncomfortable with individualization, with those closed off from the community because of fear or arrogance, or those who have a lack of faith in the students' ability to do high-quality, responsible work. It will blossom with teachers who can look at any community and see resources, people, and material which can be brought into the classroom, or with teachers who can learn that perspective. Cama-i will succeed in the hands of adults who believe in giving responsibility to kids and who realize that the young people who wrote this book are no more and no less spectacular than the students they see in their classroom every day. Finally it will work with any adult of the type Wig dedicated *Foxfire 3* to:

"This book is dedicated to those adults who love young people and demonstrate that affection every day. Without these men and women, the love already within all kids would shrivel, for it would have no pattern to go by."

This book provides a perspective on the personalities, the heritage, and the lifestyles of a rich corner of the world—Southwestern Alaska. It is a perspective presented by the people who call it home, by the elders and others who provided the information, and by the young people who preserved it.

AKV

Kodiak Island

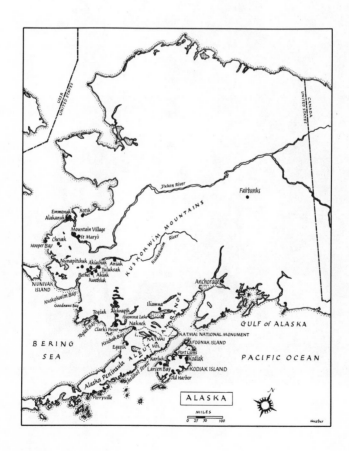

1. Introduction

THE KODIAK ISLAND REGION

by: Leonard Charliaga, Sue Covey, Fred Fogle, and Sandy Lowry

Kodiak Island lies in the stormy Gulf of Alaska, somewhat more than 250 miles from Alaska's largest city, Anchorage. Kodiak is a mountainous island, with numerous bays and a rugged rockbound coast. Only partially forested, our island is a welcome green in the summer and forbiddingly gray and white in the violence of winter.

The city of Kodiak is just about the right size for people to live in. It is not crowded like many other places. There is a unity among the people here for many reasons: our isolation, our reliance on fishing, our shared misery when the weather is bad, our joy when the sun comes back.

There is diversity, too. The Koniag and the Aleut lived a hunter-gatherer lifestyle here for centuries before the Russians came. After the Russians had taken the sea mammal wealth and displaced the Native people, Kodiak, as part of Alaska, was sold to the United States. The Russian-Native influence remained. Then came the fishermen and prospectors. Cod fishermen, herring, halibut, and salmon fishermen, came from Scandinavia and elsewhere. World War II brought thousands of GI's and construction workers to the island. When the war ended, some stayed. The great earthquake and tidal wave of 1964 destroyed and altered much of the town and Kodiak's villages. A modern façade began to dominate Kodiak. But under it all, the insider can see the influences of the hunter-gatherer, fisherman, builder, businessman, adventurer, often in the same person.

Kodiak is a special place because the rest of the world is something you see on television, or read about in the papers. Perhaps it's because life here is so vital and satisfying. Our town and the island villages are a little behind the times, and this is good. We care about each other. Maybe that's why this Kodiak section concentrates on people and what they have to say.

2. Pre-Katmai

LARRY MATFAY: HUNTING WITH TEN KAYAKS

by: Dennis Evans
revised by: Tracey Reyes
photos by: Dennis Evans
sea otter photo by: Tracey Reyes

I met Larry Matfay after a salmon season out at Moser Bay. We had been laid over for days because of bad weather. Ira Jones, the man that I worked for, told me about Larry before I met him. He told me Larry had good stories to tell, so I went out and found Larry and started talking to him. He is one of the kindest persons I have ever known. He has a great sense of humor, and he always has a lot to say. Larry lives in Old Harbor for the winter where he is a bear guide. In the summer he makes his home in Moser Bay, fishing on a gill net site.

When the plane finally came in to fly us out of Moser Bay, Larry and I flew out together. On the way out he showed me where he bear guides. He told me what bays we were coming to and who owned the cabins around the bays. Larry is full of knowledge and loves to talk to people.

"About the first thing my dad and grandpa told me about sea otter hunting was [about] the people. There are two people that check on the weather during the night, by the stars. They are looking at the stars up there all night long, watching the stars and the tides. I think they can tell by the stars up there, [by the] North Star, when there is good weather. I believe it's supposed to be blinking when there is good weather.

"The weatherman is almost always right. If he says there is to be fog, the men would check at night and at certain tides. If the fog is thick, they sound with kelp. They tie kelp together and halibut hooks are tied on the end. We make these with a little bit of yarn; they look like slingshots. They use that for sounding between the islands. As it cleared, you could see where you were going.

"Early in the morning they wake the younger people up saying, 'Come on, boys, get up and cook something, especially tea.' They are kind of in a hurry. Then they get as many as ten kayaks all in one group. They go way out. The older people tell them, 'Go ahead, go way out; it will be a nice day.

Sea otter.

At a certain time of the tide, a wind will come up. It will be quite a blow, but you just get together and don't get excited. She'll die down again before evening.' The wind is that way.

"When they get way far out they watch; they also travel around, but they are not too far apart. When they see a sea otter, they just take the oar and hold it up in the air, but they don't holler. They just hold that oar up and the rest of the kayaks will come up to it, or else to the bubbles that the sea otter makes. The bubbles tell which way the sea otter is traveling.

"They take the kayak and make a circle. They make a circle around the otter with the kayaks and watch which way he goes. The guy that saw it first is the first to try for the sea otter. Not anyone . . . the person who sights it first, gets the first chance.

"When the first arrow hits the sea otter, they'll dive. The arrow's got a string attached on the arrowhead to slow the otter down, but it will dive again and again. The arrow goes crossways in the water. Everyone can see which way the arrow is going; and after the first hit, anybody can shoot it. Of course, they can't help but they get a tip whoever hits it with an arrow. Some of them don't hit and some of them do. But the one that got the hit gets the tip. My dad didn't know how many arrows were used; but some take many arrows and some don't.

"I asked my dad how easy it was to hunt otter; he told me that it's easy sometimes. The otter goes out of the circle of kayaks, but you can see the arrow gets it weak before it goes out. Then they take a long spear to pick it up with, not by hand. They hold it off with a spear, then they club it. So, if they do get one half-alive, it does not bite the kayak. Then they do the same thing over again, but they don't skin it. They put it inside of the kayak; of course, they cut the arrows out.

"They ask, 'Whose is this? This mine! Whose is this? This mine!' Whoever hits on the tail, they get more tip, that's a hard place to hit I guess. It's enough to slow the otter down. I guess you get more money for the tail. Then they skin, clean, and dry it. They don't forget who's supposed to get the tip.

"They go out the next day, and some days they get three, four, or five. Sometimes they hit a good group of sea otter out there, outside of Trinity Islands. My dad even went out there in the wintertime.

"In the winter sea otters get sick and they will lay up on the kelp. In the winter they get cold and go up on the beach. My dad used to trap out there —not alone, though. After a big storm, they make a circle around the island and walk along the beach. That is the way they find the sea otters. He said that it's awful easy to find them. They make a trail along the beach on the sand; you find them way up on the bankside. The trail goes up there in the gravel to where the sea otters are covered over by gravel, making it hard to see them.

"After all that big hunt, they come in the late evening and have a big feed. They have been out all day and then the next morning, they go out again.

"You have to keep the kayak parka wet. The parkas do wear out, however, they will last about a year. Parkas are tight so you can roll over and come up again without getting wet or water inside it. It's just a certain way you tip over and come up. We practiced this all the time, when we didn't have anything to do. When you handle the kayaks and it's rough, the man at the back has the most power to steer the kayak. The kids can go out when they are about fourteen or fifteen. Of course, when it was not a good day, they stayed in.

"They do keep wool clothing in the kayak, but not for parkas. They have other clothes to wear, like those blue cotton shirts. The parkas are made out of whale [intestines]; some are made out of bear from Alitak Bay. Certain times, in the spring, they save all the intestines. In the fall they won't save the intestines because they have too many holes. The bears have been eating a lot of salmon up to this time [late summer and early fall], but now the salmon diet is over. Most of the bears get out of the creeks and start eating elderberries and sourberries. Just before they hibernate, they eat all that stuff to heal their insides. They don't eat all winter, so all their intestines are healed by spring. They eat all the little roots; I've watched them before. The little stuff around the bushes . . . about this time, they go up and get them.

"Of course, I was only fourteen or fifteen years old the last time my dad and grandpa built a kayak. It was a pretty good-sized one . . . a good strong frame on top and bottom. There was a little bit of keel, not very much. Going up Olga Bay, we had to fight the ebb tide. We went just about up to Becker's cabin. The alder branches there are nice long ones and that's where we got those for the ribs of the kayak. They are about three quarters of an inch 'round, nice straight ones, not too much branch on them. You pick the right branches of alder and take them home and keep them wet and then peel the bark off them. Then whittle them down to the size that you want them. Some of them are a little bit flat, some a little bit round.

"Then my dad braided them with his mouth. He put them together and lashed them as close together as he could. It was certain alders that my dad used, nice straight ones with no knots on them. He shaved the knots off by biting them; then he made them round. The long ones you don't tie too tight either.

"I asked my dad, 'Why don't you use nails?' He said, 'Nails wear out and cut the skin because nails won't ride with the sea, and they won't give when running in rough weather.' My dad liked the kayaks better than the dories. He didn't ride in dories very much because he was afraid of them because he was half-blind.

"I used to ride up to Olga Bay. That is where he worked after seal hunting. We would just paddle way up there. When one of us got tired, we just fell asleep, then the other one took over. Like I said, you kneel down in the kayak; but when you kneel down too long, you get numb because you are not used to it. After a while, you get used to it. If you sit right down in the kayak, you can't handle the kayak very well. You have to have something to kneel on, like a blanket or something like that. Some riders can handle it, but others can't. Doing it this way [sitting], you cannot handle the kayak in rough weather. That is what my dad told me."

For centuries, these people have been building kayaks. Building kayaks was what you could call their specialty. Back in their time there was nothing that could match the kayak. It was fast, light, and it floated on very little water.

Larry Matfay: "Of course, I was only fourteen or fifteen years old the last time my dad and grandpa built a kayak."

FATHER KRETA: THE STORY OF ST. HERMAN OF ALASKA

by: Cindy Merculief, Theresa Carlough, and Maryann Wilson

If you had made the longest land journey possible to arrive at your destination and discovered no preparations whatever had been made for your arrival, wouldn't you complain, especially if you had been traveling for over a year? This was the experience of Father Herman and the seven other monks that left the Valaam monastery in Russia in 1793.

When they arrived in Kodiak no one seemed to care particularly. Someone allowed one of them, Archimandrite Joasaph, to sleep in an old storeroom, but still no one knows what accommodations Father Herman and the others found.

This little band of monks, even though their welcome in Kodiak was less than warm, took their mission of spreading the Gospel seriously. They didn't hesitate to send accurate reports back to the Holy Synod in Russia regarding the treatment of the Natives by the Russian American Company. Because they insisted on speaking out against this treatment, Father Herman and the monks were, at one point, put under house arrest for two years and forbidden to hold services because the Russians felt that every time the monks got together with the people, it only stirred them up.

In spite of all this, Father Herman managed to establish Holy Resurrection Russian Orthodox Church here in Kodiak. Holy Resurrection, which is still a very lively parish today, was the first church of any denomination established in the state of Alaska.

Eventually, Father Herman was the only one out of the band of eight monks still left here in Kodiak. The others either died from illness or went back home. Government harassment became so severe that Father Herman went to Spruce Island to live. Being used to poor accommodations by this time, he dug a cave in the side of a hill where he lived during his first winter on Spruce Island. Gradually, a small community grew on Spruce Island where the simple monk made his home.

The University of Alaska credits the monk Herman with making one of the first successful attempts at farming in the state of Alaska, as well as being the first to discover the value of seaweed as a fertilizer. Among his other works, Father Herman established an orphanage on Spruce Island.

He also began a small school to teach people how to hold services in the church when there was no clergyman available. Students from his school went regularly to different communities on the island to hold services. So there is a traditional and historical reason for naming the present theological seminary, located in the city of Kodiak, St. Herman's.

Besides agricultural innovations and good works, Father Herman was also known for performing many miracles. Once, the people in the little Spruce

Island community were frightened because there had been an earthquake and they asked Father Herman to pray for them. He took the icon of the Theotokos, the Mother of God, down to the beach, knelt, and said a prayer. He then informed the people that the water from the coming tidal wave (generated by the quake) would not go beyond the point where he had placed the icon. When the tidal wave hit, the water stopped exactly where Father Herman said it would and went no further. Monk's Lagoon is still known to many today as Icon Bay.

During a forest fire on Spruce Island, Father Herman declared that the fire would go no further than a path through the woods which he and his disciple had made. The trees on Spruce Island are much too tall for this path to be considered a fire wall capable of stopping a forest fire, but, nevertheless, the fire did not go beyond Father Herman's path.

The miracles continued even after his death. Bishop Innocent, who figures prominently in the history of Alaska, kept a diary. He wrote in his diary that while he was traveling to Kodiak Island a terrible storm boiled up and Bishop Innocent's ship was being blown toward the rocks. They were doomed. Bishop Innocent prayed, "Father Herman, if you are a saint as people say you are, please help us!" Immediately the wind changed, turned, and blew the ship safely into St. Paul Harbor. There are fishermen in Kodiak today who can relate similar experiences.

Father Herman foretold that after his death he would be completely forgotten for about 100 years, but eventually a monk would come to live there on Spruce Island to watch over his relics and pray. In 1936 Father Gerasim Schmaltz came to live on Spruce Island. He died in 1969 and there are many in Kodiak now who still remember Father Gerasim for his kindness and his gifts of intricately worked embroidery.

In 1970, the Orthodox Church in America, after extensive study of Father Herman's life, including verification of many miracles that occurred both before and after his death, canonized Father Herman. He is now venerated in the Orthodox Church as a saint. His relics, or remains, were moved from the grave on Spruce Island to a reliquary in the Holy Resurrection Church here in Kodiak, the parish that St. Herman established nearly two centuries ago.

EUNICE NESETH: BARANOF HOUSE

by: Pierre Costello and Eric Pedersen

"In the year 1792–93, Alexander Baranof was sent by the Russian American Company from the settlement they had in Three Saints Bay [on the southern end of Kodiak Island] to look over Kodiak for a future site. Well, they decided on St. Paul's Harbor, where the city of Kodiak is located, and began constructing a new village and this building."

We were sitting in Kodiak's famous historical museum—the Baranof

The Alaska Historical Commission took over the house in 1967, after the city bought it for one dollar.

House—overlooking the ferry dock with Near Island a short distance across the channel. It was a nice, clear afternoon as we began interviewing Mrs. Eunice Neseth, a long-time employee of the museum. She began the story of the museum's past and present along with some interesting facts. Soon our carefully planned interview became a nice, casual discussion which we found very interesting.

"Baranof had the reputation of being a hard man on his people. In a way, when I read about him, I feel he was a very sincere and dependable worker for the company and for Russia. His main concern was that he did a good job, and he had to sometimes be a little harsh to get the Natives to understand that they had to do certain things and meet certain demands from the company. The Natives had a quota of furs to reach, and Baranof just simply had to be a little hard on them sometimes; he wasn't well liked for that reason, no doubt, by the people that worked for him. You get that feeling about him; but I think, at the end, they all liked him. He was a good leader —sometimes a leader can't just be coddling people.

"In 1793, this house was built for a commissary for the Russians here, and a storehouse for the furs. The furs were kept in a loft of a shed down at the dock below the house here. The entrance to that shed was through a covered walkway connected with this house, so that one man would have been in charge to get any furs in or out of there. The Russians had a dock for their ships, which was right below this house where the Standard Oil building is now. The Standard Oil building, in fact, is built over the remains of the old dock, which is still buried there. [NOTE: The original Russian stone dock was uncovered by the tidal wave which hit Kodiak after a major earthquake in 1964.]

"After the Russian times, this building was used as a warehouse for a Russian American Company store down below. Later, Erskine, an employee of the Russian American Company, bought the store, the house, and its grounds when the company gave up their business.

"The house was then used as a rooming house. Walter Kraft, the owner of Kraft's Supermarket of Kodiak, once told me that his grandfather, Otto Kraft, was, when he first came to Kodiak, working down at Erskine's store and lived in this house for his quarters. So it must have been fixed for living quarters before the Erskines moved in in about 1911, and once they had, the house was gone over thoroughly. They built on the sun porch and they did a very complete work-over on the house. They built the back part into a kitchen, bathroom, and bedroom, and this front part which we're in right

Mrs. Eunice Neseth.

Inside Baranof House.

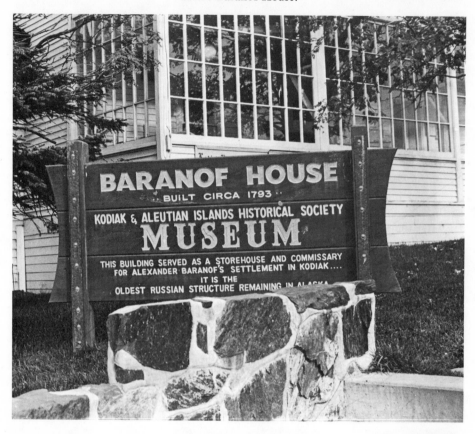

now was probably the dining room at that time. I haven't any definite information about the location of the living room at that time.

"In 1967, the Alaska Historical Commission took over the building as a museum after the city bought it from the Alaska State Housing Authority for one dollar.

"The Baranof House is the oldest known wood building on the entire West Coast. These logs are what those men cut right here in the forest. These are spruce logs cut and put together in Russian fashion with moss in between for insulation. The floor underneath is made of half-logs with the flat side up. Someday we expect to open up a section which will show the original floor also. The ceilings are also not the original ones, but the wood is California redwood, which was brought up by the Russians at a later time when they were up and down the coast for supplies and so on. That was in connection with Sitka, too . . . after it was going already. They brought vegetables, lumber, and maybe cows from California and exchanged them, of course, for furs. Furs are what they were busy with up here and possibly spruce lumber.

"The house has been altered throughout its history. For instance, the roof was not like it is now in the beginning. It was a flat roof and just a little bit above this first floor here. From former pictures, it seems like this house had part of a kind of hip roof. Many of the Russian houses had that to begin with, though they probably didn't have the shingles. This flooring is one of the things added after the Russian times because floors wear out and they have to be changed.

"Most of the copperware you see was made by the Russians that were here in earlier times. The Russians, by the way, are the top-notch coppersmiths in the world."

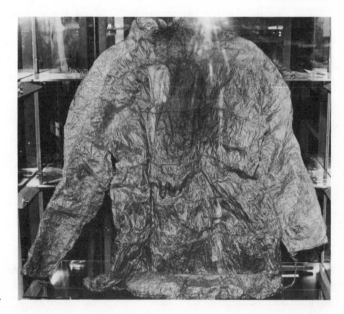

Kumlakas were made
from seal or bear guts.

"There was a time when this building was saved from the bulldozer. ASHA, the Alaska State Housing Authority, took over all these lots, including the downtown lots in Kodiak, to alter the buildings and especially to rebuild after the earthquake. This building was to be torn down and something else was to be built on its place. But the people of Kodiak got together and came to a special council meeting to discuss this building's future and, along with other people who wrote in, succeeded in saving it.

"The museum is mainly an historical museum, so the items we have, or try to have, are from the prehistoric finds of the area like the Native tools, hunting tools, and the stone lamps. These items are donated by people who are interested in the Baranof Museum. They have them and they want us to have them, for which we are very grateful. We do not like to have loans given. We enjoy having them if they pertain to Kodiak's history, but we try to make it so people actually donate what they bring. Loans can make storing difficult because the items sometimes break.

"The people are very much interested in those old gut garments that the Natives used for rain gear. These kamleikas are made from bear or seal gut strips sewed together to make a jacket and hood. Using strings from these

The brown bear, contributed to the museum by Charlie Madsen.

jackets, they tied themselves into the bidarka [kayak]. They also tied themselves in around the waist and hood so that they wouldn't be lost in case of the bidarka overturning.

"The bidarka is built with a very light wood frame—usually white cedar, which they picked up from the beach. While the sea lion hides were raw, they were laid around the frame and sewed right on. They softened the seams by chewing them soft. This was done by propping the bidarka up against something, squatting in front of it, and working their teeth across the hides. The string they used for sewing was made from sinew pulled from animal legs and then twisted into threads of different thicknesses. The Natives' bowstrings were also made of sinew; we have some examples in our showcase.

"The tourists who come by here think this is a lovely place! We like to read their notes in the guestbook afterwards; many say it's beautiful and that they're coming back. We received tourists from all over the world this summer. Quite a few Germans were here, which was interesting. This year we also had visitors from every state in the Union except North Carolina.

"Very few things have been stolen from here, but this year someone took a claw from that tall mounted bear by the door. We try to protect things from damage, wear, and theft, but it's hard to keep people from touching objects like the polar bear. Even after cleaning, you can still see where it has been rubbed right below the head and on its teeth and claws.

"I've been working with the Historical Society since they've been here. I first started working with them at the old museum, which was on Mill Bay Road. Then I helped them move to this building and I've been working here ever since. I enjoy working here very much and it's a feeling of mine that this is a very worthwhile project for the town to continue with. I think that if someone stayed with it to keep things going then the town would eventually take over. We hope that the younger people will take an interest and come and train here along with us so that they might get into it and keep it going."

3. Katmai

AUGUST HEITMAN: "THOSE WERE THE DAYS"

by: Doug Powell and Jason Otto
drawing: Scott Clark

As we nervously walked up to August Heitman's driveway, we saw him working in his shop. We didn't really know what to expect, we just put one foot in front of the other till we got there. When we did, we found a medium height, shy man who welcomed us gladly. We found out that he was a kind, patient man, and he told us this story.

"My first job was in a cannery, and I was paid ten cents an hour, thirteen to fourteen hours a day. You know, them days there was no work here—you just went to a cannery. In 1912, in the eruption of the Valley of Ten Thou-

August Heitman.

sand Smokes [Katmai], when that exploded it ruined fishing for that summer. All the fishing and everything just died down. There was three feet of ash on the ground here in Kodiak.

"During the eruption, there was thunder and lightning. When it exploded, it blew the whole top off, blew the whole mountaintop clean off. There is a big lake there now. The whole top landed there in the valley, the whole top. I was there six years afterwards and it was still burning. I went over to Mount Katmai, the Valley of Ten Thousand Smokes, and as far as you could see was smoke. It wasn't smoke, just steam.

"Katmai itself is right across here from Kodiak, and it [Katmai] is about twenty-five miles off the beach. I was guiding a movie picture party from Hollywood, taking pictures and stuff. It was a summer taking pictures, packing a camera all over the country. When we first landed from our fishing boat ride, we set out taking pictures and everything. We went over in a half-

"When it [Katmai] exploded, it blew the whole top off, blew the whole mountaintop clean off."

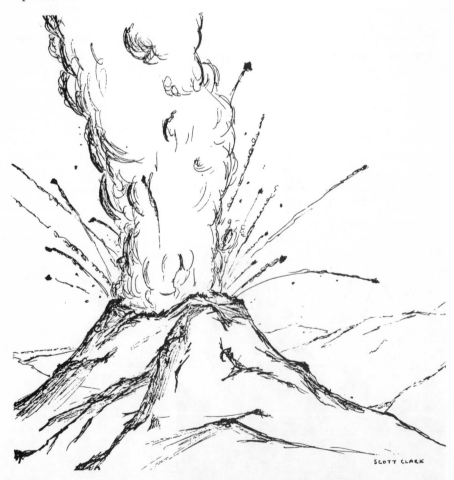

SCOTT CLARK

schooner fishing boat; they had an auxiliary motor in case of calm weather. Most of the time you sailed. We went there and it took about five days. The country there is, as far as you can see, just like a desert. No trees or green grass. Nothing. If you didn't have no grub there, you starve to death. You can't even eat bark off the trees.

"All the valley of the village of Katmai itself moved out. They all knew it was coming, so they all moved out. They took bidarkas [kayaks], dogs, cats, and all moved out. When it blew they weren't there, they were on the beach. They knew it was coming by the ground shaking all the time, so the revenue cutter came and picked them up. They moved by the boat to another village called Perryville.

"Katmai is about ninety miles straight across from Kodiak, or eight hours by boat. It takes three hours through the Shelikof Strait. It doesn't get too rough crossing over, but all the Pacific Ocean gets rough. There is all kinds of mountains over there in the Valley of Ten Thousand Smokes. There are three volcanos there: Katmai, Martin, and Mouquie, and a fourth named Nitekiee.

"They were all sheaving and shaking, blowing all the time when I was there last time. I didn't know if it was going to blow again or not. I was guiding a party at that time—a bunch of Hollywood guys again. I had to guide them in. There was two women and a small baby about eight months old. Had to take her up, too, a money-making scheme. That was Norman Doone, his wife, and his girl. It took about six weeks, I guess. There was good money in that so I stayed right with it. Ten dollars a day. Ten dollars a day was a lot of money back in them times.

"Those people were green, right from the States. They didn't know what to do; they could have starved to death if you didn't go with them. They didn't know how to handle themselves. The water was muddy; we ate groceries from Kodiak. We had to have a lot of groceries for a month or six weeks. That's a wild place. After the eruption, in some places, the ash was fifty feet deep. Then the creek washed it out. To get to it, you had to walk around, you couldn't get through it. Some places are not so steep, so you could go down and take pictures. Hot springs all over. I never saw either movie, never came to Alaska. They were silent pictures, but I never saw either one. I think they went to the East Coast, around there, showing the biggest volcano I think.

"The ashes went to San Francisco, like dust you know. Here in Kodiak the ashes were so thick you couldn't breathe. You couldn't even see your hand in front of your face. They lasted three days; on the third day it cleared up. We were all on the revenue cutter *Manning,* anchored off Woody Island. There was a radio navy station there, but it burnt down during the eruption. Lightning hit it and set it on fire. Burned right down. They couldn't send out for help or nothing.

"They didn't know what happened till they sent a boat from Kodiak when it cleared up to let 'em know what was happening. That was excitement time.

Women crying, women praying and crying. Thought it was the end of the world. It didn't bother the kids any. We were in the warehouse and had lots of candy to eat. Everything was open, help yourself.

"When I started guiding those people the first time, I was sixteen years old. I was a packer. The second time was in 1924; I was about twenty years old then. Katmai has changed since then. Dead now. A few smokes, but dead. Old Katmai Valley is a big valley about six miles long. It is all quicksand now; you can't walk on it now, if you did, you would fall in.

"I have seen quite a bit of changes in this country take place. I was here during the flu, the Spanish flu. It was 1918 and people were just dying like flies. They had it all over the United States. The flu killed more people than the First World War. You get up in the morning five or six people, and maybe two or three dead. People on Woody Island [across from the town of Kodiak] caught it too. I was lucky, I never had it. It lasted over a couple of months; it weakened and weakened till soon it was all over. Almost 150 died here, killing whole villages, just dogs left. None of our family got it. We used burning eucalyptus; when you stepped inside your eyes would just water. We bought the eucalyptus from the drugstore; but most people didn't use many drugs them days, most people used herbs and stuff from the country. It was better than the stuff you bought.

"My mother used to grow her own. If you had a cold, she made tea out of the herbs. I was about fifteen when the first doctor came, Dr. Sylvan. The

Early photo of
August Heitman's
father.

Johnsons came up twenty years later. He came up from Bristol Bay, a cannery doctor. Dr. Johnson and Dr. Jones came together. No doctors, then all of a sudden we had two.

"The town before had about 400 people, plus a big village on Woody Island. They used to ship ice to California from there. They wanted California to have ice machines too. They cut blocks on the ships, then put a layer of sawdust on it to make it last longer.

"During the tidal wave [in 1964] I was sitting across from Kraft's store watching everything. My wife, daughter, and I watched. The rest of the town went around the mountain someplace. We stayed to watch. Houses were going up and down, canneries, warehouses, everything. Dogs howlering, it was a mess. Some of the boats washed up to the old school. The tide came clean in to City Market. When the earthquake hit, the ground was like waves. After the earthquake, I went down to the beach where the boat harbor once was. All the boats were in the harbor, but [resting] on the bottom. The bottom of the ocean opened up, and when it closed up again, that's when we had the tidal wave. The dogs and cats were all swimming around.

"Nobody had time to take pictures; they couldn't even grab anything, they were just glad to get to high ground. My house wasn't washed out when the wave came. It was where the Berg garage is now. Urban Renewal built over my house, though; they tore down my house and only gave me sixteen thousand for it. I couldn't even build a little shack for that. When they built Community Baptist Church, I was building my new house.

"Before the tidal wave, this was a nice little town. It's no good now. Too many strangers, too many long-hair guys in the harbor now with long beards. Never seen them before.

"I had a small boat and fished awhile. My boys helped me fish; they enjoyed it. Now they don't fish no more. My oldest boy is working at the post office; my youngest is working in the back of the post office. I now have twenty-eight grandchildren and two great-grandchildren, so I'm okay."

August Heitman passed on about a year ago. Since then there is an empty spot in our community. He is missed by all.

GEORGE KOSBRUK: "WE WERE VERY LUCKY . . ."

by: George Kosbruk
translated by: Mrs. Shangin of Perryville

This is a story by a man who lived through the Katmai eruption. It was translated word for word from Aleut.

"What took place in the month of June, year of 1912, where two villages were combined together and located [on the Alaska Peninsula] west of Kodiak Island. Population was estimated at about 300. The salmon run was great as always in those days and the people were salting, smoking, and drying both for commercial and home use. Men were always out and one day,

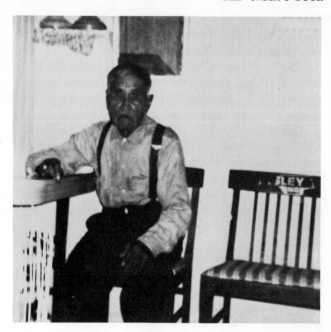

George Kosbruk.

just when they were ready to go out before noon, a strange sight was seen. In a few minutes there was an excitement as smoke came out from the volcano. Some people were saying to each other, *'Poo-yu-luk, poo-yu-luk! Tung-hoo poo-yu-luk!'* [which means in our dialect, 'Volcano, volcano! See the volcano!']. There was lots of excitement after that.

"The older men knew what was to happen later and knew what to do. The first thing they thought of was water, so they filled up every container they could find. They knew once the ashes started falling they would be in need of water and no one knew how long it would last. Some men climbed hills to get a better view and us young kids followed behind. We had fun at first before we discovered what it would be like later. Roaring thunder followed, then a mushroom-like cloud shot up real high. No difference from a bomb picture we see in magazines today. By then, people were busy putting food, or whatever they could get ahold of, away. Men turned their kayaks over in case the ashes fell. Sure enough, as the cloud spread, the pumice ashes began to fall; some were big and some were small, but we were very lucky we were not hit.

"Before we even realized what was happening, it got dark. The heat became unbearable. We gathered in one building where there were no smiles anymore; women were pretty scared and we were, too. As roaring and thunder-like noise became worse, we could hardly hear each other. We had to go real close to one's ear to talk to one another. There we were trapped in one building by total darkness; the quake followed, and quake it did. No cup could be placed on the table and we couldn't stand up on our own two feet.

We had no flashlights in those days, but we made torches from pieces of cloth wound up at the end of a stick and dipped in seal oil. These were used for lights.

"The roaring, rumbling thunder and quake was all in one. As I have said before, there were no smiling faces. People believed in the Bible, and how it would be when the world came to an end. So we all thought this was it. We had no hope of surviving; we gathered this from older people. Prayer was our only hope. We gathered together and made a special prayer to the Virgin Mary. We had never prayed before as we did now, believe it or not. As red ashes fell over the village, the heat became terrible; we hardly wore clothes, we were partly naked. Night and day for three days, we faced the thundering, roaring quake as if there was no end.

"Finally, on the third day, a speck of light was seen on the horizon. It didn't brighten up fast, it took quite a while till we had daylight. No one knew the time. The men thought of sending a couple of kayaks to Kodiak for help. For this place where we spent our good years was no longer a place for humans, as well as creatures of any kind, to survive. It was some time before we finally saw a boat and the kayaks that left here coming. What excitement! Hollering *'Para-hoo-dak! Tae-yook Para-hoo-duk!'* [which means in our dialect, 'Boat! Boat is coming!']. You could imagine us meeting the arrival of the steamer to evacuate us.

"We all boarded the boat. To where? China? We had no slight idea of where they were taking us. We felt pretty safe though. Looking back, our home was disappearing where we had enjoyed our life. We arrived in Afognak, the village on Kodiak Island. We were placed in vacant homes, in schools, and some people brought us into their homes. We spent about two weeks there till the Coast Guard boarded us to proceed on our journey west. Where? Japan? We never knew where they were bringing us.

"Well, we landed here in Perryville, but didn't stay very long. We decided to travel west and came to a place called Ivanof Bay. We stayed for a while, put up more fish. But some people did not agree with the place and the man who lived there complained it was no place to live for anyone—it snowed quite a lot and was no place where they could build houses. Today we find out that this was not true. But we were heading back east, but not to Katmai again. We came back here to Perryville where we first landed and this time many tents were pitched.

"This seemed to be a permanent place so they furnished lumber to build houses for us. They also furnished food to eat. They left one carpenter to help people put up their houses, which were built in one pattern [a square box type with skylight on top and a couple of windows on the side]. When they were done, they looked pretty neat all in a row. Before winter, we all had our homes and were very happy to own them.

"This place is called Perryville, after Captain Perry, the captain of the Coast Guard ship that brought us here. We often think of our home we left in the year of 1912. I am proud to be a resident of Perryville today."

4. Pre-World War II

NICK WOLKOFF: SCHOONER DAYS

by: Marlene Deater

Nick Wolkoff is a very nice and open person. He has a way of making life into a story. His life seems fulfilled to us because of the way he takes things so calmly now. For a man of his age, we thought he would be grouchy; instead he was calm and polite, inviting us in without knowing us, then sitting down and telling us about his life. There he sat for as long as we talked, smoking a cigar that covered the room with its aroma. He sat telling us a life and we, like journalists, were getting our historical information for *Elwani*.

We have at last completed, with no questions, Nick's life and the happenings around him. We would like you to read for a taste of history.

"I was born in 1895, here in Kodiak right by the electric shop, up the road a bit. There was a house there. Most of the houses were by the water. There was nothing back here, just all woods. There were sixteen in my fam-

Nick Wolkoff.

ily altogether; I was the oldest. I had to take care of the others. There was Pete Wolkoff, Paul Wolkoff, Sam Wolkoff . . . but mostly all of them are dead. The others had no names because they were too young to do anything; they were just kids. Yeah, I'm the orphan in the house, you know."

"Well, my father was a seaman, sailing on a schooner during the summertime. My father lived here in Kodiak. My mother was from Ninilchik, she was a Native woman. My father's name was Wolkoff and my mother's was Kvasnikoff. She was born in Ninilchik, then my father brought her here to Kodiak.

"When my mother would spank me, I'd run away to Grandma's house, you know. My mama wouldn't spank me there. If I did something wrong, they'd whip me with a willow. Spankings that was pretty hard. Hurt like hell, especially when they took your pants down, then it was worse.

"Oh, police punished me, too. See you got punished not like now. If you go down the street and see an officer, you stay on one side of the road and salute him. If you don't do that, they wouldn't tell you anything. [But] they'd send two guys and these two guys bring you there and whip you for that. That was for not saluting them, you know.

"My mother and father were good people. They're both Russian people. I spoke Russian and English. My father and mom spoke Russian. My mom spoke just a little Aleut, but I don't speak Aleut. I never talked with them in Aleut; we never learned it. All of Kodiak spoke Russian, just areas around Kodiak spoke Aleut.

"In my day we'd go to dances; we used to have a good time and go dancing. Used to go all the time we could. Dances were the same as now. Got to get yourself a girl to dance with. Yeah, used to do waltzes, three-steps, minuet . . . that's the one I liked the best, that one, the minuet, mostly French minuet. And if a guy scratches a girl's hand like this, that means he wants something. Then the girl pulls away fast. That was the most fun.

"We used to go on picnics, too. Used to go over to Woody Island and make something to eat there. Afterward we used to play ball, that's about all. You know lofka? It's with a ball, you know. Go in parts like four to one side and four on the other side. That is how we used to play it. Then one would throw the ball and someone hits or kicks it before it touches the ground; but you got to hit that ball before it touches the ground or you're out. If you do, then you got a game.

"Besides that, we used to chop wood. There was no oil in them days. We used to go up into the woods, chopping wood and carrying it home, then saw [ing] it off in blocks for stove wood. That's all you can do; there was no oil. Not too much work in them days, salmon fishing, other salmon fishing, nothing to do but go out fishing. From the beginning I was a fisherman. In them days there was a lot of fish. The Buskin River was full of fish. When the tide went out there was about that much [gesture], around two feet high, along the mile-long beaches. All dead, you know. Come down the river and died. Stink! Oh, would it stink from that rotten fish.

"My parents worked. Both my parents did. The workers had to load the ice on the boats; they got paid twenty cents an hour for it. I couldn't work; I was a small boy then. I had to take care of my brothers and sisters and stay home.

"The schooner *Wolfe* came to hunt sea otter. Every schooner had ten bidarkas, two men to one bidarka each. They would go all around Kodiak Island and come back, come up and out into the channel and wait for ice. The ice came from Woody Island in those days. Ice was sold in blocks, and then taken Outside [to the Lower Forty-eight]. They would bring sawdust for ice from Outside. You've got to have sawdust for ice, you know. With the sawdust, they would load up the schooner and head back down to San Francisco again. Do it every year like that, come and hunt the sea otter, get the ice, and head back down. That's all they used to do, they never fished. They just get the ice and go back down to San Francisco.

"The ice was for the rooms, to keep the meat cool. Usually in San Francisco they cut all around and the room was inside the ice. That's where you kept the meat for preservation. What else you could do was salt it. The schooner *Wolfe* had sails and small machines, small power. It was made out of wood.

"I was only sixteen years old when I first went sailing. I sailed from here to San Francisco and back. You got a little money for that. Then, in a year, my daddy got sixty dollars and I got forty dollars a month. Exactly comes to a hundred dollars a month for us. Anything I made I gave to my mother. Then they put me in Father's place, because he was a mate at that time.

"We used to go trapping in the wintertime. We'd trap foxes and sell the skins; some people would keep them. And ducklets, we used to go hunt ducklets and sell them. Fifteen cents a duck to people, those who could buy duck. We never sailed in wintertime. Too tough, you know. It would blow and was cold all the time.

"I also used to tend gardens. I had to keep the field clear of weeds. The gardens, some were near the house, but most were out where Beachcombers is now. Used to call it Potato Patch. There were gardens from one end to the other. Gardens, everybody had gardens there. Some people had gardens planted near their house.

"There was a store, too. The first store was the A.C. Company, then another man bought it and it became S.C. Company. The same store. I don't know who has it now. It had groceries, toys, and everything.

"There's been a lot of changes. Before, there was no radios at all; seamen used to come in by no radios. A fellow would go up on the mountain and watch if a boat come in. They would go up on the mountain and look around. If they look outside and see smoke, then they yell, 'Seaman! Seaman!' Then everybody in town would know a seaman was coming. This was because there was no radio in them days—that's how they told if someone was coming to Kodiak.

"Same as with measles. Oh yeah, we had the measles, measles were dangerous. If you got a cold after the measles, that'll kill you. I had the measles myself but that never happened to me. Just laying down and keeping warm that's about all [you could do]. Never had any medicine back then to help like now.

"Later on, I got married and lived with my wife for ten years. I got no kids from my first wife because she had TB; when the baby was born, it had TB and they died. Her name was Sally Todulla, she was Polish and Aleut. Then I met my second wife and [she] was Polish background, too. Her name was Alexandria.

"If you want to marry, you have to ask the parents. The parents call for the girl. The girl comes up and sees the boy; then the parents ask if she wants to be married to you. If so, you gotta make a banya [steam bath] in three days. Build the banya for the parents. It's a lot of work.

"After I married I worked, same as I did before. Longshoring—when a schooner came in we unloaded or loaded it. No machinery at all, no winch, we used to use two horses. And I helped the carpenters, that's all the work you can do. I'm no carpenter myself but I did help build things. Went out fishing, halibut, codfish, salmon, and herring. No cannery, so we used to salt our fish; the cod we would brine.

"There was a lot of coal back then, no oil or gas, just coal. That's why they called it a steamer, because it made a lot of steam. That was in order to make the engine go. I used to work in the coal. They used to bring coal in on big barges; I don't know how many tons of coal, but a lot of it. It used to fill two schooners. Work was for two weeks. I used to unload it to the dock, then from the dock to the coal bunkers. Then, if you wanted coal you can go up and get it.

"Besides what I've told you, there was no other jobs to do. Some people would trade with each other, like dig ditches. It was harder to get a job then than now.

"We used to have fun, too. We used to go out dancing, and [spend] twenty-five cents to see a show. Tony's Bar was here then; you had to lean up against the bar. They didn't make drinks like they do now. You never saw a fancy drink, drinks then were served straight.

"I had a house made out of logs, just a common house. The logs were crossing each other. Had around six rooms. There was a cooking room, kitchen, bedrooms, living room, and then the area on the porch for storage. We had the bathroom outside, not far from the house. You can't make it too far. My boy was born in this house, the log house. In this house my two girls were born, by doctors and midwives; they're to help bring the baby into the world. I've lived in this house say about fifteen or twenty years.

"I remember one time we were on the boat and the boat went down in five minutes. We were coming from the Bering Sea and we ran into bad weather. Smoke blowing in the air, so I went to see the skipper. 'How far from here to Kodiak?' The skipper said, 'Pretty far and we're pretty short of gas; another couple of miles and we'll be out of gas.' So we had a flag out—that's the way a seaman can tell if something happened to us, just by moving it different ways. There were a lot of schooners going by. There was one going north and one going south. One came and their skipper asked if we were in trouble. Our skipper said, 'Not in trouble, but we could get lost.' Then he asked the name of the place. Their skipper asked, 'How long you been here?' Our skipper said, 'Not long, it took us forty days to get from Frisco to here.' The other skipper told us how many miles to Kodiak.

"Then we couldn't get out of the storm, so we had to do something. We went around an island to anchor up for the weather. That's when we went on the reef. Nobody died. Then we rowed to shore. Six or seven days after that we rowed in two dories to Chignik 'cause we were right out of Chignik. We got to the cannery around midnight or quarter to one. Someone said, 'Where have you been?' We told them we were on the island for six or seven days, and all we had to eat was mussels. So they took us up to the mess hall, we sure done a cleaning there. All around the table, we were eating everything. Then we called Kodiak to come pick us up.

"Well, that's about all I can think of."

WASKA BOSKOFSKY: "YA, I'M GETTING YOUNGER"

by: Jackie Madsen and Michelle Bergeron

When we arrived at Camel's Rock (near Ouzinkie), Waska rowed out to the boat in his dory. He was very talkative, and invited us up to his cabin. Waska is short, rather small, but not at all shy or weak in personality or

Waska Boskofsky with Michelle Bergeron.

strength! His cabin reflected him perfectly; warm and cozy and smelling of woodsmoke and fresh-baked bread. We started talking right away, and laughed a lot. Whenever we would start to take his picture, Waska would notice and smile straight at us. He loved being interviewed, but it was very difficult because Waska has trouble hearing and we had to yell right in his ear whenever we asked a question.

Our visit lasted two hours, and he served us tea and alotuk (fried bread), and we all got a chance to try out Waska's four-foot wood saw. We could see that Waska was tired of talking, so we had to leave. But, not empty-handed! Waska gave each of us a gift of canned smoked salmon and a great interview! Back on the boat, as we were pulling out, we were sorry there weren't more people in the world as kind and warm as Waska Boskofsky.

We are up at Waska's garden and he is showing us his root cellar. "Well, you want to take a look at my banya, too? And my cabin? My cabin's all messy. Weasels always come in, you know. That's what that's for—weasels. [He's pointing to a weasel trap.] The bait—where they bite the bait—the thing sets off. We always used these traps before. See this little stick? He bites there and the trap goes off and squishes him! I keep traps when I'm gone. They always come in when I'm gone, you know. They chewed the boards right through!

"Once, I had a rock duck right here on the table bench. A fresh one. It was sitting right there and I had a cup of tea in the other hand, and all of a sudden my duck fell down. I picked it up. Another three minutes, it fell again! The weasel must have been right under the table. And then I see him running that way towards the door, under this plywood. I pulled out my .22 and I put the duck down. He came back and I just shot him! That's the ones we always used to use. I'll show you how it goes, eh? You know where the weasel bites? They get the bait, you know. In winter they're white, in summer they're brown. They have black tails. Old-timers always know everything! [Laughs.]

"Maybe you would like a can of smoked salmon? Dere's my smokehouse down dere—it's full of junk! Ship gear and everything, you know my boys! I had the salmon in jars first. I got the cans last part of September; 'twas too late, I'd already canned dem. Ah, you're gonna tell dem you were eating smoked salmon at Camel's! You know, I had 'em in jars first, but they say they get moldy so I put 'em in cans. Two-pound cans there those are.

"Well, here's my banya. Take a look! That's my heater, you know. To heat the water on, too. You sit here on a bench and you close the door. Then when you all through, you can come and dress out here. I build it myself. Nobody help me with nothing. I do myself; no carpenters do anything!"

"How do you smoke the salmon?" (He doesn't hear the question.)

"See this is my smokehouse. I always keep it filled with real wet cottonwood so it won't flame up, you know."

"How long do you smoke the fish for?"

"It takes a couple of weeks. I was going to smoke lots of fish, but the fog came in and I didn't get any fish. If you smoke them or soak and can them, they are really good! Sometime I am going to let you try some right after I make it. Boy, they are *really* good if you smoke them! [We are back at his cabin.] You know, canned salmon—I always cook them four hours. I got a whole big case of cans in here."

"Do you have a machine to can them?"

"Ya, you want to look at it? See, here's the cans. Six cases. Here's my canning sealer. [It was under the bunk.] I stick it on the bench here and can.

"Yesterday I went up the river and got one silver. Don't know what got into me to go out and fish. [It was really big.] Summertime, you know, salmon all over here. You don't have to go far—just around here. But this year I didn't get nothing, just a few fish.

"Yesterday I had to fix my roof. Boy, nothing beats this wood. It does best in this wood stove burner that I made. At least I won't run out of it, I got a whole woods full of it. It just burns all night. I bet you girls are cold. You just have to get used to the dampness up here. I got to put more wood in, and it will get warmer in here. It won't take long."

"No, no, you don't have to. We're fine."

"See this [holds up his ancient teakettle]? They are hard to find now. It's hard to find cedar, too."

"How long did it take you to build your cabin?"

"Oh, it take me two weeks. If you have all the materials, it don't take long. Couple of weeks, I build this one. It took me three weeks to build my smokehouse. I had to beachcomb. This one here, I had everything.

"You know what? We used the roofing paper before grass. We used to make barabaras [sod huts partially underground]. We put the tree bark, and we used roofing paper, and then we put grass over it. That's how we used to make barabaras.

"Roofing paper, you know, it don't last long after those heavy blows. Now I'm going to line it up. I'll put the roofing paper . . . it got strips on the seams and I fold the strips back, that's the only way it'll stay. Ya, I'm planning to put roofing paper all around. And then I'll put insulation up. I want to stay the winter here. I like it here.

"There's my other foundation up there I was going to build—twelve feet by twelve feet. I couldn't get the materials though.

"Boy, it's nice! You can see all the boats traveling from here, my window. Wide open—everything. Whole thing's open, everything. I live up here all summer, too. I don't stay long over there, Ouzinkie.

"Is it cold in here? See how thick a wood I got? I go someplace else; I come back in three or four hours, still burning! Last year I tries to make a root cellar. Boy, did my back hurt! I guess it was the digging. Maybe I am getting old. Dig water hole for three months. But, anyway, in here there is good water. It was worth it. In here is good water—no chlorine—it's really fresh. You got to try it sometime."

"Is it cold?"

"Ya, it's real cold, comes right up from the ground up there. Spring water.

No matter how hot it's outside, the water is very cold. Maybe you care for some orange Kool-Aid? Here's the cups. I just made that yesterday. Help yourself!

"[Referring to tape] You'd better open that as soon as you get to Kodiak! You let everybody in Kodiak hear that! They listen to that!

"Maybe you want some alotuk? Alotuk—fried bread. Try some! I just made these yesterday; I made them myself. I never need no woman at home. I do it all myself. I cook and everything. How are they?"

"Great!"

"Have some Kool-Aid. Help yourself. There's the cups—anyone you want. Boy, they're gonna hear Boskofsky talking all the way! You walk in the road and let everybody hear Mr. Boskofsky! You know that this place will all be cleaned out soon. Have some more! Don't be so shy! There is plenty. Here!"

"Waska, how do you cook that bread?"

"That dough, you know, you put some lard and hot water and let 'em melt. And then put a pack of yeast sugar in it lukewarm. Put a yeast in so it would cook. Mix it up, you always put the yeast right in the water. It raises real fast. In 'bout a couple hours it raise up the dough. Have some more if you like 'em, there's plenty more! Help yourselves! It don't take long to make 'em."

"Do you fry them in the pan?"

"Ya. I use my Coleman stove."

"What kind of oil do you use?"

"First you gotta get it real hot, then you turn it low. So they won't burn ya."

"How much lard?"

"Gotta put lard in there. Oh? How much? Gotta put lots of lard. Oh, depends on how much you want to make. When you put a tiny, little bit they burn. But you gotta put quite a bit. When they done, you know, they float up. Ya, when it gets real hot it don't take long. Like . . . did you ever fry doughnuts? Same way you know. Once in a Russian Christmas I made some doughnuts. And all the guys were out masking. They came in; I had some doughnuts on the table. 'Twas the Third Night Masking. And all the guys came in. They had to take their masks off to eat! I saw who they were!"

"Do you go into town often?"

"You know, when I go to Kodiak I go on morning plane. I take afternoon plane back. Sometimes, like a shareholder's meeting [of the local Native corporation], I stay for two nights. That's the only time I stay two nights in Kodiak. I just don't like to stay there. No fun! If you get your room, costs lots at Shelikof [hotel]. It's good when you need something. Like, I go to town, I go to the bar, to the bathroom. Once in a while, I'll take two or three drinks. That one guy I was telling him he'd just better quit drinking. It's no good, that liquor stuff! Twice he take me for a drink, again he starts! No good.

"I always get groceries from town. I got twenty-five pounds today. I got flour and that, you know, sugar."

"Waska, what do you do for a living? For money?" (He has trouble hearing us.)

"By golly, you should have brought me some ears! Help yourself! More tea?"

"What do you do to make money?"

"Me? Uncle Sam pays me Social Security. Ya, I'm getting younger. I'm sixty-eight! I'll be sixty-nine on January 12. But I don't work like I used to —no. I don't know how come I slow down.

"I had eight gill nets. I used to get more fish than they do now with only one of my nets.

"One time I had to help the father with the church. I was young. My mother told me that it would make me closer to God. He took me out and showed me around the church. At that time not many people were there. After I got done, I went back home. At that time I lived on the other side of the island; the whole village was just moving around. It was just a three-hour ride, rowing by dory, now my mother let me work!

"I had nine boys and five girls. One girl, she was three months old when she died. And one boy died, too. I have a big family I tell you! And there's a big house. In 1935 I got married and I build a big house up on the hill behind where Alice stays, in 1936 in the spring. First week of Lent I started,

Waska shows Michelle Bergeron and Jackie Madsen how to use the four-foot wood saw.

and was done. We spent Easter there. All by myself—log house. And then in '42 I built behind the father's place. That one was thirty-six feet long and twenty feet wide. Ya, all by myself. And after tidal wave, I built a house right by community hall in Ouzinkie. And a couple of days after tidal wave, the planks from Dell Valley's saw mill . . . I was picking over all those two by fours and two by sixes. I was sure lucky! Then, when I went down and I see one coming, I say, 'What is that? That's planks! Another one right behind!' Boy, was I lucky then! That house of mine was built of nothing but planks from floor. Just cover them up and sixty penny spikes in that! My son, Alvin, he's the only one who helped me with that. He used to be gone, you know. Right after he came back from school.

"You know, a long time ago Father Herman's grave was coming up! Everybody went to go hide. They all went to Ouzinkie to hide. After that, it must have gone down. That was Father Herman's grave in Monk's Lagoon. That's what my grandfather and grandmother used to say.

"You know that little bridge over [by] Father Gerasim's church? When I went there, the planks were broken. So I stayed three days beachcombing. It is hard to find planks nowadays. So I fixed it all up like it was before. There was a path, real narrow, about ten inches wide. It took me about two weeks and five days to finish working for Father Herman [on the church and bridge]. When I got done, I put moss all around.

"I had to go [to] the lagoon. I built my first home there. The wind was so bad that every time I had to nail something, the wind would blow it down! When I came back [from Monk's Lagoon] a lot of people were carpenters. Boy, you know, first year when I moved from outside there were lots of visitors. Boy, I was busy talking in Russian then!

"At Sutliff's [Hardware] a long, long time ago, I had them fix my motor. Cost me sixty dollars. I was stuck for two weeks here at my house. I had three motors, everything's broke down. It was blowing every day. I got disgusted and took the morning plane to town. If I make it, I'll make it. I got a ten horsepower [motor] for $818.

"Before tidal wave I went to my fishing grounds. You know those Andersons [his neighbors], they had a cabin right across there [points across the cove]. See that place there? They used to have a cabin there. But the tidal wave washed it away. And I went to my fishing location. And when I came back, the house was up there. I was wondering who built a house. Andersons must have built that. I didn't know nothing about tidal wave!"

"Waska, when you were small, where were you?"

"No, I gotta lot of grandchildren. Twenty-three grandchildren."

"Where were you born, Waska?"

"Who me? I was born in Afognak. That's where I was born. I was born in 1908 and then in 1933 I go to Ouzinkie to my grandfather's. I used to stay there with them all the time. My grandmother was eighty-seven years when she died; and the grandfather was ninety-two. He got the paralyzed stroke. He was just like young, though, before; two weeks only he was alive after.

He lived till ninety-two and I never saw him get mad! I take after my grandfather. I never get mad! And I never like to argue, I just turn around and walk away."

"Did you like Afognak?"

"Ya, it was good place. Afognak no good no more. [NOTE: Afognak Village was destroyed by the 1964 tidal wave. Many residents relocated to the new town of Port Lions.] Boy, there used to be more people in Afognak than in Kodiak. There was a lot of Russian people. Six hundred and seventy-two people in all, including children! And they used to have three stores in Afognak. And later they got four! Ya, it used to be big village before. About two miles long that village used to be, Afognak!

"My dad died in 1926; and my mother died in 1921. You know, my dad died when I was in Uyak with my aunt in August month. I spent a whole winter in Uyak. And when I came back, he was done. 'Twas no fun.

"When I was a kid, I worked real hard. I just wanted to do everything. I worked on a boat for a while. I worked hard when I was with this man; that's how I learned to be a carpenter. When I was thirteen, me and my friend went to Afognak and built a cabin. Dad used to teach my older brother; he used to tell me to go home and help my mother! Now Mother stopped it. When we went to school, he took us. He would stand around with the storekeeper and tell stories with him. Sometimes for three or four hours!"

"Do you speak Russian?"

"Ya, ya, I speak the Russian language. But I don't talk Eskimo or nothing like that! In 1961 I used to stay all over. Whenever I go hunting, I used to build a cabin. I just don't like to stay in tents. Anyplace I stay, I build a cabin. In tents it's all right when it's sunshining; but when it's raining, then you can't dry your clothes. But in a cabin it's dry. Like, see the hangers I got there [above the stove]? And when your boots are wet, you just put them there on the hearth and they dry fast.

"By goddy, you know what, Mr. or Mrs.? If you had traveling machine, you could travel all around and see all my cabins that I did!

"In 1975, October month, I went to Anchorage. There I stayed the whole winter. My son Allen wouldn't let me come back; he always worried about me. April, when I came back that year, I had to pay for water! In November month, I give forty dollars. Boy, it made me mad! For two months, isn't that something! Last year [1975] in April month, the doctors wasn't there—in Kodiak. There was nothing wrong with this ear, you know. That's what ruins my hearing. This one was good, but that one was too far gone they said. I was in Anchorage for a whole month for my eyes and ears. You know, they used to have doctors to operate on eyes and ears. There was nothing but haywire doctors there. Takes a whole month, and there for nothing! When I go to Ouzinkie and try to hear what they are saying to me I have a hard time. So you better talk louder.

"Last night I went out and got some clams. See how big they are? Real big ones. The digger, they dig right up to the Camel's Rock."

"Waska, do you use that big saw there [pointing to a four-foot saw by the door]?"

"Ya, I cut a lot of wood with that saw."

"Can we try it?"

"You want to? All right!" We did! Then it was time to go. . . .

"If I knew you people were coming, I would have baked pirok [Russian rice and fish pie] last night! Good-bye! Come back and visit me sometime— I'll bake you pirok!"

BOBBY STAMP: BUILDING A BIDARKI

by: Peter Olsen

At the tender age of seven, Bobby Stamp left his home in Cordova. Under Bureau of Indian Affairs (BIA) care, he boarded the Valdez-bound steamship *North Western*. Bobby acquired many acquaintances during his six-month visit and especially appreciated the help that a family by the name of Keetans gave him by housing him during his short visit. Destiny then took him, by way of the mailboat, to the isolated village of Chenega. Here, about ninety miles southwest of Valdez, Bobby grew up in an uninterrupted

Bobby Stamp.

Alaskan environment. The tidal wave of 1964, which destroyed the village of Chenega, marked the beginning of development in Alaska.

Before the introduction of microwave ovens and the television set, Alaska, the "Last Frontier," contained very natural people. It must be understood that the closeness these people had with the environment produced a satisfaction that cannot be imitated and is increasingly hard to attain. They lived in a day which demanded that they recognize and understand the instinct in the animals and the cycles of life that were found abundantly around them. As man replaced the surroundings made by his Creator with those of his own invention, a loss of satisfaction with life began. The following article is my attempt to preserve some of the knowledge that our ancestors depended on. The fact that kayaks were greatly depended on by the hunters who fed the village shows what tremendous differences in lifestyle the last thirty years has brought.

During the days in which Bobby was raised, Chenega, and villages like it, were isolated from most of the "outside" world. There were only a couple of diesel-powered boats, which the people in the village used as transportation for grocery runs. The nearest store was nearly twenty-five miles away in La-Touche. "My stepdad owned one of those boats, but they were more or less community property. Every time it was borrowed, they generously replaced the fuel. Every family had a bidarki though, and they were the chief source of transportation."

The frame is usually constructed of spruce; however, willow and alderwood are also used. The bow and stern stems are made out of natural crooks. A natural crook is at the trunk of a tree where the roots begin. There are usually two or three larger roots on a tree that can be used for this purpose.

Bobby was told that, before his time, spruce roots were used for whipping the frame together. "That and strips of sinew from a bull sea lion" were used. After the bark was removed, the roots were boiled until they could split them. Cotton twine was used when Bobby was growing up and, since then, the longer-lasting nylon twine has replaced that.

The skins were from the large female sea lion. The female is used because of the damage the bulls do to their skin when they fight. "The female seems to be easier to stretch and not as tough as the male," Bobby recalls. The skins were thoroughly cleaned and washed in warm water, and then buried. Moss from trees was wrapped in with the skins and left there for three or four days. This enabled you to remove the hair from the skin. It was "just like wiping it off" after it was dug up and was allowed to dry in the smoke of the campfire. The skins shrunk to about a quarter the original size, and Bobby recalls them being used for years after they had been dried.

"When they got ready to make the skin for the bidarki, they would soak the skins in seawater, sometimes up to ten days before the skin would be soft enough for them to work on it." On a big stretcher made out of natural crooks, they would cut little holes on the hide's edge about an inch apart.

With rawhide seal strips, the skin was strung to the stretcher. Each time they would pull it tighter, they would scrape off all the fat and wash it with warm seawater. This was done to both sides until the skin was cleaned. It generally took about eleven female seals to cover the frame of a bidarki.

The frames were made of spruce or alder and lashed with strips of rawhide. In the Chenega area, the bidarkis were eighteen to twenty feet long and most of them had three holes. For the long trips people would sit in the front and back holes and use the middle one for packing supplies.

Making a bidarki usually turned out to be a community affair in which everyone would chip in. The men selected and prepared the wood for the frame while the women handled the skins. The frames lasted eight or nine years until they had to change the lashings and a rib or two.

"The women would all get together and cut the hide and sew it together. The older women stretched the hide over the frame and sewed it with porpoise sinew. Not the porpoise that goes so fast, it's a different porpoise. I remember seeing them when they got a porpoise. They would remove all the fat and it had an awful lot of sinew." They would take this sinew and soak it in seawater for three or four days until they could scrape all the flesh and muscles off.

The younger ones who were learning how to sew would, with the aid of the elders, sew a part of the skin which wasn't critical. An elder would look it over and correct it if it was necessary. "After they would sew it together, they would put it on the frame. There was a way they had the strips sewn around it." The skin was sewn so that it fit over the bow like a sock. It was then tightly pulled over the frame and lashed.

The bidarki was set on a stand where dogs and mice wouldn't get at it. To cure the skins they poured seal oil right in the boat and soaked all the ribs, lashings, and the hide. It was then filled with seawater and washed out. This was repeated as many times as necessary to completely soak the hide with seal oil.

"I've seen these hides last up to four years, but they would take the bidarki and completely sink it until it got real soft." Again they would pour seal oil into the boat and this would be enough to preserve the skin. When the skins were too old, they were cut off the bidarki down the keel into two strips. These strips were placed inside a bidarki and used as matting. That way oars, guns, and knives could be placed in the bidarki without tearing a hole in it.

A kamleika, which was like a hooded sweatshirt made out of sealskin, was used to keep you dry. Drawstrings around the hood and wrists kept water from seeping in, while the waist was tied with strings around the rim of the bidarki. "You could take a wave over you and you wouldn't get wet." Inside the bidarki, bear or mountain goat hides were used as a mattress. The thick fur padded the knees and doubled as a sleeping bag when needed.

With the increasing cost of energy today, maybe the bidarki is not the anachronism that it seems.

WALTER PANAMARIOFF: OHLOCK

by: Maryann Wilson and Theresa Carlough

Many tales are told about a hairy, manlike being called the "Ohlock." The Ohlock was a name originated in Alaska. There hasn't been any proof or pictures taken of it, but these tales are heard by a lot of the people in many Alaskan villages. These tales have been heard from generation to generation by the Natives here. The Ohlock resembles the Big Foot in many ways; but unlike the Ohlock, the Big Foot is often heard of in the Lower Forty-eight, especially in California. There have been many stories told of both the Ohlock and the Big Foot. In this article, there are a few stories about those who have experienced the bizarre creature.

Many people have heard of the Ohlock but are afraid to talk about it. In this article there are two people who were willing to talk to us. Although Eunice Neseth couldn't supply us with enough information for a full story,

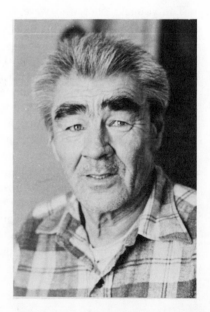

Ted Panamarioff.

we thought since we did ask her to tell us about it, we should print what she told us.

"This is from old times, the stories of what the Natives call the Ohlock. They're told from way back when about the presence of some being, whatever it is.

"There was a Coast Guard Communication Station on an island which was under command of the navy base on Kodiak Island. There were several men on duty over there at the time. It happened when they were on duty; they saw the Ohlock and they caught him, tied him up and put him in a shed. But sometime during the night the Ohlock got away. Just by coincidence a guy that was missing was the same guy that tied the Ohlock up. They don't know if he was in the shed with the Ohlock or not, but they never found him or the Ohlock."

Since we couldn't get that many people in town to talk about the Ohlock, we heard that there were some contacts in Ouzinkie who would talk. So we decided to take a trip and we chartered the mail plane to Ouzinkie. On our arrival the people there were very friendly. We got acquainted with the people the first night.

Late in the afternoon of the next day, we went to see Ted Panamarioff. He was a very shy man about five feet two, fairly muscular with broad shoulders. He was wearing Frisco jeans, a plaid shirt, and boat slippers. He talked quietly and was very polite and expressive in his storytelling. He talked about his experiences, which were told in story form. This is the way that the village people pass on their experiences. We thought that they were really interesting; we are sure you will, too. So the rest of this article concentrates on Mr. Panamarioff.

"We had moved to Akhiok and I had no trapline, so I asked the people if anybody trapped in Deadman's Bay. They said no, they don't go there, it's a bad place. I went in there in the dory and it turned out to be a pretty nice trapping ground, so I took it. My brother Alex and my brother Lawrence hunted there for a couple of years. We had a cabin there. One night it had snowed about a foot; I got up in the morning and it was still dark. So I just opened the door and I reached around. There was a box by the wall and I looked for the bacon. I had a big slab, full slab, and then a half slab. I couldn't find the bacon, so I just made sourdough hot cakes.

"I got my brothers up. My brother Alex said, 'How come you didn't cook bacon?' 'Well,' I said, 'I guess we finished it.' He said, 'No, there is a slab and a half there.' So then I reached for the bacon. I didn't step on the porch, there was an extra foot of snow. Alex said, 'It's in there.' He got up and opened the door and said, 'My God! What is this? What's the tracks? There's tracks there about the size of my foot, but they look like they were wrapped with either gunnysacks or canvas.' Then it came to my mind that the people told us not to come into the bay, so I got mad. I told Alex, 'Let's eat and track him to the beach. He came from the salt water, came on the porch, took our bacon, and followed the dry stream bed up. Go get your gun and we'll track him.' We tracked him maybe five hundred yards and then the tracks disappeared—it looked like he flew away. We backtracked him; he didn't step off any place. The tracks just stopped so we left, then came back about a week later. The same tracks were on the porch in the morning and the rest of my bacon was gone.

"He came from the bay again, from the sea. So this time I told my brother Alex, 'You get your gun loaded, take plenty of shells. He went up the dry stream bed again. If we see him, shoot him, whatever it is.' We walked maybe five hundred to six hundred yards up and the same thing. The tracks went and disappeared. He took a slab and a half of my bacon. Whatever he wrapped around his feet I don't know, it could be gunnysacks or canvas, but his strides were about the same as to human beings. We didn't see it or nothing, just his tracks. And that's what you call it in Old Harbor, Ohlock; they talk about Big Foot. Whatever he was, it was not a human being.

"Then another time I had a partner; we were trapping in Red River. His name was Davis Peterson. We lived at the mouth of the Red River; his mother and stepfather lived there. We had a four-day trapline. It was getting close to Russian Christmas and Davis said, 'To save time, you go one way and I will go the other and we'll meet up the river.' Which was an eight-hour walk. I got back to the cabin in Old River, that's on Red River Beach, and I looked at the traps. We didn't have anything. Anyway, I came back to camp, made supper, and then went to bed. At midnight somebody was knocking at the door. I said, 'Who the heck is that?' He said, 'It's me, Davis.' I jumped up, opened the door, and said, 'What are you doing here? You're supposed to be in Red River.' He said, 'Walter, something happened. I killed a man.' 'You killed a man?' 'Yes. I cooked supper, layed down. Then somebody knocked on the door. I said, 'Come in.' I thought it was you. Then a little man come in. He was about four feet high with a white beard. I gave him some tea, some bread, and some leftovers. He ate that, but he wouldn't eat the bread; he wouldn't touch it.' So Davis got to thinking that the man's not a human being.

"So Davis told him to lay down in my bunk and layed down in his, but he had his rifle with him under the blanket. Davis pretended to be asleep and snore. The Ohlock got up and picked up a stick from the woodpile. He was just going to hit Davis with it, then my partner shot him. He had a box of shells, which is twenty shells. He shot him twenty times, with every shell he had. My partner ran an eight-hour walk from his camp to my camp in three hours, he was that scared.

"He told me all about it and I told him, 'Let's go back!' He told me to cook something to eat, he was hungry and tired. I said, 'We've got to see what the heck you saw.' He told me, 'No. It was just a little human being with white hair, white beard, and long hair.' After he finally ate, we started back slowly. When we got back to the sod hut, barabara, he wouldn't go in. So I loaded my gun and I kicked the door open, but there was nothing in there but a weasel. The weasel was shot all to pieces. It was the man that turned into a weasel. But my partner swore up and down it was a man.

"I went to Olga Bay, by Alaska Packers Cannery. My brother Alex was gone. He was in the village and there also with him was an old man, Alex Nekeferoff, but he was gone too. So I was alone there. Across the river were two cannery watchmen. One dark morning I got up. It was real brisky so I thought I'd go up to Akalura Lake and track foxes. There was two and a half feet of snow. It took twenty minutes to walk to the lake. I picked up a fresh fox fur. I didn't walk one hundred yards more when all at once I just got sick. I felt fine when I got up that morning, but now I could barely make it back home.

"Around noon, I cooked some bacon and eggs and it made me sick to look at them. I left them on the table and I left. The cabin had three rooms, all in a line, the kitchen, a bedroom, and another bedroom. I undressed and went to bed. I was really that sick. I woke up and it was dark. I had a coal lamp burning and I was laying on the bed. I saw something round, with probably fifty to sixty sets of feet. He just went right by me into the other empty bedroom. I just layed there and thought, 'What in the world is that?'

"I had a .45 Colt pistol laying there; I took it and I loaded it. With the lamp, I went into the other bedroom. There's nothing in there but beds with springs and an empty trunk. What the heck's the matter with me? I thought maybe I was reading too much and I saw it in my eyes. So I sat down. There's that thing coming out of that empty bedroom; it went back in the kitchen. I could see tracks, I could see him.

"He was about four feet high, and completely black. He went back into the kitchen. I got my pistol, took the lamp into the kitchen, and looked everywhere, even in the sugar bed, in the flour bed, and in the oven. I looked all over, even on the ceiling. Nothing. Well, the second time I saw it I knew it had to be something. I came back and sat down on the bed; I was just going to put my feet up.

"I saw the stove wood coming up in the air, then he threw it at me, I ducked. He just missed my lamp, coal oil lamp. The Natives told me never to get scared. I was a little nervous all right, all alone in the dark. I just sat up and covered myself with a blanket. I held like this my hand and my arm and I had my flashlight; I was waiting for him to come back.

"He didn't, so that's how I woke up in the morning. I was sleeping with my gun loaded and the safety off! I was holding the gun and the flashlight on my lap. I was sound asleep. When I got up, I looked the whole house over. What was it? I don't know. That stick of wood was laying there, right where I saw it fall, so it had to be something; Something threw the stick 'cause I saw it fall.

"One other time . . . it didn't happen to me, but it happened to one of my friends, Nick Phillips. He was very dark complected. He had a camp, a cabin in Camp Bay, and I had a trapping camp in Red River. Nick asked me, 'Are you going to your trapping camp in Red River?' I told him, 'No, I have to cook bread.' I had all my winter food already there. 'Well,' he said, 'I'm going to Camp Bay early to my camp, then I'm going to walk across the Quail Lagoon; so when I get up I'll bake the bread.' I started to go and I walked a couple of miles and I looked and I see Nick Phillips. (I told you he was going to die from cancer.) I see him. He was running big, wide strides and his face was white like this here. He come to me and he grabbed me and I said, 'What's the matter with you?' He couldn't even talk. Finally we sat down and finally he could talk. 'You know that old village not far from here? I was sitting there out on the slopes and I was going to eat lunch. I heard people talking in Aleut.'

"He didn't pay any attention for a while and then they started singing in Aleut and he looked over there. He gets up, leaves his lunch, his rifle. He just started running—he knew I was coming by that time. I told him, 'Where's your gun? Where's your pack?' 'It was over there.' 'You're going to get it?' 'No. You get it from the village.' We had a seven-hour walk in front of us so I had to go and get it.

"That's about all the main things that happened to me there. Nothing else really. That's something I don't know why. Whatever it was, it was playing with us, stealing our bacon, and doing it. It has to be something."

CHRISTINE LUKIN: FURRY FOODS

by: Craig Baker, with Peter Olsen
photos: Peter Olsen and Leon Francisco

Living through the Katmai eruption of 1912 and tidal wave of "'64," Christine Lukin experienced hunger and hardships during the early days of Afognak. These were the days when rowing around the entire island of Afognak on a single hunting trip was still common. Bringing in cotton nets by hand and salting and smoking the salmon to last the windy winters were the seasonal goals.

Picture yourself in the early 1900s in a house on Afognak preparing a

Christine Lukin.

pirok on a wood-burning stove while others are outside splitting salmon for smoking. The smokehouse is down the path to the village and just a little further is the banya [steam bath] and the nushnik [outhouse]. Ebb tide is in half an hour so shovels are to be gathered to dig a few clams and maybe pick a few bidarki chitons [gathered at low tide on the beach]. Deer and elk are a thing of the future because they have yet to be transplanted by the government.

As a writer and high school student at sixteen years of age, I am not fully qualified to place you within these surroundings. It is equally hard for me to picture these settings because I have not lived in that day and experienced hardships these people have gone through. It certainly wasn't a question of being comfortable through the winter, but a much more burdening thought, which was the question of survival. Nothing was taken for granted as we do so much today. Physical labor was demanded of everyone. Along with the physical labor and constant demands for food, natural disasters also took their toll.

The eruption of Katmai volcano on June 6, 1912, set back many. Livestock died within hours after the first of the ash fell. After three days, the snow that wouldn't melt finally stopped falling. Five-foot drifts were common and the tremendous weight of it weakened and dropped many a roof. We are reminded of that day by the thick layers of gray ash found most anywhere on northern Kodiak Island.

More recent are the tidal wave and earthquake of 1964. March brought along its twenty-seventh day and the Good Friday disaster. As I remember, the water in the channel had risen well above the brown tide marks on the rocky beaches, this being my way of recognizing at which stage the tide was in. The moment I mentioned it to Dad, he turned on the radio and tuned it to the Armed Forces station. The broadcaster was repeatedly saying, "Tidal wave, evacuate immediately!" Our family then hurried into our old Chevy pickup and made our way up the already crowded Pillar Mountain. I vividly remember the buildings and boats which cluttered the bay the next morning. Having actually witnessed the happenings of that day and realizing their importance, I doubt I will ever forget them.

This is the situation my grandmother is in, she has much more to say than I do; to those who will listen it is interesting. Lend yourself the time to read and understand what she has to say.

"When I was in Perryville, one elderly man, whose name I can't recall, was responsible for hanging the salmon that had been caught by the fishermen in the smokehouse. That's how they lived back then, they helped one another when help was needed. Another man I remember, he brought salted salmon belly, a very good dish, and shared it with others until there was no more. Men would go duck hunting and give all their ducks to others. People were very unselfish in those days; they shared and helped because someday 'they' might need help.

"When a visitor would come to town, he would also receive food. I remember, when staying with my friend Barbara and another girl, the people would bring us all types of Native food. Angelena Smallma would come and visit me often when I was in Perryville. She was my friend. She taught me something that I thought very interesting. When the salmon are in the smokehouse but not quite done, you'd cut them up in slices and stick the slices in the oven. That's what you call 'kippering' and it's very good that way. We had never done it that way in Afognak; we didn't know about it.

"On Afognak we mixed shortening with something. I don't know what it was but it was fluffy, probably some sort of wild oil and lots of berries put into it. We had food very different from that of today. One such dish was 'furry food,' seal flippers cooked up and it was as good as pigs' feet. Unfortunately, there was no way to take the fur off. My little sisters disliked the fur part, and the table would be full of fur. As you can see, we lived off the land, wild, you know.

"I can remember when the elk were first transplanted. They would come up to the house and chew on clothes hanging from the line—they seemed to like my undies.

"Back in those days we would eat sea lion and seal till we got sick. I don't know what happened but I often developed a terrible stomachache. We were so desperate for food in the summertime that once another woman and I, we had nothing to cook, so we went to an old man's shed to steal some salted salmon. We had to break the lock. I didn't feel all that guilty about it because we were only trying to survive. Other foods we used to live on were seafood, including clams and gumboots [chitons].

Afonie and Christine (Grandpa and Grandma Lukin) enjoying a cup of chai.

"I remember they would serve smoked salmon at the parties, at least it was supposed to be smoked salmon, little pieces, skinned, with toothpicks. I told them that it wasn't the way we ate it. It didn't even taste like smoked salmon to me, it was too fancy.

"Grandpa was an excellent trapper, he really enjoyed it. Two men were planning on going trapping and they asked Grandpa if he would flesh the animals for them. He said that would be the last thing he would do. Once, way back, Grandpa had I don't know how many skins brought to him by a local man. He wouldn't touch them—they had all the fun and he'd be here doing the dirty work. He said, 'Why don't you learn to clean them like I had to?' I admired him for that. It's nothing but work, you know.

"Just last year when Grandpa was seventy-nine years old, he shot himself a seal, a six-footer, and without his glasses on. He had to hang it with a nail on the wall so it wouldn't touch the ground. Just the other day he dropped three ducks. His brother said, *'Dee-lets!'*—that means 'good shot!' He must be—after all he was shooting from a skiff at almost eighty years old! Before he brings a skin in the house, he washes it in cold water. This is done because when they are caught in a trap, animals often struggle and get their fur all muddy. After that, he hangs the skin, lets it drip, and then works on it.

"Last time Grandpa was trapping on Afognak, he set a trap between Sharatine's house and the shed. He completely forgot about the set and, when he did check it, a big silver-gray fox was in it. He had to kill it, so he shot it. It was a mess, a big hole in it. He said that I could have it and I said, 'Afonie, what would I do with it!'

"When I was just a small child I loved to fish for sculpin. I was always getting into trouble for running off and fishing the whole day away. One day I was gone until it got dark, and, let me tell you, I was more than a little scared to go home. Anyway, I made my way back to the house and noticed we had a visitor. Naturally, I didn't think Mom would spank me while a guest was over, but visitor or no visitor, she gave it to me and sent me to bed without any supper. She would whip me with those darned deck slippers; they really hurt, but it must have been hard for her to spank.

"Fishing for salmon is a job and a half. Late in the years we found that we could can our catch. In the summertime, pink salmon would come very close to Afognak, right in front of the village. I used to fish myself, you know; me and two other girls would make a set near the creek when the tide was right. We would often catch two hundred fish at a time. After catching them, the wheelbarrow would be used to haul them to the creek where they were cleaned and hung in the smokehouse or canned.

"The Fish and Game would have gotten us if we would have been caught, because we didn't have a permit. The way I looked at it was that the Lord gave us a big supply of salmon which the big boats were taking from us and we needed them to survive, so it wasn't really wrong.

"Many women knew how to fix salmon eggs to eat, and they were really tasty. I never did manage to pick the correct recipe. Years ago, they would

smash them up, set it aside, and let it rot. It doesn't sound very appetizing, but we didn't eat it like that. It was used for a flavoring in various dishes. We didn't have flavorings like those you buy on the shelves today.

"One dish called sheszook used seal oil for flavor. It was made of potatoes, all whipped up nice and fluffy, a little seal oil added, and then you stir in berries, either blackberries or blueberries. It was delicious! I'm sure the younger generation wouldn't understand such a dish, but to us it was a treat.

"I believe in learning by watching. That's how I learned to split salmon. I would watch Mother's techniques and practice on my own. She was very good; she could split those fish and not leave a bone, not many people know how to do that! She also would make red salmon oil. She would boil heads in five-gallon cans and skim the oil off the top. The oil wasn't very tasty, but we had no choice. Mom could cook wild celery, pushki they called it, and wild rice very well. I was never able to, it was always bitter.

"One of my favorite foods was a small, white-meated fish called a sculpin. Its meat was very sweet and it was, in my opinion, much better than codfish. I doubt that many of today's fishermen know the quality of this little fish because its skin is very rough and its food value is overlooked. It was good most any way you cooked it, but when it was put into soup with wild onions, it was extra good.

"We would often cook with potatoes. We would buy big thirty-pound sacks of these potatoes and store them for the winter. Not those red potatoes because they were too watery.

"People really burn me with the way they turn their noses at our lifestyle and foods. I remember the halibut would come right up to the beach and my son, Jacob, would throw a small line to them and catch a nice big halibut. Lots of people would pick watons, or as you call them 'mussels,' when the tide was out. The table was set when the tide came in. You would really be surprised at what you can eat when you don't have food like that of today. We ate most anything, raw seal, seal blubber and their fins, and it was good. I just can't explain these things to people who have never been without. We didn't have even half of the food we have today; it was just too expensive. The first time I ever saw bacon was when the volcano erupted and the big navy boat brought us supplies. Boy, we must have eaten bacon day and night.

"I'll never forget the eruption. It happened when I was only twelve years old. A huge, dark cloud came overhead and then it settled on us. Animals were running everywhere, trying to find shelter and there was none. I had no idea what was happening; people were fetching water in pails, I was very scared. It lasted for three days I think. We stayed in our house for the whole time. Some other people were there with us and we had to sleep like sardines in a can.

"One thing I'll never forget was my mother would save skins from dried fish so when we had nothing else to eat, she would toast them in the oven. They were crispy like bacon rinds and oh were they good when we were hungry!"

Because of these hardships, I often wondered why the past is referred to as "the good ol' days." I asked Dad about this and after a few moments of silence he answered that today the mental burdens greatly exceed those of the early days. . . . "We had our peace of mind. . . ."

HENRY NESETH: SAILOR, FISHERMAN, AND PROSPECTOR

This story was compiled from three other stories on Henry Neseth:
  –"*Mining Along the Ayakulik Beach*" by: Paul Collar and Geff Peterson;
    photos by: Paul Collar
  –"*The Life of Henry Neseth*" by: Larry Hellemn and Leonard Thomas;
    photos and drawings by: Larry Hellemn
  –"*Fishing With Sailboats*" by: Loretta Shangin and Jon Peterson
This story, "Henry Neseth: Sailor, Fisherman, and Prospector" was edited
by Matt Freeman.

Henry Neseth is a very self-reliant man. He came to America from Norway in 1914, learned to speak English, then went on to sail the Great Lakes. He's trained in the military, been a fisherman, a miner. . . . Today, at the age of eighty-six, he still likes to go prospecting when he can on the Ayakulik River. He is a proud, self-sufficient, and energetic man. Here is his story.

Henry was born in Norway on May 30, 1894. His family had a ranch there. "I remember when I was a young boy we didn't have any oilstoves; we had wood stoves then. We had to get wood. That's all we did, go to school and get the wood. Sometimes my older brothers and I went out. We had little boats, went out fishing and had lots of fun. Always got enough to eat. We also had meat. I was twelve or fourteen then. When I went to school in Norway, we just went up to the eighth grade, that's all the grades we had.

Henry Neseth.

"My father's parents, they were dead when I was little. My mother's parents, I remember them. My grandfather was a carpenter. He built houses." Henry's father was a shoemaker at first, but later became a tax assessor.

"When I was nineteen years old, I came over to America. The year was 1914. You had to work to eat—you couldn't run around getting food stamps like you do now. There was lots of Norwegians that had come to America. My brother was here and my uncle had a ranch in Red River Valley. That's in northern Minnesota between Ida and Crookston."

When Henry first came to America he couldn't speak any English, "But it didn't take long to learn." His older brother worked as a cook on the big steamships on the Great Lakes. His brother's wife was a waitress and when Henry came to Chicago, he washed dishes. He lived there with his brother for several years. He sometimes sailed on a ship that hauled logs back and forth, until the lakes froze in the winter and they stayed in Chicago.

Henry Neseth enlisted in the military service in Minnesota during World War I. He spent three months in Fort Snelling for training. They were going to send him across to Europe, so they gave him a physical. They discovered that Henry had TB and gave him a medical discharge. "That was a long time ago, but I'm still here. Whether they made a mistake or not I don't know, sometimes they do."

He went from there to a place they call Laverne, Minnesota, and worked in a restaurant as a cook. He left there and came west to the Black Hills in South Dakota. Henry worked on the road gang there for a while. From Dakota he went to Casper, Wyoming, and worked in the Salt Creek Oil Fields. When he quit, he came to Seattle. He came late in the spring and then shipped out with Captain Becklin for Point Barrow, Alaska, as the cook.

When Henry came back to Seattle, they got paid off in gold and silver, no paper. From Seattle Henry went to California and stopped at a restaurant in Sacramento. "You could buy half a day-old pie and a cup of coffee for ten cents, or [you could have] two great big cinnamon rolls." Returning to Seattle with Captain Becklin, he had ham and eggs and hot cakes for breakfast, all you could eat for thirty-five cents.

Henry sailed to Alaska on the vessel *Star*. It was a mail boat that ran from Seward to Umnak. "Went to Unga, Sand Point, and all them places. There was only three or four houses and a store out at Sand Point then." He went down to Unalaska. "There was just a pool hall, a church, and a few houses there." The next year he traveled to Sanak Island and was going to go cod fishing on a sailing ship, the *Progress*.

The *Progress* had two cabins, one with eight bunks on the deck, and one down in the fo'c'sle. (Fo'c'sle is the abbreviation of forecastle, the place where the sailors live.) "The engineer, he was from Ketchikan, he slept down in the fo'c'sle. Everybody put a curtain in front of their bed, because someone would have the light on so they could read, and the curtain kept the light out of their eyes and they could sleep. One evening that engineer was laying down, he wasn't sleeping, and somebody started to pull the curtain back. It was this Peruvian that came up with the dress gang. He was using narcotics and he had a great, big butcher knife in his hand. After that, everybody had hammers, hand axes, and clubs.

"One morning this Peruvian, he ran out of narcotics and he went completely crazy. Between the fo'c'sle and the deck by the mess room, back aft, there was a deck load of 100-gallon distillate drums to use for motors. The drums had boards laying on top of them. We were standing there waiting for the breakfast bell to ring. All of a sudden we see this Peruvian come out of the fo'c'sle and he put his hands on the rail and dived head first overboard. Somebody threw a lifebelt out and we saw his head bob twice, that's all, and then he was gone."

Henry only worked one summer as a cod fisherman. They used dories. "Them dories were built on the East Coast. We only had one man in a dory. Under the seat we had a pair of oars and a little sail. Most of the time we used the oars; when a little wind would come we'd put up the sail and do a little sailing. Right behind the seat there was a board across from one side to the other. There was nails about a foot apart in the ends of the board and there was two hand lines, one on each side with two hooks on each line. You had what they call the spreader that separated the hooks. Every time you pulled up a fish you took a turn around those nails so it didn't go down as far as it did the first time. The codfish followed the bait up and pretty soon you can see them down there."

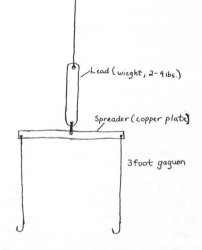

Hand lines used for cod fishing.

When the fish were unloaded from the dories they were weighed. "We got thirty-eight cents for a hundred pounds of fish, fresh fish before it's cleaned. Of course, we didn't have to pay room and board, we didn't have to pay for anything, if we did we wouldn't have had any money left." One day they had twenty-seven thousand fish on board the *Progress.* "There was three dress gangs working that day—the dress gang cleaned the codfish. First, they would cut the head off and pull the insides out, then they split them and took the backbone out, and then layed them flat and spread salt on them."

Henry Neseth also did quite a lot of salmon fishing. When Henry started to fish in Naknek with the Pacific American fisheries, he got twelve cents apiece for a whole red salmon. He fished in Kodiak for a year with a man by the name of Pete Iverson; they had a boat that belonged to Neils Christianson. They fished for the Trinity Packing Company, which had a cannery in Three Saints Bay. Henry and Neils had a seine skiff that you pulled around with a pair of oars and they took 75,000 humpies and dog salmon out of Port Hobron. "There were so many fish that you couldn't hardly tell where we had taken any." They got three cents apiece for "Those great big dog salmon."

Henry Neseth lived a little over two years in Seldovia before he came to Kodiak to live. He built a dory in Seldovia and put an eight-horsepower two-cylinder Cliff motor into it, the kind of motor they used for codfish dories out around Unga. A man by the name of Hank Russell went with him. They had the bow with canvas stretched over it so they had a place to sleep and eat. They had a little coal oilstove to make coffee and fry stuff on; they were called Swede stoves. "That's what you had in all the fishing boats out in Bristol Bay. They could make coffee in just a few minutes. They used coal oil instead of gasoline." They have a small tray around the top. "You put a little coal oil in there, touch a match to it, and you could preheat them." The stoves had a small handle that you pumped them up with. "They would burn real hot and didn't use up a lot of fuel. They were something like a blow-torch, only a much wider flame."

When they left Seldovia they went up to Anchor Point, came down the west side of Cook Inlet to Kukak. They stayed in Kukak for a day and then went from there to Takli Island, across to Uyak, down to Karluk (on Kodiak Island), from Karluk to Alitak, from Alitak to Old Harbor, and then to Kodiak. "We never had any trouble at all."

"I came to Kodiak in 1928. I was thirty-four years old then. I've been here fifty-two years. There was a school here with two to three teachers. They had a school lunch station up on the hill out there; that was the only one. The only people that had work was one postmaster. [There were] two stores, Erskine and Kraft's. Kodiak's population at that time was around 500 or 600. There were only two pickup trucks; Kraft's had one and Norman Noble had the other. The beach was clean, no processors or canneries on it except for Kodiak Fisheries and a small shack.

"I fished in a sailboat in Bristol Bay near Naknek. When I first came from Naknek they had eleven canneries there in that whole area. There was over 1,000 sailboats fishing there. They came to powerboats in 1953. Sailboats were wonderful to fish in. There was only two of us that worked on a sailboat; someone steers the boat and one pulls in the net. We had a roller on the stern to pull in the gear and pull in the net and the fish in the boat.

That's all handwork, we pull it in by hand. Sometimes it was hard work, and sometimes not.

"There was small powerboats called monkey boats. When there's no wind they pick up them monkey boats and tow the sailboats to the tally scow. Each cannery had seven tally scows and fish scows. Tally scows were house scows the crew lived in; fish scows were regular open scows tied up behind them. When they got a load, the motorboat comes around and picks fish up and takes it into the cannery. We had rough weather sometimes, not always. When the weather got bad, we went in.

"I built a dory or two, I built houses, too. The material was cheap. When I started fishing, we got twelve cents apiece for red salmon; now they get a dollar a pound. But you can buy something for your money them olden days. Fifty cents apiece for king salmon. Now they give a dollar for a little slice of king salmon. I remember in Port Hobron we got 75,000 humpies and dogs. We made one haul, took off for the cannery, and come back again. We make another haul, load up, and head for the cannery. After we took 75,000 fish in, it was enough. There was dog salmon that weigh twelve pounds and we got three cents each for dog salmon. That's all anybody paid. Couple years before that they only paid one and a half cents, that's all.

"The canneries had big traps, so many fish you don't know what to do. A boat could only catch so much because canneries couldn't handle any more. So they put up the limit flag on the scows. So many canneries couldn't handle all of it. The cannery I fished for had eighty boats fishing for them. It's easier on powerboats now. It doesn't take that long. You can take the fish to the scow anytime you want. Well, now they have motorboats all year round. Now there's four canneries left; there's hardly any fish. In my years of fishing there wasn't a cannery that didn't have 80,000 fish.

"Now some people can't afford to buy fish. I remember it didn't cost so much then, but the prices started going higher. We made enough money from fishing to have enough food to eat the rest of the year. I built this house here in 1938 after I came back from Bristol Bay. I made enough money to pay for almost everything that's in this house . . . furniture, bathtub, bathroom stuff, and other stuff that came later."

Henry was also a bit of a prospector. "I started mining on Kodiak Island in 1932 when a man by the name of Bill Castell and I went down and prospected the Red River beach. Well, back then we called it the Red River, now they call it the Ayakulik River. We mined that beach for a distance of about five miles on either side of the river. The whole beach was pure sand with gold in it, and even a little platinum. The gold was usually right on top of the sand. Well, not right on top, sometimes you may have to dig six inches, sometimes more or less. It all depends, you see.

"There's quite often a fine layer of sand, black sand, and that's where you find the gold. After a storm, though, you quite often find the gold right on top of the sand and gravel, mixed in with the black sand [magnetic iron]. We would work the beaches down to, I would say, half-tide. That whole

"I started mining on Kodiak Island in 1932 . . . The whole beach was pure sand with gold in it . . ."

beach there is a glacier deposit. That's why there is so much gold there. The glacier, God knows how many hundreds of thousands of years ago, ground out veins of gold and minerals and dragged them over the countryside to where they are now.

"To extract the gold from the sand we would use a device called the rocker. It uses a rocking motion to get the gold out; gold is much heavier than sand. Then we used an amalgam to make final separation of gold from other minerals and sand. To do this, we would use an electroplated copper plate upon which the amalgam [mercury and rough gold] would go. The way we got the mercury out was to retort it. We would put the mixture into an airtight container which had a copper pipe going out of it into a water container. When you heat it all, the mercury comes out in fumes and when it hits the water, it liquefies again; not only do you have your pure gold, but the mercury can be used over again.

"We could have used a sluice box on those beach deposits, but to do that we would have needed a water pump. A sluice box has to have a source of running water because that is how the lighter material is carried away. A sluice has riffles all along it so it can catch the heavier particles, such as gold. The lighter stuff is just carried away. The bad thing about the rocker is that it only holds two to four shovels full of sand, and out of that you get a very small amount of gold. If we had used a sluice box, we could have done in four hours what it took us a day to do with the rocker."

Almost all of the mining on Kodiak Island was done in the 1930s—practically all of the mines were opened in that period of time. Henry Neseth did most of his mining between '32 and '36, as did many other prospectors. One likely reason for this is because the United States was in the middle of a depression at that time. Many people came to Alaska to try their hand at gold mining to make a living for themselves. Some succeeded; many didn't. Henry Neseth describes the situation. "Where I was working there were many people who would come and go. Some got gold; most didn't though. At one time there were seventeen different people working the same stretch of beach. The standard price of gold was $20.67 an ounce. Later, Roosevelt raised it to $35 an ounce, and still later it was raised to $42 an ounce. One time I took thirty-two ounces of gold in eight days. Then that was $660, now that would be tens of thousands.

"We'd take all our gold over to a storekeeper in Alitak where we would trade it in and get our groceries. Some of the men that worked that stretch of beach sand down there around us didn't last the week; I was there for four years, while Frank Peterson lived and mined there for forty years with his wife. He died a long time ago, and his wife followed him. We buried her up on a hillside. Frank was a Finn and she was a Native.

"There is also a small amount of platinum on the Red River. You could get it the same way as the gold. I never bothered with it, though; there was never enough to amount to anything. Platinum is a grayish color—it looks just like an aluminum coffeepot. Most of the time it comes in round pinheads. Sometimes they are flattened, but usually they are round. You also find platinum on Sitkinak Island. Besides these two places, there is no other area you can find it in in any large amount."

Gold has been mined here on Kodiak Island by individuals for many years. There has been a lot of gold recovered in that period of time. Some people say that as much as $185,000 worth of gold, more at today's prices, has been taken from placer deposits alone. Others say this figure is low. However, there is still much more remaining than has ever been taken. The State Geological Commission tells us that less than 20 percent of Kodiak Island has been adequately prospected. That remaining 80 percent probably has enough gold and other minerals to keep prospectors busy for many years. But for anyone to completely succeed, he needs to accept failure as part of the game. Henry Neseth is a perfect example of a man who will not quit. He has mined since 1932 and will return to that same mining site every summer for as long as he possibly can.

JOHNNY CHYA: "IT'S ALL DONE BY HAND!"

by: Peter Olsen, with Phyllis Flick

Let us take you back a little over four decades ago when fishing, the backbone of Kodiak's economy, was very basic, and calloused hands were the sign of a long, hard-working season. Power blocks, radar and outboards, which are the essentials of a modern-day fishing boat, weren't around yet. In no way am I belittling today's fisherman. I fish myself, but recognizing the added risks which the fisherman of yesteryear constantly worked under, I respect the sea because of the awesome powers it possesses. To work with and on the sea with the skills and the gear that they used would give me a great sense of pride in my past. The gangs, as Mr. Chya would call them, worked hard all summer only so they could make it through the cold, windy winters.

I was told of Johnny Chya's success as a fisherman through the scuttlebutt passed around the boat harbor. This inclined me to share him with you through the pages of *Elwani*.

Not wanting to give off a bragging impression, Mr. Chya didn't want to talk with us at first. I was persistent though, and finally got him to agree to talk. His modesty and memory were clear throughout my visit with him and

Johnny Chya.

the warm atmosphere of his home made me feel very welcome. After he recognized my ignorance of his fishing days, he took great joy in reminiscing about his past. I've yet to hear of someone bringing in almost 300,000 salmon in one year and making only $4,000 at that. Today, the work he did would be worth almost $1 million. The rest of this story is every bit as interesting; we'll let him tell it to you.

"I started in 1931 and I fished with some guys around here like Harry Morrison and Johnny Morrison. Then I fished with my brothers in '33 with what they call a beach seine or siwash seine. We never did make much success that year because the traps were taking all the fish.

"We were fishing in the Buskin and the Woman's Bay. We'd go out in the morning and we'd come in with three dories loaded with as much fish as we could pack. Several of these other gangs would be fishing there and they'd come in, or else we would tow them in. Each dory was loaded down with as much as they could pack. They'd come in and the superintendent would say, 'Dump 'em all.' They couldn't take ours because the traps were getting too many fish. They wouldn't even give us a count. None of us, and all the gangs would fish.

"In the morning he'd tell us to go out and bring in the same thing, over and over. For a week or more we never got any count for our fish. I would say we lost, oh, around 18,000 fish a week. We were fishing for Kodiak Fisheries, they were the only cannery here at that time. The only time we had a chance was when Alaska Packers brought a scow in from Larsen Bay.

"They told us to load our boats up and get out to the scow. We had six or eight dories in tow, trying to help somebody else out. Well, by the time we got out there, in back of the scow there was already a string of dories waiting for unloading. Even they couldn't take our fish. There it was again, not only ours, but the rest of the gangs that were fishing.

"The real fishing started in '28, but I was fishing on a tender then. I was assistant engineer on that for a while and then I went down to Shearwater. In '34 I fished in Shearwater for Kodiak Fisheries. We had a power dory which had a four-horse Cliff inboard motor in it. We used to tow a seine skiff and two dories. A seine skiff was about fourteen feet long with a twelve-foot bottom.

"Them dories held close to 1,000 fish apiece. I say there were times we left our net out there and put fish in the seine skiff so we could tow 'em in. Then the next boat would go out there and put the seine into the skiff. We never had no luck, though, because we didn't get a count for them. I went to Shearwater and fished there from, I'd say, '39 till I quit fishing. We did very good down there. One summer we fished there was eight or nine of us in the gang that was fishing in 1935. We fished off Kiliuda Spit then. We fished something like they do in Karluk now, big nets across the creek. Except there's no creek at Kiliuda Bay. We fished off the sand spit, and you talk about jellyfish! Man, oh, man, they'd come in with the tide.

"We fished for two or three weeks, I guess. Then the fish commissioner came along. He was standing there watching us, then he said, 'Well, fellas, this is your last haul.' This was on a Saturday. 'It's the last day of fishing like that here. If you fish anymore like that here, you're subject to arrest because I'm closing this area. With a big seine like that, you could cut it in half and fish in two gangs.' Which we did.

"When we totaled up the catch, whatever species we had, they never added one or took one away from the amount. It totaled up to 100,000, *even*. That's exactly the catch we had that year. That was the last year I fished like that. After that, the three of us brothers fished together. I think our share that year was $200 apiece. Then in '37, that was the big year. We fished Kiliuda Bay; never left Kiliuda. One Monday morning, the *Minnie B* came in. We had a bag of fish and we were just gonna start to brail. We used to deliver 20,000 to the *Minnie B* three times a week. Whatever they wanted from us in the cannery. If they say, 'bring in 6,000 or 1,000,' we'd take that from wherever we were fishing.

"That year we had almost 300,000 fish. The fish that we got that summer —that's all different species and with our spring work and fall work which we used to do every year down there—we got paid off with almost $4,000. The *Minnie B* used to come in in the morning around noon maybe, and it wouldn't be till ten o'clock in the evening that we'd finish unloading. We'd have to wait till it got a little light in the morning so we could see. Sometimes we'd be going along and we'd look at the fish and say, 'No, that's not

The *Minnie B* in her berth.

enough for 10,000.' Of course, we didn't hit 'em every time. We'd make a haul and figure we had 10,000 in that one haul. Sometimes we'd have to make another haul in order to get 10,000.

"The nets were made of cotton. They weren't like the new nets now, those nylon nets. We used to use what they call copper oleate on the nets. And then there was that brown stuff before copper oleate came. We fished company gear all the time, we never fished independent. In them days you had to pitch every fish out of the boat onto the *Minnie B*. We had different kinds of brailers [for this]. We had what they called a dago brailer they used in the skiffs. You take and dip it into the fish with the web and you pull up. One man could handle that, but most of the time it was two of us. The fish roll right into the dory, just like they used to do in the trap. It's all done by hand and you keep on doing that and you can get all the fish out of the net that way.

"We used a power dory to take us around to different places. This power dory wasn't made for fishing, it was a pleasure boat. We lived right on board it. They started using the outboards in '37 or '38. You really didn't need them because a lot of the fishing was done by beach seining. The outboards were used mostly around Karluk and Red River so they could tow the net

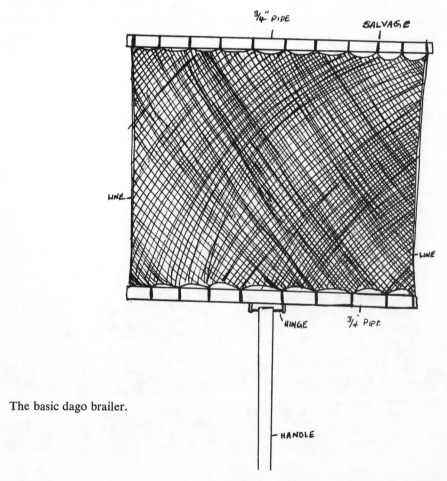

The basic dago brailer.

out. Outboards, they didn't use them too much, they weren't dependable. Days like we've been having lately, all rainy weather, they were just nine-horse and they might go out.

"A lot of the fishing was done just on beach seine. In '37 when we were fishing, a bunch of guys had tents ashore camping. Every Saturday evening we had to quit at six o'clock. Saturday evening they'd take and back up the skiffs to the beach and pull their nets up above the high-water mark. They'd spread them out so they would dry and then Sunday evening, or whichever way the tide went, they'd put them back into the skiffs so they would be ready for Monday morning.

"In '37 we didn't have no power, all we had was oars. We set out with oars. We'd pull the net up by hand and we'd purse it by hand, too. Only thing was we'd brail onto the boat with a winch; we used power then. We set the regular trap to be making those tow hauls. About forty-five minutes to a tow, you use your own judgment. In an hour and a half you'd probably have enough.

"We made a set one time and, as far as I know, we had 26,000 fish in that one set. We brailed onto the boat, loaded the boat up, then we took and tied the corks onto the skiff. We were in deep water so when the *Minnie B* came in we called them right over. So they dropped their anchor and we just tied up to them and unloaded. When we got through unloading she backed up so the other boat could come in. Then we filled up our boats again, in the same set. We'd load up till the stern end went down and drop the fish through the hatch. The fish worked their way back in between the beams and you could stand on deck and feel them kicking underneath. We'd put a top on the back hatch and then fill up in front of that. When the fish started knocking that hatch over again, you just about got a full load.

"We got that second load like that and they wanted 6,000 at the cannery. The way we used to go, if they wanted 6,000 at the cannery, we'd take a brailer full and we'd count the fish. I don't ever think we had under whatever they wanted because we always put on ten or twelve extra brailers. Then, after we'd get that 6,000 on board—whatever we figured was 6,000, we let the rest go. I don't know how much we let go; I know we had a 26,000 haul that one time.

"On your way to Kiliuda, on the left-hand side, is a pinnacle. One time we made our set right out against the tide. The fish were all along the sandy beach there. It comes out like a little spit there and then it goes in a little ways; the fish were all in the spit. But we set from the pinnacle and went clear around with a running line. We had a 200 mesh deep seine, sixty-five fathoms that was 200 mesh deep. That point there was just like a bunch of soap bubbles when the fish were jumpin' and, oh, man, was it something. We got quite a bit of the seine closed up, then we started pursing, so that they had lots of room. We couldn't pull them up very easily, no room in there. Of course, we didn't have to get that much in one haul; I don't know why we did it, we just did.

"Same way with those dog salmon in what is now called Dog Bay. It's there on the right-hand side as you come out of Shearwater. We run past the rocks there and you turn in a ways, just as you come out there's kind of a bay, then comes Dog Bay. We went over there and there were lots of dog salmon. Oh, it looked like millions! So we set and I guess we picked up around 5,000 dogs in that one haul and it looked like we didn't even bother them.

"Most of the dories we had the cannery owned. They usually didn't have too many either; tenders were so close that we didn't have to have too many dories around. But there were times too that the tender wouldn't be around and there you were . . . stuck. There was one time in '37 that some of the Old Harbor guys made a set and they had enough there to last a week because you could take out only so much a day in each delivery. See, the *Minnie B* never came down every day and she was the only one that used to go down that way to Kiliuda Bay for fish. When there were a lot of fish we were on a limit and it was very easy to get what they wanted. Like if you had a dory [that held] say about 1,000 fish and they wanted 2,000 fish, then you figure two fillings are enough.

"I can't really tell you how to fish because everyone that goes fishing has

The *Fedair 4,* sister ship of the *N&S,* John Chya's boat.

their own ideas, but I'll tell you about an incident that happened to us one time. . . . I don't know if you ever heard of him, Captain Larsen they used to call him. But anyway, he started fishing and he had a little power dory which had a sixty-five-horse inboard Craftsmen motor. We were in Santa Flavia and we had a little four-horse McGlaughlin. Heck, you could almost stop that thing with a pair of oars. We were going along and all towards the river the fish were jumping, but we were way over in the opposite direction. It was just like a little island there. By the little island was a bar, kinda flat, and the humpies were there; but, just as luck would have it, they wouldn't jump. I don't know why, but those on the other end of the island were jumping on the creek. They'd stick their noses up and once in a while they'd shine like they do. I said to my gang, 'Gosh, look at him. He's gonna beat us to that set. Point over there, point towards the river.' And we kept on going like that.

"Captain Larsen came along in that rig that he had and away he went, over towards the river. Of course, what I was trying to do, what I was gonna do, was get over there to the edge of the sandy beach. We backed in there and we set clear around. We have 3,500 fish there in that one haul. He hardly got anything in that one haul. So he said to me, 'Next time I see you pointing like that, I'm gonna look to see where you go.' But that rig that he had, honest to goodness, it was just a shallow-bottomed, round-bottomed lifeboat. It was something they used in the Navy. But they had it rigged so that you could purse from either side.

"We fished in Seven Rivers; that Seven Rivers is a shallow place to fish for salmon. There were times I'd get into the back and help the boat along. But we were there all summer, often we were there alone. That's the year Karluk had that big run of fish, humpies.

"Don Edwards came on his boat with our purse seine on board. He said to me, 'The boss wants you guys to go to Karluk. The east side closes on Saturday.' So we went to Karluk. We had a net in the boat and everything. When we came back the following year, a foreman down there at the cannery said, 'I want to show you something.' So he showed me a propeller. They've got a hub on them where the blades stick out. This one had three blades and when he showed it to me, one blade was out and about half of it was gone. The other two blades were broke off near the hub. I didn't know what was going on and I said, 'What the heck is that?'

"He said, 'That's from your K2 on your boat. How in the heck did it ever run?' It was surprising that it did go with that one-half of a blade. So I said to him, 'I'd better go to the Seven Rivers to see if I can pick up those two blades.' That's how shallow it was and you could almost hear it grinding. We were the only ones in Seven Rivers, I think. We got up to 75,000 fish there.

"You know, in the spring, from the time the cannery crew starts coming up, you meet them and when they come back next year you know them. A lot of times they come up to me, 'Well, how many fish this year? How much, Johnny? . . . 90,000, 70,000, 75,000?' 'Oh, maybe more than that.' "

Today we not only have faith in such things as the outboard, we depend on them. If they break down we lose fishing time repairing them. Mr. Chya, and all the other people of the gangs, we salute you, you and your past. There is nothing we could give to relive those days because they are now past. Thank you for sharing them with us.

ELI METROKIN: BEAR HUNTING

by: Richele Weaver, Dave Chavez, and Mario Agustin, Jr.

It was on a rainy cold day when we went to interview Mr. Eli Metrokin. Eli, a very kind and humorous man, was born here in Alaska in 1901. Most of his life has been spent in Alaska. He enjoys hunting, fishing, and trapping. In his earlier years, Eli was a hunter and bear guide, which he enjoyed, but now he says, "I'm just getting too old for that kind of stuff!"

As we arrived at his door, he greeted us with pleasure and as we entered his house, our bitter feelings toward the rainy day turned into warm feelings. At first, which is natural, it was hard for us to get Eli talking; but as we got to know each other better, our nervousness disappeared and our relationship grew. Eli told us about so many different events, exciting and serious, that he had experienced. It seemed as though he'd done everything. It was a memorable experience to talk with this man.

On one particular hunting trip, Eli's partner had shot a bear and the bear had fallen down. "I said, 'I'm gonna keep away from this bear; I think that he is still alive.' He was laying down there and I could see his ears move. 'No, no, no, I shot him right in the neck!' I picked up a rock, threw it, hit

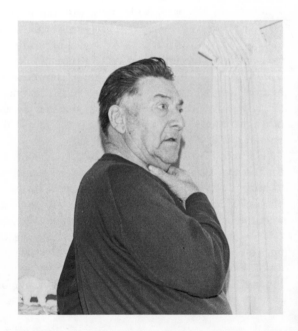

Eli Metrokin.

the bear right in the back. Holy smoke, that thing jumped up! He was coming right for me. Just as I started to put my gun up, Fred started running. The bear spotted the movement from the corner of his eye. Just as he swung around, I shot him. But my shells, I had army steel jackets, went right through him."

Fred fell to the ground and raised his arm to protect himself. The bear bit Fred's arm close to the shoulder. Fred had a pack on and when the bear tried to bite the arm, he bit the pack, too. He would have lost the arm if it wasn't for the pack. After the bear bit Fred, Eli shot it once more, killing it this time.

Eli kept himself busy with his hunting, trapping, and fishing. In the spring he would trap foxes. In the summer he would go fishing. When September came, bear season opened and he would hunt bear until November when he would start hunting the foxes again.

Eli remembers Kodiak as a small village that was nice and quiet. He remembers only eight houses on half of Mission Road. There were only two stores; you never had to wait in line for groceries. There were no roads, only trails three or four feet wide. By the Russian church there was a barn on the edge of the trail and you had to push a cow out of the way to get by.

"The fur trading started in 1930," Eli recalls. "We went out to Karluk Lake. You could count bear; I bet you could see maybe forty, fifty bear on the shores of that lake. They were fishing. The fish were all along the shores of the lake spawning. The bears came down and fed on the fish. We were on the island across where we could look with our binoculars and count the bears splashing all over the shores.

"That's when we first started. The bear really started going down when they started hunting and taking sportsmen in there. They used to have as many as six hunters at a time in a camp and they'd take two apiece. Two bear apiece and that went on for quite a number of years. Boy, that kind of thinned 'em out and they finally stopped that. They only let the hunter take one; that's the way it is now, you're only allowed one bear."

We asked Eli where a good place to find bear would be and he told us where he would go. "You gotta go someplace where there's nobody around, no traffic of any kind. You got to go to Uganik Bay, Uyak Bay, or Karluk Lake. Around here with this traffic, you won't see any bears. The farmers and ranchers killed a lot of them because they were killing their cattle. They killed quite a few bear, those ranchers did, at spring and fall. That's why there's not a lot of bear around. Even if right now one happened to come around, they'll go after him until they get him."

We asked him if he thought it was right that the ranchers go and kill bear and he replied, "I don't know. I guess so. If you don't, you're going to lose quite a few head of cattle. Takes money to keep cattle. It's hard to keep them all out like that. The bear was here first, before the cattle or the ranchers ever got started. There were bear down at the Buskin before the cattle got started. Buskin, Middle Bay, Kalsin Bay."

Eli with Kodiak brown bear, the largest bears in the world.

Eli: "This is when I was young and handsome."

Eli displays two of his prize bears.

Next we asked Eli to tell us how he prepares the skins. "You gotta work the whole thing over. You gotta take it back to camp and take all the fat out of it. Then work to the joints and claws so the salt can get to them. The head, you gotta lot of work to do. You split the ear; you split the lips. There's a lot of work on that thing. You salt it, forty-eight to fifty hours of salting; then take it out and dry it. After it dries up, you just roll it up·and take it to the taxidermist." He told us that the size of the skin determines the price that the taxidermist will charge. Maybe a seven-foot bear would cost $1,200; a ten-foot bear would cost $1,300.

"There were a lot of bear here on the island, no more now. Oh, there's a few, but not now, very seldom you see a bear here. It takes quite awhile, quite a few years, for a good-sized trophy to grow. Eight, nine years, maybe ten. But they kill the cubs two and three years old. They might look big to some hunter that never saw a bear before. One about that size, why heck, that's only from here to the chair [four feet] if they're only two or three years old. Well, that's what makes it bad. There may be some ten-footers roaming around, but you don't get many of those. You get about one or two a year from the island.

"Afognak's got them. Afognak Island's got the bear, the big bear. Nobody hunts there and it's hard to hunt. Very seldom will anyone go out there and hunt, too much wood. You come down to the beach in the open and you happen to be there at the right place, right time, you get one. Otherwise, it's pretty hard."

We asked Eli if he had any trophies. "No, no, I never keep them. Do you know why? They are nothing but dust collectors. For a person collecting trophies, you gotta have a special room, a big room. They take a lot of space —you gotta have ten feet. A bear's just as long as he is wide with his arms out." And referring to his living room, Eli Metrokin told us, "You'd be likely to squeeze a weasel in here!"

HAZEL NIXON: FORTY-ONE YEARS IN KODIAK

by: Lynnette Strahle, Rhonda Gossage, and Lillian Bradshaw

Her life began near the turn of the century and has brought her to a new and different technological age. She has become wise from her experiences in our world and can speak of both the past and present with vivid knowledge. Few are left who can remember early Kodiak, so one can learn much from the reminiscing of Hazel Nixon.

She was born in a small mining town near Duluth, Minnesota, during an era when wood fires were their main source of heat and horses their transportation. Hazel feels strongly that the ways of the past will one day be the ways of the future. "I feel sorry for you. I really feel sorry for you—if you ever lose your can opener you'll be in trouble. We can't go back to what we were, but I would like to see everybody trained in some way, for self-preser-

Hazel Nixon.

vation in case something happened. I wouldn't like to see people starve to death because they don't know how to start a fire without matches. Lots of things you really need to think about."

Hazel and her husband Al moved to Kodiak in 1939 just before World War II. "We heard about the base going up; there was nothing here at the time and the fishing was good so we decided to stay here a year, but that was forty-one years ago."

The Nixons came to Kodiak on a steamboat. Boats were the only means of transportation to the island and they brought the one line of communication—mail. They still play an important part in the function and life of our town. "When I came to Kodiak there was nothing unusual here. It was a nice, small town with about three cars and a team of horses. A boat came about every three weeks or so and everyone in town came down to the dock to see the boat come in. There was about 500 people living here then.

"The first thing we did when we got here was look for a place to live. We finally found a little log house next to where Blackie Patterson had his old garage. It was on the corner of Benson and Alder Lane; but you couldn't

"I wouldn't like to see
people starve to death
because they don't know how
to start a fire without
matches. Lots of things you
really need to think about."

find it now, there's nothing there. Early Kodiak had no telephones or electricity. Kerosene lamps were used for lighting. There was only the road to
the base, which was just a wagon road.

"There was no bank in town so when you came in with your fishing
money, you'd deposit it with Krafts. When the boats would come in, Ben
Kraft would go down to the boat's purser and get what silver change he
needed. Then he would walk back up the street with two bags of money.
Nobody bothered him, everybody knew Ben was coming up from the boat
with money. He made no secret of it; that was before crime was invented
here. We had no problems. There was one policeman who worked both day
and night. He didn't carry a gun but he carried a 'wop you over the head
thing' and that took care of it."

In 1939 the Army arrived in Kodiak and began building a base on the
peninsula between St. Paul Harbor and Old Woman's Bay. The base boosted
the economy and the population of Kodiak, but wasn't finished when war
was declared. It would be completed later on in the war. "Kodiak didn't see
any war. Everybody was scared and they made us black our windows out.
They wouldn't let us run any lights or even have a flashlight on the street.
Nobody got hurt, but a woman did shoot herself accidentally when they issued guns. We were under martial law for some time, but I was never fright-

ened because if the Japanese were going to attack they would have done it at Pearl Harbor. Kodiak was too small for them to bother with, but we were prepared.

"We had an outpost in town where the post office is now. It was a small dugout with four men watching the bay. There was another one where the Kodiak Electric Association building is now and then the big gun emplacement at Fort Abercrombie, but it was closed to civilians. Then after the attack on the Aleutians the war left us and moved south."

Hazel and her husband moved quite a bit around Kodiak Island but spent most of their years at Bells Flats working on their ranch raising cattle. The cattle industry is a hard life in Kodiak, as well as expensive. The land is good for the animals, but not for farming the support crops needed for them. Most of the supplies are shipped from Seattle. Besides the high cost of feed, the cattlemen lose a lot of cattle to bears. "The first year we were here a bear killed eleven head of cattle. We never hunted bear, though we did kill one bear while we were out there. He came right into the yard and ate some pig feed so we killed him."

It was during her time on the ranch that the 1964 earthquake hit the island. "I was out on our place about twelve miles out of town and my husband was in town. We had about forty head of cattle on the ranch. They'd been down towards the beach and they came home a little early. They stood around the house and they were there when the quake struck. I was just about to go outside and feed the chickens and do other things when the quake hit. It was Good Friday, five o'clock in the afternoon. It didn't sound too good but I wasn't frightened. I stood by the window in the kitchen looking out but there was nothing to see; I was standing there dodging cups that were falling. The tin roof made some noise, and one old cow looked back, then she called her calf, and all the cows followed her toward the barn. There was a pan of milk and a pan of water sitting up on the table; they jumped up and spilled all over the floor. The earthquake lasted five to ten minutes and not an animal made a noise except for that mother cow.

"After the quake died down, I went and got a mop so I could wipe up. Al got home in twenty-five minutes, it usually took longer. He started for home as soon as the quake was over because he thought I'd be frightened out there all alone. The earthquake didn't really affect us much. It shook down a little calf pen and it shook the nails out of the roof. As far as water and any other damage, there was none.

"When Al got home he had heard that there would be a wave, so we listened to the base radio. The broadcaster was the last man off the base peninsula and he let us know the size of the wave. First it was eighteen feet coming around Cape Chiniak, then it increased to twenty-five feet. Of course he warned everybody to high ground. I sat down and started pulling my boots on and Al said, 'What do you want your boots for? Don't you know you're twenty feet above sea level?' Then when the wave hit, we didn't see it. We never did see the water till the next day when we walked out."

"Everyone makes such a fuss about people growing old, but you can't stop it. I think old age is beautiful."

Hazel's husband Al died in 1966 and she continued to live at Bells Flats, running the ranch for four and a half years. In 1971 Hazel packed up and moved into town. She now resides at the Senior Citizens building where she operates the switchboard. Although her life has been long, Hazel Nixon is still as vigorous and intense as ever. "Everyone makes such a fuss about people growing old, but you can't stop it. You're gonna get there somehow or other. They seem to think that old people need so much. We don't need much, we like to talk, most of our talk is in the past. For me my life is much happier now than it was when I was young. I think old age is beautiful. I have much more fun now than I did when I was sixty years younger, so it's all in the way you live."

5. World War II

FRANCES BARTON: "I'M GOING TO BLOW THAT LIGHT RIGHT OFF YOUR CEILING"

by: Francis Costello

Frances Barton is an elderly lady who has lived in Kodiak for almost forty years. Mrs. Barton was born and raised in Tacoma, Washington, and came to Alaska in 1931. She lived in Anchorage for nine years and came to Kodiak in 1939. Kodiak was completely different then, there were few cars and people used horses instead, due to inadequate roads. Kodiak was a nice little town then, something like Port Lions or the little villages around here. People helped each other and everybody knew most everybody else. If somebody arrived in town, the people of Kodiak would usually be having coffee with them and getting acquainted within the hour.

The population of Kodiak was 600 to 650 people; that didn't include the navy base because it wasn't finished yet. In fact, it was said that the war discovered Alaska. Mrs. Barton begins her story at the time she came to our small town.

"I left Anchorage and came to Kodiak in 1939. I came on a freighter boat that carried passengers. It was a nice trip and I met Mrs. Freida Blinn and her daughter, Marlys, who was only two or three years old. We had quite a nice talk aboard the boat; she said she had lived in Kodiak all her life. Then as we stopped at the dock, I looked as if it was kind of disappointing to come from Anchorage to this, so Freida says, 'Come up and see us sometime when you have nothing to do.'

"We stayed at Madsen's Hotel. It was just a one-story little place. No lights, just candles. They had lights but then they burnt candles at 10 P.M., and you had to pay to take a bath. We stayed there about a week and finally we moved in with some friends. Then we built our own home, and got acquainted with the people here, and they were really fun. Freida and Jess owned a great big dance hall. We would go there to dance and have fun every weekend.

"We knew everybody and the best dancer that ever danced with us was Kyle Lunde, and she really could dance. We were all pretty young then and we all thought it was pretty cute.

"Then the town started to boom, and we knew the war was coming. Civil Service people came here to work at the base. They were pushing up tents everywhere so they could live. They built the navy base, Fort Abercrombie, and another camp and we used to go up there and have a Sunday dinner with the boys. We used to invite them to our house and have a little lunch because they were so lonesome for their mothers. They told us the war will be hitting us and it is coming closer and closer.

"Then one Sunday morning, a friend of mine came to the house and said, 'Oh my God, what are we going to do? Japan has hit Dutch Harbor!' It scared the wits out of me. I said, 'Oh my God, they ain't got far to go!' [NOTE: Dutch Harbor is in the Aleutian Chain, several hundred miles from Kodiak.] Then I found out that it was Pearl Harbor, so we all felt a little at ease. The Navy came to our house and gave us numbers on our houses; they said they would take all our keys so if we had to evacuate, they would come to the house and pick up things we needed. This was in the wintertime and they told us we had to have a sheet to cover ourselves in the snow. If we heard them dropping bombs, lay flat, or get under a tree and lay flat. My number told me to go to the Harvester restaurant, which was just under construction. So my girl friend and I ran up the road to the Harvester as fast as we could when there was an air raid warning. When we got there everyone was just hysterical because they didn't have any medicine if anyone did get hurt. We went in, looked at each other, and said, 'Let's get out of here.' I had a cabin at Island Lake, so we went there.

"We were afraid to walk the roads, so we cut through the woods. We got there and we weren't supposed to have any lights, but we did have lights. We were rather stupid. A couple of days later someone came up from Fort Abercrombie and told us to turn off the lights; he said the Japs might think it was a place to drop a bomb. We had to stay there in the dark and in four or five days, we came home.

"Then the evacuations started. We would get so scared; we would have to run up Pillar Mountain, get halfway up, and hide in the bushes. We could see everything so plain, we figured the Japs could see us and they were going to come. We were scared that they might pick us off on the mountain; so we figured, no more, we just can't go up that mountain. But you never knew when you had to evacuate. Sometimes once a week, or maybe twice a day. When we would hear the siren, we would run up the mountain. There was supposed to be a big Jap aircraft carrier out in the bay somewhere. We were scared because we knew how many planes they carried and we heard the Japs were going to drop bombs. Then it got so that I was scared to stay in the house. I found a big hole under one of the trees in the backyard; I took a sleeping bag and slept under it.

"The siren blew again and we had to run up Pillar again. We found it was a false alarm. The boys that would come to us told us that if it ever got so bad that we heard a bugle blowing, that was the way they would let us know that the Japs were coming. He said, 'If that blows, make it the best way you can through the woods to the base, because everybody is going to be evacuated to the base.' We prayed we would never hear it blow. My girl friend and I would sit in the bed and she would say, 'Did you hear a bugle?' and I would say, 'No.' Then we would get out of bed and go listen outside.

"We just ran so much and got so tired of running. We would get up at twelve o'clock midnight, have to turn the oil off, and get old clothes on. I had mukluks and I could hardly put them on. I was so scared of running. We were allowed one suitcase and a pet with one can of food. We had our numbers where to go where they could bring us up some food—which they never had to do because the Japanese never did drop a bomb. All the evacuations we had were in total blackout. We had boards put on our windows that we would leave off during the day and put up at night. A lot of the times I couldn't sleep and I kept it totally black in the house. It seems like every time I looked out the window, I would see big trucks going by with big guns on them, all night long going from base to Fort Abercrombie and the other two camps. It really was a shame how we had to keep evacuating, it just scared us so much.

"When we had the blackouts and had to have plywood over our windows, my husband had them on all the windows except the kitchen. Instead we had a green curtain. I left it down once and I let the light burn, but not too bright. Then an MP guard came along and said, 'Lady, if you don't turn that light off or hold this curtain down, I'm going to blow that light right off your ceiling!' He meant it. At first I thought he was kidding. He said I had a streak of light coming down the side of the window and if a Jap plane was flying above, he could see it just as plain as day and I wouldn't be here. Then I really taped her down; and I wouldn't let that curtain up from there often. They meant business when they tell you to keep them off."

Frances tells of other things affected by the war threat. "When I first came here there was a restaurant called Dunny's Café. A girl named Edith Dell took it over and was running it during the war. You had a blanket that you would come into like a front door, then another blanket after that one, and then the door. This kept light in. That's the way you would have to enter the building.

"Because of the blackouts during the war it would be dark, so dark. You had to have a flashlight, but you put a blue cellophane over the glass part and then you could use it to see where you were going. But it didn't help much because during that time there was a lot of cows here, and I would walk around and fall over a cow.

"The Army left and they left the Marines and the Navy. There was a big camp up on the hill right about where the park is now; it was a beautiful big camp and they tore it down. You would never believe that there was a big camp there. I also wondered why they destroyed that big gun, a beautiful big gun and I saw them work it. I can't say whether it was a fifteen- or twenty-foot gun. The boys said they were going to destroy that gun when they were through here because they don't want anyone to have it. They did, you know, they blew it up. Why I don't know. It would have been nice if they would have left them there for the park because there were four or five of them.

"After the war, the people were happy; they were making improvements with their homes, trying to make things more modern. But we liked it like it was. We lived in Kodiak, and we were on an island. We did not want big, beautiful buildings. What for? We're not in a big city. I left the city to come to an island and loved it."

6. Pre-1964

ED OPHIEM, SR.: FOX FARMING

by: Susie Pedersen
photos: courtesy of Ed Ophiem, Sr.
revised by: Tracey Reyes

Ed Ophiem has done a lot of things in his life. Building dories and skiffs are among them. Fox farming was also something which Ed enjoyed, at times, doing. It was hard to feed so many foxes; every day he had to go out and catch food for them.

"My first fox farming adventure was on Nelson Island, near Pleasant Harbor, the year during the Second World War—1941. Doc Pryor, owner of Nelson Island, had proposed a half partnership raising blue foxes. He was the first I know of in Alaska to breed platinum foxes through mutation.

"As I had not been around fox farms where different kinds of foxes were raised, I did not know too much of fox farming. I knew that it was a seven-day-a-week chore, feeding and taking care of foxes in all kinds of weather. Even a small size fox farm, with only several dozen foxes, consumes a lot of food that has got to be caught or hunted such as fish or sea lions. Or run a

Ed Ophiem, Sr.

trawl line to catch halibut, cod, flounder, or bullheads. It's a job in its own. Plus cleaning and cooking all this fish to feed a bunch of hungry foxes each day.

"In the summer months it's catching salmon to dry and salt for winter feed. Having to handbarrow this fish from the boat to drying shed, or salt house, was nothing but work, with the hope there would be a good increase of pups and a good price for pelts. For years the increase of pups were small, of poor quality, and the price was way down. A possible chance of breaking even for a year of toil, for nothing.

"I was for only a year with Dr. Pryor on Nelson Island. I bought an island from a man that was in need of money. It was an island that held a lot of loose foxes, plus several pens full of breeder foxes. The small island was Wooded Island, on the north end of Spruce Island. There was an old log house that had seen lots of living, a real cozy home with several gardens for growing vegetables, which we did. As there was several good gill nets nearby, it was a two-way thing. But, as anyone knows, gillnetting is all work, just as fox farming is. I had more than one man's share of work to do.

"In years before, I had been around many fox islands and knew how much work there was to fox farming. My father had tried raising foxes in pens on Unga Island back at the turn of the century, possibly 1906–7. He had to dig the silver-gray foxes out of the dens to get his start, and then try to pen-raise wild foxes. The pens were close to the house where his wife, my mother, could take care of them while he worked or cod-fished. This was three years before I was born.

The early days of fox farming.

"Here is a story my father told me later when I was growing up. There was in the community of Unga some hard cases. The fox venture was a going thing as the wild silver-grays increased and the price was good. It was getting to the pelting season when a couple of men, of questionable character, got to thinking about pelting the foxes for my father. As they had been around casing the joint, as they say nowadays, my father got to thinking why men of this caliber would give his place a visit. After they left, father put up a light line around the place, with the trip so a bucket of pebbles would fall on some cans and tubs. After dark, he sat with a double-barrel shotgun and waited. It wasn't long to wait and the trip line did its thing, scaring away the fox nabbers. They were bold enough to come back the next day with an excuse that they were passing by. As father had hid the trip line and noisemakers, there was a wondering look about them. Knowing these men of no good reputation, he pelted the whole bunch of foxes. Knowing that these men would not give him any rest, he could not work *and* sit up all night with a double-barrel shotgun to protect his foxes.

"As I was only three years in fox farming, I could see that there was no future in foxes as Russia flooded the world market with all sorts of fur. The best I got for my blue fox pelts was $35 a skin. Doc Pryor got as high as $1,400 per pair for platinum live breeders. But so many people started raising and breeding platinum fox, the market for long-hair fur went out of style.

"Why would anyone want to try raise pen-raised foxes? Back fifty, sixty years ago new people were coming to Alaska and settling on islands that were ideal for fox raising, as no wire pens were needed. With so much fish for fox feed, it was a means of making a living during years when salmon was so plentiful and there was no market or price.

"Fox pelts made into fur pieces was the fashion years back then. It was common to see a lady with two or more fox skins around her neck. Back in those days, a pelt worth ten or fifteen dollars to a fox farmer was a way of eating regular with no other means of making a dollar. I started fox farming only because there was nothing else to do except fish in the summer. As the island I bought had blue fox in pens, and the woods full of them, I thought there might be a future in such a venture. I knew about the work and problems of catching enough fish to feed such a bunch of foxes.

"I never did know how many fox I had. I had my pens on a small, low point on Wooded Island. Fighter planes would fly low over the pens passing on patrol, this was during the war in '42. The noise was so loud that the mother foxes ate all their pups. This put me out of the business of pen-raising. I did pelt a few during the fall season, as I had let the breeder foxes out to roam.

"During the next year I packed up our belongings and left the island, foxes, gardens, never to go back, with no regrets. I had fed them a small herd of sea lions plus enough fish heads to keep the foxes alive. I never knew what happened to the foxes left on the island. The blue foxes fed on mussels

"Most all foxes
contained on a small
island become pets."

when the tide was out. When I left the island there could have been 100 to 200 foxes roaming loose.

"Most all foxes contained on a small island become pets. Not that one could touch all of them, but tame enough to walk around unconcerned. Our son Edwin had a number of pet foxes that he would set the table for out in the yard and feed them scraps on old dishes. Some would be polite and stand with their hind feet on the chairs with their front paws on the table. Blue foxes are very curious animals, watching every move one makes. I would see them on the rock bluff above the smokehouse, peering down, thinking up some sort of mischief.

"During pelting time, I had box traps that I would put feed in to catch them. If the fox was not well furred I could let it go and set the trap for a better-furred fox. On killing them it was no problem, just a light tap on their snout with a small stick the size of a broom handle. The amount of money received, at that time thirty-five dollars, was a fair price, but good pen-raised blue fox brought sixty to eighty dollars or more.

"Most fur trappers and fur farmers sent their pelts to London, England, to Lomson Brothers, one of the largest auction houses. I sold mine locally. As there was such poor demand for blue fox pelts, I pelted only about thirty foxes each time.

"Back in the twenties and thirties there was a man by the name of George Hoag living at Blue Fox Bay on Afognak Island. He raised island foxes and made a good living from his time spent. Also Fritz Lorenson on Bare Island was one of the early fox farmers. The largest fox farm was Whale Island and the man who owned this large fox island was Dr. Parker. As there were so many foxes, he had to have help to do the catching of fish to feed such a large amount of blue fox. Feed would be distributed around the island by use of a small boat.

"Dr. Parker was a character. He owned a small boat, which he called *Prickly Heat;* it had a small heavy-duty gas engine to drive it. But this one day he came to Kodiak to get supplies, and at leaving time the engine wouldn't start. After some time and sweat, straightening up from bending over hand-cranking, he looked us over and declared, 'So, she doesn't want to run. Well, I'll fix that so she won't run again!' Leaving the oil float and going up to Erskine's store, he came back with a sixteen-pound sledgehammer on his shoulder. Stepping aboard his boat, he took off his coat, folded it, and pulled up his shirt sleeves. Spitting on his hands, he hefted the sixteen-pound sledgehammer and made a swing at the cylinder heads. The crowd stepped back as pieces started to pop off and sail through the air. After demolishing the engine, he tossed the larger pieces overboard. Looking the audience over, he declared, 'There is one engine that won't give anyone cranking problems!' From then on, when anyone was seen cranking a hand-starting engine, the onlooker would declare, 'Doc Parker it!'

"During the early years of fox farming, Long Island had several owners. I remember a Barret Willaby who wrote a story named 'Island of the Rocking Moon,' referring to Long Island. This story was made into a movie and one of the characters is still living at Ouzinkie. Mrs. Alexandra Smith was the heroine of this story, a daughter of Nick Larionoff, who was also one of the story characters. Long Island has seen a lot of people come and go. There was a lot of local moonshine made and sold; fox farming was just a front, as so many fox islands were.

"Nelson Island near Pleasant Harbor had a combination fox farm and moonshine still going. It was a way to make ends meet, as the price of fox was down to $10, with no buyers. Moonshine was down to $1.50 a pint, and very few people with money to buy it.

"Captain Johnson on Crooked Island was the only one that I know that made money fox farming. Of course, he built his breeding stock up and the price came up in later years, to make up for the years of work. Chirikoff Island had been a fox island and cattle ranch, but as far as I know, no one ever made any money on the cattle or foxes.

"Fox ranching was a passing thing and I doubt that it will ever come back. I personally never liked the idea of raising foxes and then have to take their hides to sell for a few dollars—one of the reasons I could never make a trapper, though I tried trapping for a few seasons. When I was growing up there was no other way to make a living, it was a way of life for so many people in Alaska."

HELEN NEILSEN: LIFE ON A BLUE FOX ISLAND

by: Susie Pedersen

Helen Neilsen is one of the greatest aunts I have; she is very easy to get along with and is considerate of others. She tries her best at everything she does and has a lot of experiences and knowledge that she is willing to share with people who are interested. Helen has a lot of character and, just by looking at her, you would say the same.

Helen was born January 31, 1916, at Chignik Lagoon, Alaska. She is one-quarter Aleut and the rest Danish and Norwegian and has lived in Kodiak twelve years now. She has four children still living; all are married with children of their own. Helen does not have a job—she does a lot of baby-sitting and just takes it easy. She has no future plans, she just takes life as it comes.

"Our fox farm was located on Nakchamik Island, or Fox Island as we called it. We lived on the island for many years; I'd say we were out there about ten years and we fox-farmed all that time. There wasn't anything else to do [at] that time in Chignik. People didn't fish for a living, you know, so we had to trap or fox-farm, either wild animals or fox.

"Papa started building the fox farm around 1925, but as the years passed, the prices dropped so low that we couldn't keep the fox farm going. Everybody had foxes, raised them on their own islands, but we had Nakchamik. Living on the island was nice, I liked it. We had some fun on the island, not just caring for foxes. Wintertime we would go skating, sliding. That was fun.

"When we started, we bought a pair of foxes from another island, and they increased. There was a lot of foxes after they grew—they increased fast. I've never seen a lot of foxes, but there were quite a few around. I've never seen a litter of baby foxes either, but my papa has. We never could catch the little ones; they were always there, but they were hiding. They look like little kittens running around, cute, but I've never seen them myself. I'd say the female fox had about six or eight pups, something like a dog you know, and they had babies only once a year. We didn't keep the foxes in pens or anything, they would run wild on the island. It wasn't very hard caring for foxes. We did a lot of walking, but it was okay.

"The foxes weren't real tame, but they were planted and fed by us; you couldn't go out and pet them or anything though. Some of the foxes were tame on other islands, but ours never got that tame. I don't think you can really tame a fox, they don't get that tame. If we had a fox for a pet, I wouldn't trust it; it probably would bite. We never kept any as pets; some people did, but we didn't. We had other pets, like chickens, pigs, and cats— no dogs, but lots of cats and chickens. The foxes never bothered the chickens or anything; they were so wild they never came near the house. We never had any problems with the foxes as far as I know.

"While my brothers and I went to summer school in Chignik, my mama

and papa stayed on the island and cared for the foxes. In the winter, they would come and get us and bring us back to the island.

"The foxes survived real good in the winter; we'd see them sitting outside their burrows, just sitting there, watching. They would burrow into the ground, under the rocks, or into a bank or something. Sometimes they would walk the beaches and look for food along the waterline. They would find dead fish and clams and things like that—they ate all that. Sometimes the foxes would burrow in on the beach, in the cliffs, under the rocks, and the tide would wash in there and would wash them away. A few got lost like that. We would see where they had been and the water had gotten up to them. There was no real danger to the foxes, animal-wise. Only the eagles, I think, carried the little ones off if they were out in the open. Other than that, we didn't have anything else on the islands except squirrels and mice, no big animals.

"We enjoyed feeding the foxes, taking care of them, raising them; that was pretty nice, easy to do. The killing part wasn't very nice, but we had to do that because that was our living. We had no one helping us raise and care for the foxes, just my brothers, me, and my papa, that's all. While my brothers, my papa, and I cared for the foxes, my mama cared for the family, like cooking and caring for the younger children. She also helped cook food for the foxes when she had time.

"The foxes depended on us for their food, we had to feed them to raise them. We carried lots of food with us when we'd go to feed them. I guess it was hard, but we were young at that time so it didn't matter. We'd take our sled, load it up, and take off. We had a bucket of food for each place we went to; there was a group of foxes in each feeding place. The foxes would sneak around so they saw us, and they would come and eat as soon as we'd take off. They knew when we'd come, they'd be waiting around. We could walk past them while they were eating, but they didn't let us touch them or anything.

"Every day we'd go around the island to every feeding place and feed them. I'd say there was about a dozen different places we had to go each day. Some of the places we didn't go to every day; we'd go maybe once a week 'cause we had to go far away to the other side of the island. The feeding places around our big lake we'd go to every day 'cause we could cross the lake on a sled over the ice and bring the food.

"We'd feed the foxes bran mixed with fish or sometimes meat, like seal meat, sea lion, and fish; mix it with bran and cook it. We'd always go fishing and bring home lots of fish for the foxes. We'd go seal and sea lion hunting also. The foxes ate anything wild. Sometimes we'd bake the fox meal into loaves of bread, then we'd slice it up and give the foxes so much each day. 'Course they ate that!

"Once a year, in the fall, we had to go into Chignik and load up with bran and stuff, and take it back to the island. The bran wouldn't last if we didn't mix it with wild food. We had this meal, it's a fox meal with all kinds of grain and bran in it; we mixed it with wild food to make it go further, that way we'd have enough food. I can't remember us ever running out of food for them—we always had some.

"When it came time to kill them, we'd set the box traps where we regularly fed them before, at the feeding places. The way we caught the foxes was we'd set a bait in the box trap, and the fox would get in and get the bait. When he gets the bait, he shuts the door, it automatically shuts him in. We'd go there every day, get them out of the trap, and kill 'em. We'd use tongs and get them around their necks, and haul them out through an opening at the top of the box. Then we laid them down and put our knees on their hearts until they died. I didn't like to do that, but we couldn't hurt the skin, we couldn't hit them or anything. This was the way the places that bought them wanted them killed; we couldn't damage the skin. I didn't mind trapping so much because most of the wild animals were already dead when I came to my trap. I didn't have to kill 'em. But when you fox-farm, you have to take the fox out and kill it, that wasn't very nice. That was the bad thing of fox farming.

"The foxes were full grown when we killed them, but I really don't know what age they were or anything. We didn't kill the very young ones; they had to be maybe a year or so. I don't know how my papa could tell, but he used to know. I think we could kill them about December; I'm not sure but it was in the middle of the winter sometime. I think my papa killed about fifty foxes each time, once a year. I think it was around that much.

"I didn't do much of the cleaning on the foxes, my papa did that. I had to kill the foxes, but I didn't help clean them. My brothers and Papa did that. After we skinned the foxes, we just threw the carcasses in the dump; my papa had a place to throw them. The eagles and crows would eat them.

"We sent the furs in and would get a check back from the company who bought 'em. At different times, we got fifty dollars for some furs, and I guess forty. I think they went as high as seventy-five dollars a fur. We got a good price, I know! Some were better than others, thicker fur. The heavier the fur, the more they cost. We sent our furs to, I think, Seattle Fur Exchange and to New York. We sent some to New York, but most of them went to Seattle Fur Exchange. It wasn't very easy at that time to get a check back; we would get mail maybe once a month. I'd say it was about two or three months before we heard from the fur company since we had sent the furs out.

"Before we sent the furs out, we had to clean them, stretch them, and dry them perfectly dry. Then we turned them fur side out, folded them up nice, put them in burlap bags, and sent them out.

"When we quit fox farming, we just left the rest of the foxes on the island. There was a few foxes on the island when we left, and right now there is still some, but they haven't increased too much. I don't think!"

NICK NEKEFEROFF: BEAR HUNTING

interview by: Mary Webber and Mary Greene
story by: Tracey Metzbower and Donna Royal

"I didn't go hunting the first time I came here year of '40; it was '42 or '43 and I went with Charley Madsen, then Alf Madsen. I'd been with Alf Madsen, cooking for him. Then I went out with Charley; I hunted bear with Charley up to the time he quit. I don't know what year that was. We used to go hunting and then we broke in Munsey [another well-known Alaskan guide]. That was with Bill Poland hunting for him. I hunted all my life over the mainland and all over before I ever came to Kodiak.

"We were actually born here. The rest of my brothers and sisters are dead; buried alongside of Patterson's garage, up here. There used to be an old graveyard there, way back before volcano time [Katmai, 1912] even. The other house of ours used to be down there by Icy Cape, where Nick Wolkoff used to live before; that used to be our place before, and in Chiniak.

"I hunted this Kodiak bear for a long time and then they had [as guests on] some of those Madsen boats the guy that killed Dillinger, and that big oil man by the name of Borden, and the guy that mixed penicillin, the Frenchman. I got his name in the book somewhere. And Roy Witteveen, and a lot of other fellas that I know pretty well that are big shots now. Also Jonas Brothers, they were hunting here before. I've been all over. Well, that was when there were lots of bears around; we were killing two or three, four bear a day. They had a fella here and he'd skin it. And then I took the hunters out some other places and [we'd] get another bear in the same day.

"I weren't scared of the bears or anything; I was used to them. The first time I shot a bear it was with a .25-20 on the mainland. I was only sixteen years old and there was a great big bear, ten-footer. I was a good shot at that time. I used to get them dolls from magazines and set them on a pole and shoot their heads off. About fifty-five yards away, oh, sixty yards. I was pretty good. I could shoot the ptarmigan right in the head when I used to go

Nick Nekeferoff proudly displays one of his bears. "Some of those [Kodiak bears], they weighed about 122 pounds of skin alone."

with the other guys. That's how I used to handle a gun all the time. I had the gun anywhere I went.

"To tell you the truth, I didn't want to be a registered guide, didn't need it. But they told me I had to go registered guide or else get out of there altogether, so I had to do it. I got my registered guide [license], and I've been a registered guide ever since. I don't know what it would cost now; it's more, you know. Doubled, it's just doubled what it was before. I had cabins, I put places up there for myself, but they ruined them, tore them all up. I don't know if I got any more left up there now. If there is, it's nothing but nothing. Some guys built 'em for me, you know. I couldn't leave stuff to cook, no way, they'd steal every bit of it.

"I captured many of Kodiak's brown bear, but they were crippled. That will happen, if you cripple a bear and you follow it; and if you didn't know how to follow it, you'll get chewed up. The only way to do it you gotta keep on walking, every step you make just take it easy, walk on the safe side. When you start stalking the bear, you don't know how you're gonna get to him. You see you got an open space, and you gotta get to him in order to shoot him. Sometimes the big ones will lay down if you can catch 'em just in time. They'll lay down around between nine-thirty and eleven [at night]. And then, if you've got the right friend with you, you can get to the bear. You got to know how to get to him; the first thing you gotta learn is how to shut your mouth, and lay off cigarettes. After you get through with the game, then you can talk until the cows come home. The sow is the only one that will attack you most of the time. The male will attack you if he's crippled, you shot him, or something like that.

"But other times we used to go out and get the young ones. Me and Griska used to go out and get a couple of young ones. Sometimes you have to shoot the mother; and sometimes you don't have to, you just chase it away because they'll come after you. Well, anyhow, I got the three little cubs, and put them in the sack; they squeak and make all kinds of noises. They'll fight between themselves. You gotta put them in separate sacks and then they won't fight. If it's never gone without its mother then it'll never stop crying; I had to shoot one.

"The neck is about the best place to hit the bear. But if they're standing sideways then you hit 'em here [points to the underarm area]. And then he'll drop, just like that. Very seldom do they get up and run. Yeah, it hits 'em right through the tube, and it tears everything right down to the heart. I usually only had to shoot 'em once, that's it, very seldom twice. I used to use a .30-30 before, that was my favorite anyway.

"Once I went up and chased a bear when a Mexican guy came to hunt. I told him where to shoot the bear, but he didn't shoot where I told him. He decided to shoot the bear in his own way. That was the same bear we chased along that gulley. By the time I got through it was about one o'clock in the morning, it was dark. I could hear the bear breathing alongside of me, but yet I can't see to shoot him. So I had a lighter and I would light my lighter;

you know, I smoked cigarettes then. I would pull it up like this with one hand and hold my gun in the other hand. If I could only see that beast in front of me, I could shoot him. But I would wait for a little while and I would listen and I can't hear him breathe anymore, so I keep on going ahead and at the same time I was lighting my light to see if I could see him. I could hear him making noise ahead of me, maybe a few feet away.

"Well, I cut him off and there was a big pool of blood. If I had only left him alone right there and come back in the morning, I would have found him right there dead. I disturbed him and he went across the creek and I never did find him. But that crazy guy came along and he went aboard the boat and he told the people that I was chewed up by the bear. Everybody from the boat came ashore looking for me. That was two o'clock in the morning! And I came down below and I could hear hollering. They tried to find where I was because they thought I was tore up pretty bad. When I seen one guy I said, 'What the heck is the matter with you fellars, this time of the morning?' He just looked at me and said, 'That fellar told us the bear tore you up.' I says, 'How can he tore me up since I got a gun?' I never had a chance to even shoot him. I missed him, you know, 'cause the gun got caught in the brush.

"I hunted Kodiak bear on the mainland; they're hunted over there greatly. I'm covered for all those game. But only thing, I don't go and get them; I'm getting too old to hunt now. I can't go out anymore, I'm better off here. I don't do much—you know, when you go out bear hunting you have to work. Some of those, they weighed about 122 pounds of skin alone. And when they put the head in there, it goes up in a hurry. Sometimes skin and head goes to 205, 210. That's what I used to pack, two of them when I was younger, and it was hard. Together that was over 422 pounds.

"Ah, Griska and Dick Malutin, we hunted together all the time, all in one group for a long, long time. We could go up there, look at the tracks and would know what we got. We would know where to find them.

"A long time ago I had a lady from Canada there. She was supposed to get a bear that day. I seen a bear on top of a big hill going over and then I told the lady, 'You better get ready; we're gonna shoot him when we get a hold of him.' So we went ashore. She told Charley Madsen that, 'If you don't take me out this afternoon, we're going back in.' Yeah, I had to take 'em out, so I took 'em out. But accidentally, somehow, the bear turned and came back. I told her to keep the gun loaded, handy ready to shoot. It came to us all of a sudden, you know.

"It wasn't attacking or nothing; it was breeding time for the bear in the spring that time. And the bear stopped about ten feet, anyway ten to fifteen feet, away from me where I was standing. And she was standing about twenty-five feet away from me and the bear.

"I told her to go ahead and shoot. Well, she shot, [but] first she couldn't get the gun fired. She was so scared she couldn't get the gun to go off because she forgot to pull the safety off. She took the safety off and let her went. It hit them alders way on top instead of the bear. And I hollered to her, 'Quick, you better hurry up!'

"Anyway, this thing was just about ready to spring. I shouted, 'You better give her up.' And she shot again, almost the same way, and it hit the same tree. And finally the third shot, she was screaming already then. I said, 'Forget screaming, you better shoot that bear quick!' Her old man was gonna shoot and I said, 'Don't, don't bother with it.' He was standing right alongside of her. 'Let her go ahead and kill her own bear.' So she shot and down goes the bear. While I was standing there, her husband says, 'Stay there, stay there.' He pulled a tape out and he measured out where I was standing, and me and him standing together, it was ten feet, ten or twelve feet to where the bear fell down.

"I've had other experiences on seal and walrus, both. I used to ride on a walrus on Round Island. I used to go ashore there and play around on a walrus. Ride on their backs, but they don't go ahead; they go around and around and then they go back the other way. Once you get on their backs you have to work hard so that they don't run over you. Their teeth sound like a jackhammer! [He imitates with his teeth.] I rode on a walrus on the other side of Togiak. Me and Carpenter. I had a boat and we would go out there in Togiak. We'd go out to Round Island and take a lot of pictures. Bunch of walrus laying all around over there at Round Island. I would sneak up to them and jump on their backs; I sneaks right up to them and they can't hear because the wind was blowing. Sneak right up to them and jump right on their backs. He gets right up, and his teeth are going, same time he's heading for the boat. Round and round, if you jumped off, you almost got it. It almost ran over me; he tore my pocket.

"They're sort of a funny species, you know, like the sea lion. They won't bite, you can even pet them. The walrus, his teeth are steady going like a jackhammer. They're trying to bust you, trying to hit you with those paws all the time, but you can touch them. They're a funny animal. They don't smell like a sea lion, they smell like a pig. That's just what they smell like, the odor.

Eli and I used to be up at Uganik Bay with Alf down there, too. We used to go out there hunting all the time. I was cooking two seasons for Ralph down there. It was easier, I didn't have to go out to the field or anything. I hunted all my life. And that is how I used to make a living."

KATHERINE CHICHENOFF: "I WENT THROUGH A LOT OF THINGS"

by: Rhonda Gossage

I interviewed Katherine Ckabal Chichenoff, who lives at the Senior Citizens home with her youngest daughter, Ruthy. She is a very kind and sweet lady whom we enjoyed talking with very much.

Kaba Chichenoff.

Kaba knows so much about the Russian Orthodox Church, and about the Russian holidays. She can speak the Russian language extensively, and also understands Aleut. Her interesting background has attracted many other students in the *Elwani* class because she has been in several of our past issues of the magazine.

When I arrived, Kaba made me feel very welcome and comfortable, and she stopped everything she was doing to sit down and talk with me. We hope you, our readers, enjoy this as much as I did.

"I was born and raised here in Kodiak, eighty years ago. I went through a lot of things. Of course, I didn't live here all the time. I was brought up in the Russian mission because when I was three years old, my mother died, and my father couldn't take care of me. So he gave me to some old lady to take care of me. She was very mean. My father used to pay her a lot of money. He was a sea otter hunter and made a lot of money. He'd bring this bag, I saw it. Bring those canvas bags full of those great big dollars, like silver dollars, but gold dollars. He'd give that old lady a whole bunch of them to make me dresses and things. She'd make prettier dresses for her, and what was left for me. Of course I loved them. When I was at their place, I never sat at the table with them. I never laid on a bed, I laid, just like a little dog, on a mat. That's how I remember it. They finally found out that they were treating me mean, and the priest took me. They took me for a month before I was seven years old, and then they put me in the mission. I remember my first confession and Communion. I lived there eleven years, at St. Herman's Orphanage. That was the best time of my life. Other people were at the mission that were orphans I guess, or their parents deserted them. They all came from around the islands, and I'm telling you one thing! It was hard to teach them Russian 'cause they all spoke Aleut. We didn't understand them either, so we had to teach them. 'Course, it's a hard thing to do. But they learned fast the prayers, because we all said prayers all at once. But the language is pretty hard to teach them. We went to English school, public school, from nine till four. We came home for lunches though. And then from four till five we went to Russian school, so I read and write Russian.

"There used to be twelve of us in the mission, but after the natives came over from Russia, they cut down to eight of us. They kept us in the mission till we were eighteen, and after that you had to go. So they didn't know what to do with me. They must have wrote a letter to my father, because he sent me the money to come to Seldovia. I didn't want to go to my father because I heard he was married and not a very good person. So I didn't want to live with somebody else for a mother when I didn't have my own. In the meantime, there was a letter from Afognak to the priest here in Kodiak that the oldest son of their friends wanted to marry me. I didn't know how he knew me. So, instead of going to my father's, I gave word that I was going to marry him. So, we were married! I went to live with my husband in Afognak. You know where Afognak is? The one that the tidal wave took. We lived there for eighteen years, had eight children there, then we moved to Ouzinkie and had two more! I was married to him for thirty-seven years! I really enjoyed it, he was the best person. He loved his children and grandchildren.

"We lost a son in Korea. He was missing in action for three years, then all of a sudden they found him. I don't know how many of them there were. He was only there for two weeks. Then we lost a little girl. She was only five years old. Just before she started school, she got pneumonia and died. No doctors or nothing. The rest of them are living. Only one son I have now.

"One time a long, long, time ago, 'twas in February month, 'twas the last day of the blini week. That's a week before the Lent starts. We had a big snowstorm. It was on a Friday, too. Oh, my, I was heavy with a baby, and my brother-in-law said, 'Why don't you make us some blini?' His grandpa and him were going to the store to get some cigarettes. That was in Afognak. So that's okay. I said good. I fix good, you know. They like my blini. They wouldn't ask his mother to do it. When they were in the store, I started fixing them, and all of a sudden, I started to have pains. So I told my mother-in-law. There was a bad blizzard outside. Two of her sons were out duck hunting, too.

"She went to her husband, he was napping, and said to go and get the midwife. Right away he gets up and runs. As soon as the midwife comes, I'm ready to deliver. The boys started to come in from their hunting trip, and right through our bedroom. So she said no, this won't do. So she took me upstairs where the boys sleep. It was cold. We lit the heater right away. She put the mattress on the floor. She didn't want me to get up in the bed. I never even had a chance to undress, and the baby was born. That fast! The midwife took my apron off me and she said, 'She'll be a good cook and a baker,' and sure enough that's what Alice is! My second daughter. All my children were born at home, all ten of them. The midwives were so good. They'd do everything for you, clean you up, clean the babies up. Then for a while, they'd be coming over to attend you.

"Have you ever heard of blini? Gee, I haven't made blini in ages. Well, the way I always make it is I take a bowl, put in eggs, I use about a half a dozen, little sugar and salt and very little baking powder. Then of course you beat the eggs, put a little bit of milk in. Beat it up all together and put flour in. Enough to make a smooth batter. Take a ladle after it's all done and see how it is, that's how we used to do it. I used a frying pan, put the frying pan on the stove and I always fried mine in butter. Melt the butter and of course you melt the butter for the pancakes, too. Put the butter in the pan so the batter doesn't stick. Then you take a ladle, not a full ladle, just as long as it goes around even. I used to use a knife to put under the pancake and turn it fast. Then when it browns a bit, take it off. Takes a long, long time to make a stack. Oh, people would eat twelve at a time!! Woo! I think two was enough for me. They'd take one and spread butter and put syrup mostly. And then they'd start eating them. Roll them and then, oh, they'd just love it. Blini is only fixed at Easter time.

"The tradition in the Russian Orthodox Church is at Easter time everything is white, the altar, the priest's robes, and everything's on the stands. Then fifty days after Easter they change it into green. Before, when we had the old church, people would cut fresh grass and flowers, then spread it all over the floor. That's all called Trinity. Then on August 28, the Virgin Mary passes away and everything turns into blue. Blue robes and things until December 4, when the Virgin Mary is going up to church by herself. Up the thirteen steps. Then, after that the colors change to red, for Christmas. Everything then changes to dark colors for Lent. They have dark purple or dark brown maybe, but no blues. That's for a whole seven weeks of Lent. That's the tradition in our church. Also, when the bishop is here, everything is in yellow.

"We celebrate Christmas with three days of the star. We always celebrate holidays with three days, like Easter and Christmas church services were held in the evening, the next morning and on the third evening at four. We would carry a star from house to house. Of course, other people had stars, too. First they'd go to the priest's house and to church. This was in the villages, you know. It took them three days and after that, masquerade time. A whole week of dancing and masking. Oh, that was good. See, the masking was when King Herod found out that Jesus was born, so he sent his men to kill all male children up to two years old. Somebody heard it and they came to Mary and Joseph and told them to go someplace where they could not find them, because they wanted to kill Jesus. And so they went to Egypt. That's why masking is, masquerade. Oh, there used to be devils and everything. I loved it, I loved it! Did you ever hear of that in the Bible? It's in the Bible you know, too. They don't masquerade or anything like they did before. They go with the star for three days, but no masking.

"I used to dance a lot. When I got married, I didn't know how to dance. My husband never danced so he'd send me to dances in Afognak, which was good because his parents owned a dance hall and so we lived with them. My mother-in-law said, 'Go ahead and dance!' Then after I started to dance, I never missed one. Boy, I'd dance, dance, dance. Big with babies, I'd be dancing! I never gave up. I love to dance.

"My maiden name is Egoroff. That's all died out now though. But then somebody was here not long ago from our church and asked what my maiden name was and I told them Egoroff but I think it's dead now because my brother is dead and so is my father.

"Oh, you know it seems to me we have some Egoroffs in New York.

"You asked me how I got the name Kaba. Well, our three oldest grandchildren used to call me Babooka, that's grandma in Russian. When my third daughter had her first baby, she wanted to say Babooka, but anything she said she turned around, you know. Well, she said Kaba. She couldn't say Babooka, just Kaba. That's how it came out and everyone just picked it up! My husband, everybody called him Papa. None of our grandchildren called him Grandpa. From the first one, he's forty-one years old now, to the last one, they called him Papa. They loved him so much. Not only his grandchildren, but other people's children. Our place would be full of children always 'Papa, Papa, Papa!' My husband was very comical. Oh, he was a nice man. Up to now I don't even have a picture of him. We lost our house, which was by the beachcombers. Big house, four bedrooms. Living room, dining room, big kitchen, and the smaller bedroom was his. I was downstairs, that's where he died. He died over twenty-five years ago now. I've been a widow since then.

"When the air base here was started, my husband worked there. That was after they started the war. Good thing, too, 'cause we never had anything here before. When this Japanese attack on Pearl Harbor came, we thought they were going to do something to Kodiak, too. But I'll tell you, I think Father Herman stopped them because when we were living in Ouzinkie, we'd hear the planes flying and it would be all over Ouzinkie, maybe Kodiak, too, I don't know. It was just like fog. They couldn't find it. They were flying all over, but they attacked Dutch Harbor after they attacked Pearl Harbor. If they'd see a little light in your window, they'd come and tell you to close your blinds or something. They had to, in case of an attack. That's why I've always said, 'Father Herman, protect us.' It seemed like every time we'd hear planes, there'd just be fog. Can't see nothing, and then, blackout. Right after that they started that air base. After the Army moved out, there were Marines, and Navy, and now it's the Coast Guard. I hope they never give it up. It sure helped.

"The only games we used to play were tag, maybe hide-and-seek, that's all. And if anything else we had swings. The summertime seems like hardly had any rain because after supper we'd go up Pillar Mountain, every day except Saturday. Saturday we'd go to church. Seems like there was little rain, I don't remember not going up the hill.

"I remember that Halley's comet. You know, it should be on pretty soon, too. It comes every seventy-five years. It was quite a while ago. I don't remember though because when we were kids, every time after supper, we'd come out to watch it, right over Pillar Mountain. You could see the star, but always just like a flame. Big, long, with a tail. Every day after supper, I don't know how many days, the comet would be there. It should be here in a few years. I don't know when was the last time, I can't remember what year it was, but it should be soon because I'm already eighty years old! We were lucky to see it, you know.

"I'll tell you one thing, too, I'm the oldest Kodiak born in Kodiak. Most of them died. Yeah, all of us used to think Nick Wolkoff, but we found out that he was born on Woody Island. His brother Peter, who died, was the same age as I am. He was born in Kodiak.

"Once I thought about moving to the States, but no, I'd rather stay here. Ruthy, my daughter, and I were there about two years, but we came back. We had a home, and after the tidal wave, they built me a nice little place on Mission Road. I don't think we'll move to that new place either that they're building, 'cause I like it here very much. So close to everything, very close to our church.

"When we lived in town, I wouldn't say we were really poor because we worked a lot. We worked hard all our lives to support our children. We did all our gardens that were in Afognak. I'll always wish we had gardens here in Kodiak. We usually had chickens all the time and had our own eggs. We also had cows, grew our own potatoes for a whole year and for seeds for the next year. That's the way it was, we didn't have to buy anything. We grew our own cabbage and rutabagas, carrots, turnips, and stuff like that. Now we go to the store and pay so much for everything. We did our own fish, too. We'd smoke salmon. I'd put it away for winter and salt salmon. Got a lot of salt salmon. Before we didn't have any freezers, so we salted them. Maybe some canned, too, I can't remember. Anyway, we'd start saving eggs before the Lent starts. We'd have about eleven or twelve dozen eggs for Easter, and enough for dyeing eggs, too. Children would come and knock at the door early Easter morning and trade eggs. They'd come out about four or five o'clock and you'd want to sleep.

"I think people think I'm crazy, you know. First time in Kodiak there was measles and they came just fast! They were quarantining people and right away they thought no, they better not quarantine, how could people get help? So they quit quarantining people. I think we were the last ones to have measles, all of us in the mission. Anyway, all the eight girls were in bed except me, and all of a sudden, I was washing clothes and everything else, and some nurse says, 'You better go to bed, you have measles,' sure enough, I went to bed with measles. Do you think I was sick? I wasn't even sick. Everybody was sick but me. And here I'm in bed laying down with measles, not sick, all kinds of things I could be doing. I was the last one to have measles and after I got well, first thing, what do you think I had to do? Wash clothes again!

"I'm telling you, I always thank God because I've never had a sick day in my life. He was really good to me. They'd have whooping cough and all of that, didn't bother me. So I think I was just lucky, that's all. I was just lucky 'cause I never had any sicknesses or anything.

"I was working at a cannery here in Kodiak, in '62, December 21 or 22. I was going down to get my check from the Alaska Packers, and I didn't even see this small piece of ice on the road as you go down by the old post office. And I slipped and fell! Good thing some people saw me. These people came to help and I wanted to get up and I couldn't get up. I broke my right knee-cap. They put me in a car, and let my people know of course. Then they took me to the hospital. I found out I broke my kneecap and Dr. Bob said he doesn't know how to do anything about it so they kept me overnight at the hospital here. My first time in my life in the hospital.

"In the morning they sent me to Anchorage on a plane, my first flight out of Kodiak besides Afognak and Ouzinkie, you know. I went just before Christmas and I was there three months. I came home just before Easter. Good thing there was someone to take care of Ruthy and all of that I didn't have to worry over that.

"My good knee bothers me now. Both my legs are bothering me. I think I'm just getting old now. I know I am getting old. I'll have to give up soon, I guess. My eyes are going. My eyes are the ones that bother me, because if my eyes go then I'm ready to go. My ears are good. Yeah, I think I've had a good life, a very good life. I've no complaints. God gave me a good life. When I was a youngster of thirteen or fourteen, I gave God my word, prayed to God that I'd never smoke, never drink, and I'll never give myself to any man unless my husband. That's how I've lived up to today. My friends used to say, 'Try a smoke.' Oh, gosh, no!"

ORAL BURCH: "BOTTOM BOAT GOES BROKE"

by: Scott Ranney

This is the story of Oral Burch. Oral is one of Kodiak's pioneer fishermen. He is a short, husky man who is always helpful and very trustful. He has a highly developed sense of humor and his own special laugh, a rough, broken chuckle. He loves the outdoors and has a black Lab that he takes along while hunting and fishing. Oral and his brother, Al Burch, own the boats *Dawn* and *Dusk*. Oral runs the *Dawn*.

Oral was born in Deerlodge, Montana, on June 13, 1919. He first came to Alaska in 1942. He was in the Army Transport Service at the time, and was in for three more years. Immediately after, he started fishing and has been fishing ever since. He also ran a tugboat for several years. Oral has seen all of the fisheries grow and change and has himself contributed to their growth and change.

"I started fishing in 1945 out of Cordova, fishing dungeness crab out of a skiff. I was fishing dungeness crab, pulling the pots by hand. That's about the hardest work I've ever done, but it built us up to what we have now. That took a lot of years.

"I went from that skiff to the *Ruptured Duck*. It had a little winch on it. I'd load that thing down—I sank it three times. I went from that boat to a better boat; each boat has been a little bigger. After that came the *Rena, Billy H,*

Oral Burch.

I-Leak, P. J. Endeavor, Vida, and I know I've forgotten some of them. There was about twenty of them.

"I've fished just about everything around here. I've fished halibut, salmon, scallops, commercial razor clams, king crab, and shrimp. I like shrimping better than anything else.

"Fishing has gotten much easier; now it isn't even in the picture. Take the Fathometers and sonars. When we fished there was a lot of shrimp, but we had to send them into the cannery 100 percent clean. Now the canneries pick the fish out. At that time I was fishing out of Seward. We had to run from the south end of Kodiak Island clear over to Seward. That was with the *Celtic,* the *Vida,* and the *Endeavor.* We fished out of Seward for a year, and after the tidal wave, moved to Kodiak. The tidal wave took all of the processing facilities out of Seward.

"I rigged the *Endeavor* for crabbing and I just hated that. I've had bitter experiences with king crabbing in the formative years. I was fishing just thirty pots and I'd load up in a pick and a half and come to town and wait a week to deliver. There was also a lot of pot robbing. I got to the point where I was ready to shoot somebody and I decided when I get to that point, I might as well quit. I've never crabbed since.

"I didn't like halibut fishing, but I did enjoy salmon fishing. I gillnetted for salmon on the Copper River Flats. I'd go out all alone and I really liked that, fishing in the breakers." Oral also fished salmon out of Kodiak with the *P.J.* and the *I-Leak.*

"I hunted seals and really enjoyed that, but there were also a lot of hairy experiences. Getting the skiff caught in the ice, glaciers coming down kicking up big waves and knocking holes in the skiffs. It kept you on your toes all the time."

Out of all of the fisheries Oral has chosen shrimping as his favorite. Shrimping has changed a lot from the formative years. "The price for shrimp was four cents a pound for years. The first time I iced up the boat, they had a D-8 Cat and they dug ice out from under the sawdust in the old-fashioned icehouses and threw it out on the dock. Then they ran back and forth on it with the Cat and shoveled it aboard. That was crude ice. We had nothing but a Fathometer on the boat; back then we learned by trial and error. We were mending web all of the time and we lost a lot of nets. We have nets strewn all over this country. There is a lot of ocean out there and it fools you once in a while.

"I personally think that the shrimp are just as thick now as they were in those days; now we just have more rules and restrictions. We can't go where the shrimp are. We used to shrimp out of Katchemak Bay with trawls, but now we can't even go there. We used to take two tows and then quit and pick fish until midnight to get the shrimp clean. We could have loaded that boat in a heck of a hurry, but we had to keep the shrimp clean. We couldn't deliver one fish—period.

"When there was only eight or nine boats on Kodiak, they used to tell each other hot spots. It's an awful big country for a few boats; but now with forty boats, it's a very small country. With sonar and everything you can go to a spot that used to take us a month to survey and start towing right away."

Although Oral has had a lot of good boats, he did have one that could be called a jinx, the *Vida.* "The *Vida* was a big boat, an eighty-six-footer. It was awful big in those days. We spent more time fixing it than we did fishing it. We owned a one-third interest in it, and gave it to the partners. We said, 'Take it, we don't want anything to do with it.' If there is a jinxed boat, that was it for me. That boat was trouble from day one. You'd go into the dock and back down and the shaft would slide out of the coupling and stuff like that. It makes me appreciate what we have now."

Now that we have heard about the worst boat that Oral has owned, let's hear about one of his better ones, the *Celtic.* "That boat was better than any other boat I've ever seen or had. It was a good sea boat. I made forty-odd trips across the Barrens in one season so you know I hit every kind of weather. She took every bit of it. She even went through the tidal wave. The day before the tidal wave hit, I had gotten off of a boat here and flown to Anchorage. We were just going down the highway when the earthquake hit. That was the first time I'd seen waves on a highway. The lakes were all frozen over and they just exploded. Trees were coming down, rock slides, and everything. We walked from way out the road clear to Seward. When we got to Seward, it looked like the whole town was on fire because the tank farm was burning.

"The *Celtic* ended up on the airport. We had to dig a deep trench from the tide flats clear to it. Later on, I piled it up on Spruce Island in a southeaster one night. I swore that it couldn't be torn up, but it didn't take but a few minutes for that sea to get it. It was a schooner-type shrimper built in 1928. It was just the fact that I'd been working too hard for too many hours. We were on the boat a very few minutes before we got picked up, otherwise we'd have been swimming."

The boat, the *Dawn,* that Oral now owns with his brother, Al, is at least as good as the *Celtic,* maybe better. "The *Dawn* is the first double-rigged stern trawler with a stern ramp in the world. Everyone said it couldn't be done, but now everyone down there is copying it. When we were putting the stern ramp in it, I was standing on the dock watching and this guy comes along and says, 'What damn fool is cutting this beautiful boat all to pieces?' and I said, 'This one!' When I told them to put it in, they said I was crazy, but we paid for it so they put it in.

"I've been hurt several times. Once a boom came down and pinned me between it and the winch. It squeezed me a little and bruised me from one end to the other. Another time, this thumb was cut off. A guy dropped a door on it. I put it back on, threw some sulfa powder in, and tied a cedar stick to it; there it is, it still works.

"The one thing that everybody should be deadly afraid of is icing down. If

Oral with his brother Al, co-owner of *Dawn*.

"If I had to do it all over again, I would do exactly the same things."

you aren't afraid of it and you fish in the winter, you're not long for this world. I will not monkey with icing conditions. If I'm close to land in icing conditions, I go and anchor up, because ice can build up so fast."

Although fishermen don't agree on everything, there are some things that are pretty standard and most fishermen agree. One of these things is helping each other. "If you see somebody in trouble you go for them right now, you drop all else and go for them. I think that's pretty much standard all over the fleet, taking care of each other. I think it's beautiful that they do. Another thing about fishermen is I've never seen a fisherman yet that isn't trying to be a top fisherman. The name of the game is the more you catch, the better off you are. Top boat is in the money; bottom boat goes broke."

At the end of the interview we were left with these words. "If I had to do it all over again, I would do exactly the same thing. I wouldn't make some of the mistakes, but I wouldn't hesitate to start over. In fact, I'd choose that instead of anything else. It doesn't get boring, you never know what's going to happen next, and where in the world can an uneducated man get up to the position to where he makes the money he makes right now? I don't know of any other field unless you're a prospector and strike it lucky, and that's a great deal of luck. This is just work."

TED LIEDORF: A WAY OF LIFE

by: Shawna Lindberg

Dog Ear Mountain stands off to the left as you enter Mush Bay. At the foot of the mountain is a long circular beach maybe a half mile in length and inside of the spit is a lagoon. It's a fairly large lagoon about three quarters of a mile long and shaped like a wine bottle. At high tide it gets two to three fathoms (six feet to a fathom) deep. At low tide there is a big sandbar in the middle with a wide creek running down each side of it, meeting at the mouth and traveling way out about 100 to 200 yards at low tide. At the base of Dog Ear is our house. Not very attractive on the outside, I admit, but my mom keeps it looking homey on the inside. We have all the modern facilities when our light plant's working. Lights, tape decks, iron, anything like that. When it ain't working, we work out all right on Coleman lanterns and kerosene lamps. Even if it isn't working, we have cold running water.

The banya stands behind the house and up about fifty feet away is a big stand of cottonwoods. No spruce grow around here. It's all cottonwood, alder, birch, and some weird-looking trees in the valley. We have a big valley up back of our house. It looks exactly like a valley should look. It has a big, smooth brook running in the middle with a sandy bottom. Now and then we'd get a couple of nesting mallards back there. Those weird-looking trees stand off on the far side of the creek, all hunched over and crooked. In the spring the trees get cottony-looking things clinging to the leaves. The valley gets flowers on the floor of it; all colors, white, purple, pink, yellow.

Well, up the bay about three miles is the Finley's place. A big, old house standing up on pilings with an old-type porch that could use a rocking chair on it to make it look like the old-timey houses.

Out in front of our house about one mile off is Mink Point, which leads you off into the South Arm. The South Arm is the prettiest place in the summer or winter, spring, or fall. There's only a few places on the left side that you're apt to hit a rock at low tide. On the right side is a different story. There's more'n a dozen spots where you'll hit rocks if you aren't careful. Up at the end of the South Arm is a large lagoon also. You would have to see it yourself to be able to describe it. I would describe it as being very creepishly beautiful. Very bear-infested in summer, and very deer-infested in the winter.

I'm getting too far off the track now from what I meant to tell you about.

Ted Liedorf lives out here with us. He is a tall old man, has silvery-white hair, and he's usually always busy down in the warehouse doing handy things. Sometimes he sits in his green chair down there and has a smoke break. When we sit down to dinner and somebody will mention something that starts a fuse in Ted's brain, BOOM, he goes off into one of his long-ago tales. Maybe we heard them before . . . maybe not. He's been a very good friend of ours and numerous other people in town.

From bush pilot to rounding cattle on Sitkalidak, he's been around Kodiak a long time. So finally I worked up the nerve to ask him for an interview, and after two tries and a bribe of a bottle of brandy, I finally got one from him.

"I came to Alaska in February '41. I worked at the Ketchikan Spruce Mill as an electrician for a little over a year. Then I went to work for the CAA, which is now the Federal Aviation Administration (FAA). Annette Island [in Southeastern Alaska near Ketchikan], a man would have to travel from there to the whole territory of Alaska. There were seventy-eight CAA stations at that time, during the war, and I made all but one of those stations durin' all of my time with CAA. Some of them as high as three or four times. After I left CAA I worked at Post Engineers at Fort Richardson [in Anchorage] for approximately a year.

"Then I went back to CAA for about a year, little over a year. During the time that I was working for CAA, why . . . we was loaned to the Army. My crew and I sent out to Dutch Harbor to help the Army out, and we were there at the time of the bombing of Dutch Harbor, and it was a very unpleasant situation."

The clock started chiming and I happened to notice that Ted was scribbling on the table with a pencil in his nervousness. He was sittin' there puffing on cigarette after cigarette. "I was also on Attu after the third day of the invasion, and that was a very . . . very, very horrible situation." There was a long pause as he took a last drag on his cigarette before grinding it out in the ashtray.

"Then from CAA I went to work for an electrical contractor, Alaska

Electric. I worked for them for approximately a year and a half, then I went into business for myself, truckin'. That was kind of a sad affair. Then I bought into a roadhouse called the Big Timber Lodge, 130 miles out of Valdez, 205 miles out of Anchorage. From then on, I just worked here, there, yonder.

"I came to Kodiak; well, I was on Woody Island in Kodiak durin' the war for a couple of months. That's when they had the submarine nets out. Between Woody Island and Kodiak . . . it was just right above where Kodiak Electric Association is now; they had to open the nets a'fore you could get in from Woody Island to Kodiak."

Ted glanced over at me and said, "Okay, ask me something." I guess he'd read an *Elwani* before. I thought I might get away with not asking any questions, but I guess not. It took me a moment before I could think of any.

"What was the most exciting thing that ever happened to you in Kodiak?"

"Well, I'll tell you, the earthquake in 1964 was the most exciting thing that ever happened to me." He paused again as he lighted another cigarette. "I was in the Breakers Bar, the old Breakers Bar, at the time it happened. Well, people all run out of buildings and everythin'. They were out in the street and they was hollerin' and screamin'; I thought it was kind of comical, I wasn't very shook up myself. I been through a couple minor earthquakes in California 'fore I came to Alaska. I was kinda laughin' about it, and ol' Lou Iani, he was kinda standin' in the door of the old Breakers Bar with his hands up braced against the door. I was standin' out on the sidewalk in front of the door and about that time the whole door, facing and all, fell out and hit me in the back and knocked me down."

He snorted at the memory and went on. "But it was an awful mess. When the tidal wave came, that's what caused so much of the damage, was the tidal wave. Took out . . . there was the old high school, or the old school, only had one school at that time besides the Catholic school. It set up back of whar' . . . I don't know just what would be there now. Anyway, it set up on a kind of hill down whar' the telephone office is now. Approximately thar' 'bouts there was a kind of tourist place. I forget what they called it. That ol' power barge the *Selief* was settin' up there the next morning. It was right even with that old school building in there 'bout where them fill-up stations are now. There was boats all over.

"The boat harbor, it went completely dry, and . . . One friend of mine, he went to walk out to the boat he was on, the *Stranger*. It belonged to Ed Lenigon. He was going to walk out to it and one of the tidal waves came back in and caught him and they never did find any trace of him. Nicky Anderson's wife . . . she was trapped in a boat and they didn't find her until a long, long, long time later. Found her in the hold of a boat, old hull of a boat, what was left of it. I think it was around fourteen, or something like that, people lost their lives in the tidal wave.

"Ask me something."

"Well, what adventures did you have in Kodiak?"

"Oh, outside of that tidal wave, I didn't have too many adventures. Had some purty rough boat trips. Got caught in a blow . . . awful uncomfortable for me 'cause I get seasick when it gets really rough. Usually if I take the wheel, why it don't bother me, but if I'm laid down on a bunk or sit at a table I'll go to gettin' sick. I never have heaved, but I been awful uncomfortable.

"Why, before the time I was truckin', I flew a couple of years up in the Interior Alaska bush . . . bush flyin'. Had a few experiences in that deal. One time I was comin' inta Anchorage through Rainy Pass and was goin' backwards. Looked off on the wing tip at the rocks and the plane was goin' backwards and the gas gauge was goin' down, down, down, down! I finally got through and I got on the radio and told 'em I didn't know where I could make it. And they said try to keep to where I could make an emergency landin'. So when I finally got into Merrill Field [in downtown Anchorage], I landed because I run outa gas an' I couldn't taxi. They had to tow me offa the field. That was my greatest experience I had flying. I've had some awful uncomfortable feelin's, get into whiteouts [zero visibility because of weather conditions] an' you'd swear the compass was wrong . . . an' 'course it was just the other way around.

"I've fished with Ed Lenigon, crab-fished with him two seasons. First season we fished, them days, they didn't have square pots like they have now, they was all round pots. Yuh got lot bigger crab. The first year I fished with 'm we had a twelve-and-a-half-pound average. An' we got the big sum of eight cents a pound fer crab. Next year we got ten cents a pound. This year they opened the season at a dollar-thirty a pound. You kin see the difference in 'bout twenty years ago, 'bout eighteen, twenty years ago.

"There was no shrimp fishing in them days, amount ta anything. A few people tried it, experimenting, but there wasn't a market for 'em like there is today, by no means. We salmon-fished. Got twenty-five cents apiece fer humpies first year I fished. Then they went to thirty cents. Now everythin's by the pound."

"Did you have any experiences fishing salmon?"

"Oh, one time we wuz fishin' down below Karluk and we made a set, and we got awful wet before we closed up, we just closed up an' we had a big shark in the thing. So we had two days mending seine after we got through with that. There was three boats come up alongside, they seen it an' they came up an' they shot it several times. We finally got the line on it, just holes all over it, but it was still alive . . . like to have tore everything off the deck."

"How long was it?"

"About eleven, twelve foot, big one for its kind."

"Where'd you fish around mostly?"

"We fished mostly on the west side of the island, here, all the way down from Litnik clear on down to Alitak. We fished 'em all. I only fished, well, I fished here on Packers Spit with Jim Esky one year. Was no houses or no shacks or nothin' here then."

"Did they have tenders that you could deliver fish to?"

"Yeah, they had tenders. If you was close, why you'd have to deliver 'em to the cannery. Like here we'd deliver to the cannery. One year I fished with Jim Atwood and his brother Russ, we's fishin' fer the old Parks Cannery over here. We had ta deliver all our fish ta the cannery."

Ted paused momentarily to light a cigarette.

"Was New England cannery here?"

"Yeah, they was a cannery there, but we had an agreement ta fish fer Parks. Jist like, ya know, some people fish fer New England, some fer another outfit. We kinda had more or less an agreement ta fish fer Parks. I fished with ol' Tiny a couple a years."

"Bear huntin'?"

"Well, most of my bear huntin's been when I had ta hunt 'm when I was down on Sitkalidak's ranch, at McCord's there. Every spring we'd get one, maybe two bears, swim acrost at the narrows over there by Old Harbor, get on the island, then they'd get after the cattle and we'd hunt 'm. I killed three . . . three down there. One winter we had one down there, he never did hibernate. We'd track him down in the snow and he'd still get away from us. Next spring I finally got him up. Seen 'm chasin' some bulls and I . . . me and Harry Revell, we went after 'm and got 'm in between us and the brush. He come out on my side an' we got 'm. That was the last one we had, but after I left there why . . . heard they got a couple more down there."

"Any of 'm get too ornery?"

"Ornery? Yeah. But they never did come around, never did come around our house, or anything. They'd jest bother the cattle and chase the cattle . . . kill 'm. One time we had one, we could never corner him anywhar an' finally Fish and Wildlife, they sent a guy down there ta trap 'm. He'd just killed a cow an' this guy tried ta trap 'm but he never did. Bear was too smart, he never would get in his traps. He'd come up ta his kill, but when he'd smell the traps he'd never get in any of 'm.

"Yeah, I like it out here. I had to quit my job in town. Worked in Alaska Packers and I couldn't get a place to live . . . couldn't afford it on the wages I was makin', that's why I'm out here."

Ted (Lowell) Liedorf was born in Missouri and has traveled quite a bit from what I've heard. He's crab-fished, salmon-fished, and has flown a plane quite a bit. He helped build Kodiak as most of the old-timers have.

CHARLIE JOHNSON: "I WAS TWENTY-EIGHT THEN"
by: Phil Johnson

Living in Alaska is in itself a challenge. However, living in Alaska plus running a ranch for a livelihood approaches impossibility. Very few have been financially successful. To Charlie Johnson, success has not been measured in financial gains or losses, but in the amount of experience acquired through his overall dealings with the people involved, the livestock, and the surrounding country.

Charlie Johnson was not alone in this venture. His partner, Don Becker, saw it through until his death in the late seventies. His death left a definite void in the operation and Charlie soon initiated the selling of the livestock and lease. He is as of now a retired rancher with only a couple horses and forty acres.

The following article describes events that occurred during his earlier life, events that would ultimately shape his future.

"I was born in Virginia, in Birchville, and about when I was nine years old, I moved to Yorktown, Virginia. From there I moved to Hampton, Virginia, where my family is now residing. I went to school at Poquosen and when I left school, I ran a newspaper stand and sold magazines and newspapers to the veterans' home and hospital. I also had a dry cleaning outfit, but I sold that soon after.

"I left Virginia and came to Alaska in September of 1949. It took eleven days to get here on the *Denali* [Alaska Steamship Line, the only passenger ship they had at that time], which ceased to exist soon afterwards. On the way up, eight of us slept in steerage because it was cheaper. Steerage is the hold in, or near, the engine room where they used to bring up Chinamen from Seattle for labor and things. Conditions weren't very good, a few lice and so forth. And you were right over the engine room, and when you're in rough seas, you get all the engine room smell up in the galley. You'd sit there and hold your nose and try to eat. I particularly remember on this trip one of the Bell's kids from the Bells Flats people, the oldest boy I think, he always walked around with a beer in his hand and he was the only one who didn't get seasick.

"When we got to Seward, they needed people to offload the salmon cases. We worked for about twenty hours there and then went over to Homer where we worked for a few hours and then back to Seward and loaded some more. It was exhausting work.

"On the way to Kodiak it was so rough across the gulf that I kept my knees in my belly to keep from getting seasick. When I finally got to Kodiak, I looked like a tramp, I really did. Here's Hedly and Pearl and all the kids down there waiting for me and they didn't even recognize me I was so tired.

"Just as soon as I got here I was looking for a vehicle. Vehicles were very

Charlie Johnson working with cattle on Kodiak Island.

scarce; you couldn't find a vehicle to save your neck. But I met a friend, name of Buck, he ran the army diesel and had a 1941 half-ton command car with a canvas top on it. I gave him $425 for it, which was a lot of money at that time. I'll never forget the night I went over to pick it up. It was a snowy, wet night. I went into the power plant, paid him off, and he signed the title. I started back to the house. Suddenly I hit a bump and the canvas top split and dumped all the water and snow right down my back. It just covered me good, it really did. Anyway, I remedied that. I built a plywood top on it.

"When I first got up here, the game hunting was wonderful. There was no deer season or beaver trapping at the time, and fox weren't selling for anything, so the main things were ptarmigan, eagle, duck, rabbit and seal hunting. We were getting, I believe, six dollars for seal scalps and two dollars for eagle's feet. All you had to do was shoot the seal or eagle, take the prize [scalp or feet] and send them into Juneau. The reason the eagles were being shot was because they claimed the eagle was destroying the game and fish, which they probably were. I've seen them do it. I've also seen eagles attack ducks and destroy them. I've seen the eagles attack newborn calves and newborn sheep and destroy them also. The eagle's a glorified buzzard, that's all it is; it's about a worthless bird. It's a good scavenger, but seagulls do that, we don't need the eagles.

"To get back to hunting, it took a four-wheel drive rig, high off the ground, to get out to Chiniak, Pasagshak, or Narrow Cape. You could start out in the morning before daybreak, and get your limit of ducks out in Middle Bay in about an hour. Then you could proceed along and look for rabbits and ptarmigan and, say you had four people, you'd have your limit by noon. Meantime, while you're traveling around, you're getting thrown all over because of the terrible roads. I remember particularly Bitch Creek was a bad one because it was always washed out and had a gulley across it. Especially in the fall when the duck season was on, it was frozen and you had to jump a ditch. There was no road maintenance at all. The Army built the roads in the forties and was gone in '49. So the roads were left unmaintained, like Saltery Cove is now. Passage was pretty well impossible in the winter. They didn't even start to maintain the roads until I'd guess 1954. And, even then, they let it go for a length of time, and when they decided to come back, they had to use a bulldozer.

"When I went bear hunting I didn't have to put up with the roads. I'd take a boat. In '51 I went bear hunting in Uyak Bay. We saw thirty-three bear in one week. We'd planned on a two-week hunt, and on the fourth day we had our limit of four. We didn't even have to climb a mountain for them, we got them right along the shoreline. One of them was nine feet, one was ten and a half feet, and the rest were eight and a half feet. When we first started out the bear smell was real bad, so bad that the four of us went up the trail and one looked ahead, the two in the middle looked to the side, and the one behind looked behind. Because the bear smell was so strong, we decided to set on a knoll on the right-hand side of Brown's Lagoon. We sat there all afternoon. We were sure a bear was gonna show up, but none did. So we got into our little fourteen-foot skiff and we started back to camp at Amook Island. We got to the spit that closes in Brown's Lagoon and here's a bear sitting on his butt like a dog. We shut off the motor and drifted into the beach. When we hit the beach, he took off and ran into the brush; so we sat there and made a bunch of plans on how we were gonna attack the bear. We finally took off in pairs, like a bunch of fools. The guy with the poor eyesight, glasses about a quarter-inch thick, heard and followed straight up on the bear. My brother and his partner were about 100 yards to our left, and all of a sudden we came up to a little gulley, with just a few bushes between us and what turned out to be the bear. The old bear was standing there broadside to us, eyeballing us, about fifteen feet away.

"It startled me so bad I wouldn't even raise my gun, thought maybe he'd think I was vicious or something. I waved my partner up and said, 'There he is, there he is!' He kept saying, 'Where is he, where is he?' And ya know, I still didn't raise my gun to shoot in self-defense, I was so excited. About that time my brother and his partner had an opening between them and the bear. They could see him clean about 100 yards off and they started firing at him. I started yelling for them to knock it off, 'cause if they make that bear mad, he's gonna make one jump and eat us alive. I still didn't raise my gun to shoot that bear 'cause I figured if he hit the alder patch, I'd be done for. But when they fired, right past us, the damn bear took off through the bush. We got together again and chewed ourselves out. Anybody fool enough to run after a bear is a nut. Then we heard a crack in the bush and all four of us took off running hard as you can after the bear again. I think if that bear had been smarter, he'd of ate all four of us.

"This whole trip started off when Pete Wolkoff, the man we hired to take us over there, dropped us and our skiff and all our gear off at Amook Island. He was supposed to have gone back to Larsen Bay, but we hadn't even got all our supplies up to the place yet, and here he comes back. He's got a small bear hanging from the boom on his boat and he wants to know if we want the skin. Well, it was too small for a keeper, and we couldn't keep it if we wanted a bear apiece, so we turned him down.

"The next day a Fish and Wildlife boat anchored right off our shore. We got to talking to him and he recommended we go to Zacher Bay, which is right next to Uyak Bay. So we loaded up the skiff aboard his boat. When we got there, we immediately went up on a mound to look around. Suddenly, my brother and his partner took off running; we thought they had spotted a bear. All we could see was the huge mound, and you could see where a bear had climbed up the vertical side of it. It didn't look inviting, with alder and everything, but my partner and I went clear around the back end of the mound. We figured we had a bear up on top of it, so he and I started through the bush. We were parting the bush with our gun barrels it was so thick. Then we started hearing noises coming our way. They grew louder and louder. We had our guns off safety and everything. Side by side, fighting through the alder, when suddenly about ten feet in front of us, the other two hunters show up doing the same thing. Stalking the sounds, just as we were doing. They never did tell us what they ran off for.

"Anyway, we ended up staying there all day, and just before dark we spotted a bear on the left-hand side of Zacher Bay as you come in. My brother and his partner ended up getting that one before we even got there. It took off before we could get a shot at it, and here we go through the brush. After all the promises about not chasing a bear, here we go, right after him. I ended up in front of the rest of them and the bear sat down somewhere. When it did, I ran up on it, not knowing, of course, that it was there. As it jumped out and went one way, I went the other. So much for that bear.

"We ended up going back to skin out the first bear. Once it was done it was too late to do anything, so we headed back to camp. We were gonna build a fire and cook supper, and here we had misplaced the groceries. Somebody got the bagful of potatoes that had been placed in the same place as the groceries; so all the food we had was potatoes. We ended up going to the cannery and getting put up for the night. Boy, what a night! The next day we went back to Uyak Bay to where our camp was. We picked up our forgotten goods and headed back out. We didn't get more than two miles when we decided to get out and walk. So we parked the boat and started walking and walked right into a bear. A beautiful blond bear. I fired the first shot, but because of the gun's safety, I shot the bear through the wrist, on the left front leg. Left nothing but the skin holding it on. The bear took off like it never did bother him.

"Then my partner shot him and he done a flip-flop and got up and ran again. I finally shot him in the neck and finished him. He turned out to be the most beautiful bear I'd ever seen. After we skinned him out, we went on down the bay a little further. Suddenly we spotted a bear on the hillside. As soon as he heard the motor, he took off up the hillside. So we pulled in a little lagoon. The bear wasn't in sight. He had gone up a well-worn trail so we didn't know what to do with him. The guy that spotted him got the first shot. So all four of us were standing there looking for the bear when my brother spotted him. His head was sticking right over the top of a log, right off the trail. I don't know if he was waiting for us to pull up after him or was just curious.

"Anyway, my brother pointed out the bear to the guy, and the guy shot right at his head and missed. The bear then jumped right up and took off running. My brother fired the second shot with his .270. The bullet hit the bear and it came rolling down the hill, breaking off alders two inches thick all the way down. We all got so excited that we emptied our guns at the bear as it came down the hill rolling over and over and clawing the ground. When it finally hit bottom, it was dead. There was only one bullet hole in it and that was the first one my brother shot. Everyone of us had missed it.

"Next morning we took off down the head of Uyak Bay and we had gone only a short distance before we saw another bear on the beach. So we parked the boat and stalked him and got within twenty feet of where we saw him. The whole trip we saw thirty-three bears we could've got and we were done in four days.

"Anyway, we headed back to Amook Island and camped there. We were ready to go home, but we still had several days before Pete Wolkoff was supposed to pick us up. So my partner and I got into a little boat and started out to Larsen Bay to radio in that we were ready to come back. On the way we spotted a whale ahead of us. He was surfacing and going the same way we were, but we figured he'd be long out of the way before we caught up with him. When all of a sudden, about four or five minutes later, he surfaces right beside us. We could've touched him with an eight-foot oar. Scared the daylights out of us.

"Anyway we got to Larsen Bay and radioed Pete; he came and picked us up the next day. This was probably one of the most enjoyable hunts anyone could ever have. In fact, when we landed on the island, Charley Madsen with his ninety-seven-foot yacht was anchored right off our shore. His men came ashore and we visited. They said they'd rather hunt the way we were than the way they were, which was all luxury. We totally agreed with them.

"The Korean War started in, I think, June of 1950. I'd been in the Naval Reserves since '48 and I knew I'd probably have to go in, but I didn't particularly care about the fighting we were doing over there. And besides, I was trying to establish a trade. But as it goes, I ended up getting a notice the first of December. I was to report to a draft board in Newport News, Virginia. This was kind of impossible so I wrote and told them that. They came back and said report to Anchorage, or somewhere in Alaska. Meantime my boss in engineering thought I was vital to the war effort and didn't want to lose me. He wrote a letter to the draft board explaining how he felt. On Christmas Day I got the best present I ever had—I was reclassified, I didn't have to go. But about two weeks later, I got another little card that said I had been reclassified and had to report to Anchorage, Nome, Juneau, or several other places for a physical.

"Well, I wrote them back and said, 'Now be specific, which place do I report to?' Quite a while went by and another notice came back and it said, 'If you don't get over here in about two days, we'll have the marshal pick you up.' So I called them and said, 'My instructions had been to report to any of these stations, so I think I'll take the steamer around to Bethel and then a dogsled to Nome, and check in there.' Well, I didn't get too far with that approach. Anyway, they finally got me to Anchorage and I took a physical and then went to army boot camp. The first meal I had was cold ham, cold coffee, and cold mashed potatoes, so I said to myself, 'This ain't me. I'm going to sign up for active duty.' So I went over and volunteered. Well, this lieutenant commander said I couldn't do it. I just happened to have a *Reserves Newspaper* on my desk, so I went and got it and showed it to him. It said, 'For the first time, Alaskans can achieve active duty, from Alaska.'

Once I showed him that, in four hours I was on the plane via Seattle to San
Diego. I was then sent to Japan, after boot camp, then to Adak, Alaska, for
a year. After Adak, I went back to the States and got discharged. Soon after,
I came back to Kodiak and met my wife-to-be, Carole. I was twenty-eight
then."

NORMAN HOLM: NORWEGIAN STEAM

by: Brent Sugita, Greg Shafer, and Gilbert Wilson
photos by: Brent Sugita and Norm Holm

"Let her go," yells the captain. Suddenly the skiff man begins to row towards the shore, while the captain tows the net into the path of a school of
herring.

We interviewed Norman Holm not as a marine surveyor, as he is known
in Kodiak, but as an old Norwegian herring fisherman. We began our interview with some biography on Norm and his family. "My dad's name was
Oliver and my mom's name was Louise. Both of my parents were from Norway and settled in Petersburg [in Southeastern Alaska] at the very early part
of the twentieth century. My father was a herring fisherman all of his life.
My brother and I helped him out until we finished high school. My brother
didn't like fishing too much so he quit. But I continued on in the fishing
business. . . ."

Norman Holm was born in Petersburg and was raised there. "I went to

Norm Holm at home with photos of marine disasters taken on his job as a marine
surveyor.

grade school and high school there, and then to a place called Pacific Lutheran University in Tacoma, Washington. My dad died while I was in the service during World War II.

"I liked fishing in Alaska and after the war I came back as soon as I could. Ever since then I have been in one aspect of the fishing industry or another. I've been fishing as far back as I can remember. I came to Kodiak because the fishing in Southeast Alaska was very seasonal. It was primarily salmon and halibut, but the crab up this way was starting to develop. It was a year-round fishing industry and I wanted to be active year round also, so we moved up to Kodiak like so many others did in those days.

"I saved enough money when I got out of the service to buy a fifty-two-foot wooden seiner. It cost $13,000. It was fairly old but in pretty good shape. The name of it was the *Phoenix.* Then I bought another boat called the *Estella,* which was a little bigger than the *Phoenix;* I paid $19,000 for it. That was what we called an Alaska limit seiner; it was about fifty-six feet overall, forty-nine on the keel. It had a seventy-five-horsepower Atlas diesel in it and it really traveled, too—it went at least eight or eight and a half knots. Both of these boats were about average for Petersburg. I probably owned a dozen boats over my lifetime in the fishing business."

Then we went on to talk about the fishing gear used in going after herring. "We used cotton seines in those days, but we had to dip them in tar and let it dry. You had to be pretty careful so you didn't burn it. When it got too hot the cotton would disintegrate. If we didn't soak it in tar, it would soak up too much water and get pretty heavy because everything was done by hand in those days. The nets were about 175 fathoms long and 5 strips deep, which is about 15 to 18 fathoms deep. A strip is about 200 meshes deep. You had to be careful for snags and hangups because cotton would tear very easy. Our lead line was basically made out of manila with leads slid over it. Purse lines were also made out of manila. We didn't have such things as nylon or polypropylene lines. Instead of using synthetic floats, they used Spanish floats made out of cork.

"We never had power blocks like they have nowadays, but we had power rollers. Most of it was just plain old muscle. Norwegian steam, we called it."

Then we asked Mr. Holm how he spotted the herring. "It was a little different in those days, we didn't have any electronics. It was quite a science. We had to row around in the skiff and we would have a very thin line over the stern which we would hold in our hand. The line had a lead on the end of it and we'd row through the water and that very thin piece of cotton line would go through the water. If it hit a school of herring, the herring, of course, wouldn't see it and we could feel them when they hit the line. A guy could pretty well tell how much herring there was in that school by rowing around it. We would set the seine around where he indicated that the school was. We didn't have electronics to tell us where we were. We would have to know the lay of the land and take soundings by hand, not easy to do when you're chasing a school of herring.

"We sold them for bait. It was either direct to halibut boats for bait, or to

The *Phoenix*, Norm's fifty-three-foot wooden seiner.

Norm's son Oliver and Dave Kubiak transport the herring from the dock to the cannery.

Norm and his crew checking on the
brined herring roe.

Norm's wife, Dottie, working with the
herring catch.

cold storages who froze them for halibut bait, or to a reduction plant that turned them into fish meal and extracted the oil from the herring. These were the three markets. We used to get about three dollars a barrel, which would be about thirty dollars a ton. When we sold them to the cold storage we used to get about one dollar a barrel, which is about ten dollars a ton. We sold live bait to the halibut boats and got three dollars a barrel, which held about 200 pounds.

"I still like herring fishing, especially now when you have electronic gear, sonar, and depth recorders. It makes it a good deal easier. There is more competition now as the prices of herring have gone up to $500, $600, or $700 a ton for the spring roe herring, depending on the quality of the roe. I guess it makes it a pretty desirable product. When we first fished herring up here we got $35 a ton delivered to cold storage. That was in '64. Then there were those who were fishing for herring roe and were getting $17 a ton. That was the cheapest it got, then I think it went up to $22 a ton. Now it's up to $500 or $600, depending on the recovery of the roe. Things have changed a lot since those days.

"We would start herring fishing in March and the spawned herring would probably be over into the last of May. That would be the spring herring. It came in at different times and different localities. Sitka used to be the first place they would come into. We didn't fish much for fall herring. When we herring-fished we had three or four crew members. You didn't do all that much setting, usually an evening set and a daybreak set.

"While we were in Southeastern Alaska, we didn't have much competition. There were probably half a dozen boats there that fished herring for bait, small boats like ours mostly. At that time there was a big herring reduction plant industry going. These big boats—they were big then, seventy-five feet —many of them are still in the crab fleet and most of them were wooden crab or herring boats. They would start in June and fish all summer into the fall for reduction plants. Of course, they had eleven-man crews and packed about 100 tons. We would pack about 20 tons. Sometimes they would pack 150 tons, some of them with a deck load. That gives you some idea of the difference. Basically, we were fishing for bait and they were volume fishing for what we called the fertilizing, fish meal, and the herring reduction plant.

"When we first moved to Kodiak, which was in 1962, my boys and I fished late herring for three years. Then we started in with herring for roe. We were one of the first ones to start it up here. I think about the same time Zacher Bay started in with herring roe. We were about the only ones in Alaska, I think, that were doing herring roe at that time.

"Our best year for salmon in Southeastern Alaska was in 1937. We had 120,000 fish. We shared $2,200, which that year was the highest boat out of Petersburg.

"I pulled a lot of seine and corkline in my lifetime. I don't know if you ever noticed it, but when I walk down the street and I let my arms relax, they drag on the ground because I was doing so much pulling when I was a kid."

7. Current

NICK ALPIAK: NOTES FROM KARLUK

by: Nick Alpiak

Karluk is a village on the west side of Kodiak Island. A long time ago Karluk used to have seven canneries. When the canneries were still up, there were three big warehouses that were used to put seines in during the winter when fishing was over. The people used the warehouses to have big parties in after fishing season. A few years back there were so many fish in the river at Karluk that the people would have a hard time getting around with their skiffs. Way back when the canneries were still up, Karluk used to be one of the biggest villages around the island; there used to be something like 700 people living in the village. Now there are less than 100 residents.

Before, the people in Karluk did not have outboard motors to haul a seine around with. The people used to have to get together in a skiff with four or five people rowing and towing a seine at the same time. The men would get together and go fishing, and the women would wait for them to get back so they could split the fish. Some of the kids would help carry the fish up to the fish racks for drying.

Sometimes the men would hike over the mountain to Sturgeon Bay River to hunt for deer, mallards, ptarmigan, and rabbits. The food in Karluk used to be pretty cheap back when the canneries were still up. The people home used to tell us kids about how they used to get a dozen cans of milk for one dollar. People lived in barabaras back when the canneries first started to operate. Old people used to tell us that there used to be barabaras all over Karluk!

The village of Karluk has two sides. The people in Karluk do not live all on one side; there are two sides and a sandbar and a spit that separates them. The side where the store is they call the Spit, and they call the other side Old Karluk. In Karluk there was a bridge built a long time ago to get from the store side to the other side. We have a church in Karluk that was built by Charles Smith Hursh over 120 years ago and it still looks very nice. Some of the graves behind our church are so old we can barely make out where they are at.

A couple of years ago when the ocean washed over the spit in Karluk, it really messed up our path going down the spit and to Old Karluk. When it washed over the last time, it knocked the beach gangs winch house over. The beach gang had a winch that they used to tow their seine up on the beach.

The skiffs that they used to use were driven by a water wheel attached to the stern of the skiffs.

For recreation in Karluk the people go to movies, play pool, bingo, and Ping-Pong. We use oilstoves and wood stoves during the winter. My family uses a homemade sled to haul fifty-gallon drums of oil from the store to Old Karluk where I live. In the wintertime, the kids always hike halfway up the mountains with toboggans and slide back down. During the summertime, my dad, my brothers, and I all go fishing. When the fishing season is over, I give my dad and mom a few dollars to buy oil or whatever they need to get.

In the spring, just before my dad goes fishing, he goes hunting for Park Munsey. When my dad is done hunting during the spring he goes fishing; then when he is done fishing, he goes hunting in the fall again. After my dad is done bear hunting, he usually takes my mom, my little sister, and my little brother into town to shop for whatever they need at home. When my other brothers and I get done fishing, we usually come into town [Kodiak city] for a trip, too.

My dad does not hunt for himself; he is a bear guide for Park Munsey. I have an uncle who is also a bear guide for Park Munsey.

During the winter in Karluk the people do a lot of ice skating and they build a bonfire to keep warm with. In the fall when the cannery is operating, and the people dump all the fish guts on the beach, a few bears come down during the night and eat everything up. Just last year, someone in Karluk left their dried fish out too long, and a couple bears came down during the night and ate everything. My grandma and her little grandson were walking up to Old Karluk one day and there was a bear that followed them all the way from down the spit. My two brothers were down the spit visiting one night and when they were walking home, a bear chased them all the way back. Just this summer, John Craddack was walking around down on the beach and a bear chased him.

I can remember when we used to live up the river in Karluk. My brothers and sisters used to walk three quarters of a mile to get to school even in winter. Some of the kids would walk up to the riverside after school with my brothers and sisters to visit. When my brothers and I started going to school, my dad bought a house that was closer to the school. When I was in the eighth grade, my brother got me a bicycle for not flunking once in grade school! After he got me a bicycle he showed me how to use his 125 Hodaka and he used to let me run to the store for him.

When my dad was hunting in Sturgeon one year, he took some hunters out. They wounded a bear and it hid away from them in the brush. My dad did not like it. He had a .30-06 rifle and a .44 magnum pistol with him. He was going into the brush to see if he could get the bear out and all of a sudden the bear came charging out at him. He was just going to shoot the bear when his rifle jammed on him. The bear got stuck in the brush somehow and my dad took his .44 pistol and shot it three times to kill it. After my dad got the bear for his hunters, one of them gave him a brand-new .375 rifle with a scope.

My brother and I went to Sturgeon last summer with a friend from Karluk, Tim Sugak. When we went over, we saw about thirty reindeer. My brother wanted to get a couple, but my dad said not to touch them because of mating season. We were helping some bear hunters pack their gear over to my dad's cabin. Some of the hunters started over about four hours ahead of us and they shot a couple reindeer on the way over. They gave us three hindquarters to take back with us.

When the canneries were still up, Chinese people used to work over in Karluk because they were skilled workers at canning salmon. Also, when the canneries were still up, people did not have a hard time catching fish like today. Before, when the people would go fishing with a seine, they would get about 2,000 fish in one haul. A little while back, they did not have planes flying in and out of the villages like today. The only thing they had to haul mail and freight in and out of the villages was a mail boat. Herman von Sheeley was the guy that used to bring the mail over to the villages; the first boat was the *Phyllis S.* and the other boat's name was the *Shuyak*. The *Phyllis S.* was hit by an army tugboat which broke it in half and destroyed two lives. This happened during World War II. I think Von Sheeley's nephew has the *Shuyak* today and it is still running.

Things today have changed quite a bit since a few years back. I guess some of them in Karluk kind of miss how things used to be a little while back. Before, people used to walk to Larsen Bay and back to Karluk. When they used to have parties in the warehouses, they used to have about three barrels of beer in each warehouse.

When I went fishing last summer, my skipper anchored out at Tangle Point right next to Karluk. My skipper was checking the oil in the engine and dropped his screwdriver into the bilge. He was reaching for it, when all of a sudden he lost his balance and fell into the bilge. My brother, my cousin, and I all started laughing and I guess that was what got him mad.

The summertime is the best time to be over in Karluk. In the summertime everything over there gets just green and it looks very nice.

A few years ago, Karluk had a real good dock, now it sure doesn't look too good. The only thing left of the dock is the piling, and it sure doesn't look too good. It would be nice if the people in Karluk would tear everything down off the old dock and rebuild it. If the people would have taken care of the dock a few years ago, it could have still been up. Most of the people that lived in Karluk moved to different villages and some time they might be back again.

It sure is bad living in Karluk during the wintertime. It's hard to haul fuel over to Karluk then because of the bad weather. When the radios are out, it is hard to call in and out, especially when someone gets hurt or sick. Sometimes it gets really cold over there and the school's power plant goes out; the teacher has to call off school till they get the power plant running again. Willie Pete Wasilie is pretty good at fixing power plants and they usually get him to work on it. When the store's power plant goes out, he fixes that too and gets paid for doing it; otherwise he could be doing something else up at his own house.

Willie and my dad are pretty good friends and when our plant goes out, he comes up to the house and helps my dad fix it. When the nights are boring at home, my dad, mom, and Willie usually play pinochle all night long sometimes. Then my dad and mom wake the rest of the family up and they go to sleep for a while. Then my brothers and I usually go out and cut wood for our heater, while my sisters clean house. When we finish, my dad gives us a few dollars to go to the movies and play bingo.

During Russian New Year's at Karluk, the people usually have some kind of devil dance. They have three volunteers to put Wesson Oil all over each other and then they cover themselves with soot from wood stoves. When the people clean their stoves, some of the guys get them to save soot. They cut a couple pieces off old boots and they make devil's horns out of them. To let the people know about the dance, someone dresses up like our old year. An old year is someone who dresses up with old clothes and makes himself real big. Then they tie a sign to his back and one in front, telling the people when they are going to have a devil dance and where it's going to be. For the music they have someone playing an accordion. If the people can find a guitar, they will have someone playing that, too. The devil dance will last for about forty-five minutes; when the devil dance is over, they will have a regular dance. The dance will probably last for about three to four hours.

Karluk is a very good place to live in because it is always very quiet. I think it is a lot better than living in town because at night when everyone goes to bed at least we don't hear cars and trucks driving around all night. The only time the people have a hard time living in Karluk is during the wintertime. The mail plane always has a hard time trying to get into Karluk because of the cold weather freezing up the river when there is no other place to land.

GILL JARVELA: FLYING BY THE SEAT OF YOUR PANTS

by: Bill Fox and Marc Howard
photos: Bill Fox and courtesy of Gill Jarvela
revised by: Paul Greenlee and Tracey Reyes

We decided to interview Mr. Jarvela because we were both interested in the subject of bush piloting in the Kodiak area. We were told that he was an exceptional pilot with lots of experience in bush piloting. We then contacted him, set up an interview, and found out he had a lot to say about his flying career.

Gill Jarvela served as a bomber pilot with the Eighth Air Force during World War II and saw action in Europe. He arrived in Kodiak in 1948. He served as a state representative from Kodiak District during the second and third state legislatures and was a member of the Kodiak School Board for ten years. After twenty-five years of flying in Alaska, Mr. Jarvela became airport manager of the Kodiak airport.

His wife arrived in Kodiak right after he came here. Bonnie Jarvela has been secretary for the junior high principal for the past six and one-half years. Three of their five children were born in Kodiak.

"I started flying commercially with Kodiak Airways when it was just beginning. At that time the operation consisted of two Sea Bee single-engine amphibious aircraft. There was just Bob and Helen Hall and myself. Helen

Gill Jarvela by the type of plane he flew for Kodiak Airways.

Hall was dispatcher, bookkeeper, mail handler, baggage girl, hostess, ticket agent, chief cook and bottle-washer. Our hangar was just a little building, and to get an airplane into it you had to take the wings off.

"It was a beginning and the Kodiak Western you see now is what the beginning amounted to. Along the way, of course, one has a lot of memories of interesting experiences that we had. Back in those days things were pretty crude. I remember we had to roll our gas down to our planes in fifty-gallon drums, then fuel them with a hand pump, then roll the can back up the beach. Every time we worked on our airplanes, it was out in the bad weather.

"To begin with, the people around the island were not very used to flying. It took a little time to get everybody interested in flying. There was a mail boat that went around the island run by Bob von Sheeley; soon after we started flying we contracted to deliver the mail and that was the beginning of the demise of the mail boat. When the aircraft entered the picture, our business consisted mainly of getting cannery workers and fishermen to and from canneries. This was important work in the beginning. Also servicing the villages, getting the mail around, that was very important, and getting the people back and forth.

"Then along with that type of flying, since Kodiak is a 'hunter's paradise,' there were a lot of people coming here to hunt the Kodiak bear. We became more and more involved in taking people out hunting. We never did any of the guiding as such, but we worked with the guides in getting the hunters and their gear to where they were to go.

"I remember one experience that was very interesting. Up to that time there had been bear hunting going on, but on a very small scale. When bear hunting started to really become more and more important, hunters that came up here began taking effect on the numbers of bears to where pretty soon they had all the big bear hunted out. Any more you don't get the size bear you used to get. But it was the number of bears that astounded me. I remember one occasion going into a place called Little River and I took a Fish and Wildlife guy in there. He was going in to look for tagged red salmon. Since there weren't many airplanes around, it ended up that I took him in with a plane that I was using to teach flying.

"This was before I even began flying for Kodiak Airways. When we went into this lake, there was a whole mess of bear fishing in the lake amongst a big mess of red salmon. This was where the guy wanted to go because this was where the tagged fish were. When the bear came into this lake, they would come into a stream where they all congregated around the mouth of this one little stream. He wanted to get off where the bear were, so I taxied up to the beach and turned the plane around and gave a blast of the prop to scare them out of the water. I could have come up and hit them; they didn't want to leave. When I turned around and hit them with a blast of the prop, they moved. Then we turned around and were facing toward shore and saw over thirty bears standing on the bank. They were shoulder to shoulder.

There were light ones, dark ones, little ones, big ones, momma bear and papa bear.

"They were all standing there and it was so strange to see them that way, and we didn't have a camera! Nowadays you just don't see sights like that.

"I remember flying two live bear cubs to Kodiak from one of the hunting camps. I had them in a gunnysack, and I worried all the way to Kodiak as to whether that gunnysack would hold out or not. It did. Those two bear ended up going to a zoo in Hamburg, Germany.

"To show you just how safe flying is, I have flown a good many hours up in this country and have never had a really dangerous situation where the aircraft failed me. I had situations where I lost an engine in a twin-engine aircraft, but I was able to get to where I wanted to go.

"I had one experience that I remember very well; this happened in a Sea Bee. I ran out of gas because I didn't check my tank. Another experienced pilot supposedly had checked the gas tank and I took his word for it. It happened to be an emergency flight. I had been out on a flight with another airplane, so when I came in he had this airplane all ready to go to a place called San Juan, on the west side of the island, to pick up a sick cook. Since it was an emergency [big rush, rush] I asked him about the gas and he said that he had checked it and there was plenty. I went over, got the guy, and was on my way back. There was a pass you had to fly over. I had just got past when the engine quit; I was fortunate enough to be close to where I could get to the water and land. When the engine quit I was able to land safely. I then sailed the airplane to a beach by just letting the wind blow me. We just waited until they came and picked us up.

"The sick cook was so frightened by the forced landing that he completely forgot about being sick. When we finally got to Kodiak, he left on the first plane for Seattle and said he was never coming back.

"I had a couple of accidents where I hit reefs in areas where I wasn't familiar with the water, and I wasn't careful enough. As far as having any serious accidents, I really never did. I wasn't fortunate enough, I guess, to have a bad accident and live to tell a tale of it. I had some very thrilling flights, like everybody that flies up here has.

"The weather is one of the things that draws a person to doing this kind of work; it's just the excitement of challenging the elements. I had one particularly exciting emergency flight that almost got me in trouble, in danger of losing my pilot's license. I was called on one day to go to Point Banks, which is on the north end of Kodiak on Shuyak Island. There was a lone attendant guarding the FAA station and taking care of the equipment. The station has now been decommissioned. At the time there was a radio station up there. This fella had gone out seal hunting and a bank gave way and he fell off a cliff onto the beach. He got a compound fracture in one leg, and it also knocked him out. When he came to, he had been there awhile.

"There was a small road, about a half-mile long, from the building that housed the installation down to the beach where the airplanes brought in the

"As far as having any serious accidents, I really never did."

supplies. They had a four-wheel-drive jeep that hauled the supplies back and forth. He had parked the jeep down on the beach and he dragged his body, using the butt and the barrel of his gun, until he reached the jeep. He couldn't get into the jeep, so he put the jeep into low gear, hit the starter, and it started going. There he was, laying on the seat of the car with his leg dragging on the ground, and he could just barely see where he was going. Fortunately, he knew what little road there was very well.

"You can imagine the pain that must have gone through him, although maybe he was in shock and didn't feel the pain. He drove himself up to the building, and when he got there he turned the jeep off and dragged himself into the house. When he opened the door, his black Lab, which hadn't seen him for a while, was so happy to see him he jumped all over him. There he was suffering with this broken leg, and he thought he was going to have to shoot his dog to get it quiet. Then he went to the radio room and managed to get hold of the microphone. The radio was always on, so all he did was call Woody Island and say he was hurt; he then passed out.

"The FAA manager, Darrell Chaffin, called the Coast Guard to go up to Shuyak and pick this guy up. The weather was exceptionally bad and they didn't have the type of aircraft that was needed to go into this area. They didn't even have a chopper then. They were going to send one of their boats up there to get him. If they had sent it, he would have been bad off because it would have taken so long to get there.

"Darrell had found out the Coast Guard couldn't get there in time to help the guy, so he called us up; I told him I would go ahead and try, if he had someone to go along with me. So Darrell, a navy corpsman, and another guy came along. We managed to get up to Shuyak and land there.

"We got up to the house and found the guy. He was in very bad shape, really sufferin'. He was in deep shock, and the medic tried to put his leg in traction, and then got him into a big web basket. We had to carry him down to the airplane and we couldn't even touch the guy until after we had given him some morphine. We got him back down to the airplane, and back out into this horrible storm. We managed to get out and back to Kodiak.

"After the trip was over, Darrell wrote a little blurb for the newspaper about this experience he'd had. He mentioned the bad weather and how we had saved the man's life. The article was picked up by the FAA in Anchorage. They sent me a letter saying they were going to cite me for violation because of flying in bad weather. I let Darrell know about it right away, and I said, 'Thanks a lot for getting me in all this trouble.' Of course, he got very excited about it and let the FAA know very quickly what the score was. They decided not to press any charges, but that was kind of a different twist to an exciting flight.

"My flying up here has been all amphibious and float plane flying. I have very little experience with flying with skis. I have flown on skis before, but I haven't done any glacier flying, or mountaintop flying, or things of that na-

Gill with a drugged
bear on a Fish and
Game survey.

ture. I just never had the occasion to be called on to do something like that. I'll leave it to braver souls.

"The last year I flew I did a bear survey with the Fish and Wildlife. I had a picture taken of me next to a bear that was drugged and couldn't do anything about it, fortunately. I also had my first beach landing accident. I flipped my wheel plane over on its back when I mistook a soft mud hole for solid ground. The only thing that was damaged was a prop and my pride.

"During the tidal wave I wasn't on Kodiak. At that particular time I was in Juneau, but I got here the day after the earthquake, so I saw the aftermath. I was a member of the legislature and we were in session, so I missed all that excitement. We recessed after the earthquake so everyone could see what the devil happened.

"We had our home out at Spruce Cape, right out on the beach. We had just finished building this new home and my wife and five children were there. My wife had been with me in Juneau just prior to the earthquake and was home during the tidal wave, just opening up all the goodies she bought in Anchorage before she came home.

"I got a flight out of Juneau to Anchorage, but I couldn't get out of Anchorage to Kodiak because the runway was littered with trash and they weren't sending a flight out right away. I was fortunate at running into Dave Henley, who still flies for Fish and Wildlife. He was coming to Kodiak at the time, so I got a ride with him. We flew over Ouzinkie on the way down. There were buildings all over the place in the water. It was quite a sight to see.

"I was quite concerned when I came around Spruce Cape because we didn't have any word of what transpired in Kodiak. The only word I could get was that Kodiak had been completely devastated. I could just see everything gone, including my family. When I came around Spruce Cape, lo and behold, there was the house! It hadn't even been touched; it was quite a relief to see. The bay out in front was littered with stuff, so you couldn't land an airplane there. There were houses, boats, you name it and it was floating there.

"The small airstrip was available there in Kodiak, and we landed. Kodiak Airways was completely wiped out, the only thing left was about two concrete posts that were still in the ground. Everything else was completely gone. Just prior to the tidal wave they did move all the airplanes up to the strip, and they were in the process of trying to take a Goose out of the hangar. We had a hangar right on the beach, and the hangar was kind of small, so you had to move that airplane a certain way to get it out of the hangar. It was always a problem getting it out. One man had to tell everyone else which direction to push. While they were trying to get this airplane out, the water was splashing back and forth, and making so much noise with the rocks rolling on the beach and everything else going on, they couldn't hear the guy giving instructions. They kept getting it screwed up, so they couldn't get it out. Finally, the water got up real close to the hangar, then somebody yelled, 'I'm getting the hell out of here!' After that they all vacated the place. It wasn't long after that when building after building kept bumping into one another.

"The dock at the old Alaska Packers place tore loose and it came charging down, barging into building after building. That's what happened to our hangar, with the airplane half in and half out. It went out to sea. Somebody said they saw it once, way out to sea, but it certainly didn't end up around Kodiak. We never did see it again. It was quite a 'low blow,' destroyed with all those tools, parts, and that beautiful airplane. It was quite a sad thing to lose absolutely everything of Kodiak Airways but the planes that were saved.

"When coming through Anchorage the day after the quake, I had an opportunity to go all around town, and I saw the whole bit. That was quite a terrifying thing that happened back then. It was a terrible devastation, and there it was in front of me.

"I've seen a great many changes and feel young people settling here have a bright and interesting future. Kodiak is coming into a new era and there is a very strong possibility that we will see changes that we never dreamed of. What we need is a new generation of well-educated men and women to manage this change so that we might be spared the many pitfalls that these changes can bring."

When asked what his feelings were towards Kodiak, Gill Jarvela said, "I came here in 1948, but I feel like I've lived here all my life."

"I came to Kodiak in 1948 but I feel like I've lived here all my life."

LINDA TERABASSO: NIGHT RESCUE
by: Joe Descloux

The Terabasso family moved to Blue Fox Bay on Afognak Island in 1971 when they left Kodiak. The next year they moved to Packers Spit in Mush Bay because they wanted to be closer to their fishing grounds. In the summer months, they fish the tides. In the winter, they trap and get deer across on the South and East Arm at Mush Bay. They live inside the lagoon at the base of Dog Ear Mountain. The mail comes by Goose or Widgeon seaplanes to the Village Islands about two miles up the bay and about thirty-two miles west of Kodiak on the other side of the island. It takes about twenty-five or thirty minutes by Goose or Widgeon, and about five hours by skiff, depending on the motor size, to get to Packers Spit. The Terabassos come to town about twice a year for groceries and equipment for repairing the seines and gear for the summer fishing.

The winds of Kodiak Island can blow regularly up to sixty miles per hour. The worst blow is ninety-five to one hundred and twenty-five miles per hour with thirty-foot swells. The Terabassos have had some bad experiences with the straits, rip tides, and reefs of Kodiak. There have been quite a few deaths in the waters of Kodiak. If it wasn't for the Coast Guard, there would be more deaths, including those of my aunt, uncle, and cousins.

Joe Terabasso is always yelling but he's a nice guy. He has a positive attitude toward life; when you get on a subject he'll talk himself blue in the face, but he won't give up his argument. He is short and stocky and looks something like Grizzly Adams. Linda is kinda quiet when she is in town. She takes life the way it comes to her; she can take a bad situation and make it better.

Robin was fifteen at the time when this happened. Shawna was thirteen; she helps around the house and fishes—she does her share of work. Kelli was eleven and she helps with about everything. Joey Ann was three and Dusty was eighteen months; she most likely doesn't even remember what happened. Mike was nine, he's about the same as Kelli. Linda is telling the story of what happened to her and her family.

"We left Kodiak March 24, 1974, around 4:30 P.M., bound for home. It was a nice day for travel and the first time the kids and I had gone around Spruce Cape when it was nice. We could see the remains of the *Martin* where she was lying upside down on the rocks. We made fair time to Ouzinkie and stopped to stretch and restore some circulation after sitting for an hour in the cold. The temperature was 27°.

"We picked up a bit of speed after leaving Ouzinkie since Joe added a bit more gas to the fuel tanks. The oil was thick and hard to mix. The weather was still nice, no wind, no spray, and the eighty-five-horse was going good. We figured to be in Port Bailey in another twenty minutes; this is when Joe checked the time after coming out of Whale Pass at 7 P.M. The tide was high by this time, and there were some swirls and tugs at the twenty-one-foot Whaler as we were traveling, but nothing to get excited about. About five minutes later as we were nearly even with the end of Raspberry Island, Joe suddenly hollered to us to, 'Hang on—here comes a big one!' Nobody had time to wonder what he meant, we just held on. Then a huge wave came completely over the Whaler from bow to stern. The battery was submerged and immediately blew a fuse.

"Joe tried to start the kicker again with only a click for a response. The next wave turned us broadside and the Whaler was full of water. Joe started throwing everything out to lighten the boat so it would rid itself of the water. Once everything was out of the Whaler, it kept trying to flip over to dump us. Joe said it would right itself like a cork. He had the kids keep shifting their weight back and forth to keep from dumping. He tried to row us out of the rough water, but it was like trying to row the *Tustamena* [the Alaska State Ferry that serves Kodiak Island]. It was impossible! Then he lost one oar. After about fifteen minutes, but what seemed like hours, we were once again in calm water. We could still see the big waves that hit us, but all the rest was calm.

"By this time it was nearly dark. The current was carrying us down Kupreanof Strait toward Port Bailey. As we floated along, some of our clothes and food would swirl by on the current. The phosphorescence in the water seemed to dance along beside us and played tag with the various objects floating by. As we were drifting along, the waters started going out of the boat and we were beginning to feel the cold somewhat. Robin, Kelli, and Mike all had lost their hip boots and were standing knee-deep in freezing water.

"Still close to the middle of the strait, we had drifted down to the flasher buoy across the way from Port Bailey and were just drifting back and forth in a short circle when Joe said, 'Hey, I see some red lights over by that mountain. If that's a UFO I hope they come down and take us up to Mars!' The lights disappeared and we sat for another five minutes without saying anything except Dusty, eighteen months, who was mad because her security blanket floated off.

" 'What's that light?' Bright as day was Whale Island as the Coast Guard was checking their new high-intensity light. 'Maybe they will see our stuff floating around and come and get us!'

" 'Naw. There they go the other way!' We drifted back over toward Port Bailey, even saw the cannery lights, then they were out of sight again.

"Joe dug around and with Shawna's help opened up two three-pound cans of coffee and Tang and dumped the contents. He poured gas from one tank and with a 79 safety match, he lit the two makeshift flares.

"All the kids were okay as far as I could tell. Joey Ann was in some shock from all that cold weather, but otherwise they were able to move around a bit now that there was only six inches of water in the skiff. I had just stood up to ease a cramp in my back and was trying to straighten up when again Joe said, "There are some red lights up there toward the end of Uganik Island!'

" 'Really!'

" 'Where?'

" 'I don't see anything!'

" 'Me either. Wait I hear a motor!'

" 'Look—the light!'

" 'Yay, we're saved!'

"Joe picked up one of the cans that was burning and waved it around, dipping it and turning it so they could see us. They came down closer, circled us, then hovered over the water near us. One of the crew used a pole with a hook on it to hold the skiff since the wind from the rotors kept blowing us away. Joe put us all on board, then threw a drag anchor for the skiff in case it drifted to the beach, to keep it from traveling too far."

While they were boarding, one of the pilots radioed in and contacted Dr. Jellerson and sick bay for an ambulance and medical personnel to attend them on arrival. They were taken back to the base and transported to the hospital in town. Joe Terabasso, his wife, and six children were all treated and released. Not one case of frostbite and they were out there four and one-half hours, most of it standing or sitting in the freezing water.

"Commander Potter of the helicopter that picked us up told us they didn't know we were in trouble until they saw our flares. The Coast Guard helicopter was on a return trip from a rescue mission to a lake up around King Salmon for a downed aircraft. Potter said they usually come around Malina Point and up Kupreanof to check, just in case something is wrong.

"After the helicopter picked us up, a few short hours later the wind picked up and by the next day was gusting to eighty-five miles per hour through Kupreanof Strait. No boats were traveling. The next day we got a call from a friend of Joe's; in passing Outlet Cape in their fishing boat, they spotted our Whaler on the rocks. Darrell Short from Bare Island went over and got the Whaler for us and towed it over to Tom and Grace Malmberg's. Brian hauled us over on the *Karen Sue* to Bare Island and we spent the next month patching the Whaler. It had some huge holes in it, especially in the middle where it had pounded on those big, huge rocks at Outlet Cape. It also had a big crack across the bottom.

"Again, the help that people gave us was great. All I can say is I'm glad I live in Alaska, especially on Kodiak Island."

U. S. COAST GUARD: IN ACTION

interviews with U.S.C.G. pilots G. Blain Brinson, James D. Stiles, and Mont Smith
by: Lillian Bradshaw

"It was October 17, about 1615 (4:15) in the afternoon. We got a call from the *Comsta.* They said, 'A boat is reported sinking. It is up just south of the Kenai Peninsula.' We didn't think too much of it, until about two minutes later. They said, 'They are taking out a life raft and putting it on deck.' We immediately launched a helicopter and a C-130. The C-130 got on the scene first, of course, because they are a little bit faster than the helicopter is. When we got on scene the winds were high, from seventy to eighty knots. The turbulence was moderate, which means they were bouncing around pretty well on the way up there. We got up there and the C-130 hadn't found the boat and the helicopter didn't see the boat. The C-130 started to search the southeast and those of us in the helicopter started to search northwest. We made a couple of passes.

"The daylight was getting real short. We were really strapped for time. We had about fifteen or twenty more minutes on the scene because of our fuel situation. We looked at a buoy in the distance, there wasn't anything there, so we started down our next leg. A few minutes after that Commander Addison saw what we called 'another buoy.' We said, 'Even though it looks like a buoy, we'll take a look at it. We would rather look at a hundred buoys than miss one boat.' So we took it safe, and, sure enough, it was the boat we were looking for. It was just turned bow away from us so it looked like a superstructure buoy. There were no signs of life on board or anything else.

"We assumed they had abandoned ship. No life raft or anything on board and the raft looked like it was riding rather well. We made a circle to take another pass on it. We were rolling out of what we call 'a down wind,' which means we were going parallel to the boat's course, but not going any closer to the boat, just 'rolling out on down.' As soon as we rolled wings level, we saw a little orange life raft right in front of us. There were three people in the life raft.

"The ferry *Tustamena* was in the area searching also. We thought about diverting her over to pick the people up since the sea was extremely high. We were worried about the ferry's 'freeboard,' in other words 'the amount of distance between the waterline and the deck of the ship,' being able to get the people on board safely. We decided to hoist them. We pulled into a 'hover' right over the people and lowered the basket to them. The basket, the seas, and everything else including the raft were moving around quite a bit due to the sea action and high winds. There was a couple of times I was looking up at the tops of the waves, they were actually that high. They were the biggest waves I have ever seen.

Coast Guard helicopter hovers over the ship, about to lower a basket.

"We lowered the basket and one man grabbed hold of the basket, jumped from the raft to the basket, and it went immediately into the water and we hoisted him aboard. The raft wasn't an open raft, it was a covered one and the people were all inside the raft. We did that three times; we pulled all three survivors up. We then took them to Homer, which has a little airport. We landed there and spent the night. We found out that just after they got in the raft, it did a tumble act on them; it went completely upside down. They didn't have any survival suits. I don't know if you've seen them, some people carry them. They keep you dry, totally dry. They didn't have any so all three were soaking wet. It was a cold evening.

"The interesting thing is that the boat was afloat the next day. The only thing I can figure is they were going from the Barren Islands up to the Homer area. The waves and wind were from the northwest. They were taking the seas on the port side. Apparently, once they abandoned ship, the ship turned around so the starboard side was to the waves, winds, and everything else. I would imagine that was the only thing that kept the ship afloat. This is one of our cases with a happy ending. I think they went out and tried to tow it in. The boat was almost gone the next day.

"If we hadn't had any wind or anything like that, it would have been doubtful that we could of hoisted all people aboard. Helicopters are funny animals; it takes more power for us to hover than it does to fly. It takes more fuel to hoist. We weren't really hovering when we were doing the hoisting; we were actually flying because of the wind.

"When you have a hurricane coming, you have to fly the airplanes and the helicopters away. Up here it is rather strange; we have the same amount of wind, in fact these were hurricane-force winds, but it is rather strange we don't worry about the winds as much. It is always windy here. We hangar the airplanes when we expect hurricane winds; it is not that seldom that we have seventy knots of wind.

"In rescues, the C-130 will usually wait until the helicopter comes to the scene. It would be more hazardous to go from one life raft to another, so they will probably just leave them in the same life raft and let the helicopter evacuate. Now, if it looks like it will be awhile, the MA2 kit [is dropped]. I think it has a seven-man life raft and a lot of food and other neat things you would want for a long period of time. In other words, it makes it comfortable. It is certainly better than what they had. A big raft is harder to tip over.

"The main thing we work against is darkness. If we know exactly where they are and they are within helicopter range, and we know they are safe in a raft or what have you, we have plenty of time. The difference between the helicopter and the C-130 is the speed with which you can get somebody on the scene and find them. In that rescue I described, we wanted to get them found so we wouldn't have to search for them and the C-130 did get up there much quicker than we did. The C-130 flies 100 percent faster than the helicopter. The C-130 moves along at about 300 knots whereas a helicopter can move along anywhere from 120 to 140 knots at altitude.

"The C-130 is a search vehicle. It can get into smaller and shorter runways. The main thing is that it is a communications station. It has very sophisticated communications ability, including a teletype machine. You can actually sit up there and type a message out and they can reach you back from the ground station—they type a message from the ground. It is very effective communications relay.

"When we were circling the ship, the C-130 stayed on scene until they knew we had all the people on board. They hauled for Kodiak and we hauled for Homer to drop the people off. The C-130 didn't only hang around for communications, it hung around in case something went wrong. They carry a little more survival equipment than we do, 'the MA2 kit.' They can drop down at marker buoys, they help you locate a certain place. They just wanted to make sure everything was running smoothly.

"When we are doing a hoist, especially a hoist like this, we have absolutely nobody to talk to on the radios except the co-pilot and if we had an emergency flight where we had to land in the water, we might never get out of the haul. So they hang around mainly to keep an eye on us, to be sure everything is going smooth. They could talk to the world for us. If we were to have an emergency they would know we were in trouble, especially in a situation like that, because if we lost an engine and put it down to the seas, I doubt seriously how long the helicopter would have been able to stay up even with the rotor. With the seas that high, I think we would have taken seas through the rotor system, and, once that happened, the rotor blades would just come apart and the helicopter would have capsized. It would

The C-130, a search vehicle and airborne communications station, carries a fuel load of almost 63,000 pounds and flies at 300 knots.

have been very obvious if someone saw a helicopter upside down in the water that we were having trouble. With that kind of wind we were having, though, if we had lost an engine, we would have been able to fly it. We couldn't have come back for people in a raft; we would have had to send another helicopter out to pick them up. In which case the C-130 would have had to stay with the raft. We would have gone and taken the people we had aboard to Homer, landed there, shut down, and they would have flown another engine to us.

"We don't take pictures on all our cases; we try and get as many pictures as we can, however, when we get a search and rescue case. A lot of times, especially on helicopters, we leave so darn quick we don't have time to grab a camera. We do carry a little camera in most of the helicopters. Those pictures there were taken from the C-130 and we had plenty of warning that they were gonna go out, so we made sure they had a camera aboard. We try and document it because it makes a news story as far as the downtown papers and the wire services are concerned. A lot more interesting, it gives you a very good graphic description of what's going on with search and rescue [SAR]."

This is Mr. James D. Stiles. He works at the air station on the Coast Guard base. He only flies the helicopter. Mr. Stiles has been in the Coast Guard for eleven years and has been flying the helicopter about nine years. He enjoys flying the helicopter. He flies in the C-130 as passenger quite a bit. "A lot of times, if there is no SAR case going on, I'll fly along with them, just as a passenger, so I can take pictures and things like that." He is going to tell us more about SAR.

"Right after I got up here, I think it was May of 1976, we had a sailboat 1,000 miles south of here that got caught in a storm. It whipped over and broke its mast and it was an instance where there's nothing that a helicopter could do because we don't have the range. We can go maybe, at a maximum out and back, 275 to 300 miles, depending on the weather.

"One boat, the *Sea Fair,* which sank, was a seventy-foot fishing boat. They started to take on water and the initial response was to send out the C-130 and also send the helicopter out with pumps on board so they could help [control] the flooding. We carry a pump on board at all times. If we know that we are going out on a boat that is sinking, a lot of times we will stop before we take off and throw an extra pump on board."

Mr. Stiles also talked about the survival equipment they carry in the helicopter and what it is used for. "Normally we carry special equipment in the helicopter. We carry a sling, which is a padded piece of strap that you put behind your back and under your arms and it hooks onto the hoist. We carry a basket, which we lower down and the people sit in it and we raise it up with them in it. We also carry a litter and that way if someone can't walk, we can stick them in the litter and strap them in. There are three straps which go across them, it holds them in good and tight, and that way we can hoist them up off the deck. It keeps them fairly stable and keeps them from getting jostled around as much as if they were sitting up. A lot of times this is important, say a person got a broken leg or a back injury, you would want to keep their movement down to a minimum. That's the reason we use a litter. Those are the three basic pieces of equipment.

"In addition, we carry the pump. Another piece of survival equipment that we carry is an exposure suit. Some people call them poopy suits. They are a one-piece dry suit; you slip it on over your clothes and it's got feet in it and one zipper down the middle of the suit. It looks just about like the flight suit with the exception that it has a rubber collar around it and rubber cuffs on it. It's kind of a neoprene with a nylon overlay. It keeps you dry most of the time. It's probably an early forerunner to the kinds of suits that a lot of the fishermen have, exposure suits. Survival suits are more of a combination of a wet suit and an exposure suit. This is more like a heavy raincoat with nylon on the outside of it."

Mr. Mont Smith also works at the air station on the Coast Guard base. He also only flies the H-3 and has been flying about seven years. He talked some more about the SAR cases. "We carry a sled on board the helicopter. In our sled we have four sleeping bags and a cooking kit. We have a tent and a small survival weapon, a little rifle. It is a combined rifle-shotgun. We also have fire starters, extra pieces of rope. We also carry a seven-man life raft, emergency food, so if something were to happen to the aircraft, we have enough things on board the aircraft that we could sustain ourselves.

"Just about everybody up here goes through a survival training and it amounts to a week, a day and a half in the classroom and you go out for three nights to Cliff Point in the winter when it is snowing or when it is like it is outside. You spend about four days out there. You take the survival sled just like we carry and you're pretty much on your own. You build shelters and it's good training, especially [since] a lot of the fellas that come up here have never had any type of survival training at all.

Survival equipment on the helicopter includes a sling, basket, and litter for the hoist, a pump, exposure suits, a life raft, a tent, and emergency food.

"Each person on the helicopter carries his own survival kit. In there you have winter survival clothes, special boots, a parka, a special winter flying suit, big fur mittens. Also, we carry a wet suit, one piece, you can wear it in the event that you have to abandon the helicopter in the water and survive in a life raft. It is also a good idea to carry dehydrated food in a bag in case you get forced out someplace and have to survive for a couple of days before somebody can get to you.

"Maximum fuel load on the H-3 goes up to around 7,000 pounds, which is a little over 1,000 gallons. I think the maximum is around 1,100 gallons and it burns roughly 180 gallons an hour, so we can get a maximum of about six or seven hours. When we keep them on the ramp here, normally we keep about three hours of fuel in the aircraft. A lot of these cases, especially here where we have what we call tremendous distances for a helicopter, we will have fuel trucks available and what we have to do then is stick a hose in one spot on the thing and if we need fuel in a hurry we can pump in as much as we need. A lot of times, like Mr. Smith was saying, we go to places like St. Paul [Pribilof Islands] and we have to hopscotch from here to Cold Bay and maybe refuel. There's a lot of places that we have to go to.

"If it is inside 300 miles normally we will send a helicopter; but if it is an emergency situation, really taking on a lot of water and going down fast, probably what we will do is send the C-130 out. The C-130's have a dash speed. They can get 300 miles in roughly an hour, where with the helicopter the same 300 miles would probably take about two and a half hours to get there. We send the C-130 and follow it up with the helicopter. They both do the work. It's very much a team effort. You have to initially send the C-130 out and they can drop the pumps; they parachute it out of the back of the C-130.

"Probably as far as our Search and Rescue response up here, normally the helicopter is the backbone of our response. It has a lot more capabilities, we can go in and out of the villages around here and a lot of our Search and Rescue involves going into villages. Going in and getting people off the fishing boats who are sick, or plane crashes, sailboats, things like that. We have capabilities with the helicopters, they don't know we see them; but then on the other hand, we're limited to how far we can go and how fast we can go."

Mr. Stiles is going to tell us about how many men fly, what kind of men, what they are trained to do, and when they use people on the C-130. "We fly with a crew of four, two pilots and two crewmen. One is a hoist operator and the other is a navigator and radio operator. In an instance where we have one person aboard a boat and he is really hurt bad, what we try to do is put down one of our men. Now a lot of times, if we know that we'll be going out and someone is hurt, we will take a corpsman [medic] along and we'll put the corpsman down. He will prepare the person, you know, get him on a litter, get him on board, and then bring the corpsman up. If something happens and we don't have time to get a corpsman, if we happen to be flying around on a training flight or something like that and get diverted, then we will just send our avionics man down, or a flight man. Some radiomen are qualified as hoist operators, some aren't.

"Mr. Smith's job here at the station is enforcement of laws and treaty officer. See, in addition to being pilots, we have other jobs. I am the public affairs officer; Mr. Smith is our fish man or fish cop; and over here Mr. Finess takes care of all our flight records. Mr. Sand takes care of all the charts and things so we know where we are going.

"The C-130's prime responsibility is fisheries patrol and to provide a long-range response. The C-130's capabilities are limited; they have the distance but once they get to a scene they're basically limited as to what they can do. The C-130 is able to go out 1,000 miles, they drop rafts and emergency provisions and medical supplies to the people, and still make it back to Kodiak. Maximum fuel load on the C-130 is 62,920 pounds. They burn about 5,000 to 6,000 pounds an hour, which is about 9,500 gallons and the load lasts about ten to eleven hours. If we are going on a long patrol, as we burn down some fuel, we get our weight down a little bit and we can shut down on two engines; it cuts fuel consumption to about 3,000 to 4,000 pounds an hour. We have regular Search and Rescue equipment that they carry on the C-130. It's a box which has everything, pumps, survival kits, and all that stuff. They just roll it in the back of the airplane and we carry it with us anytime we go on a mission that might involve Search and Rescue.

"I have not flown very many training flights. It is pretty hampered up here, and influenced a lot of times, 'cause we are pretty busy and the weather a lot of times is kinda adverse to go out and train. But when we do fly them, probably in the average of about three to four training flights a month, we try and carry two pilots. The helicopters usually carry as many as three crewmen.

"The kinda training flights we like to work on when we get them are to practice instrumental approaches into Kodiak and other airports where we would have to get into during bad weather. We also go out and practice boat hoisting and simulating taking people off a disabled boat. We have a forty-one-foot patrol boat here in the boathouse on base. We'll have them get underway and go out here in Chiniak Bay. A lot of times we will go out and practice delivering the basket, and the litter, to the small boat. That gives the pilot and crewmen a chance to practice their technique. Of course it is not realistic doing it to a forty-footer a lot of times, but it is the only way we can simulate so people can do a real situation-type hoist. Those are the best training flights.

"We also occasionally practice things like external cargo. Usually the external cargo sling can pick up about 3,000 pounds of cargo and carry it around. We do that occasionally around here, both in practice and for actual operational missions. We have a flight coming up here and it is going over to Valdez and picking up a tower. It is about 120 feet high and is a radar tower. They want to move it so we will go over, pick it up with the sling, and carry it onto the Coast Guard base there. We get a lot of interesting jobs up here and a lot of varied kinds of missions for the airplanes.

"The helicopter in general is used primarily as a recovery type of vehicle. You can use a helicopter in confined areas for search. Say we had somebody lost in Ugak Bay or back by Saltery Cove, we can get in and search it much easier with a helicopter; where the C-130 takes a lot of turning room for them to get in, with a helicopter we can do it a lot more efficiently.

"I think the really more interesting aspect is using the two of them. This has happened to me; I think it has happened to Jim. On several occasions it is kinda leapfrogging with the H-3 and the C-130 when we go long distance. We took a helicopter up to Nome on a medivac type case and you can put a spare crew of pilots and crewmen of the helicopter on the C-130; one crew can fly it for three to four hours to some point, then the other crew can jump in and fly it for the rest of the way. From here to Nome is about 900 miles, so you can really cover a lot of ground by doing that, kinda leapfrog-ging the airplane along. Out to St. Paul we went by way of Cold Bay, and that was a total distance of 750 miles. So we can get to a lot of areas that they couldn't cover before until we got these two types of aircraft.

"There are many different cases. There are medivac cases which concern medical supplies, doctors, and hospital, if needed. There are cases where ships have problems and many more. You know, each case is different. The two we had here last weekend, they were two separate cases. We had one on Friday and one on Monday. In both cases, we had the C-130 aircraft over-head. The H-3 can navigate offshore without assistance from the C-130. But many times, the C-130 can provide a lot of services, like navigational services. It can refuel a helicopter when you get stuck in a place; maybe a nearby airport does not have jet fuel for the helicopter, so we can refuel from the C-130 on the ground.

"They work well together as a team. For instance, in the second case we had last weekend, they didn't exactly know where the people were in the life raft and the C-130 was sent ahead. They can go out to sea a lot faster than we can; they can help the H-3 navigate right to their position. The C-130's a lot of times do the large searches, offshore, where the helicopter cannot feasibly be sent. Other times, the H-3 will go offshore a short distance, pick somebody up, and come back where we really don't need a C-130. They work pretty well together on major efforts, when you have to have a lot of support to get the job done.

"The main thing is that the C-130 is designed primarily as a search air-craft. In Alaska there's a lot of places that have gravel runways and things like that. We really don't think of airstrips down in the Lower Forty-eight, but here the C-130's can get in and out of a lot of places that you just wouldn't think that large an aircraft can operate on. With the helicopter, and we got the option of the H-3 or H-52, we can go out and hoist off a boat or we can land in the water if we have to and pick people up. The H-3 and H-52 both have a boat hull on them; as long as the seas are not too heavy, you can pretty safely land in up to a five- to six-foot sea. If it gets much heavier, then it gets pretty shaky, pretty hairy trying to get off water."

Mr. Smith tells us about what they do on spare time. "We work a lot on occasion helping out the local agencies, like we did some work for the Alaska Department of Fish and Game down the Karluk River where they have their fish weir. We carried some construction materials for them to help them with their research projects that they are doing down there. This is what we call cooperation with other agencies. The Coast Guard is not really funded for this, but we will do it when we have an aircraft and crew available, to try and help out the local people in the community. We also have a flight Jim was on last year right around Christmastime each year where we go to some of the villages. We have what we call a Santa of the Villages Program; we take some donated gifts and visit the village children and we have a Santa Claus. Last year Jim dressed up as Santa Claus and went in there and passed out some gifts and talked to the kids for a while. We feel it is kind of a nice program for the kids to be able to see somebody come in like that. We are hoping to continue that in the future.

"I think you find that 95 percent of the pilots and crew up here enjoy flying in Alaska. It is a challenge and it is interesting; the conditions change from day to day and season to season. It is rewarding flying and it is a lot of fun really. In a lot of cases it is a lot of work, but it can be exciting."

OLUF OMLID: ANOTHER WAY

by: Emil Norton and Charlie Lorenson

For years salmon fishing has interested many people. However, we thought they focused more on purse seining than gillnetting. Seining involves, in most cases, one large boat, thirty-eight feet in length upward to fifty feet on the keel, and a skiff. The purse seine is towed by the skiff into a hook, after a while it is then drawn to a close and pursed up. Here the fish are caught in a sack called the money bag. Unlike the purse seine, the gill net has lighter, synthetic mesh. Only skiffs are used to tend the nets. The gill net catches the fish around the gills and suffocates them. In the process the fish try to escape by fighting savagely, tangling themselves into awful messes. It's the fisherman's job now to come along the net pulling parts of it into the skiff, getting the fish untangled and throwing them into the skiff.

The gill net comes in several different mesh sizes. The Alaska Department of Fish and Game puts a limit on the sizes, types of construction, and materials. The type of mesh commonly used is green in color, stranded loosely, and made of synthetic fibers. The mesh is measured stretched out and varies in size depending on the species fished. Before it becomes a gill net, the fisherman orders it by length and depth. To tell the difference between length and depth you look at the knots and the way the mesh lays.

A gill net is not mesh alone but also depends on other functioning parts. At the top of the net the selvage is hung onto the corkline with tarred twine. The selvage is the heavier mesh at the top and the bottom for more strength. This is where the weight is carried. Corks are used to hold the net up and the twine is called hangings. The corks are fastened onto this twine· with heavy inner tube strips approximately two inches wide. They are used for easy removal and to let the scum and debris in the water flow over the top. The mesh is hung even with the corkline. The bottom selvage is hung to the lead line; the line has a core of lead to weigh the net down. To make the net spread out, the lead line is hung farther apart.

For the first few fathoms of the gill net the small mesh from a seine line is used. When the tide goes out and the net goes dry, gill net would be ripped if it were used there. Floating lines are used to tie the gill net onto; the gill net is tied on with regular strapping twine. The floating lines are anchored to keep them in place and buoys are used to mark the anchorage spots. Anchors used vary from 100 pounds to 300 pounds depending on tidal activity. The lines are arranged in a trapline pattern; the triangular pattern is called the trap. The net is tied on following the opposite side the fish are coming from—fish usually follow or go with the tide. If the fish are coming from the right it's tied onto the buoys following the left all the way around. Likewise with the left.

Every gill-netter has a different operation depending on the area he fishes. Opinions vary on how the fishing should be run. Oluf Omlid has been living in Alaska since 1965 and is originally from northern Minnesota. He teaches wood shop in the junior high and in the summertime gillnets at Moser Bay on the southern tip of Kodiak, and has for ten years.

His setup is like this. "I use about three to four skiffs for my operation but I have eight," said Oluf. "After the fish are caught in the net, they die in about one to two minutes. When it comes time to pick them, I go along the side and pick up the nets gradually. Some days I spend eighteen to twenty hours off and on the water. The fish are then thrown into the holding skiff, which is a heavier sea-type skiff. My wife and I run my operation; I could probably run it alone but I'd have to cut down two nets."

A variety of marine life gets into the net and some cause problems. Types of "junk" fish caught include flounders, bullheads, codfish, halibut, and many types of crab. Porpoises and seals trying to rob the nets are seldom, but sometimes, caught. Seals chew their way through the net and porpoises are very clever, so aren't usually caught. Seals are protected from being shot by law, but fishermen are still allowed to shoot them. Oluf's opinion is that this is a bad law because the population is getting bigger.

The Fish and Game protects and enforces laws pertaining to fishing. We asked Oluf what he thought of Fish and Game. "I think they are doing the best that they can, but I don't know. I think they could watch things a bit closer. But what they are doing now is finding concentrations of fish and watching them by sending someone behind the markers where fishing is not allowed."

Emil asked Oluf's opinion of creek robbers, fishermen who take fish in illegal waters, usually close to the mouth of a stream.

"The first time I'd give him a fine and I mean a stiff fine, not a little one like a couple grand, but one about twenty-five to thirty grand. And that should cause a little ice on the puddle. And the second time take his boat, license, gear, and permit. Confiscate everything until fishermen get worried. Otherwise they are going to keep on having problems."

Limited Entry is a law used to cut down the amount of gear in the water. A Limited Entry permit is your license to fish. We asked his opinion of this law.

"I think it's something that we're gonna need or we will wind up like crab and shrimp fishermen have in the past. They're getting much shorter seasons and quotas stay the same. The seasons are extremely short and there aren't enough fish to go around.

"But my place has produced very well. Really all I've done is bought myself a summer job and it's actually produced sometimes better than my winter job. And my settlement—payment at the end of the summer—really all depends on who I fish for. I like to fish with the one that pays the most and gives me the best services. I am completely independent and I owe no one anything."

EMIL NORTON: TAPPING A RESOURCE

by: Emil Norton
illustrations by: Emil Norton

Shrimp, abundant in Alaska, are finally becoming fished by boats of all sizes. The nets used are manufactured especially for shrimping.

On this particular day, the water reflected the blue hull of the boat, ripples were made by the wind. The *Gladiator,* a well-known little boat, is owned and skippered by Steven Horn. This Chignik thirty-eight-foot tunnel seiner was rigged for beam trawling. We were going to a spot about thirty-seven miles away from Kodiak. Food had been put aboard and all that was left to get was ice for the shrimp to keep them cool and fresh. In the afternoon around 1:30 we were out and on our way with three tons of ice in our hold.

The Caterpillar diesel pushed the boat at ten knots. It took two hours to get to the Triplets, the islands near where we fished. To find the right spot on the bottom we used a depth sounder with paper readout, which gave us the contour of the bottom and told whether it was rocky or muddy. Radar can put the boat in an approximate location above it and keep the boat traveling in a straight line.

We were ready to set the net and by then we would only get one tow in before dark. The net was wound on a hydraulic reel. I took off the brake and let the net out slowly. The end of the net was thrown over while the boat idled along in gear. I operated the reel while Steve piloted the boat. Upon setting it out, the net is checked for knots that have slipped and for holes, then it is thrown over. The brake on the wheel is released and the net is watched so that it does not twist. The reel is stopped and weights are hooked to the wings at the mud rope. The net is let out some more till it gets to the bridle; one end of the bridle is tied off while the beam is hooked to the other end. The beam now is let out till the other end can be hooked up. The cable is played over fast so the net won't flip over. The reel is stopped when it comes to a line spliced in the cable. A double block hung from the mast is hooked to this and there are about three to four feet of cable let out between the reel and the block. The block is used to relieve pressure from the reel and make the steering easier.

Stabilizer poles were put out before this started and then the stabilizer fins, called fish, were thrown into the water. The only reason we had them out was to see how fast we were going. Using radar and the depth sounder, we kept the boat on course. It was time to take it easy for it was our first drag; usually we would be washing and shoveling shrimp into the hold.

After about an hour it was getting dark, so we decided to pull it up. An hour is rather short, but when it gets dark the shrimp tend to rise to the surface. A 110-volt generator supplied power to the quartz iodine lights that shone on the deck. Pulling the net up is just as simple as letting it out. When you let the net out, and have the weight and then the cable put on, the cable is let out fast so the cod end of the net doesn't flip over through the bridle. When pulling it up, the one end of the bridle close to the beam is tied off. The beam is then unsnapped, the bridle is untied, and the net is pulled up and the beam following is tied onto the mast. The weights, which are chain links weighing 120 pounds apiece, are disconnected and put on deck. A bite is taken around the net with the single. Enough net is left in the water to distribute the shrimp evenly. The net is towed around in the prop wash to get the mud out of the shrimp.

The boat was turned hard starboard to bring the net around to the side. I grabbed the net and broke it over the bulwarks and Steve took another bite with the single. The lazy line, which is connected to one wing and runs down above the cod end at the splitting strap, cinches the cod end so you lift only a limited amount of shrimp. A double block is hooked to an eye on the splitting strap and lifts the cod end out of the water onto the deck. The sack, called a split, weighs up to 1,000 pounds full of shrimp. A special slipknot is tied to the opening at the cod end so it is easy to untie. This is tied up again and dumped over and the process is repeated.

We had a good tow that night and had six splits. Steven didn't think we'd do that good. It was dark so he decided we'd go in and anchor up at Pineapple Cove. It was glassy and the water reflected the moon like a mirror. While we were traveling, I shoveled the shrimp around the deck. The bright lights

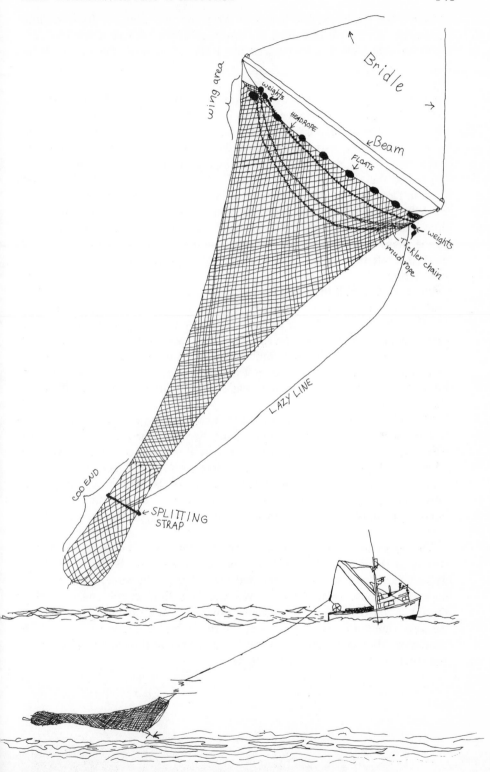

attracted the sea birds; one flew into them and was stunned. As it waddled around the deck it got into my way. It wouldn't fly away so I threw it over.

About nine o'clock we anchored up. I started to wash the shrimp to get the mud out; this took about a half-hour to do. Then we started shoveling them into the hold. For every few shovelfuls a little ice was sprinkled over the top. At a quarter to ten we were done and washed up. We ate and went to bed right away because we had to get up at a quarter to six. During the night several boats had come in and anchored up also, and when we woke up it looked like a harbor. The stove wouldn't boil the water for the coffee fast enough for us, so Steve took out the propane torch and helped it along.

I pulled the anchor up, a fifty-pound Danforth, and we were on our way. It wasn't rough, but it was coming up fast. The swells were long and we headed right into them. We towed for two hours and during that time the sea lions had come around the boat and were playing, but there weren't as many as the night before. I cooked breakfast and it didn't fill us up because we worked it off fast. Snow flurries came and went fast, and the seas slowly grew larger.

We started to pull the cable up and the hydraulics started to squeak. Steve said this was a good sign of a heavy load. When all the shrimp were dumped on deck, Steve took the boat back up to the same starting point to make another tow, keeping the wind on the stern for easier steering and working conditions. During the night the shrimp lost their blood and juices which made a green slime in the hold. We washed the shrimp and shoveled them into the hold, then stood back and knew it was a good haul because it was filled two thirds of the way.

We had to turn the music up loud to hear anything over the engine noise. But it's always good to hear the engine because when it stops, then you worry about it running again. When we were done with our work it was time to pull up the net, and this time the hydraulics squeaked and groaned a lot because of the tremendous pressure on them. As the stern would go up and down on the waves, it would slap. This was caused by the tunnel when air would get trapped in it. The sea lions would play by the net as we pulled it up.

The boat was in the troughs now and as it lurched to one side the ketchup flew onto the floor and made a red mess. As soon as all the shrimp were aboard Steve said we had to stop and take pictures, because when you have a good haul you usually forget. We ran in a little calmer waters behind Ouzinkie Narrows. Here we washed, shoveled, and cleaned up the boat. As we were running in, spray flew over the flying bridge and got us wet, so we headed inside for the rest of the trip home. Several days later we unloaded our catch and hung up the net until next season.

JOE BLACK: "YOU SHOULD STAY OUT THERE . . . UNTIL YOU STOP THINKING IN WORDS"

by: Beth Lindsey, Elaine Dinnocenzo, and Elizabeth Pohjola
photos by: Joe Black, Beth Lindsey, Elaine Dinnocenzo, and Elizabeth Pohjola

You may have read the article "Hunting with Ten Kayaks" at the beginning of the Kodiak Island section of this book. This will be a very different kind of article because the main shooting Joe Black does is with a camera.

When you first see Joe, he strikes you as being rather wild, but once you meet him you see that looks are deceiving. Joe has black hair and a black beard and is rather large. He is sensitive, observant, kind, and almost a shy type of person. Joe is building a seven-sided cabin out at Monashka Bay. He has been working on it for a year and a half now. He plans on getting a 200- to 300-gallon fish tank and creating his own little ecosystem so he can observe nature in the comfort of his home. A large part of the cabin will also be a photography studio.

Joe is very fortunate in that he has had some wonderful and truly valuable experiences. I must admit that I am rather envious of him. We began by asking Joe what made him come to such an obscure place as Kodiak.

"I think I saw a picture one time of a guy holding up a king crab or something. I was headed toward Europe and I went broke in New York. I tried to get across in a boat, but I couldn't make it—I used to hitchhike around a lot. So I hitchhiked over this way and I worked in Juneau. From there, I went to Kodiak. I heard Kodiak prices were high, so I bought a big box of groceries in Juneau. I hitchhiked all the way up with that big box of grocer-

Joe Black.

ies. I got here and found out prices were cheaper! I had rice and cornmeal and all that.

"When I first came here I sat up on top of Pillar Mountain [the mountain right behind the city of Kodiak]. I was watching traffic go back and forth, watching one shift come out of the cannery and the next shift go in, watching boats coming in and going out. And I asked myself, 'Do I want to join this?' You know, you sort of see the whole pattern and see where you can fit in, or if you just want to bypass the whole thing—'cause you can get wrapped up in anything, and it's all important. What you want to do is an individual choice and that's what's important."

When Joe first came to Kodiak in September, he didn't have anywhere to stay. He got a job at a cannery, and found a place to stay.

"I worked there three weeks. It rained nearly every day, and I earned about $800. Then I thought, I've never hated a place as much as this. So I came back the next summer to see what it was like because I thought 'It's got to be better than that,' and at the time I had some money.

"I worked on a fishing boat one summer. Every time you pull up a halibut, you think $50. Then when you watch one swimming underwater, you can't put a price tag on it. We'd come real close to land, maybe a beach, and anchor up for the night. It was beautiful, then we had to clean fish! Then you leave early the next morning. I'm wanting to get on the land. It's so pretty and you're out there two, three miles away. So the next summer, I got the gear. I didn't make any money fishing, so I came back upset.

"I was working up on the North Slope. It's beautiful. I always think of it as an ice virgin up there. Then you come out and destroy it. I worked up there in '69 where in every camp you left great piles of garbage.

"There's some beautiful sunsets there on the slope in the winter. It's a very religious experience to watch one; it takes sometimes fifteen to twenty minutes to go down. You're up there seeing it for the first time and it's fifty below. You could never be up there on your own. An oil company is paying you to be up there. You're seeing something and at the same time destroying it. It's a self-consuming thing. Then you get to thinking, well, what do you do? Go back to nature? You live out in the sticks and you have to kill things more. Just what line do you draw between being a hypocrite?"

Joe plans to do some professional wildlife films in the future up here. "The opportunity is right here, but it's hard to do filming up here. Cousteau came up here, but had a lot of money behind him. One time I was out filming and I thought, 'How can I compete with these guys?' There's a chopper flying over me with a wildlife guy in it. It costs $460 an hour for that helicopter. It costs me about $70 to go on a whole trip. That guy could spend $1 million getting to a place he couldn't have gotten to any better than I did.

"The summertime around here is an especially good time to go. Right now in January and February, everything's kind of frozen. It's cold and you wouldn't have much fun in a kayak. You can live for about a dollar a day if you're eating a lot of fish. So food is not a problem. You've got your little four-pound tent and your sleeping bag there . . . you can go anywhere. Just go by those $50 hotels. Even if you're in a big hotel, you don't see anything anyway. That's no way to live. There's no memories there for the most part.

"When you first get in a kayak you'll almost fall out. It takes about two or three days before the boat becomes a part of you. Then you also learn to read the water. When you go out you don't have to really make an endurance thing of it. You can go two or three miles a day; you don't really have to go fifty miles. If the weather's too rough, you can stop or just go around the corner. As long as you don't start programming yourself and say, 'Well, I've got to get there,' then you don't really enjoy it.

"If you go slow, you have birds pass over you. They always check you out. A lot of birds do that and everything comes to you; you don't have to try to sneak to them. Especially if you go out with a wet suit. You can stick grass up through your goggle straps, that sort of camouflages your head. When you get in the water just the top of your head is sticking out. I've been about two feet from ducks with young. You watch them blink or wink at you. You can also get up close to hear that way. They loooook at you, smell up in the air, loooook down. They know you're human, they're afraid of you. You sort of have power over them and as long as you're not afraid it becomes fun and you can move up to something kind of big. It is just as challenging, though, to get up to a duck or something else.

"I don't eat meat when I'm out. I just eat a lot of rice, because if you start

eating meat the animals can smell the blood and won't get close to you. But if you eat a lot of rice, fish, and that kind of food, you have ducks just right next to you. They think you're a cow or something because you're a vegetarian and you don't threaten anybody.

"You find out a lot of times if you're with somebody you'll do things you wouldn't ordinarily do by yourself, and sometimes vice versa. Sometimes you have to prove something to yourself. It's important that way.

"Other times you say, 'I'm not going to go out there.' It's a self-learning process. But the most important thing, I think, is to spend at least three weeks out there 'cause then you don't think in words anymore. That's when you start enjoying what's out there. But if you just go out there and you've got a gun and a fishing pole, catch a few fish, shoot a few birds, make a lot of noise, and got your radio plugged in your ear, you haven't learned anything. Sometimes you're out camping like that and you see a boat passing by and they're talking, shooting, fishing. You think, 'These clowns don't know what's going on.'

"In a regular boat you have to stay off a quarter mile from the shore and figure out where you're at all the time. In a kayak, if you get too shallow, you step out into the water and you don't have to worry about it. You can go in water about six inches deep if you get out of the boat and pull it. They're ideal boats. Even in the rain they don't get much water in them and the opening is only about two square feet. I have canvas over mine and if it gets raining too hard, I just put canvas over my head. Usually you get used to it and just row and forget about it. You keep warm by rowing, or you can have a little fire on a camp stove to keep your tea warm.

"These kayaks are made out of Naugahide and you feel the water pressure coming in on you when it's rocking. In a kayak your boat will turn and twist with the water. In a big boat you just go through the water and it's no fun. You start rowing in a kayak this way and your boat will be twisting as it goes through each little whirlpool. It's like being on a motorcycle going fast. If you're in a car, you don't feel the wind; you don't feel anything as you go down the road. If you go on a motorcycle or a fast bicycle, you feel every dip and turn. That's the way a kayak is. The water is right there; you can dip your fingertips in it and feel it. After you're in awhile, it'll take the water as good as a skiff will. Then you can have a skirt on the kayak so you're tied in. I never could in mine because I had so much gear. I just had canvas over the top and never had trouble. With a boat like this you can pick it up, take it down to the water, go into the water and come back, and you don't have to have a boat trailer or motor.

"You can make a big adventure out of going three miles in a kayak. It can take you all day and you see more than if you have a speedboat and zoom across here and there, and all you end up doing is getting wet. Those speedboats are nice, too, in their way, but they don't compare with seeing the country.

"Folboats, I think, are the best for up in Alaska. They're wider and you can stand up in them. On the Yukon, which is a mile and a half across, you can have a little gas stove going and heat the water for your tea and rice. Kleppers are about $1,000 now but they're narrow. These Folboats are about $300. In a Klepper you've got to sit down low and do everything carefully because they tip very easily. But you probably want something with a wider beam on it, then you don't have to be so careful.

"Animals all communicate. I was after goats and I got a few lousy goat pictures. You can see them from way down below but they're smart and they've got good eyesight. It took me almost all day to get up there. But wherever you're walking there's marmots all over the place, and they all squeak and that tells everybody what's happening.

"When you're walking, the goats can tell just where you're at. And you say, 'Ah, just over this ridge'; you look up over this ridge and they're not there. You see them up there running like mad two miles away. But everything communicates. You don't notice that if you just stop and make a lot of noise when you're out trying to shoot something. If you go out just trying to understand, then you sort of see where you fit in with the animals. We're all a part of this world.

"Over on Afognak I was sitting down eating dinner one night and this fox came around. I started watching him and he got real stiff. After a while, I didn't even look at him anymore and started eating some fish. There's a lot of dolly varden out there, and every so often I would throw a fish out, he'd come back and sniff it and eat it. Pretty soon he's about five or six feet away and his tail is down. I was just eating, making lots of noise. He stayed around for three days. I took pictures of him.

"One time I was portaging over from Red Lake to Olga Bay. There's about a three-quarter-mile portage between these two lakes and I had the kayak. It was a late September, frosty morning. I just drug the kayak across and it slithered really fast. I had a pack on my back with a lot of stuff in it. It was so heavy when I got the pack on, that one time I just knelt down to rest and fell over. The whole pack was so heavy that my hands and feet went up in the air; I had to take it off and put it back on again. I took the pack off my back and sat down to rest. I saw a little isopod in the water; it had a little cone house of sticks and rocks put together. He's got his little four or five legs out there and he's pulling upstream, moving about an inch at a time. And I said, 'I know how you feel.' Then pretty soon I realized my work was easier than his. He's doing it in cold water and I'm doing it in halfway warm air. I picked up my stuff and started off again.

"When I was floating down the Yukon River—I got out about the fifth of October—it was starting to ice up. It takes about two weeks for that river to ice up, and it's a mile and a half across. You can camp along the side of the river, wake up in the morning, and the ice is thick. It gets down to about zero to five above. The ice is about one inch thick and about fifteen feet out. You have to get your boat and work it like a surfboard. Stick everything in it, just kind of lay on it, scoot out, and drop down in the water. Then after

about the first week these big patties of ice that are about 100 yards in diameter start hitting each other. They form upriver and they float downriver.. You've got to watch it when you get one behind you and one in front of you. They're moving at four or five knots; and the one in front of you will stop and the one in back will keep moving. They hit with such force they pile up five to six feet in about ten seconds. With these kind of boats you can learn to walk. You keep your weight right in the center, and you lean back a little, raise the bow up, dig in the ice real hard, and shoot the bow up on the ice. Then you paddle like mad and work the rest of the boat on the ice—these little metal tips on the ends of the paddle help.

"One time I saw this arctic tern that had its eggs down pretty close, but, I seemed to think, not too close to the water. The next morning I was making my rounds to see which of the eggs had hatched. I always keep an eye on them and try to get pictures. It takes quite a while to get up close to one and then they fly away. This big chunk of ice fell off the glacier during the night and swept away all the eggs. Then I saw a pair of these arctic terns flying around the ice; you knew they had lost their chicks. After you stay on the beach awhile you walk around and are very careful not to step on the eggs.

"The worst experience I've ever had with animals was on a beach where I lost all my food. So the next day I shot a little seal, with a .22 I had with me. A seal hunter has to be a good shot because you're moving around and the seal is usually moving around, too. I shot this seal just as he was jumping in the water and I hit him in the back. I was aiming for his head but he was moving fast, so I went in the water and stayed with him. He'd come up, and I'd shoot all around him and make him go back down in the water again. I couldn't hit him very well. He'd come up over here, he'd go down, I'd go over here, and he'd come up over there. He was wounded and needed air. Pretty soon his mother came up underneath him and held him up to give him air. That's when you really feel rotten. His mother trying to save his life and you're thinking of food! Meat! Finally I got over close to him and he had to stay up and breathe. I shot him and put him aboard. His mother followed behind me all day. I really felt rotten. It's just sad; it's like a parent losing a kid, they have feelings, too. Then you think, 'Here I am out in nature trying not to destroy it; but when it comes to food I end up being a hypocrite.'

"I got on the beach and then I skinned it out and I ate it for about three or four days. I ate the whole thing. And right when I was barbecuing it—I had a little spit—it was just meat then. It wasn't seal anymore, it was just meat. So then I didn't feel so bad. Pretty soon here came a little fox. He dragged the skin away and was chewing on the fat thirty feet away. I laid the skin down on the beach and the tide came in and the skin started floating

Joe talking to *Elwani* student: "Here I am out in nature not trying to destroy it, but when it comes to food, I end up being a hypocrite."

away. He swam out and got it; he brought it back and he chewed on it. So there's a fox eating that's probably feeding its young. You start seeing the cycle all over again.

"Well, one time I was going out of King Cove around Afognak and I saw something out there in the water. I didn't know what it was and I got to looking at it and it looked like a serpent. You could see half circles [coming out of the water] for about thirty feet, forty feet, and so I tried to get a picture of it.

"I started going after it. I finally got about two miles off the shoreline in between there and Marmot Island, and then I could see that there were two sea lions. They were swimming in tandem, heads moving and midsections. The closer I tried to get to them, they just kept going away. I got too far and started to go back. Before I knew it, they were right alongside the boat. I got pictures of them. You could almost reach out and touch them, their eyes about that big [gesture] looking at you like that, and then they went sneaking off. They're curious, they followed me for about half an hour.

"Another time, I floated down Karluk River twice and then from Karluk, I went down between Karluk and Red River. As I was crossing I could see this storm coming up, black clouds, and I figured maybe I could make it. I had about two or three miles to cut across and the wind caught me. You're rowing just as hard as you can row. You're staying in the same spot, not moving, and if you stop you go backwards. That's when kayaks are no good.

"With a kayak I came across from Raspberry Strait into Kodiak just in one trip. I go out between Whale Island and Ouzinkie; it's about a six-mile crossing. It was a calm day, but the swells were up to eight feet. I came across and this fishing boat was going by. He was about a mile away, and saw me and turned. Everyone ran up on the deck and, boy, here they came to the rescue. I was just rowing along. They thought I was sitting on a log.

"One time I came across on the ferry from Seward and stopped in Port Lions. I was planning on going to Afognak. I had been there before so I didn't have a map. I camped right close to Port Lions, and the next morning it was foggy. I could hardly see anything. But I took off for Whale Island. I found out later I was going in the opposite direction towards Kodiak, and I thought I crossed Settlers Cove, but it was just a little indentation near Port Wakefield. I thought, 'Well, now I'm at Whale Island.' I was going to get over to Raspberry or Afognak and everything seemed right. I crossed Kizhuyak Bay and I thought, 'This is it! This is Whale Pass.' You could hardly see anything. Sometimes the fog opened up and other times you could see maybe thirty or forty feet just cruising right next to the shore.

"This fisherman and his crew were out there; they were setting up their net and you couldn't even see them. You could just hear them: chug-chug-chug. So I cruised up to them, and I said, 'Is Afognak River around the point?' He looked at me and said, 'It's over there.' [Laugh] I thought, 'Well, this guy is nuts, he's joking, or lost, or something.' 'Cause I knew where I was at. So he brings out his chart. I tie up the boat and when I get on he says, 'Ouzinkie is back this way.' [Laugh] And I didn't know where I was then. He said, 'Hey, fella, you're way off, you'd better go back on shore till the fog lifts.' He thought I was from California or something.

"Then I finally got my bearings straight. I went a little ways that day, then the next morning it was still foggy, and I headed back towards Port Lions again. Then I passed this other fishing boat, and this guy with a big voice comes out and says, 'Where am I?' Then he laughed. What could I do? So I just waved at him."

DANIEL BOONE REED: A VISIT TO THE VILLAGE ISLANDS

interviews with Daniel Reed, Chief Asicsic, and Ted Pestrikoff
by: Scott Ranney, with Sandy Lowry

Early one warm winter's morning I left Isthmus Lagoon on Cape Chiniak and headed the bow of the dory toward town. While passing a small group of islands on the east side of Kalsin Bay, I watched two emperor geese fly overhead signaling the start of another day. A little later on I reached Kodiak harbor, tied the dory up, and went to school. After school, I found that the dory had taken on some water so I decided to pull it out of the water and see what was wrong. As it turned out, a scrubbing batten had

Daniel Boone Reed.

fallen off, allowing water to pass through the nail holes. With help from Dave Kubiak, the dory was fixed and set to float off on the next tide.

The whole purpose behind this experience was to interview the people from around the Village Islands. I brought my dory from Isthmus Lagoon, Chiniak to Kodiak, and from Kodiak on the crab boat *Linda Jo* to the Village Islands in Uganik Bay. After waiting for a storm to pass over, the dory was loaded aboard the *Linda Jo* and I was on my way. Heading to Uganik Bay I saw a bunch of sea otters in Viekoda Bay. The trip took about eight hours and we arrived around four-thirty in the afternoon.

The dory was launched off of the *Linda Jo* and I was on my way. The sun had just gone down and dusk was approaching. The snow was coming down hard, but I only had to travel about a half a mile to the Reeds, where I was to stay. I surprised Nan Reed when I appeared because my arrival had been delayed by the storm. She brought me in and showed me to a small cabin where I was to stay for the next four days. We ate a codfish and mashed potatoes for dinner and I hit the sack.

The next morning I went to Ted Pestrikoff's house and waited for the mail plane which would bring Daniel Boone Reed back home from his Native corporation meetings in Kodiak. The plane landed and while mailman Ted Pestrikoff was sorting the mail I went and met Daniel Boone Reed. Later on, he told me about himself.

"I was born up north, where I lived for a while and I am part Eskimo. I came back to Alaska quite a few years ago, 1937 or '38 or somewhere in there. Before, I had been living on a reservation in Idaho, and I had lost my wife to smallpox. I had gotten over the smallpox myself and I started to have vomiting spells. The reservation doctor said after serious examination that I might be having stomach cancer and would there be someone that I might want to go and visit before they got around to getting it straightened out for me to go to Rochester or wherever they were going to send me to have the operation. I came up to Seattle and worked on one steamboat after another, one small boat after another. I went down to Lake Union and got a boat that was coming up to Kodiak; I figured, well, from there that would be a jump-off place for going further.

"When I arrived, Kodiak was kind of wild. There was cattle running on the streets. If you weren't stepping in mud, you were stepping in cow manure. When the fishing boats would come in, there were all kinds of characters getting off of them. There were all kinds of characters living here as well.

"I worked a little on the south side of the island, getting a little money ahead to go to the mainland and go from there home. Well, I got to drinking a little bit, like everybody else who came to town. I was going to go out and work for Jack McCord for a while; he was living on Sitkinak and was trying to proposition me to come in ranching with him a little bit. I don't know how he got wind that I might have a few shackles in my pocket, but he seemed to

"When I arrived, Kodiak was kind of wild. There was cattle running on the streets." Now Dan lives in Uganik Bay.

smell money no matter what. Whether he had been told or not, he could smell it.

"This was all before I came to Uganik Bay. Anyway, as a result of meeting Jack McCord and going to Kodiak and drinking a few beers, I woke up in jail. They put me in for six months and in the time I was there I was on good behavior and trusted. I'd go out picking berries and so forth and so on. I had free run to go in the women's quarters every once in a while and make fires. In the six months I was there, one of those women that was incarcerated from Afognak was found pregnant, so the marshal caused me to marry her. We were married and went to Afognak before the child was born. From Afognak I went to Bristol Bay.

"There was a character from the mainland who said he had a fishing boat in Bristol Bay and so . . . heck, I decided I would go in with him to fish at Bristol Bay. Well, I had to stake him before I could fish. So I took him up on it and paid his fare up there. When I got up there, he didn't have a boat and I had to go work for a cannery and when I got paid off, I only had ten dollars. I had to hitchhike back to Afognak. When my wife greeted me and said she lost her baby, I didn't have anything to look forward to. Only perhaps to continue on and go and get my operation.

"The only way I could break away from her was to hurt her feelings by saying I didn't love her and so forth and so on. She broke up and caused me to go into jail and then to prison. The child is the existing cause of putting me into jail, railroading me there, holding me against my will. For six months I was in Valdez, and I burned down the jail. Then I found myself in prison. Now then, if that's the case, that child is still existing. Jails and prisons were used to kidnap the child in me, and I find myself back here in Kodiak on my own—the law didn't bring me back, I came back on my own.

"After I had come out of prison I married another Indian woman in Yakima. I left her and came up here just on my own, just bullheadedness. A good friend of mine named Macardny met me in town and he said, 'You're back, Daniel. Well, I got a job for you. I want to advise you to stay out of town. These people will put you in jail. They'll put you back there if they can.' He said more than that but I won't reveal that. So I went on one of these scows in Cook's Inlet and counted fish. When I came back from there, Macardny paid me off and said, 'I got another job for you. It's a watchman's job about halfway down the island. If that part of the country looks good to you, anchor yourself down and stay out of town.' And that's just what I did. That's how I find myself in this bay.

"I was watchman for two winters. The first year my present wife came out to cook and she and I kept company and got married, but I was married to an Indian woman in the States and I had to annul the marriage in order to marry this one. We've been together ever since 1950. We brought in livestock and everybody that didn't like me too well, my enemies, said, 'Well, he'll go broke, he'll be back in jail, he'll be back in prison, we won't have to worry.' But I'm still free, a Native for my own purposes of existing and trying to exist and maintain a semblance of balance and mind, as well as a semblance of fitting myself into general society. That's about my life's story.

"Here's a story that was told to me years and years ago; I was seven or eight years old, I guess. We were living at Kiana, that's on the Kobuk River between fifty and seventy-five miles from the mouth of the river. The Kiana Native village was about half a mile, I guess, from the main Kiana settlement. It's on the riverbank.

"The old folks would be sitting around, carving wood or making snowshoes, making fruit baskets for next year's fruit crops, and fleshing skins that they had gotten from their traplines and stretching them, and while they're doing all this, why they're telling stories to all their kids. I'd come and be one of the kids and they'd tell me stories to kind of scare me, for going home spooky. Ha!

"They told one about the 'Crybaby.' You'd never see it but you could always hear it. It would float down on the river along the bank and it would be swishing around crying like a crybaby or it would whoop like a screech

Dan Reed's home, overlooking the Bay.

owl, like a snow owl. It would float along noiselessly, just like a snow owl would be floating along noiselessly. You wouldn't hear the swish of the wings or nothing, but it would be floating along and as it would float along you could hear it crying, making this particular noise. So I'd be going home, you know, a moonlit night. You could hear that snow crunching under your feet and all the eerie noises crackling along on the willows and the banks of the river; it was spooky and eerie just to be out in the night. You're hearing something you're not hearing at all. There was great times in those days.

"There was little people and they lived in squirrel holes and were no bigger than your thumb. But they had great mysterious powers and so there was a medicine man living in the country who was wanting to secure this mysterious power that the little people had. So he brewed up a brew and drank it and it gave him the power, or you might want to say the stimulus, to want to go out and meet those little people. He seen one of these little people standing up straight like a stick, on a little dirt mound outside of his home. He was living in the burrow with a squirrel; the squirrels accepted these little people to live with them. The medicine man says, 'Looks like I see something.' 'Yes, your eyes are good,' the little man said. So he deliberately turned around and he started to throw a basket or something over this little man, but the little man had a piece of bone in his hand and he threw it up in the air toward this basket that was coming down toward him. The basket mysteriously disappeared. It exploded in pure air.

"So this giant of a man told the little man, 'Why, I never seen anything so mysteriously done as that. You were not looking at me.' He says, 'I can see you without looking straight at you. Why were you trying to catch me?' The medicine man says, 'I would like to have some of your medicine. One of the medicines you have already demonstrated. You have shown me one of your medicines to destroy my efforts to catch you. I would like to know that.' The little man told him that he would never give it to him unless he would get from him first something that the medicine man possessed and would be an equal trade, providing that he would use his power for the good of all mankind. So that was the end of that story.

"Back in the time of the beaver people, wolf people, fox people, etc. . . . Cold, cold weather, real cold, and the beaver was in his house nice and snug. He was having a good time sleeping and he had a lot of food there. He wasn't worried about nothing. Then all of a sudden, he heard somebody knocking on his door or scratching and growling and so he went to his lookout place, his smelling place in the house. He knew. It was the wolf people come to get him. So he spoke real loud for a little while. Then he talked to the Great, Great Spirit to bring on a storm that would discourage the wolf people. In a storm they would have to go and look for a place to stay out of harm's way. He didn't anymore than get through praying and talking to the Great Spirit, when a big ice fog come, big ice fog. From that time to this day when the ice fog comes, everybody says in my part of the country, well, the beaver must have talked to the Great Spirit to chase the wolf people away."

Chief Asicsic lives in a small cottage about a hundred yards from the Reeds. He eats with the Reeds and helps out on the chores. "I lived in Norton Sound since I was sixteen. I left home in 1938 and got back in 1941. I was working for construction up in Fairbanks but it got too cold, so I went back to Seattle to look for another job and I signed up with the Navy for eighteen months.

"I first came to Kodiak in 1948 after I got discharged. I really like it here. It's nice and quiet, better'n in town because you can go up on the mountain to the lake. It takes about three hours to go up there. Dan and I went up there about a month ago for ptarmigan; I got one.

"I remember the first time I went fishing, I went with a guy from Larsen Bay. We didn't have any 'kickers' [motors] them days, all we used was a pair of oars. I fished commercially with a seine. Cripes, they let me out in the skiff with the end of the seine and I thought that thing was going across Shelikof Strait—I never seen a seine so long, 200 fathoms of it. I had to hold the hook with a pair of oars. The seiners were sailing vessels and they rowed the skiffs. There were lots of fish then, but we didn't get but four bits apiece [for them]!"

Chief then told me about home. . . . "We used to make these dogsleds in a day. They didn't turn out this good. We used to use common pins and used a claw hammer to bend the runner. I think the earliest thing I can remember was when I had a little boat, a sailboat. It was about twenty inches long. I used to take it to the pond in the summertime when my mother was picking berries. I'd look for a bird's nest and put it on my sailboat and let it sail. That was when I was only two or three years old. Also, when I was a kid, I used to spend most of my time down at the river in the wintertime. We would cut a hole in the ice and we would have a slide and it would end right at the hole. It was about eighteen inches wide, the water was two to three feet deep, and we'd take our sled and go down and just before we got to the hole we'd turn off. Some guys never made it. They'd go into the water and then they'd go home crying. Once I held my little brother over a hole in the ice and I slipped and he got his head all wet. I couldn't go back down to the river. I was just trying to scare him but he slipped from my hold.

"There was an old lady. We used to go to her house and listen, four or five of us kids. She had this kerosene lamp so we'd put the lamp in the middle of the floor and she'd sit in the middle with us around her and she would start telling ghost stories. Oh cripes, one time it was time to go home; we'd go home in pairs. There was a friend of mine, we lived a couple hundred feet apart, so when we got there we'd pace it off from his place to my place, we'd get in the middle, turn back to back, and run like hell.

"One time my friend and I were out hunting rabbits with bows and arrows. Well, one of us shot an arrow and it stuck in a tombstone. When we

Chief building a miniature dogsled.

The finished sled.

started to walk away we heard a noise like a baby crying, but nobody was around. We stood side by side and one of us would walk and stand on the other side and then the other would do the same because we didn't trust each other to run, one of us might run faster.

"Another time I was running a dogsled by myself and it was getting late. I was sitting in the sled when I felt a lurching like someone was pushing the sled with one foot and riding with the other. The dogs looked back, put their tails between their legs, and took off. I never looked back. Those were the only times anything like that happened to me, but I've had other experiences with bears.

"I've had bears walk up to me, about ten feet away. I'd just wait for them to walk away. Once I saw a bear below me. I think he smelled me, but he never saw me. He started walking back and forth, coming up. When he got too close I scared him with my rifle and he came right back to where I saw him. He never stopped, he just turned around and took off. Another time, I had to holler at a bear. He was about fifty feet away from us, me and two other hunters. We went after a bear up in the mountains and while we were climbing we saw this bear coming up. I told the hunters, 'It's too small.' We just watched it and it came around behind us on the trail and started coming towards us; I had to holler at him, then he took off.

"I guide for hunting bears and plan to go out again this April. There were some astronauts out at Afognak Lake once. Conrad, he was out there. There were six guys from down below hunting, they were hunting all right . . . playing cards all day, drinking booze, beer, 800 pounds of meat, all the steaks you can eat. They were hunting bear and elk.

"Once I saved the Village Island beavers. About four or five years ago, there were some trappers here and they set some traps. I was going down to check the house one day and I ran into these trappers. I asked if they set any traps for the beavers and they said, 'No.' So I told them, 'If I find any traps, I am going to pull them out.' When I went down to the beaver pond, sure enough they had three traps set for the beavers. I pulled two of them out and the third one was frozen in the ice so I took my hatchet and chopped it up. About a month later they left here and they pulled their traps anyway. A month later they came back. Cripes, this one old guy, he was mad. He didn't like it because I pulled his traps. I told him not to trap here. We want to try to build up these beavers. They built a new dam last year. They built a big house."

Having talked about wildlife, what about wild weather . . . "I remember one storm in particular. It was about ten years ago. I was living with Lynn and DeeDee Hans. DeeDee used to give the weather report in the afternoons around four o'clock. One afternoon she got the radio going and she was going to look out the window to see which way the wind was blowing. It was southwest. She looked out there and said, 'Cripes, the boat's gone from its mooring and it's snowing and blowing.' So Lynn and I went down to the dock there and got a kicker. They were all winterized. We just grabbed one and put it on the skiff and went out looking for the boat. When we found it, we went alongside. Just then the kicker quit and it wouldn't start again. It quit because it was winterized and had some oil in it. Anyway, we were lucky, we got alongside of the boat and we tied up the skiff, started the big boat, and took off. We had to spend the night down at the old cannery because it was blowing so hard. While we were going down the channel the boat would list right over on its side. The boat's about thirty-four foot long."

Ted is the mailman. I met him while waiting for the plane to bring Dan home. Ted is a nice man who lives in an old hut and loves to tell stories. "I was born in Ouzinkie in 1903. I had three sisters and two brothers. Only one brother left, Johnny Pestrikoff; he lives in Port Lions with his wife and his son.

"I didn't get far in school, only to fifth grade, then I dropped out. A lot of people died of flu when I was young, my dad, granny, grandpa, uncle, and auntie all died of the flu. This was around 1918. When I was nine or ten years old, Katmai exploded. For three days and three nights there was no daylight, it was coal black. There was explosions and earthquakes.

"I used to be a tough kid, no shoes, even in the snow in the winter. Ran to school with no shoes. One time I ran into six big geese. They bit me and I ran to my mom and she put the geese out. Now I can't ever go barefooted, not even in a little bit of gravel.

Ted Pestrikoff, the mailman, in front of his house, in the Village Islands.

"I've been here in Uganik over thirty years. I used to work for the little cannery that was here before; I was the winter watchman. In the winter I was the watchman and in the summer I would fish. I used to make damn good money fishing. I had 300 fathoms of gill net all alone, work like hell. Sometimes I caught 1,200, 1,800 fish a day. Then when the tender came I had to deliver the fish, all alone, then wash my boat and go home, go to sleep. Four o'clock in the morning I get up, maybe drink some coffee, then I go out to my 300 fathoms of gill net. I got tired.

"I gave up fishing in 1970. I didn't know what was wrong with me. One time I was getting ready to set my net, to set the anchors out. I got short breathed and I couldn't move around; I breathed like hell till I had to sit down on the beach. I was alone, too. If I was going to be like that, I can't fish anymore. I might lose my season [a year's income]. So I went to East Point. I was waiting for this guy to come and buy everything; but there was these two brothers across there and when I told them what I was going to do, they said, 'Sell it to Daddy, sell it to Daddy.' And I sold it to him, cheap, too. I sold him three boats, all my gear, and fishing supplies.

"I used to go hunting down at Shuyak Island. That was a long, long time ago. I used to love hunting, but after I lost my family I gave up everything, all my guns. I like it here, especially in the summertime. It has nice beaches. In the summer people come around after fish in fishing boats. They give you some fish, then they reverse and take off and go look for more. Then if I get too much, I salt it down. You live cheap around here. The shrimp draggers, they're good, they'll give you a big shopping bag heaping full of shrimp, halibut, and some bottomfish."

After a search for Joe Darling on Valentine's Day, I boarded the *Linda Jo* and headed home. The snow was falling so heavily that it was sticking to the water. Good weather favored us and we tied up at the King Crab cannery the following morning. I can't say enough about the kindness and good hospitality of the Reeds and the other people of Uganik, and I left with a sourdough cookbook and sourdough starter, presents from the Reeds, and some new friends.

MARY HERNDON: THE NEW ENGLAND FISH COMPANY

by: Sandy Lowry, with Bonnie Greenlee, Gwen Sargent, Kim Jewett, and Tracey Reyes

My first real knowledge of how the canneries operate was given to me when I went to Mary Herndon's house and interviewed her. As I talked to her, I realized that she knew her business very well. She explained all the different steps and processes that the products have to go through at the New England Fish Company. Later she was our guide on a tour of the cannery. When we decided to visit NEFCO, we had to get special permission to take pictures; everyone was very nice, and they set up a time for us to visit the plant. When we arrived, Mary gave us a very complete tour.

"I work at New England Fish Company, at Gibson Cove. I'm a foreperson there. I instruct, work, and teach beginners how to work with the products: shrimp, crab, and bottomfish. I also hire workers. I started in a pear cannery in Oregon, then after that I came to Kodiak. That was in 1966, and I started into crab at Pan Alaska. From there I worked in almost all the canneries. Then I went to Alaska Ice and Storage and stayed there for three years, working steady in halibut, peeling cheeks. Next I went to Gibson Cove, where I work presently. I've been working six years, in April, for New England; I've worked at that same plant for about eight years. It was formerly owned by American Freezerships. Before it became a plant, it was used as a ferryboat between Seattle and Bremerton, Washington. It was brought here to be used as a cannery in 1969.

"I've seen a lot of improvements over the years. When I first did or watched shrimp, shrimp workers had to hand peel all the shrimp. Now, you know, we have sophisticated machinery that peels 'em. There's been quite a lot of improvements in packaging, wrapping, stapling, and banding for shipment. All that is the new equipment that the canneries have improved. In the way they fish, they've got larger boats and they bring in more products. The canneries can do it [process] faster because they have better equipment.

"We have better freezing facilities for our shrimp and bottomfish; we have an individual quick freezer which freezes the products individually. They run a special amount of time in the freezer, and they come out down a chute,

Shrimp on a boat before reaching the cannery. The raw shrimp are peeled by machines, frozen in blocks, and shipped to Seattle.

into a box for packaging. We don't do any canning, we just freeze our products. Our brands are Ship Ahoy and Icy Point. Our raw shrimp is frozen in blocks, put in boxes, and shipped to Seattle in Sea Land vans. With cooked shrimp we put it in a tank and wash it, then we run it across a belt, and that's where they pick all the fish out of it. Then it's run through the peelers and peeled. It next goes through a separator and that gets out the rest of the shells that are left over from the peelers. The shrimp is cooked right over the peelers; it's steam cooked. It goes across the shakers, where there's a blower that blows some more shells out, then onto a belt where workers pick out whatever is left on the shrimp.

"It's dipped in a brine and then drained. Then it goes into an IQF freezer and it takes about seven minutes to freeze. From there it goes to a holding freezer, packaged in fifty-pound boxes. Then it goes on a van to Seattle. Our raw shrimp goes through the same process, but it's weighed in sixteen-and-a-half-pound blocks and put in a plate freezer and frozen solid. The next day, or even the same day, they are broken out of there and put in cases, shipping cases, and put in a van to be shipped to Seattle. Very little of our products stay here, most of them go to Seattle. Sometimes we get special orders that are sent on planes, but not too often. We put them in Styrofoam boxes and ship them down on the direct flight. If it has to go to Seward or something, we use the ferryboat.

"People call and ask for orders. Our plant in Seattle will get special orders. Occasionally, they'll have to ship something overseas; we might be doing a lot more of that because if they think it'll pay, they'll start shipping directly from here, straight to Germany or Japan or whatever country might want to order. They're talking about it. It will probably be done by plane straight from Kodiak. I remember that when I used to work at Ice and Storage we used to ship whole crabs to France by plane. All we did was cook them. But first we opened up their backs and cleaned all the bad insides out. They were then put in special made boxes and packed frozen, then we shipped them straight out. They didn't get rotten or anything because it doesn't take very long to ship them; if they're packed in Styrofoam, they won't thaw out. I know one lady in town who ships by mail to her relatives. She gets the ice that comes in packages and puts it in the Styrofoam boxes with the crab and it keeps.

"In the processing of crab in other plants, they roll the crab through rollers to get the meat out of the legs and claws. Then they run it through a blue light to get the shells out. The light makes them glow, so they can clean them out. But at our plant we section them and send them to Seattle.

"At our plant we are processing bottomfish. The fish that feed along the bottom of the ocean floor are considered bottomfish. Cod, pollock, English sole, Alaska plaice, and flounder are a few. We were the first plant in Kodiak to do the bottomfish; we now have three boats fishing. It takes about 100 workers to do bottomfish; our boats often bring in 200,000 pounds a load. The cannery started bottomfish in April of 1978. I went to Pier 65 in

Tanner crab waiting to be processed.

A worker at the heading and gutting machine.

Workers fillet, clean, and package the bottomfish before it is sent off to Seattle.

Seattle and learned how to work in bottomfish; then I came back up and showed the people at the plant here how to do them. Also, people from Pier 65 traveled up here to help to get things started.

"We also have very sophisticated machinery that does much of the work. One of the machines heads and guts the fish. Then the fish travel down a chute and are filleted. Workers then look for parasites and trim the fish. Then it's frozen and packaged and sent to Seattle in vans for use in restaurants and other places. Lab technicians take daily samples of the fish and look for contamination and disease. So we do put out a very clean and safe product.

"Our cannery especially has good clean-up equipment so we keep our plants cleaner. We have what we call pressure equipment. We just use a pressure hose that has a trigger gun on the end. It sprays soap all over everything and really cleans it up good; then we don't have all that slime buildup and mess that you get from seafood products. All the docks now are cemented instead of wooden; they are covered with cement so that none of the dirt stays in cracks or crevices. The same's true with dirt in the machinery, the spray gun can get in every crack. There is 900 pounds of pressure in some guns and 600 to 800 pounds in others. We are putting a new foam in ours, a cleaning compound of some sort. Our drains are better now and we don't drain anything into the ocean anymore. We put it all into a big hopper where it is washed many times and then sent to Bio-Dry [a plant in Kodiak which converts waste into fertilizer and other products]. So all the waste is removed every day and we don't have any refuse around.

"OSHA, the Occupational Safety and Health Administration, checks on us to make sure we don't have any accidents. So not many people get hurt. Also, we have a program at our plant now where we are educating people on safety. We are trying to make our jobs more safe.

"We have many kinds of people that work for us. We get people from everywhere, Mexicans, Filipinos, Koreans, Japanese, and Vietnamese are just some of them. Others are from Canada, France, England, Iceland, Hungary, Yugoslavia, Poland, Greece, Italy, and Spain. I had a Swedish woman working for me at one time who never did know any English. We do not discriminate against anybody."

NORMAN HOLM: 1975—A YEAR OF HARDSHIPS

by: Scott Fuller, Mike Greene, and Rud Wasson

"The *John & Olaf* was a steel shrimp boat that was coming from the Chignik area with a load of shrimp and got in very bad, cold weather over along the mainland shore, down by Wide Bay. It iced down very heavily and, in the process of trying to find shelter, she ran aground on a little reef off the beach. They thought that the boat might possibly roll over so they got in their life raft and it got away from the boat somehow. There was a very strong, cold offshore northwest wind. It was blowing seventy, eighty, maybe more, and extremely cold, so we think they got loose from the boat and then went sailing right out in the middle of Shelikof Strait, out in the ocean where the seas and the weather were even worse. The Coast Guard found the partially destroyed, collapsed life raft up on an island ninety miles away—of course no trace of the crew was found. No one will ever know exactly what happened."

The waters surrounding the island of Kodiak in the Gulf of Alaska have yielded to man a bounty of treasures, but they have also taken their toll. With seas up to twenty feet and winds gusting to 100 miles per hour, it's no wonder man has little chance against such uneven odds.

Another tragic example, as told by marine surveyor Norm Holm, is the story of the *Martin*. "They were heading out one night and got off course and got on a reef. The vessel rolled over, bottom side up. The house broke off in those pretty heavy seas that were breaking over the bottom of the boat. The crew was washed off, I guess, one by one. Two of 'em made it to the beach and one of them, the skipper, survived for a number of hours clinging to the side of the cliff. One of the crew members made it up the cliff for a ways, but apparently perished and fell back into the bay. During the night the other two, as far as we know, never made it to the beach. They were just right outside of town here."

"No trace of the crew
[of the *John & Olaf*]
was found.
No one will ever know
exactly what
happened."

Another mishap was the halibut boat *Ilene*. "Those fellas were out halibut fishing in the ocean. It was about a sixty-five- to sixty-eight-foot wooden boat, and they had been out halibut fishing for twenty-three days; the fishing was rather poor and the weather was really rough. They got about 30,000 pounds of halibut aboard and then came in about four or five o'clock in the afternoon to Kodiak with the thought of delivering their halibut the next day at the Alaska Ice and Storage Plant. So they tied up at the face of the dock,

The overturned hull of
the *Martin*.

The *Ilene* goes down.

and they all went ashore. They went uptown, one crewman lived here so he went home, and the other three took a hotel room, cleaned up, had dinner, and stayed there.

"During the night we had pretty heavy northeast winds, quite a bit of swell coming in there, and also a very big tide. So, with nobody aboard the vessel, the bowline that they had draped over a piling with a loop slipped off. Because of the big tides and the swell, it just flipped the loop off the top of the piling so the boat was only secured with a stern line to the dock. This left the boat laying broadside with the wind blowing against it and the swells rolling in there. Pretty soon, that stern line broke and then the vessel was not secured at all to the dock. With nobody aboard it went sailing down the channel past Union Oil and the city docks and it ended up on a point outside Gibson Cove. She sank there and washed out, and within an hour all we saw was the top of the mast. So here's these fellas that had worked so hard to catch that fish, and gone through all those hardships, just to come to town and lose their boat and their catch right within sight of town—they were heartsick. There was a great financial loss with the loss of the catch as well as the loss of the boat."

Even a minor accident can become a near tragedy—which was the case of the *Kalgin Island*. "That power scow *Kalgin Island* was a crabber and she got off course. The skipper was asleep and a crew member was steering; they went off course and they ran up on a reef that was about a mile off shore. This happened across Shelikof Strait outside of Hallo Bay. The reef jutted out there and the weather was real calm. The tide was going out so they stayed there that night and thought they would float off in the morning when the tide came in. This is right out, mind you, right out in the middle of Shelikof Strait, which just happened to be calm at the time. But I was informed of it, that she was aground, and that they expected to get off early the next morning on the incoming tide. Presumably they thought they would be all right; however, the weather turned bad that night and then really blew. The weather was too bad for an airplane to go, but I arranged for a helicopter charter to leave before daylight.

"We had picked up a fella at Port Lions that was the manager of the cannery for Wakefields that had an interest in that boat. Then we headed down Raspberry Strait and it was blowing and snowing, thick weather, so we couldn't see anything and all we had was a little compass. We didn't have a chart, but we headed across Shelikof Strait. It was just starting to get light and we finally found the other side; it's about thirty miles across there. It was snowing real thick, real heavy snow, so we found the coast and we followed the coastline down out toward Cape Douglas in Cook Inlet and, by golly, it got so thick we finally sat down. We didn't see anybody or any boats or anything so we sat down on the beach there with the helicopter and I recognized a clam beach which had just a few old shacks up there and I knew we had gone past where the ship was aground. It was snowing so thick you couldn't see a hundred yards. Anyhow we headed back down the beach.

"There were several boats standing by when we reached them on the radio and asked them to turn their big floodlights on so we could see 'em when we came back down the coast; they did that and we finally picked them up. We went out to the vessel that was aground laying off the beach there and it had just floated free of the rocks. It had bounced over the rocks taking most of the bottom, which was scattered all up and down the bay there. I could see right away that the boat was a loss; but the crew was still aboard and the boat had just hit on the rocks and was just starting to lay over a little bit on its side. We tried to get in with the helicopter to get the crew off, but the rigging was in the way. As she started to roll over on her side, the crew walked up along the side of the house so the helicopter was able to get in there and got two of them off right away.

"The helicopter got one man in in a well-organized fashion. The second one got panicked and jumped and grabbed one of the pontoons of the helicopter when the pilot wasn't aware of it. It flipped the helicopter over on its side partly and they just missed the rotor blades going into the rigging on the boat by about a foot. If they hit the rigging with the rotors, they would have dumped themselves right down into the bay there right on top of the boat. I don't know what would have happened. It was really a close call. Then they headed for the shore and one of the other boats got in close enough and threw a line up to the one remaining crew member. He got hold of the line and they physically hauled him through the water and aboard the other boat. Then in just a few minutes there was just a little corner of the boat sticking up—that's how close it was. I don't know what would have happened if I hadn't had that helicopter that morning, just got there in time. The weather was so bad the Coast Guard wouldn't fly that morning; they didn't go over to the mainland it was so thick, no visibility at all. That was a very close call."

KIM BUCKMAN: "WE HUNG ON ALL NIGHT LONG"

by: Sean Huggins and Mike Miles

"Well, you see, it was not my boat that sank, it was Larry Tousignant's boat. I had just got back from Chignik. I was fishing my dory down there and the cannery burned down. Larry asked me if I would like to make a trip with him. He already had his boat up from Port Williams, so I went along with it and we went out there to fish.

"We were just starting to pick up some gear that he already had had out for a week or so, 'cause he had to come back to town to pick up his wife, who was on vacation. When we picked up his gear, it was a windy day; I think it was blowing out of the northwest more or less, about thirty. When we got the gear picked up we decided to set some gear a little bit offshore. About 500 yards offshore, the line got tangled up when Larry started setting the gear. The line got tangled up in the prop and when we went to clear it,

Kim Buckman: "They found us none too soon, you know."

there was too much weight in the stern. We had a heavy outboard, and the batteries were weak because he hadn't run the boat in about a week.

"It started to swamp, we didn't have enough time to bail it out. It happened fast, you know, and when it did swamp it took it about twenty seconds. He had the boat divided into three sections, the back part was the living section, the middle section was the fish hold, and the front part was the work section where they carried gear. As it swamped we had those big buoys that he marked the gear with, regular crab buoys—we had nine of them on board because we had just started to set them. We put them in the middle hold and that kept the bow out of the water, and we just climbed up on the bow.

"We did not have enough time to get a mayday out, we just had a CB and the batteries were too dead and in the water. When it swamped it happened so fast we didn't get a chance to get anything else. Then we tried to get everything off the boat to get it down weightwise. We managed to get out one life vest. I had my oilskins on and we decided to split them and Larry didn't know how to swim so I gave him the life vest. We were approximately a half a mile from the shoreline and there was a little island, too, but Larry wasn't really a good swimmer, so we decided to hang on instead of trying to swim to shore. This happened about two o'clock in the afternoon on the first of August in 1976. The water was not too cold, but there was cold wind coming in off the mainland. We were off the north part of Shuyak Island so the breeze was coming off of Cape Douglas. Then the breeze carried us and we drifted up towards the Barren Islands.

"We managed with some line to balance ourselves on the bow and we tied line around us so we didn't fall off. We managed to hold on and take turns keeping awake. One would sleep for a half an hour, and the other would hold on to him; the next half an hour the other guy would watch out. We held on that way through the night and I think the current carried us more or less up toward the islands. At one point at night I thought we were almost closer to the Kenai Peninsula than Shuyak Island.

"During the night the wind picked up; there always is a certain amount of tide rips off the Barren Islands and we got kind of sloppy weather up there. The wind picked up a little bit, it must have blown at least twenty or thirty knots. It was pretty cold but we managed to hold on because there was no other choice but to keep hanging on. We were hoping come morning that the ferry would see us and, well, it is coldest around morning. We were situated by then more or less off Shuyak and kind of between Shuyak and Marmot Island. We were at least a good twenty miles off Shuyak and it seemed that the current was whipping us straight out.

"We were still hanging on to the bow. Part of the cabin was below water and the midpart of the boat was still floating because of the buoys in there. The cabin was maybe a quarter of the way above the water. Larry and I agreed that I'd try to go back there and get a sleeping bag or something out. They were kind of floating up towards the windows. I was to smash one of the windows and try to get something for more protection. We only had light summer clothes and cotton shirts on because we weren't prepared for the cold and we started to suffer. I made two attempts to go back there to get something and on the second attempt the boat must have had an air pocket in the cabin because it capsized and rolled from the upward position where the bow was sitting out of the water.

"It rolled over and we had to scramble onto the back. We had to kinda sit on the, what is it called, the chine of the boat—it's where the bottom and the sides meet. We had to straddle that and it's like riding a horse or something; we had to lean it this way and lean it that way to keep it from rolling back and forth too much, so we could hold on to it. Occasionally, there were eight-foot swells that would wash over us. We tried righting it a couple of times by hanging on the sides to make it come right but there was just too much weight in the boat. We couldn't get the kicker off because it was a 130-horse kicker. There was still a lot of stuff on board that we didn't manage to get off, so we didn't have any luck bringing it back up. We just held on.

"We saw a SeaLand ship go by one time about a half a mile inside us, and they didn't see us. We saw the only other boat that came close to us before early afternoon; I think it was a halibut schooner, but it was a little too far to see the name. I'm pretty sure it came within 200 yards of us, but nobody was on the wheel watching. We were more or less out on open water so a lot of boats didn't keep a constant eye on the water. I always carry yellow rain gear with me. I got on top of Larry's shoulders and tried waving but nobody saw us.

"Then at four o'clock we saw some other boats coming, there were two of them. The guy who was on one of them was Crow [Calvin Colbert], that's his nickname, he's a middle-aged fisherman from Seldovia. They were coming straight from Gore Point to Tonki Cape; it was kind of an unusual route but they were taking it because it was kind of stormy out. We saw him coming from about a mile away. I started waving my rain gear and it was the skipper who was on watch and he kinda caught it out of the corner of his eye 'cause he was going at quarter angle to us. At first he thought it was a whale playing or something, but then finally he saw us and headed in towards us and picked us up.

"We figured we might have made it through another night but it was dubious. We were pretty stiff; our legs were getting very stiff from being underwater. They found us none too soon, you know. We both suffered a certain amount of frostbit legs. It took us both a couple of months to really recover the lower sections of our bodies, for them to come back to normal. The people treated us real well on the boat, they fed us and got us warm. About six hours later, when we got back to Kodiak, we were in fairly good shape. Larry had to stay a night at the hospital."

"How long were you in the water?"

"We figured about twenty-six hours. We weren't completely submerged in the water all the time; we managed to keep ourselves floating and sheltered, you know. Just say we were up in the bow, and the water would get our legs wet. We were exposed to the wind due to the lack of clothing. I had my rain oilskins on. I had the top and bottoms on, but I took the bottoms off and made a top for Larry 'cause all he had on was just his Levis and a shirt. We took turns handing the life jacket back and forth."

"What were your feelings out there, did you feel that you'd be rescued?"

"Well, you know, I think we just tried to keep our spirits up, we realized that maintaining them is important. We got to the point where we were accepting what happened; we had seen enough of life that we weren't panicstricken. We tried to keep it pretty calm."

"Did you feel excited when you saw boats passing?"

"Oh, yeah! We really tried waving, yelling like when we saw SeaLand. We tried waving but they were pretty far off. I'd say they were a half mile off us, maybe not that far. When we saw the halibut schooner we really tried waving. I've always worn yellow oilskins 'cause I've seen a man go overboard in the Bering Sea and just the fact that there is such a color contrast makes them safer at sea. In fact, in Norway now, it's a law that fishermen have to wear fluorescent-type rain gear, in case something does happen, other boats can see them."

Bristol Bay
Region

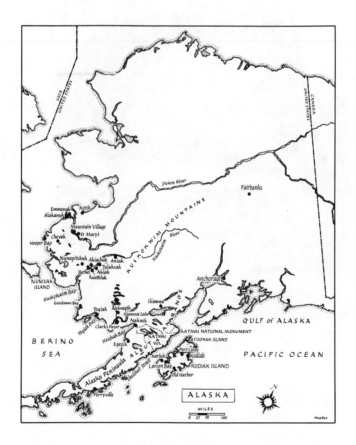

1. Introduction

THE BRISTOL BAY REGION

by: Annette Nestegard

Our magazine is called *Uutuqtwa* (pronounced oo took' twa), a Yup'ik word which translates into English as "I go home." The name was chosen because the magazine is a look at the past and the present, like going home.

The publication is important to us because we want to preserve what has happened traditionally in Bristol Bay and what is happening now. This is not an easy task since the three villages that make up the school district have their greatest activity in the summer when school is finished.

The area relies on the brief summer season when just about everyone fishes for the Bristol Bay sockeyes. The villages swell to twenty times their winter populations as an influx of fishermen and cannery workers arrive as they have for the past hundred years.

Naknek is unique in that it is the traditional meeting area of the three Native groups of Alaska. On top of this is a Russian heritage dating back to the eighteenth century. It was the canneries, however, tapping the salmon resource, that drew Scandinavian, Italian, Native, and other fishermen to the area and mixed their many customs.

Many people stayed in the area to take advantage of the schools, transportation, bush environment, and the subsistence fishing and hunting. Few people speak their original language or strictly practice their traditional customs, but what has developed is a unique culture consisting of people from all over the world.

We feel honored to contribute what we've learned about the Bristol Bay area to *The Cama-i Book*.

PLACE NAMES IN OUR AREA

by: Patrick Lind
revised by: Mary Murray

- The valley of Hollerville was sometimes called Oosklook, which means something fell over. The banks there usually slide down or fall.
- Naknek's name came from the Yup'ik language and means muddy.
- Libbyville was built by Libby, McNeil and Libby.
- King Salmon received its name from the run of king salmon up the Naknek River from Bristol Bay.
- Another name for Red Salmon Weighs is Inlawak, which means play bed.
- Red Salmon Pump Lake is connected to water pipes that go down to some canneries. The water is pumped out to be used in the canneries.
- Leader Creek was named after a boat.
- Savonoski's Native language meaning is that the place can't flood during the spring melt of the winter snow.
- Katmai's name comes from the Yup'ik language. Another name for it is Tooypulik, an Eskimo word meaning smoky.
- Givnugeuk in Yup'ik means a lot of flat or very low land. This place is mostly swampy or muddy.
- Hungries, also known as New England Fish Company, is located at Pederson Point and is named after L. A. Pederson, who built the cannery in the 1890s.
- Koggiung is a Yup'ik name meaning sandy. This place is located nine miles north of Naknek.
- Bristol Bay was named after the third Earl of Bristol, Lord of the British Admiralty.
- Paul's Creek was named after Paul Chukan.
- Eskimo Creek's Native name comes from the Yup'ik language and means crooked.
- Kertoong is a Yup'ik name for the Diamond M Cannery area and it means high up.

2. Life in Bristol Bay

SLIME TIME: SALMON FISHING IN BRISTOL BAY

by: Mel Coghill, Jr.
revised by: Sabrina Tibbetts and Joe Lind
contacts: Red Harrop
drawings by: Mel Coghill, Jr.

Salmon are excellent navigators. When spawning time arrives, they know instinctively to return to the exact spot where they were born. One of the main spawning grounds in the world is the Bristol Bay area, which is still referred to as "The Salmon Capital of the World." The major rivers in this system are the Naknek, Egegik, King Salmon, and Kvichak (Kwee-jak). Various types of salmon which return to spawn in the bay's rivers and tributaries are: chinook (king), sockeye (red), coho (silver), pink (humpy) and chum (dog).

The sockeye is the most sought-after salmon in the world and the most abundant in our area.

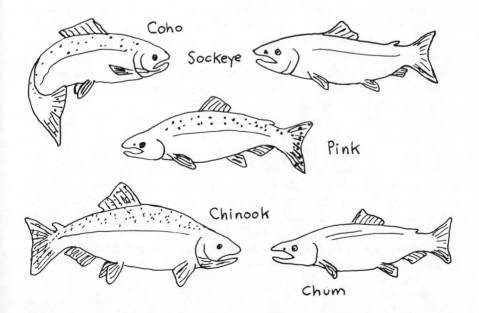

Salmon average from five to seven pounds in weight and twenty-four to twenty-seven inches in length. The salmon's color is blue-green to blue on the back of the salmon; the sides are a bright silvery color. The sockeye's color changes once it reaches fresh water and begins its spawning cycle. The body turns bright red, caused by carotene, a red pigment found in various plants which the salmon eat at sea. It is stored in the fatty tissues of the salmon. Upon entering fresh water the salmon stops feeding, so the fish relies on the fats stored in the body for nourishment. Once it starts using these fats the carotene is distributed throughout the body, thus changing the color of the fish's body from blue to silver to red. The head and tail color is changed to a pale green, which is caused by the amount of time in fresh water and the salinity of the water.

The male salmon also goes through a physical change which alters the shape of the body. The jaws become deformed, particularly the upper one, which droops and displays teeth that are longer and sharper than they were during their life at sea. The lower jaws don't show much change, but they display a set of big, sharp teeth. The salmon uses these teeth for fighting off rival males and other fish that feed on fish eggs during spawning. Once the salmon reach the lake or stream where they were born, the spawning process begins.

Often the late arrivals have to wait for a space to spawn. When the salmon begin spawning the female will swim in a circle around the place where she will lay her eggs. When the female begins this circular motion, a male will start swimming alongside her; often males will fight to be the female's partner. As the female sockeye is swimming in a circle she'll make a pass at the spot where the eggs are going to be laid and slap the gravel loose with her tail to form a small pit. When the pit is ready, the female hovers over it to signal to the male that she is ready to lay her eggs.

As she is laying the eggs, the male fertilizes them with sperm. After the hole has a lot of eggs in it, the female moves upstream and makes another pit just a few feet from the first one. The loose gravel from the hole upstream covers the one downstream, thus protecting the eggs from trout or other predators. The female doesn't spawn the next eggs with the same male. Once the eggs are laid and fertilized, they remain under as much as a foot or more of gravel for many weeks.

Sometime during the winter the eggs hatch and small salmon called fry come forth. The fry stay in the gravel until it is dark, then they wiggle free. While the fry is waiting in the gravel, it feeds on the yolk sack of the egg, which is still attached to the body. Out of some 3,000 eggs the female lays, about 30 to 100 will reach the fingerling stage. There are many problems a small salmon faces while it's growing up, including change in temperature of the water, droughts, and other fish which feed on the small fish. Fingerlings are about two to three inches long and stay in fresh water until they become smolt. After developing into smolt they head out to sea and do not return for two to five years. The salmon return in late June and early July.

Fishermen from miles around come to Bristol Bay and the surrounding area because salmon bring good money. Many years ago when people first learned of this resource, they didn't have powerboats as we do now, but had to use sailboats. These boats were made of wood and had a big sail which was used to trap the winds to propel the boat. The boats were the same; they were all thirty-two feet long and had the same amount of net and equipment. "You could get within three hundred yards of another boat, throw your net out, drift all night, and wake up in the morning with the same boat beside you three hundred yards away." Each boat had two shackles of net, each seventy-five fathoms long. The nets were linen and had large, bulky cedar corks for flotation.

To prevent the wooden corks from becoming soaked with water, the fisherman would put them in a large vat in which he then melted paraffin wax. When the wax was melted, the corks were put in it for protective covering. After this waxing, the corks were cooled and hung on the nets. Each net weighed about 300 pounds. You needed something to mark the end of each net while you were fishing so other fishermen would know where your net was.

For heating and cooking purposes, the sailboats had two different types of stoves, depending on the nationality of the fishermen. The Italians had coal stoves and the Nordics had a gas-primed Swedish stove. The Italian coal stove was about two feet tall and eighteen inches in diameter. It was like a stovepipe with the bottom closed off. The stove had a handle on top and a small door on the side for draft. The coal rested on a small loose grate that fit in the bottom. The Swedish stove was about one foot high and was made of solid brass. Three legs supported a grill where pots could be placed. It had a one-quart fuel tank and burned kerosene, but was primed by wood al-

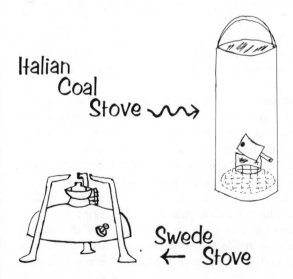

Italian
  Coal
    Stove ∿∿↝

Swede
← Stove

Two types of stoves used for heating and cooking on early salmon fishing boats.

cohol. The alcohol was placed in a small bowl which was wrapped around
the burner nozzle. This stove was pressure-operated, similar to the common
Coleman stoves.

"It was easy to tell the two different kinds of boats, because a Nordic boat
would have a white sail and an Italian boat's sail would be dark from the
smoke of the coal stoves." When it was dry weather you would have to be
very careful with a coal stove because if a spark got on the sail, it would go
up in flames.

In addition to stoves and sails, a sailboat carried a toolbox, two pairs of
oars, each fourteen feet long, picking hooks, and pews. Pews are long sticks
like broom handles with a prong on the end and are used for pitching fish. A
coffeepot, a big cooking pot, a frying pan, two plates and cups, and silverware for two made up the cooking and eating utensils. The toolbox contained a hammer and nails, a screwdriver and screws, and a hatchet to cut
lines or nets in emergencies.

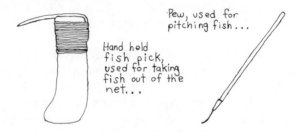

Hand held
fish pick,
used for taking
fish out of the
net...

Pew, used for
pitching fish...

The rigging consisted of a mast, a boom, a sail spreader, and a sail. The
mast was about thirty feet high and had a built-in pulley at the top for the
rope used to raise and lower the sail. There were metal rings that fit around
the mast, which were used to guide the sail. A small, wedge-shaped block of
wood located at the base of the mast kept the metal rings from sliding all the
way down.

The boom was about twenty-five feet long and had a notched end for a
rope, which was used to fasten the boom to the mast. The end of the boom
was tapered so a small rope fastened to the end of the sail could be slipped
over it.

When the sail was being raised, the bottom end of the sail was slipped
over the outermost part of the boom. When that was done, a rope which was
looped around the mast was put around the notched end and was pulled as
hard as possible. After tightening it, the rope was wrapped around a cleat
and around the boom a few times. Near the end of the boom, two rings were
located for a block and tackle to adjust the sail's angle to the wind.

Canvas, brass grommets, small rope, and a spritzel, or sail spreader,
formed the sail and its parts. The rings that guided the sail along the mast
were put through brass grommets and so were the few ropes used in working
the sail. The spritzel was about thirty feet long and had a hole in one end
and a small notch in the other end. The end with the hole in it was threaded

on small rope which went through the top of the sail. The small rope was twice as long as the spritzel and ran down both sides of the sail to the base of the mast. A block and tackle were used to tighten the sail by putting a rope around the notched end and pulling hard until it fit into a hole on the wedge block. Two rows of small ropes located at the lower part of the sail were used to lash down part of the sail on windy days.

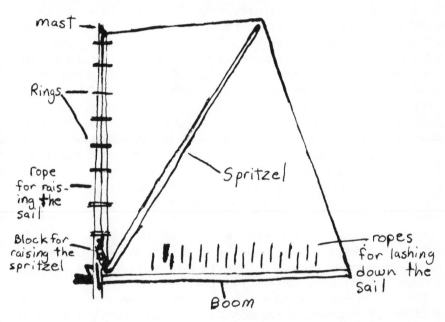

The first row of ropes was about a foot and a half from the bottom, and the second was about a foot higher. A rope was attached to the top of the sail near the mast for raising and lowering the sail. After the sail was raised to the desired height, the rope was fastened to one of two cleats located off the side of the bottom of the mast. "On windy days you'd lash the sail to the boom until just a little triangle of sail was showing and it would be all the boat could handle." There were four different sail positions: full, three quarters, one half, and just a little sail up for windy days.

The boat was steered by a large wooden rudder that had a board at the top. This was called a tiller and was made from oak; the rudder was made out of pine. The rudder was constructed with several boards which were held together by long metal bars and had a slot near the top for the tiller to slip into. A long rod was welded to a strip of metal and connected to the stern of the sailboat. The front edge of the rudder had several metal rods which were bent into about three quarters of a circle and welded onto a metal strip. These were slipped down over the rod at the stern of the boat, making it easy to remove the rudder.

Fishing was very hard work; the hardest part was sailing the boat. "When you sailed against the wind or had the wind to either side of the boat, you tacked, which is zigzagging." The sail was adjusted by the use of a block and tackle depending on the direction of the wind. "When you were sailing, you had to have either the tide or the wind in your favor. You couldn't have both against you or you'd get nowhere."

The early fifties saw the conversion from boats with sails to powerboats, which were the sailboats with engines in them. These were far better than the sailboats because they didn't have the wind and tide problems. The early powerboats had hulls with two pointed ends, which were gradually changed to a flat-sterned hull. The powerboats had bigger cabins and could hold more fish. Powerboats could hold as many as 4,000 fish, depending on the weather, size of fish, and type of hulls. The sailboats could hold around 2,000 fish under the same conditions. The powerboats were as long as the sailboats were—thirty-two feet. Today so many of the boats are custom-made that, depending on the design, they can hold a lot more fish.

The plain powerboats have bunks, a portable or a little stove, a radio, and a power roller to make pulling in the nets easier. The really nice boats have almost every pleasure of home such as carpeting, television, toilet, refrigerator, and a lot more. Some boats have power spools to aid in retrieving the nets.

About the same time the boats changed, the nets changed. The cedar corks were replaced with Styrofoam corks and the webbing was switched from linen to nylon. The lead line didn't see much change for a few years. The lead was on the line until it was put inside the rope.

The different canneries in the bay area have their own scows to pick up fish from their fishermen. The cannery scows have the color(s) of their companies painted on them so the fishermen can easily spot them. Most of the scows are anchored inside the mouth of the Naknek River. Some go out in the bay or up towards the Kvichak River.

After all the fish are picked from the net and depending on the amount of fish aboard, the fishermen head for one of their cannery's scows. Each cannery has several scows, which are large barges with housing on board for the

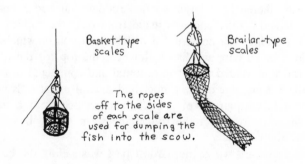

Basket-type scales

Brailar-type scales

The ropes off to the sides of each scale are used for dumping the fish into the scow.

crew. These barges are as long as 200 feet and as wide as 50 feet. The larger scows hold between 30,000 and 40,000 fish. Fish are transferred from the boats onto the scows by big baskets or by a long net tube. The tube or brailer has one end kept on board the barge and the end with the scale on it is put on the powerboat. When there are a lot of fish in the net, it is pulled up so the fish can be weighed; then it is lifted up so the fish can be put aboard the scow.

When a powerboat comes alongside a scow to unload fish, it can go on either side of the boat. If both sides have boats unloading, then the fishermen will have to wait at the stern of the scow. Years ago, the Bristol Bay fishermen didn't have a union. The outside fishermen from the other states had a union and the canneries served them first. If a local resident was unloading fish and an outside fisherman came to unload his catch, the crew of the scow would move the first sailboat back and unload the second one.

Up until a few years ago the fishermen were paid per fish instead of per pound. When Red Harrop first arrived in Naknek, he got paid thirteen and one half to fifteen cents per fish. As the years have gone by, the prices have changed. About ten years ago the fishermen started getting paid per pound of fish.

After a scow has a big load of fish and when the tide is right, it will head for the cannery. The cannery is the place where the fish are cleaned, canned, and cooked.

RETURN OF SLIME: THE GROWTH OF THE CANNERIES

by: Mel Coghill, Jr.
revised by: Joe Lind and Sabrina Tibbetts
contacts: Allen Nelson, Herman Herrmann, Edward Clark, and Red Harrop
drawings: by Mel Coghill, Jr.

"Explorers progressed their way up the Pacific coast to Alaska and finally to Bristol Bay. Each place the explorers stopped, the Natives told them that 'There is a place up north of here where there's lots of salmon.' The explorers would say, 'Oh yeah? Well, we'd better check that out.' They continued talking to the Natives until, over the years, they reached the Bristol Bay area. There's probably been hundreds of people up here to look over the land, but then there was a lot of other places. These places were warmer and easier to get to. Then those places were being fished out and they turned to Bristol Bay. It was kind of like going back to a capped-off oil well. They knew the fish were here, but didn't need them until other places started going bad."

When the salmon of this area were looked upon for processing, the companies sent in large crews of men to build salteries. The salted salmon were packed into large wooden barrels and shipped out aboard large sailing ships.

Naknek Cannery, now the location of Naknek Trading Company and Standard Oil. (Courtesy of Bristol Bay Historical Society)

The companies soon found a greater market and not enough salmon was being salted to meet demands. The new process of canning was born and many dollars would be made or lost in the building and operation of canneries.

During the early 1890s there were two big salteries in the Naknek River. The first one, in South Naknek, was built and operated by the Arctic Packing Company in 1890. Alaska Packers Association bought this operation and converted it into the first cannery in Kvichak Bay. Naknek Packing Company was located on the north shore of the Naknek River.

"The canneries could be built and operated in the same season. They were able to build them faster and cheaper because the cannery workers were paid by the day, no overtime like they have now. They used to work their men ragged. Of course, the fishermen that came up specialized in a certain trade, some were carpenters, blacksmiths, and just about everything.

"In the sailing ship days, after you had signed a contract you left San Francisco to come here. Your contract said that you'd work for, oh say, 3¢ a fish and run money. Run money was usually $50; I think the last time run money was used it was up to $225. It wasn't until just recently they cut that out. But anyway, for that run money, he came up here and that was all he got; he didn't get any more. The cannery worker had to help get everything ready for the season, load the cases, get them out to the ships, and unload them after they were home. They had to help with everything; that was all for run money. When he got back to San Francisco, he got that money plus what he made for his fish. When you docked at San Francisco you got ten dollars for shore money until you got paid from the company, usually a week or so. In those days, ten dollars was a lot of money.

"They didn't have a so-called 'carpenter gang'; the fishermen did everything. They had to do this for the run money—everyone did his share of work. Some were building a bunkhouse, or putting a roof on one. Others might be putting in a new dock or repairing boats. They usually held a meeting to figure out who was going to do what, so-and-so was going to load boxes and so forth. The fishermen all had their duties. It was a whole different ball of wax compared to today."

Cannery workers came up in the early spring, even before the ice had gone out in the bay. This crew would prepare the cannery for the coming season; the main jobs were making the cans and the boxes which contained these cans. The ships would bring many sheets of tin to the canneries and from these sheets, the cans were cut. The boxes were precut from wood and had to be nailed together. Making enough cans and boxes for the season usually took three to four weeks.

"The fishermen today might come in the day before fishing, fish for a while, and go home when the peak is over and the fish are slack. Before, they had to be nice to the superintendent of the cannery because he had the only way for you to get home. You couldn't go up to Wien's and fly home because there were no airlines."

Now the cans are delivered partially assembled and flattened out; these are put into a machine which shapes them. The boxes have changed from wood to cardboard and have to be folded by a machine and glued.

The cans which contained the salmon came in three different sizes in the early days. These were one-pound talls, one-pound flats, and one-half-pound flats. The one-pound talls were most common, but a few canneries packed a small amount of the other sizes.

Much of the high-speed machinery today operates and does the same things that the early machines did. The machinery used years ago was steam-driven; the cannery had a boiler room with steam engines. The steam engine's power was harnessed by the many belts, which operated each machine.

The machinery now is driven by electric motors. The use of electric machinery has speeded up the process so much that one line of modern machinery can do what five lines did years ago.

After the salmon are caught, they are loaded onto tally scows. When the scow has a full load, it is brought into the cannery at high tide to be unloaded.

Years ago the canneries didn't have scows and the fishermen had to come into the cannery and throw their fish up onto the dock. When the canneries provided scows for fish pickups, they still didn't have a very good means of unloading at the canneries. Some canneries lowered a big wooden box into the scow and cannery workers loaded the box with the fish; when the box was full, it was hoisted up onto the dock. Another method was a rail car, a big wooden box on wheels, which was run along iron rails. A ramp was constructed of timbers and had to be built so it wouldn't float away as it ran from the dock and out onto the beach.

As the canneries became more mechanized, an elevator was installed on the side of the dock. This was a conveyer belt with many scoops which were

Two Finnish fishermen outside Libby's Koggiung Cannery, 1943. (Courtesy of Bristol Bay Historical Society)

fastened together like chains, enclosed in a wooden chute, and lowered onto the scow by block and tackle.

The chute was fed by hand; a crew went down onto the scow and pitched the fish into it with peughs. This method damaged the fish because they were handled too much. To prevent this, a self-unloading scow was developed, which used the pressure caused by thousands of pounds of salmon. On the side of the scow there is a rectangular opening about one foot by two feet where the elevator is fed. Between the opening and the elevator there is a metal chute which guides the fish to the conveyer belt. This metal chute is fastened to the opening in the scow and narrows down to the width of the elevator. Precautions such as nets and high wooden sides around the metal chute keep the fish from falling into the water. Only one or two men are needed to unload the scow using this method.

Slime Gets Processed

Once the fish are unloaded from the scow, they are hauled to the processing lines. Before they had conveyer belts and chutes to carry the fish to the lines, the fish were dumped on the floor by the machinery.

The fish have to be beheaded, sliced down the belly, and the fins and tail removed. Cannery workers, mostly Chinese in the early days, do this by hand. Just after the turn of the century, a mechanical fish cutter was invented which saves many, many man hours.

When the fish are beheaded and dressed, they are sent to the "sliming tables." This is where workers remove the insides, any fins that might have been left, and the blood from the backbone. As the fish are inspected, they are continually doused with fresh water to keep them as fresh as possible.

Until recently, the canneries threw away the salmon eggs. Now there is a great market for eggs, so cannery workers have to be careful when removing them. The eggs are used for food and shipped mainly to the Orient.

Once the fish are inspected, they go to a fish cutter which cuts the fish into several pieces. After the fish are cut, the pieces are moved to a filler machine. The filler puts a little salt into the can and almost exactly a pound, half pound, or quarter pound of salmon, depending on the size of the cans.

After the can is filled, it goes through a machine which weighs each can to see if it has the right amount of salmon. If the can is a fraction of an ounce off weight, it is rejected and sent on to the patching table. The patching table is where cannery workers have trays of salmon pieces which they add to the underweight cans.

One-pound cans and the patched ones go to the clincher. This machine clinches a top onto the cans and sends them on to a vacuum machine which draws the air out of the cans.

The first means of creating a vacuum was to have workers solder the can top on. Then the exhaust box, a big wooden box in which the cans were moved by a long system of moving chains, was invented. This box was made out of redwood or fir and was about twenty feet long, eight feet wide, and three feet high. The box was filled with steam and the cans entered at one end and went through a maze of moving chains. There were eight or nine moving chains and every other one was moving in an opposite direction. At the end of each chain was a turntable which rotated the cans so they would go down the next chain in the opposite direction (see diagram). The can stayed in the exhauster for twenty minutes, enough time to exhaust the air

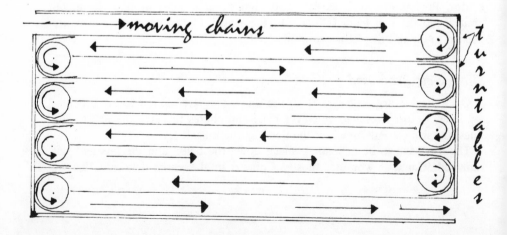

supply in the can. Today, the cans are filled, a top is put on them, and the air is removed all by one machine.

As the cans come out of the exhaust box, they move into a machine which seals the ends onto the cans for good. The cans next proceed onto a track and into a can washer, a metal tank with the chain moving along the bottom. This tank is filled with water so the cans that don't have a vacuum will float. The vacuum-packed cans are moved through the tank and put into cooler racks. After the cans are put into these racks, several racks are loaded onto carts and sent away to be cooked.

The fish are cooked in huge pressure cookers, using the same principle as a kitchen pressure cooker. These are filled with steam produced by the boiler room and have heavy doors to keep the pressure in the retort. The cans of salmon are cooked for an hour and thirty minutes.

In the early days before the canning process became almost totally mechanized, cannery workers were used for many things. Workers would slime fish, stack the cans, label the cans, or put them in boxes.

The workers were of several different nationalities, including Chinese, Mexicans, Filipinos, Italians, and Alaskan Native. The Italians didn't like Chinese or Mexican food and vice versa. The different companies decided to put up separate facilities for the workers; for example, the Chinese workers had their own cook house, washrooms, and bunkhouses.

The cannery workers now are provided with room and board for so much money per day. The fishermen can also stay at the cannery.

After the season is over, when the cannery workers have all gone home, and the packed salmon has been shipped to various markets, a local gang of men is hired to prepare the cannery for winter. This gang makes sure everything is secured and their biggest job is pulling the tow boats and barges up on the weighs. The weighs is a section of the cannery where all the big boats are stored.

"Those days we had iron men and wooden boats . . . now we got iron boats and wooden men."

"These boats that we hauled up were not small boats, they weighed quite a bit. They were eighty feet long and had big gas engines which weighed almost as much as the boats. The engine was just a big chunk of cast iron— the fly wheel alone in some of the boats weighed into the tons. There was one time we put an engine into a boat and we had to take the fly wheel off because it was too heavy to lift. They were three- and four-cylinder engines. Everything had to be done by hand, that was when we had iron men and wooden boats. Now we got iron boats and wooden men.

"Let's go to the early days. In the olden days everything was primitive. You had to pack stuff. One particular weighs I'm talking about is up at Diamond J [Cannery]. We had mud about three feet deep and you had to pack rollers. Those rollers were little iron things, usually four to each piece of wood. We had to pack these and there never were enough of them because they were always being lost. They'd go out on the end of the weighs and the waves would wash them off. We had to pack something that was seventy or eighty pounds through three feet of mud; it was quite a chore. I suppose you've walked in the mud and know how easy it is, especially when the suction gets your boot and your foot comes out easily but your boot stays down there.

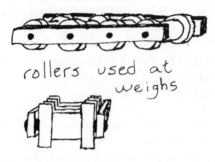

rollers used at weighs

"Anyway, we had what they called a cradle and it was made up of ten by twelve timbers on edge, for the length of the boat. Every launch had its own cradle and that cradle was made just for that boat, because every boat had a different shape to it. So when we launched them in the spring it was no problem because it was just moving the cradle down to the weighs, waiting for the tide to come in, and then they floated—so there was nothing fascinating about that. They went out there with another two boats and took the cradle off, or had the engines running on the boat and backed it off and tied it to the dock. That was if the boat didn't sink. Some of them were pretty well dried up and they didn't have these gas pumps we have today; it was just a matter of buckets or hand pumps. Oh, by the way, we had to tie those cradles down so the boat would float off, or else it would stay with the boat and wouldn't come off.

"Then we had to wait for the next tide and chop the casings and the cradle would float. We'd take a boat . . . sometimes before we had a little tugboat, we just had a skiff and oars. We had to go out with the skiff a little ways and drop an anchor. We'd pull the length of the line attached to the cradle, then row out some more, drop the anchor again, and pull the cradle out some more, for another 500 feet or 300 feet, whatever it was, and that was the way we moved those things. They were hard to tow because they were like a big raft. We put them away right by the beach or wherever we got a place for them.

"There's been times when tides and big winds have come along and our cradles drifted away. Nobody would know which way they went. We couldn't go up to Tibbets and say, 'Let's get an airplane and fly.' Course there weren't many such things as airplanes in the country at the time. So we had to go up the river and look around because we didn't know if it floated up or down. But we usually found them. One time we found one drifting

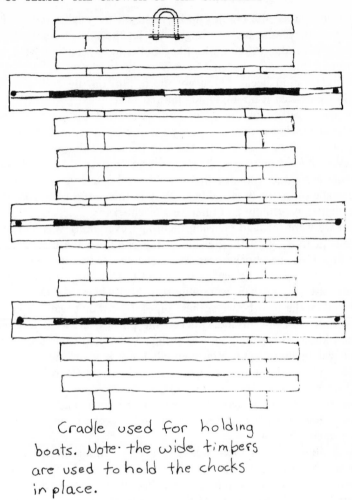

Cradle used for holding
boats. Note· the wide timbers
are used to hold the chocks
in place.

way down by Ugashik. We had to go down there and tow it back up because
they were kind of expensive, you know, lots of timber to one of those things.
That's the way it was launched. Now let's go and take one up."

"Up That Weighs"

"First of all when fall came along, and there was no more use for the
boats, we would take the cradles and put them on the weighs. By that time
we had all kinds of boats. We'd take a little launch which had a small gas
engine in it and tow the cradles to the weighs. We sat there on the bow, one
on each side to guide the rails onto the rollers that I told you about. Another
couple of guys were on the back end of the cradle. Well, we always had
quite a few guys. Not like the economics today—we took all the hands we

could get and pulled the cradles up by hand till they came out of the water and we knew they were pretty straight. We let the tide go out and hooked a rope onto the cradle. After the donkey boiler was fired up, we'd wind the cradle out of the water because it was down in the mud. We didn't like working in the mud because you got more mud on the cradle than it was worth. So we heaved it up a couple hundred feet.

"Now we were out of the water and we started getting scrapers out to scrape the channels for the chocks because they laid around all summer and got full of mud. You had to put grease in them and the grease came in big barrels. We greased these so-called chocks and moved them back and forth. The chocks were the shape of the bow of the boat, and one in the middle was the shape of the belly of the boat. Way in the stern of the boat there was another shape; we usually had three sets of chocks.

"When we were through greasing them and everything was working good, we pulled them away on the outside of the cradle so the boat could slip in without knocking the chocks over. We had lines tied to the chocks and two pipes were in the same timber as the chocks. The three timbers which had the chock assembly in them were almost a third wider than the boat, so that we had to float the boat between these pipes if we didn't want to knock these pipes over. If we came in and knocked the pipes over, we'd lost our guide and didn't know where the boat was sitting. So we had to measure and see if the boat was in there right. You couldn't lay a boat in there crisscross because the weight would shift to one side and the cradle wouldn't climb as easy.

"Sometimes the cradle would fall off of the track and, when that happened, you had to pack all of the screw jacks, timbers, and everything you got down there.

"It took about two or three weeks to get everything straightened around because we didn't have all the modern stuff we do today. So we got all that fixed, put the lines on the pipes, and coiled them up on top. These pipes were usually twenty feet long. Those ropes were to bring the chocks right into the center and up against the boat.

"So here it is high water and sometimes there was a lot of wind. This would all be done at high water because if the tide was crossways, you couldn't put a boat in there. So you waited until the tide was just absolutely still. And, by the way, you're probably wondering how we got the boat in between these six pipes. Well, beforehand a pile driver came along and put in four pilings right abreast of each other, maybe fifty feet or so apart. We had lines on these and the skiffs went along and picked up the lines and gave them to the boat. You grabbed ahold of this line and skippered it along. Then you caught another piling and they pulled them all in there. This way we had lines in control of the boat at all times. We also had a head line that came from shore to pull the boat ahead. We lined the boat up with the cradle nice and straight, then we started pulling the boat up onto the cradle, right between the pipes. We'd get it absolutely straight.

"Sometimes this was done at nighttime, so we used two lanterns and when they lined up, we knew the boat was centered in the cradle. After the boat was centered we put tackles on the lines, because when the tide started to go out the boat might slide down a little bit and you couldn't get it back up.

"As we were waiting for the tide to go out, we'd keep watching the bow of the boat for the water to drop a foot, because by that time the stern of the boat was on the cradle also. Then we pulled the ropes for the chocks; the ones in the bow were pulled first, then the middle and stern chocks. We pulled until we heard them hit the hull and tied the ropes snugly to a cleat. We got all the chocks tied up and the boss man said, 'Let's go home.' That was usually about four o'clock in the morning, because all the morning tides are big.

"Then we'd go home and sleep for a couple, three hours and come back. By that time the boat was dry and we'd check it to see if it was all right. We had to put wedges in front of the chocks and nail them down so the chocks wouldn't slip and have the boat tip over. The boiler was fired up and the men stretched along to pass signals to the winch man. We pulled the boat up the weighs and there weren't any sidetracks like today. The scows were sidetracked.

"That's what it was like to pull up scows and tow boats."

"Once Upon a Slime"

Through the years all of the canneries have changed hands, and with the changes, the names have changed. It would be very long and drawn out if all of the different names were to be included in this article.

Once there were about eleven canneries operating in the Kvichak Bay at one time. Since the early days, many have been destroyed or abandoned and new ones have taken their place. There are many sites where you can see pilings or old broken-down buildings which are the ghosts of once great salmon canning plants.

"There was never enough cargo to ballast the big sailing ships for their trips up here, so the ships were filled with big rocks for ballast. After the ships arrived, the groceries, tin plates, and other supplies were unloaded from the ships. The rocks were removed after the supplies and dumped on the beaches around the cannery, but not where they would damage any boats. Some places they'd build bins out of pilings and dump the rocks into them.

"Then of course, by the same token, they'd have poor fishing seasons and it wasn't a very practical thing to be hauling rocks back to San Francisco. They had burlap bags, so they filled them full of sand and they hauled barge loads of sand out to the ships to use for ballast.

"There were some poor fishing seasons, possibly 1924 or '25; it's kind of vague, but I do know there were real poor seasons. The fishermen made nothing and it's possible they owed the company for supplies. They had to

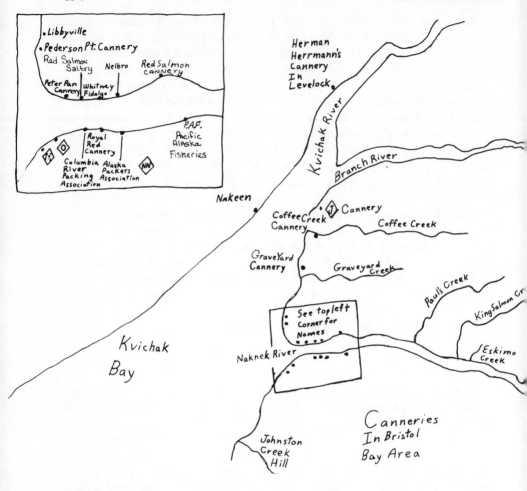

Canneries
In Bristol
Bay Area

have enough money to go home with; they made sure they had ten dollars for shore money.

"Pederson Point cannery used to be the largest cannery in the bay. One summer, in the middle of the season, the whole cannery burned to the ground. This cannery had twelve lines; actually it was two canneries on the same exact location. They had two of everything: two cook houses, several bunkhouses. It was just like walking into two canneries.

"Today the cannery is used for storage when a big ship comes in; you use the cannery to get groceries hauled up and you can buy supplies from the canneries. They are used for more than just canning fish; they have also become a part of our lifestyle.

"The difference between the canneries now and then is like night and day."

CHAILIATE: HANDICRAFTS

by: Pam Myers, Julie Caruso, Annie Newyaka, Evelyn Mike, Terri Alto, and
Linda Lehman
revised by: Diana Cook and Sheila Hutson
contacts: Vicki Peterson, Alpha Myers, and Anishia McCormick

One of the unique things about Alaska is the Native handicrafts. In the
section on handicrafts we have included articles on beading with quills and
without, kikiviks (sewing handbags), skin sewing, slippers, and cu ruks
(baby dolls).

The following combined articles are from previous *Uutuqtwa* magazines
and recent sources.

Beading: Past and Present

The predominant craft in the Bristol Bay area is beading. We don't know
when beading actually began in this area, but it was a long time ago. Before
the Russians came the Natives used to make their own beads from bird and
rabbit bones and soft stone. They'd dye the beads with native tea, berries,
and different colored roots. They'd boil the roots and berries until all of the
juices came out; then they'd put the beads and bones into the mixture and let
them soak for about a week or two.

Many years ago they used the muscles along the backbone of caribou for
sinew, which was used for thread. They would take the muscle out, separate
it into strings, and dry it. When they wanted to use it, they would soak it in
oil or water and then sew with it.

When the Russians came they brought beads and trinkets, which they
traded with the Natives for skins. After that, Natives got their beads from
the trading posts. The canneries also used to bring beads in from the States
and sell them to the Natives. They were inexpensive at that time. Many of
the old trade beads can still be found at the old Native village sites.

They used bear claws and animal teeth for making men's costumes and
men's jewelry. This was a way of showing their strength and power. The wife
of the man who had killed the bear would make him a necklace from the
claws or teeth, or would hang them on his parka.

The trade beads that were brought by the Russians varied in size. Some
were very small and others were about one-half inch in diameter. The beads
were all different colors, but most of them were white and blue. Beads today
are getting smaller and some they're making out of plastic. But you can still
find beads made out of glass today.

Most of the beadwork was worn by the women. They would never use
beaded or quilled designs or anything fancy on babies because they used to

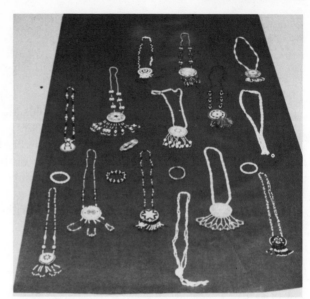

Examples of beadwork
done in Bristol Bay
area.

believe that the spirits of animals would take the babies if they saw them
dressed in pretty clothes or wrappings.

Years ago, if a woman made a design with beads or quills and another
woman from a different tribe or village saw the design and liked it, she
would make a trade bundle and trade the woman the design for the bundle.
A trade bundle was made up of different kinds of beads, needles, sinew, and
skins. The woman would take a large skin, place all of these things in it, and
wrap them up. The woman who had traded the bundle for the design could
never trade for the design again, and she couldn't copy it again. Only the
woman who created the design could copy it or trade it for something else.

Making Rosettes

One of the most popular necklaces around the state of Alaska is the
rosette. The following paragraphs outline instructions for making them.

Here is the list of materials needed to make a rosette:

1. Piece of felt or cloth
2. Bead needle or any small needle that will fit through the beads
3. Beeswax
4. Strong thread (nylon)
5. Multi-colored beads

To begin, take a piece of felt about four inches long and four inches wide.
Thread your needle and wax it. In order to do this, you must first run the
thread through the wax about four or five times. Take your needle and poke
it through the center of your felt or cloth. Put one bead on the needle and

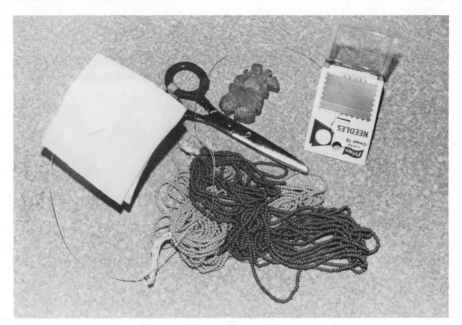

Materials needed to make a rosette.

poke your needle down again. Hold the bead down with your thumb and be sure you poke your needle down right next to the bead. Pull your needle up through the cloth, put two beads on the needle and poke the needle down through the cloth. Push the needle up again and go between the two beads so that you're splitting the thread that is holding your beads together. After that, take your needle and push it through the second bead. Put two more beads on the needle and do the same thing. It usually takes about six beads to make the first circle.

After you've made your circle around the first bead, finish your round by pushing the needle through the first two beads you put on to form the circle and then push your needle down. If your thread is too short, tie it off and add another; if it isn't, push your needle up and continue to make another round.

After you've made enough rounds and your design is the way you want it to be, take a pair of scissors and trim off the extra pieces of felt around your design. Trim it close to your design, but don't cut into the design or cut any of the threads.

When you're finished with that, thread your needle and poke it up against the beads, right next to the felt. Put five beads on the needle and poke your needle down, bring your needle up again and go through the first two beads. Add three beads to the needle. Push your needle down through the felt and up again, going through the two beads. Continue doing this until you have

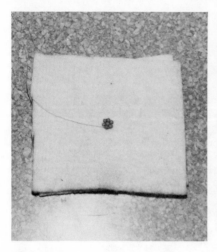

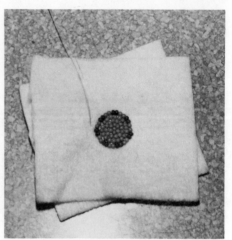

Beginning a rosette: "It usually takes about six beads to make the first circle."

After the center is complete, different-colored beads are used to create a pattern.

A modern-day rosette, one of the most popular necklaces in Alaska.

put an edge on your design. To finish the edge, put one bead on the needle, push your needle down through the two beads, and tie your thread off.

Thread your needle and push it down through any two beads that you put on for the trim. Add any number of beads and make your design; you can make it as long or as short as you want to. Poke your needle up through the next two beads on the trim. Bring your needle down and put on the same amount of beads and make the same design. Keep on making the chains until you have the right amount you want on it.

To make the necklace you simply take your string and line it up with the chains. With the string pointed to the opposite end, poke your needle through the two beads on the trim and start your necklace by adding beads. Make a design with the beads like ten white, ten blue, and five orange, and keep working the same design until the chain is long enough. After you've done that, push your needle through the two beads on the outside of your necklace and add the ten white and ten blue beads. When you come to the five orange, without adding any more orange beads, go through the five beads that are already on the chain. Keep working the chain until you come to the end, push your needle through the beads on the outside of your chain, and tie your thread off.

When you've finished the chain, find a piece of cardboard and cut it to fit the back of the necklace. Cut a piece of felt big enough to cover your cardboard and the back of your necklace and, using tiny stitches, sew it on.

Quills

This past summer Mom and I were sitting around the table and looking at some necklaces. She asked me if I knew anybody that had porcupine quills. I said no, so she said that we should go out and find a porcupine and get the quills to make a necklace.

About two weeks after our conversation I was walking down the beach and saw a porcupine. I didn't have anything with me to collect the quills with, so I ran back to the cabin to get something to gather them. The only thing I saw was a glove, so I thought that would have to do. I then quickly ran back to where I had seen the porcupine and it was still there. Holding the glove on one corner, I jabbed it at the porcupine's rear end to get the quills stuck in the glove. After I had enough, I played with the baby porcupine that was with its mother. The baby's quills were only about an inch long, too short to use. After about ten minutes I returned the squirming, scratching baby to its mom.

You can collect quills other ways by using a piece of cloth, Styrofoam, or anything handy. Some people kill the porcupine for cooking and save the quills for making a necklace. Another way, if you don't have anything else around, is to grab a large branch with lots of leaves on it so some quills will probably stick.

The next step is to take a piece of paper towel and spread the quills out. Then, take a dampened towel with a bar of soap rubbed on it so it will be kind of soapy. Wipe the quills back and forth and rub them around so they will be clean. After you have wiped the quills off, you have to cut off the tip so you won't poke yourself when you wear the necklace.

Now that you have the quills, you'll need the following materials to make a necklace:

1. Beading needle—a long, skinny needle
2. Thread—dental floss or strong sewing thread
3. Beads—small glass or wooden beads
4. Barrel clasps—clasps to hold the necklace together

Traditional porcupine-quill necklace.

To start, you have to thread the needle and tie on a barrel clasp so the beads and quills won't fall off. Then, you put a bead on; next put a quill on lengthwise so it goes through the hollow core; then you put on a bead and so on until you have a necklace as long as you want it. Finally tie the other end of the string onto the barrel clasps so the rest of the necklace won't fall off and you will be done.

If you want a real fancy necklace, you can put on different kinds of fur, such as beaver, otter, or rabbit, as spacers, and they really look beautiful.

Kikivik

The kikivik was like a small sewing kit and was usually made from scrap materials with a beaded trim. Often it had three compartments, but it could have any number of pockets in it. The kikivik usually held needles, thread or sinew, and other small treasures. These bags were used by men and women when they went on long journeys. A few women in the Bristol Bay area still know how to make these bags.

A completed kikivik.

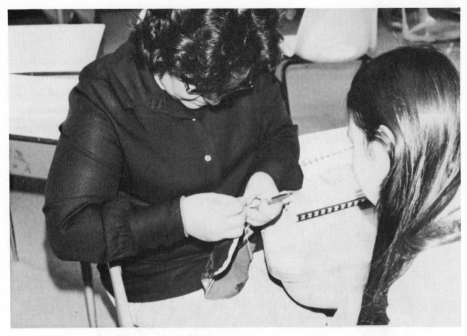

Barbara Peterson showing Emily Anderson how to sew a kikivik.

Evelyn Mike working on her kikivik.

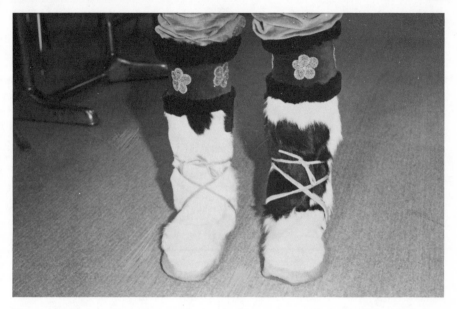

These boots are a beautiful example of skin sewing with beading in the Bristol Bay area.

Skin Sewing

The moose, caribou, beaver, and other animals have always played an important part in the lives of the people in our area, supplying them with food, utensils, and clothing. Sewing with fur was designed to look nice, to keep the cold weather out, and also to be practical. Here are some directions to make a few fur garments, which we learned from Anishia McCormick, who was born in Naknek in 1927 and has lived here all her life.

In order to make a fur hat you will need certain materials and tools. For the materials you will need about one and one-half yards of velvet, some thread that will match, yarn, and fur. Either otter, beaver, or muskrat is best because these furs are warmer and shed water. Mouton can also be used. You will need lining for the inside of the hat, sharp scissors, a skin needle, a razor blade, chalk and maybe a thimble.

Take the pattern piece that is shaped like a triangle and cut out four pieces from the lining. Sew two triangles (A&B) together. (See Diagram 1.) Sew the other two (C&D) together in the same manner.

Then sew (A&B) to (C&D), matching them carefully so there won't be a hole in the top of the hat. (See Diagram 2.)

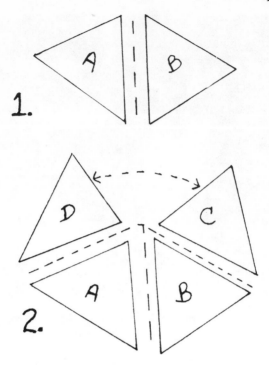

Take the same pattern piece and cut out four pieces from the velvet material. Sew them together in the same manner as the lining.

Using the pattern piece that is shaped like a foot, cut two pieces from the velvet and also two pieces from the fur. Sew the pieces of fur together on the dotted line as shown in the diagram. (See Diagram 3.) Do the same with the pieces of velvet. After you have finished sewing these pieces together, take the two pieces and put the right sides together; fold up about one quarter of an inch (to the wrong side) on the piece of velvet so the material won't ravel. Sew the pieces together using an overcast stitch. (See Diagram 4.) Be careful when sewing the fur because the fur sometimes will get caught in between the threads and will look ugly. This can be prevented by smoothing down the fur with your finger and then sewing. Do not sew over the straight line.

When sewing the pieces together, you can take a short cut by sewing the strings inside of the hat at that time instead of doing it later. It will also look better than doing it the other way. (See Diagram 5.)

Make your cloth or yarn strings, figure out where you want them placed on the flaps, place one end of the string under the velvet, and then sew over the strings.

After you have finished this, you have to connect the flap to the top part of the hat. Pin the lining and the velvet together, with the velvet on the outside. Match the ear flap to the other piece; pin them together and sew using an overcast stitch.

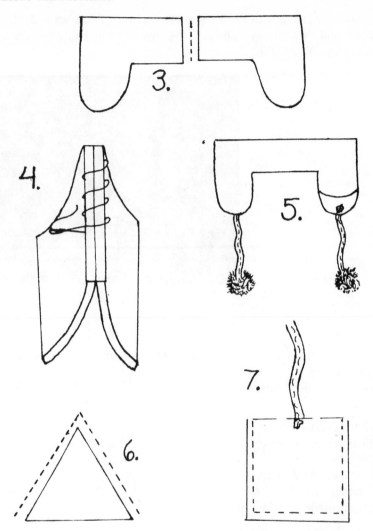

Using the piece that is shaped like a triangle, place it on the fur (wrong side) and trace around the pattern using a piece of chalk or a pen. Cut the piece out using a sharp razor blade.

Pin the fur triangle to the top of the hat, so it will stay in place while you are sewing on it. Using a skin needle, sew the triangle to the velvet, but sew only two sides of the triangle to the velvet. When you finish, there will be the bottom of the triangle to sew. (See Diagram 6.) Fold the piece of fur under the hat, then sew it to the inside lining.

The tassels for the hat can be made either from yarn or leftover pieces of fur. The yarn tassels are made like any other tassels. To make the fur tassels, cut a square piece from the fur. Sew the square on three sides; turn inside out; make a knot in the yarn string; then weave a stitch on the end that is open. Place the string with the knot at the end into the open end, then pull the needle and thread very tightly so that the fur ball will close up around the knot. (See Diagram 7.)

Completed fur hat.

Now we will describe how to make gamuksuks, or slippers. These are another example of the skin sewing done in this area.

First you will need these materials:

1. Button and carpet thread
2. Skin sewing needle
3. Scissors
4. Fur (for the uppers)
5. Leather (for the sole)
6. Razor blade (single edge)

First, trace the pattern on the wrong side of the leather and fur; then cut the pieces out with the razor blade.

Next, sew the toe pattern piece to the long strip, using the same overcast stitch as in the fur hat instructions. This completes the top part (uppers) of the slipper.

After you sew them together, sew the sole to the top part and make sure the slipper is inside out when you are stitching. This completes the basic slipper.

You may line it if you wish, and add a one-inch strip of fur around the top for trim. Roll the trim over and stitch it to the lining or the inside of your slipper.

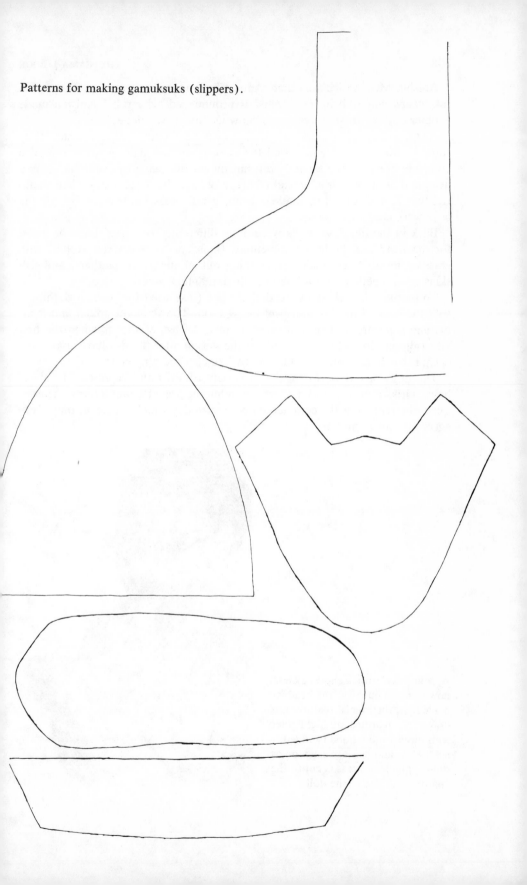

Patterns for making gamuksuks (slippers).

Anishia McCormick's mother, Anna Chukan, made the cu ruk for us. Cu ruk means play doll in Yup'ik and is pronounced "chu ruk." Anishia made another doll for us step-by-step to show us how it was done.

Anna and Anishia made the doll shown here out of rag material. They started with the head and sewed the eyes, nose, and hair. Anishia stuffed a complete body for the second doll; but the cu ruk made by Anna has only a head and arms, which is typical of many older dolls. Frequently when material was scarce, they just made a head, arms, dress, and no body. All the boys were clothed in pants.

Back in the old days, dolls were quite different. They used bone or wood for the head and body, or sometimes skins and old material stuffed with grass or moss. They made the clothing out of fur, duck feathers, and fish skins sewn together with a bone needle and animal sinew.

To prepare the fish skins for doll clothes (also used for regular clothing), split the back of the fish and peel the skin off. The skins are tough and flexible and waterproof. The best time to make the fish clothes is when the first king salmon run and in the middle of the season after the fish have spawned.

Cu ruk's dress is made of blue and white checked gingham.

The dolls of old were made in a variety of sizes and represented babies, boys, girls, mothers and fathers, grandmothers and grandfathers. This is quite different from the commercial dolls of today which represent only teenagers or young children.

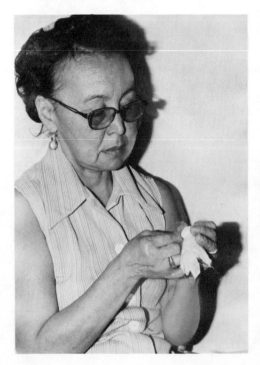

Anishia McCormick shows a class how to make cu-ruks: the head is made first; then facial features are drawn; the features are highlighted with thread and a hood is added; next, arms and legs are sewn on as shown; finally, a dress is cut to the approximate size of the doll.

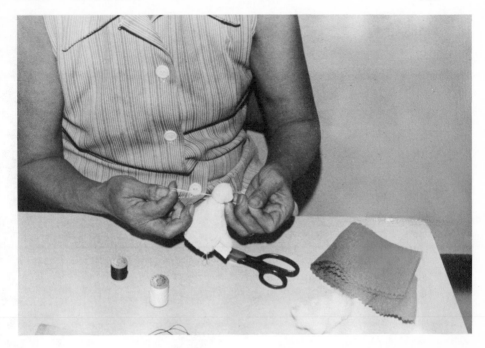

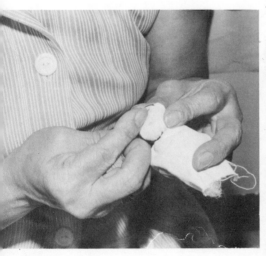

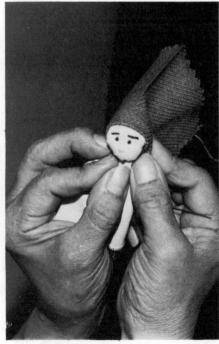

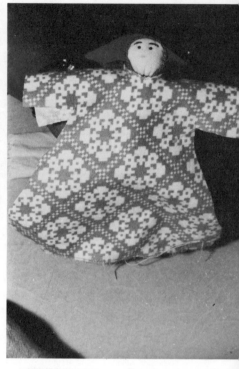

Finished cu-ruk.

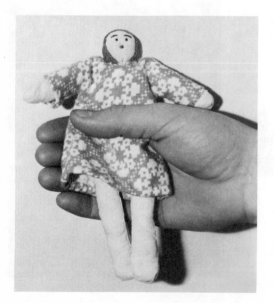

SIX CENTS A FISH

by: Carvel Zimin   revised by: Sheila Hutson

Mary Klein Zimin is a set netter, born in Naknek in 1911. She married Nick Zimin in 1929 and moved to South Naknek.

Mary's husband Nick was a winterman (caretaker) at the Diamond O cannery in 1929. He received sixty-five dollars a month working for the Alaska Packers (APA) cannery as a winterman. During the summer months Nick fished for salmon for his main income, as did a majority of the local residents.

Mary could not work because women were not allowed to work in the canneries. In 1933 Mary and some others went to the APA superintendent and asked to fish "set net" on the beach. The superintendent said he would give it a try. Soon Mary and nine others became some of the first commercial set netters in Bristol Bay.

The price per salmon was set at six cents by the canneries. In 1935 the price increased two cents because of a small union that was established in the bay. "I remember in my dad's days, he was only getting two cents a fish. Before the unions came, what the company offered, we took."

The first set netters numbered ten, mainly old men who couldn't fish on the boats, and women. The first women were Funa Tretikoff, Nina Harris, Palogia Melgonak, Lesha Savo, and Mary Zimin. The men were Nick Melgonak, Sam Krasskoff, Dan Estrada, Golia Panikan, and an unknown Greek. Their sites were located on the beach between Diamond O and Diamond M canneries.

For the first few years APA gave the set netters free nets to fish with, as well as free food. The food usually came in a box or a case containing coffee, tea, milk, cheese, eggs, fruits, vegetables, canned meats, onions, and potatoes. The canneries also gave free ropes and free kerosene for the lamps if needed. In later years, other fishermen came and moved down below Diamond M and established sites. They were Annie Hagen, Olga Kihle (Malone), Evon Olympic, Golick Issac, and the postmaster Old Man Tory. After the 1950s the beach was filled with set net sites from Diamond O to Johnson Hill. Most of the fishermen picked a place where they wanted to fish; but Fish and Wildlife regulations said they had to be 300 feet apart and couldn't move above Diamond O cannery.

A few years later Naknek opened up to set netting also, and they fished from a cannery called Nornak on out. Most of the fishermen stayed in the Diamond M and Diamond O bunkhouses and walked down to tend their sites every "slack" tide. The season was only one month long, usually from June 25 to July 25. Fish and Wildlife boats came from King Salmon to tell the superintendents when the season opened and the superintendents told the fishermen. They didn't have radios then.

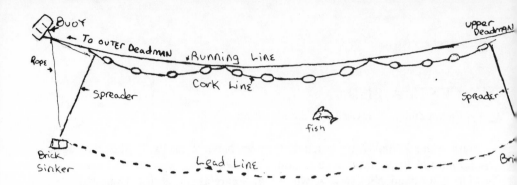

They never had to open and close the season several times a year as they do now. "I think that the Japanese have made a big effect in the change in fishing." The only time the set netters had to pull up their nets was on the weekends. Every Saturday morning at nine they pulled up and Monday morning they set their nets back out again.

Alaska Packers had a couple of Dodge pickup trucks, and they used them to pick up the fish from the sites and take them to the canneries.

To set net, you used "deadmen," which were either stakes, pipes, or coolers that were buried in the ground with a "running line" between them. On the running line you would attach your "corkline," which is the upper part of the net, by means of string. On the end of your net you would put a buoy with a Fish and Wildlife number on it. Back in the earlier days of set netting, the people had long, thin boards they used as "spreaders" to keep the net apart and to keep the "lead" line, which is the heavy bottom part of the net, directly below the cork line.

There are other factors that pertain to set netting. Considering certain weather conditions and times of the year, a person could predict how many fish he was going to catch. Usually the southeast wind would be rough and it would bring the fish out in the bay closer to shore. When it was calm, the fish would usually lie around outside in the bay. The east wind would take the fish to the Kvichak side. Also, on rough days the beach was easier to travel because the sand would get hard; when it was calm, the beach would get soft.

At the beginning of the season, the set netters would catch more fish on the outside of the nets; as the season progressed, the fish would come up the net. At the end of the season, set netters would get more fish along the rock line on the beach because they would be running for the gravel. When the season began, if the salmon were small, the fishermen would have a good season because there would be a lot of fish. If the salmon were big, there wouldn't be as many. When there were a lot of jellyfish in your net during the season, you wouldn't get as many fish.

Set netting hasn't changed much in the past forty years. Mary Zimin, Nina Harris, and a few of the first ten in the Naknek area are still fishing and probably won't let up for quite some time. Set netting is a way of life for a lot of people like Mary and Nina. The only big factor that has changed is that there are more fishermen and fewer fish.

SMELTING

by: Rosalie Johnson
revised by: Dianne Moorcroft
contacts: Emily Paterson, Alvin Aspelund, and Freda Aspelund

Smelting is a type of fishing in Naknek, King Salmon, and the surrounding Bristol Bay area. You can use a gill net and fish on the beach or wait until the river freezes and jig through the ice in the winter.

In the fall the smelt enter the mouth of the Naknek River. As the ice forms and freezes over the river, they move up the river. In the early spring they reach their breeding ground and spawn. They are anywhere from five to six inches long and are blackish-gray in color. Eight medium-sized fish together weigh approximately one pound. Some people say they smell like cucumbers.

To smelt, you will need to get a gill net or a scoop. A gill net is similar to a minnow seine. Its mesh is anywhere from one quarter to one inch. A scoop is a round hoop with webbing of the same mesh around it. When using a scoop, you stand in one place. You take the scoop and dip it into the water. The net can either go with the tide or against it. But very few fish are caught by using the scoop net. Gillnetting, one family uses a fifty-foot by six-foot net with a one-inch mesh. You'd want a lead line and a corkline on the net. You'd probably want to put sticks at each end of the net so it doesn't roll up. In addition, you will need to wear boots—either knee boots or hip boots.

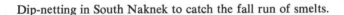

Dip-netting in South Naknek to catch the fall run of smelts.

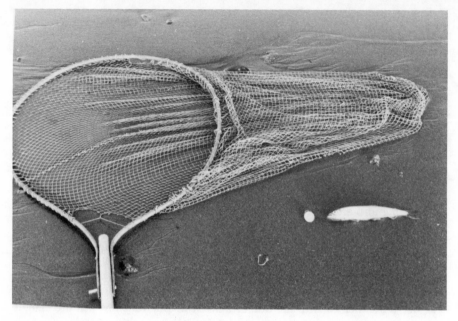

A scoop and smelt. Smelts are generally about five inches long.

The people here in Naknek and South Naknek start smelting in October. It really doesn't matter if you smelt in the daytime or the nighttime. You usually smelt on the ebb tide, which would be three to three and one-half hours after high tide. To smelt, one person stands waist-deep in the water and the other stands near the shore and then walks thirty to fifty feet with the current. After the distance is reached, the person at the deep end walks toward the shore and when he gets to shore, they put the fish in a bucket.

High Water Slack

After the ice gets to be six to eight inches thick, you can start jigging for smelt. You will need several things to jig with. Some people think Lujohns (brand name for a type of hook) seem to work the best, but anything that flashes red works—even a red piece of cloth, and if you don't have a lure, a small trout hook will work. And you will need something to attach your fishing line to, any short stick will do. You will also need something to put your fish in. Jigging for smelt is done on high water slack.

If there isn't already a hole to fish through, you will have to chop one with an ice pick. You'll have to find a place where the water isn't too deep or too shallow. A good-sized hole is six inches and it can be bigger. Just to be on the safe side, you should smooth the edges off or you're liable to get your line hooked up. After you get all finished chopping, you're ready to jig for smelt.

Jigging for smelt: sometimes you can catch four or five a minute.

When you let your hook and line through the hole you'll have to let enough out so it goes just past the bottom of the ice. Move your pole up and down with a flick of the wrist, once every three to five seconds. When you feel a tug on your line you pull your line up, but not too fast or the fish might get loose.

Smiley Knutsen showing his catch.

THE WAY THEY FLEW

by: Shawn Aspelund and Danny Seybert
revised by: Annette Nestegard
contacts: Roy Smith, Eddie King, George Tibbetts, Sr., George Tibbetts, Jr.,
Martin Severson, Alvin Aspelund, and Fred Kraun

Commercial bush flying based in this area originated in the late 1940s, although there had been frequent planes in the area from other places. In 1923 the first plane came in, and it arrived on floats. For our article we interviewed some of the resident pilots in the area.

"Hours of boredom interrupted by moments of stark terror" was the definition of bush flying we got from George Tibbetts, Sr. Speaking of stark terror, we asked a few of the pilots about some of the more exciting or interesting flights they'd encountered and we got the following from Big George. "I remember hauling Anishia McCormick to Dillingham about five o'clock in the morning when she was about to have Glenn. We went clear over there because there was no radio contact. This was in the middle of the winter. [We] flew clear over there within a mile of the place and couldn't get in. [We] flew clear back to Naknek and she was really getting close. [We] landed on the field and Gunnar Berggren was driving around in a truck. I went alongside him, got out of the plane, and said, 'Take her to town. Get her home quick!' She had the baby right in her dress when Gunnar was packing her into the house. We later learned that this story was published in newspapers nationwide."

Fred Kraun told us this story about one of his many interesting flights. "We were flying a freighter back from Cape Lisburne, Alaska, to Anchorage. We picked up a gal at Unalakleet who had problems delivering a baby. It was somewhere between Unalakleet and McGrath that the baby was born. Course we had two midwives along who took care of her, but the baby was born in a stack of lumber. They later named it Lester McGrath, Lester being the name of the captain of the trip."

George Tibbetts, Jr., gave us this response to the same question. "Exciting? I try not to make any of my flights exciting."

We asked Alvin Aspelund the same question and he replied, "Well, they are all exciting. Each and every one is different. Sometimes you push the weather. When I say push the weather, I refer to it in that manner because there were no local radios at that time to ask for weather—so therefore you had to go and see for yourself. If it was bad, you always turned back till later when the weather cleared. It was pretty hairy at times, but each one was different and exciting. When you're young like that, you seem to look for excitement. The more you push the weather, the more you seem to enjoy it."

We received this story about picking up another pilot who had piled up from George Tibbetts, Jr. "It was in a blizzard and we used rather interesting techniques to find him. I was flying around on instruments at low level, but you could see a little bit here and there. He had a radio that worked and I could hear him talking, so we narrowed down the search and we found him pretty fast. We gave the directions to a ground search crew from Egegik. It was so bad on the ground that the vehicle [of the ground crew] kept going in circles."

Some of the first resident pilots in the area were Nick Monsen, Ed Hansen, Fred Kraun, Andrew Peterson, Bill Reagon, Lloyd Zimin, Melvin Monsen, Earl Aspelund, George Tibbetts, Sr., Elmer Nicholson, Stan Chmiel, Babe Alsworth, Alvin Aspelund, John and Albert Ball, and Herman Herrmann.

Although the first resident planes came in in the forties, it is said that a plane came to the area in 1923 and attempted to land somewhere on Branch River, but flipped. When they pulled it out of the river, it was pulled apart. It took all the next summer to fix it, but they flew it out.

There was also another plane that came on skis in 1923 during the winter. It was flown in because Mrs. Christianson had become ill and needed to be flown out. The Christiansons worked for the Bureau of Fisheries.

Eddie Deigh, Frank Dorbrandt, and H. N. Evans in front of one of the first planes in the area. Early flying was characterized as "hours of boredom interrupted by moments of stark terror."

Mail plane at Naknek in the 1930s.

First plane to land at
Naknek in 1930s.

In the forties the only instruments that the pilots had were primarily an altimeter, compass, engine RPM gauge, and an oil pressure gauge. As for radios, most pilots thought that they were excess weight. Some used HF. All the flying that they did was strictly "seat of the pants flying" (VFR).

Also back in the late forties, there were very few airfields so you either flew with floats in the summer or with skis in the winter. They did not use wheels mainly because there weren't very good fields and they also thought that if their engines quit they'd have more places to land with floats or skis. Then after a while, people started building airfields and more and more people started to use wheels.

The first fields in the Bristol Bay area were at King Salmon, Dillingham, Iguigig, and Illiamna. At Naknek they landed on the beaches or at Airplane Lake. The Dillingham field (the one in town) was built in the early forties by the Air Force to fly out a crashed plane. The fields at Iguigig and Illiamna were built sometime before that. The field in Naknek was built in the early forties by the villagers with a bulldozer that was borrowed from a local cannery. They built it out of a road going to Airplane Lake.

"Most of the accidents in this area are caused by pilot error," and most of them are pilots "doing something they shouldn't be, when they shouldn't be doing it.

"You could be the worst pilot in the world, and if you know it and act accordingly, you'll never have a wreck. So it's judgment and then, of course, in this country there are a lot of bad conditions. I mean, you're not always on nice runways."

Some of the other hazards of bush flying in this area are weather, field conditions, landing on beaches, sand dunes, lakes, and places that you haven't been for a long time where conditions have changed.

In the late forties, there were very few airfields, so pilots flew with floats in the summer or skis in the winter.

One of the worst things about bush flying is the weather. Some of the types of weather bush pilots cope with are fog, ice fog, whiteouts, wind, snow, and cold weather, which sometimes can be very hazardous to the plane and pilot. George Tibbetts, Jr., said, "In the early days, kinda the rule of thumb was to fly till the visibility was down to one-half mile, then it was a 180° turn and back to where you started." We also got a comment from George Tibbetts, Jr., about bad weather. "During December, January you have nothing but fog, rain, and snow all the time. It's just part of the deal. Flying requires, if you're really going to get around, that you've got to be able to fly instruments and know the terrain to do the job right."

Most of the bush pilots started with either Taylor Crafts or J 3's since they were cheaper and easier to handle. Since most of them were just starting to fly in the late forties, J 3's were good to learn in. When the pilots became more experienced, they started trading their planes for, or buying, larger and more reliable planes.

Alvin Aspelund said, "I started in a J 3. Witters Flying Service, which is where I learned to fly, had nothing but J 3's in 1947. Then in 1948, when I continued flying in California, this guy had a PA 12 Super Cruiser and I put some time in on that. Then when I went to Seattle, Nick Monsen, Ed Hansen, and I started to really put time in T-Crafts before we got ours—which we had bought in Wyoming and were having flown to Montana. From there we flew them up here. My favorite all-around plane is a PA 11 with a ninety-horse engine on floats."

Many pilots in this area have a special type of plane that they like best. Roy Smith said, "My favorite plane would have to be a Maule." George Tibbetts, Jr., said, "I like a Cherokee with tricycle gear and positive steering."

Bush flying became a way of life in the Bristol Bay area and in many other areas simply because it was the only transportation readily available to the people.

We thought Fred Kraun summed it up pretty well when he stated, "Years ago I got tired of walking and it looked like the easy way to go."

Bristol Bay's mail
plane, which made
deliveries in the fifties.

DOGSLED EXPRESS

by: Dennis Herrmann
revised by: Sandy Coghill
contacts: Herman Herrmann

This story was told to me by my father. It is not a legend. It is a true story.

Before there were any airplanes, the mail was hauled by dog team. The dog team was hired at Dillingham, which was known then as Snag Point. There was a trader over there by the name of J. C. Lowe, who hired the dog team. The dog team started out at Dillingham; it came all the way up the Nushagak River over to Portage Creek, down to the first patch of woods—Nakeen—up as far as Levelock. They crossed the river at Levelock and then came down to Koggiung. They didn't have a post office there, but it was a mail stop. From there it went to Naknek. Then they went across Naknek River and on down to Egegik and Becharof Lake. From there they went over to a place called Kanatak. Kanatak was a port always open, even during the winter months. They had a mail boat that came in there once a month.

The mail was limited, you couldn't get parcel post or anything like that. Only first class mail for all those little places amounted to quite a bit, and they could only take a few hundred pounds in a sled.

They had to carry dog food and two men on the sled. There were usually fifteen to eighteen dogs and it took a lot of food for that many dogs.

Many times the trip was made when the weather was cold and it was fairly

Nick Zimin's dogteam in 1929.

good going. Sometimes you would get mild weather, then everything started thawing until it was all bare ground. The sled had to be pushed over the bare ground.

They took advantage of all the small lakes and swamps that were frozen to get the sled going smoothly. Sometimes it took a whole month to make the trip. There have been some winters that they got mail only two or three times because of the weather conditions. There were quite a number of hardships in this mail hauling because it was done when it was almost summer conditions. You had to go about ten miles up a creek to get across it . . . when you could have done it in a few hours when the weather was cold. So conditions stayed like this for a few years. When the mailman did come, it was a big time in the old town.

They got the mail once a month or nearly so. All the towns and villages between saw the mailman go by and hitched up their dogs to follow him. The mailman was a really good person. When he came, that meant a dance in town. The best foods were gotten out when he came and everyone had a great time. Everybody looked forward to the mail.

There were even some times that the mailman came by boat. If the dog team could only get as far as Egegik, the mailman hired a boat. The boat went up to Naknek and Koggiung and delivered the mail. Then he went on to Dillingham. Those were winters when the winter was very mild.

FISH EGGS

by: Leslie Savo
revised by: Artie Johnson, Jr., and Randy Zimin
contacts: Judy Fischer and Elizabeth Phelps

One of the delicacies around here in Bristol Bay is boiled fish eggs. During the short summer while the salmon are running, many families putting away their subsistence fish for winter will use the fresh eggs for a snack after the fish have been stored. The females are the only ones that have eggs in them, that would be about 60 percent of the fish. The eggs are in skeins that are about six to eight inches long; two skeins are found in each fish.

The way Judy Fischer prepares boiled fish eggs is this: first she takes the fish skeins and washes them with salt water and lets them drain for a few minutes; next she puts them in boiling hot water and boils them for about twenty to twenty-five minutes. They should look chalk pink when they're done. She said they remind her of seagull eggs.

Another way to use fish eggs is to make caviar out of them. To make it, you take the eggs and separate every little egglet, wash them off with water, then drain them and put them in a jar with salt and lemon juice. Let them stand for about three or four days in a refrigerator and then you can eat them as they've been cured. You can also make a gelatin mix by mixing gelatin with the caviar and eating it like that. Judy said she wouldn't want to

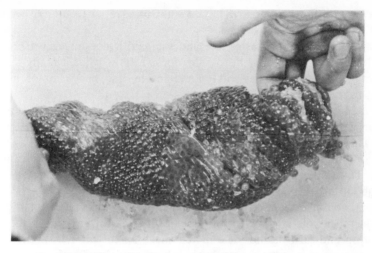

Raw salmon roe in egg case, prior to cooking.

eat too much of it, though. She said it's different but it doesn't taste all that bad.

People also use the fish milt which comes from the male fish. It has iron, calcium, and vitamin C in it. What Judy does with milt is wash it with a salt solution and fry it in butter or any kind of vegetable oil. You can cut the milt in little pieces or strips and roll them in flour and cook them for five to ten

Uutuqtwa students show advisor, Kurt Jaehning, how to cook fish eggs.

minutes until they get crispy. If you want to save some for the winter, just treat them like you do fish eggs.

I asked Judy what it tastes like and she said it doesn't taste like the eggs and it doesn't have a fishy taste—she doesn't know what it really tastes like. It's crispy on the outside, soft on the inside, and has a lot of nutritional value in it.

Some people around here use eggs for bait. Judy said she uses salmon eggs of any kind. The fish eggs don't have to be fresh but they're better if they are. The way she prepares bait is to take the skeins of fish eggs, lay them on a board, and slant the board upwards so all the moisture can drain out of the eggs. Then she sprinkles salt or borax on them and lets them stay like that for about three days.

Next, you take them off there, cut them up into little pieces, and put them in a jar; then you light a piece of paper with a match, throw it in the jar, and hurry up and turn the lid. The match sucks all the air out of there. If you want to store them, just put the jar in a basement or refrigerator.

Judy keeps her bait in a refrigerator for over a year. When you put it on a hook, just take a piece and hook it through.

A LITTLE ABOUT A "MUCKEE"

by: Emily Anderson and Charlotte Kie
revised by: Diana Cook
contact: Rose Kie

Many of the people in Naknek and the surrounding villages really enjoy taking steam baths. To some, a steam bath makes them relax. It is also called a muckee.

A steam bath, or muckee, is a bathhouse where you throw water on rocks to make steam. It can be built in many different ways and sizes. It usually has two rooms, a washroom and a dressing room. You build a steam bath just like a house with two rooms and a cement or wooden floor with holes for the water to drain through. Cement floors are better because they never wear out and they won't catch fire.

Make the walls thick and insulated so they will keep the heat in. The materials needed to build a steam bath are wood, sheet iron, bricks, rocks, a fifty-gallon oil drum, and cement if you want that particular kind of floor. It really doesn't make any difference what kind of wood you use.

To build a stove you first make a brick wall, or another kind of barrier that won't burn, around the fifty-gallon oil or gas drum. On one end, cut a square or round hole for the opening. Then, put rocks between the wall and the drum. You can use any kind of rocks, but porous rocks are good for absorbing heat and water.

Weld a door on the drum to cover the opening and make sure that two other holes are in that end of the drum and are aligned so the larger hole is

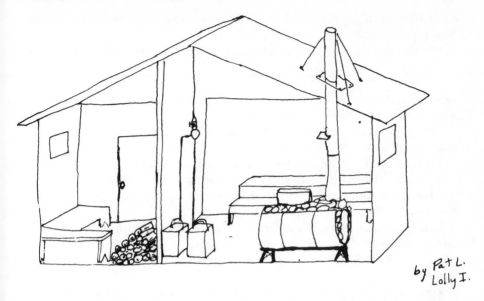

by Pat L.
Lolly I.

The muckee, or steambath, usually has both a main bathing room and a dressing room.

on the bottom. The larger hole is the damper. Now cut a hole on the top of the drum for the smokestack. (Be sure to insulate around the hole in the roof where the smokestack goes through.) After you do that, weld two iron rods on top to keep the water cans evenly flat on the stove, so they won't fall off. There are different kinds of stoves used in a steam bath and this is only one of them.

Several people have their own ways to light the stove. One way is by first chopping up little pieces of wood, then putting bigger pieces on to make the fire burn well. You can put a little stove oil on the wood so it will burn faster. After you've done that, you open the damper, which is the large hole

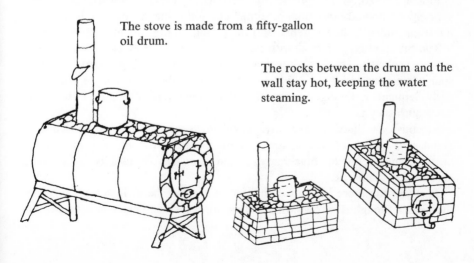

The stove is made from a fifty-gallon oil drum.

The rocks between the drum and the wall stay hot, keeping the water steaming.

on the stove, to let the fire breathe. You can close and open the damper whenever you want.

For the water system you should have two five-gallon cans or some kind of big pot or container on the stove to heat from the firing stove. The cold water could be in a fifteen-gallon metal trash can, or any other large container. Put it somewhere on the floor where it won't get hot. You can have as many cold water containers as you want.

The temperature you can get in a steam bath varies with the person. It ranges from about 190° to 200° and up.

For lights you can use candles, electricity, or a kerosene lamp. It would be best to keep the kerosene lamp in the dressing room, because it would get too hot in the washroom. Use the candle in the washroom if you don't have electricity, or candles in both rooms.

Taking a steam bath is similar to taking a sponge bath except it's hot. Some steam baths have one or more benches for you to sit on. You don't get as much heat on the lower bench. You can stay in there as long as you want.

You use basins for washing and a dipper, which can be made out of a small pot or a can nailed to a handle (stick), for getting the water into your basin.

NIKKUTIMUGKITE: FOOD INGREDIENTS

compiled by: Teresa Johnson, Mary Murray, Doreen Williams and Sheila Lind

In every one of these recipes the main ingredients, such as the berries, fish or caribou, come directly from the land. No one plants the berries or herds the caribou (although they used to herd reindeer); everything is wild. The only restrictions we have in our hunting are from the Department of Fish and Game.

Picking, cooking, and preserving the berries is a lot of work, but it is a very enjoyable and rewarding pastime. The following recipes are local, coming from students, their parents, and the people of the surrounding villages.

The first few recipes deal with berries. The cranberries used in these recipes are called lowbush cranberries. They are tiny, yellow, hard, and very sour when they aren't ripe. When they get ripe, about the end of August or early September, they get a sort of dull red; they are also soft. Later on in the month they get mushy.

Lowbush cranberries have tiny, waxy green leaves all the time. They lie about two inches off the tundra. These berries grow in slightly swampy areas; reindeer moss, blackberries, and crowberries usually grow right around the cranberries.

There is one more kind of cranberry that grows here; it doesn't grow on the tundra though. It grows where there are a lot of trees. These berries are called highbush cranberries and grow on tall bushes three to five feet off the ground.

If you handle these berries too much your hands get stained. It takes a lot of soap and water with lots of elbow grease to get cranberry stains off your hands.

The following pages include recipes for agutuk (note different spelling for this food in the Yukon-Kuskokwim and the Bristol Bay regions of Southwestern Alaska). This word always brings a twinkle to the eyes and a delightful taste to the mouth of many Alaskans. Be creative when you make agutuk. Mix berries; try salmonberries and mix them with blackberries. Just blackberries by themselves are the best.

AGUTUK

1½ cups shortening
2 cups sugar
6 or 8 cups berries (any kind)

Cream the shortening and sugar. Add berries, perhaps a cup at a time. Use your own judgment for the amount of berries.

MARY LOU ASPELUND

SALMONBERRY JELLY

4 cups juice
7½ cups sugar
1 bottle Certo Fruit Pectin

To the measured juice in the saucepan, add the sugar and mix well. Place over high heat and bring to a boil, stirring constantly. At once stir in the Certo and bring to a full boil. Boil hard for one minute, stirring constantly. Remove from heat, skim off foam, and pour into jam jars. Seal the jars at once with hot paraffin.

PAM MYERS

CRANBERRY AND WHITEFISH AGUTUK

1 cup shortening   Desired amount of cranberries
2 to 2½ cups sugar   2 cups boiled and shredded whitefish
Few drops water

Wash your hands and let them remain wet. Cream the sugar and shortening. Add a few drops of water and mix well with hands until fluffy. Add desired amount of cranberries alternately with whitefish. Don't worry about it being too sour, the whitefish and sugar take away the bitterness. Serve as a dessert.

CAROL HESTER

CRANBERRY JUICE

    2 cups water
    1 quart berries
    1 cup sugar

Heat water and berries at medium heat for eight to ten minutes, then boil
for two or three minutes. Put through a strainer. Heat the strained juice to
boiling point, then add the sugar and boil for two minutes. Pour into steril-
ized bottles and seal.

    To serve, dilute to taste one part cranberry juice and one part orange
juice, sweet apple cider, or other juices.

MARTHA JOHNSON

CRANBERRY SAUCE

    4 cups berries   2 cups water if using Certo
    1 cup water without Certo   2 cups sugar

(If berries are extra ripe, use Certo; if berries are firm, use no Certo.)
    Bring the berries and water to boil. Add the sugar. Cook approximately
twenty minutes; if this isn't as thick as desired, or it doesn't jell, add a little
Certo.

MARY LOU ASPELUND

CRANBERRY "KETCHUP"

    4 cups berry pulp   2 cups sugar
    1 teaspoon cinnamon   ½ teaspoon salt
    1 teaspoon cloves   1 cup vinegar
    1 teaspoon allspice   Dash cayenne
    1 teaspoon pepper

Combine ingredients and boil rapidly until thickened, about 15 minutes.
Pour into bottles and seal with paraffin.

PAM MYERS

FRIED PTARMIGAN

    1 cleaned and cut-up ptarmigan
    Cooking oil
    A bowl with ½ cup flour and
        ½ cup cornmeal (may need more)
    Salt and pepper to taste

Preheat the pan on your stove to about 360° (medium on butane or electric
stoves) and put in the oil. Roll pieces of ptarmigan in the flour mixture and
place them in the pan. Fry until golden, crispy, and completely done (about

fifteen minutes). Salt and pepper to taste. Serve as a main dish or cold as a snack.

Some good sauces to put on it are sweet and sour sauce, ketchup, and Worcestershire sauce.

CAROL HESTER

CURING MEAT IN BRINE

Brine: 1 cup rock salt to 1 quart water (make enough to cover meat—about 2½–3 gallons)
5 pounds sugar

½ ounce saltpeter
½ cup mixed whole pickling spice
25 pounds meat chunks (¼ to ½ pound each)

Dissolve the rock salt, sugar, and saltpeter in water, add the pickling spice, and let it cool. Add the meat to the liquid and weight it down so it remains covered. Let the mixture stand for two to three weeks. Remove the meat, rinse it, and hang in a cool dry place until dry. A fan helps to dry the meat in damp weather. Slice and use like dried beef.

GINNY LUNSFORD

CARIBOU SOUP

Caribou are abundant in this area and therefore we eat the meat often. There are many ways to cook caribou and the tasty one is caribou soup!

First you take a part of the caribou, like the leg or back, and wash it till it's clean. Then cut it into small squares with a sharp knife.

Put it in a roaster or a heavy pot and add just enough hot water to cover the meat. Let the meat cook with the water for an hour and a half.

Now you add:

1 cup rice
1 can tomatoes

Carrots and/or peas
Potatoes chopped in squares

Let this all cook together for at least half an hour.

KATHERINE PETERSON BOSTON

DRY MEAT

My mother's name is Catherine Mike. She lives in Kokhanok. This recipe for dry meat I learned by watching my mom make it.

Take the meat from the hindquarter of a moose. First, cut the meat in strips; some are seven inches long and some are three inches. They are usually three to four inches wide. Then you salt them with regular salt, but not very much salt. Next you hang the meat outside where it is warm. Mom usually makes them in the spring or summer.

In the winter she hangs them by the stove so that they can dry. To check if they are dry, she cracks them, and if they are not dry in the middle, they are put back until they are. A good way to eat them is with melted butter and pepper.

EVELYN MIKE

CANNED FISH

For this project you will need twelve one-quart jars with self-sealing lids; they have a rim to fasten them and a top piece that fits on the jar exactly. The inside part has some rubber around the rim; when the jars get to the boiling point, they seal themselves securely. You will also need about six or seven medium-sized fish.

Chop the heads off the fish and cut them into about two-inch squares. Put one heaping teaspoon of salt into the bottom of each jar. Stuff the fish into the jars and pack down firmly. Put another heaping teaspoon of salt on the top. Screw the lids on and boil for about two hours. Take them out and keep tightening the lids as the jars are cooling. Store in a cool place.

HELEN HERRMANN

BEAVER OR PORCUPINE POT ROAST

1 small beaver or porcupine
1 cup flour
salt and pepper to taste
water
4 bay leaves, broken in half
1 large onion

Cut the beaver or porcupine into small pieces. Sift flour, salt, and pepper together (you may want to add other spices). Roll meat in this flour mixture. Brown meat to desired brownness and add a little water, bay leaves, and onion chopped to desired size pieces. Let simmer over low heat until meat is tender and done, stirring every so often to prevent from sticking.

MOOSE OR CARIBOU JERKY

3 pounds moose or caribou meat
½ cup salt
1 teaspoon pepper
1 teaspoon minced garlic
Dash Tabasco
⅓ gallon water

Cut meat into thin strips of desired length and width. Mix salt, pepper, garlic, and Tabasco into the water. Soak meat strips in this solution overnight, drain, and hang them to dry, preferably in a warm dry place. Jerky is ready to eat when it is dry and crackly. It takes anywhere from two to five days.

PICKLED FISH

First you soak the salmon in salt water for a day. Then you take the salted salmon and soak all the salt out with cold water.

Cut salmon into strips of one or two inches each.

Find a glass jar or crock, or something enamel. The size depends on how much you are going to make.

Then you make layers of onions, pickle, pepper, and any other spices you might want, with fish in between each layer. Combine one part white vinegar, one part water, and ½ part white sugar; mix as much as suits your taste; pour over the layers.

Let the fish set for three days in a cool place and then it will be ready to eat.

BETTY MAE PETERSON

GUMCHALK

Get a smoked salmon or dried fish. Put it in enough water to cover the fish. Boil it until it is tender or until your fork goes through the meat and the skin.

Eat it with agutuk, Sailor Boy crackers (pilot bread), and tea.

MARLENE JOHNSON

FISH SKINS

For a little snack, burn some smoked fish skins. Just put them on a fork and burn them over a blue flame or a campfire. Do this until they are crispy. Eat them plain or have a little agutuk on the side.

MARLENE JOHNSON

KANARRTUK

This recipe is called kanarrtuk, meaning frozen fish. Take a fish and gut it, taking out all the guts and backbone blood. Wash it good and clean with cool water.

All you have to do next is hang it out to dry on a fish rack and wait until it gets about medium dry (not quite stiff).

When it is done drying, put it in the freezer or somewhere very cold and wait until it is frozen hard. Take it out, cut it into bite-sized pieces, and eat it with seal oil or salt.

KATHERINE GROAT

Seagull Eggs

by: Roberta Deigh
revised by: Mary Murray
contact: Judy Fischer

"Oh ya, it's just like Easter egg hunting in early spring," says Judy Fischer about gathering seagull eggs, a local springtime event. Judy began when she was seven or eight years of age. Another resident started when she was about twelve. They all picked seagull eggs together.

It's said about the best time of year to pick seagull eggs is in the early spring or during the last week in May and the first two weeks in June. This is about the time when the seagulls start laying eggs. You can go early in the morning and get quite a few, but, then again, you can also go in the afternoon after high noon. Actually, you can go out any time of the day, just as long as you beat the others.

They say about the best place to find seagull eggs is on a deserted island where there are no animals or other birds to harm or take the eggs. Also, it doesn't matter what type of weather it is, just so long as the seagulls are laying eggs.

You can boil seagull eggs and eat them that way, or you can mix them in pancakes and cakes or such. But you can't fry them; if you do, your eggs will turn out very rubbery—you probably couldn't cut them. But when you use them in cakes and such, they rise about half an inch higher than if you were to use a regular chicken egg.

There are a couple of ways to keep seagull eggs fresh. Put them into preservative water glasses and put them into the freezer, or you can just refrigerate them.

ONE MAN REMEMBERS

by: Dianne Moorcroft and Mary Murray
revised by: June Holstrom
contact: Paul Chukan

Paul Chukan was born in the year 1901. He lived in a house where the Red Salmon store is now. He lived in a house which is called a sod or a barabara. It was a sod or turf hut built partially or wholly underground. In the middle of the house there was a fire. Right above the fire there was a hole in the roof to let the smoke out. There was a screen which fit over the top of the hole; the screen could be open or shut. It was made of beluga gut or intestine.

For their clothing the Chukans used the skins of animals. They wore parkas and sealskin mukluks that came up to their knees.

Some of their eating utensils were wooden. Cups, plates, and other utensils were all carved from wood. Each person had his own set of dishes so he wouldn't pass germs.

Pots and other dishes were made out of clay. They were formed by hand and baked in a fire. This made them hard and a lot like ceramics.

They used seal oil lamps. The lamp was a flat rock with a dip in it. They put the seal oil in the middle of the rock, then they took moss that had been twisted into wicks and put it in the oil.

Paul Chukan said that the weather has changed greatly since he was younger. Paul can remember when the snow was so deep that you could only

Paul Chukan.

see the tips of the willow trees. He recalls there being winters which lasted until July.

The Katmai eruption was one of the greatest geological happenings in the Bristol Bay area. It was a great volcano which erupted in the summer of 1912, when Paul Chukan was eleven years old. He remembers very distinctly that the ground shook hard for five days. There were times that at 10:00 A.M. it would be just black as night outside. This was caused by the thickness of the ash flying from the volcano, blotting out the sun.

The ash covered the ground up to a foot or two. He said, "It was just like snow." They could see lava go up every two hours.

The vegetation of the area was killed off by the ash. Paul said, "It killed everything." It took two years before anything started to grow, but in five years, it had all pretty much been restored.

When Paul Chukan was fifteen, he started working. His first job was at Alaska Packers. They were the first cannery around here. He worked for fifteen cents a day. The fishing was a lot different then than it is now. They fished up the river by King Salmon. He used to fish for seven days a week. People came all the way from San Francisco, but not as many as from Seattle. Now people come from all over the world. Not just from the smaller places around.

The barabaras, or sodhouses, were built partially or wholly underground.

The prices paid for fish were much less. Fish went for three or four cents each. In the springtime when the beluga came up the river, Naknek, South Naknek, and Savonoski all went together to hunt the whales in the river.

The ways of transportation have changed considerably. They used to use dog teams in the winter—seven to eight dogs on a team. In the summer they used beluga skin boats. But most of the time they used their feet.

The first plane Paul remembers came during World War I. Everyone went out to see it. It was small with two wings on each side and no cover, just a windshield. The first car was down at the cannery in 1936. It had to be wound up to start it.

In 1918, a very contagious flu epidemic made its way over from Europe. The epidemic caused the adults and elders to become very ill, and most eventually died. People were confined to their homes and were not allowed to even talk to a neighbor. Paul Chukan said that white people came in and brought food, supplies, and medicines.

Naknek during the 1930s, drawn by Alec Peterson.
(From a photo by Paul Chukan)

The children that survived were sent to orphanages around the territory. The children were the main survivors because of their stronger resistance to the flu. Few, if any, adults survived. One million people died all over the United States.

When Paul reached the age of forty-one, World War II had just begun here in Naknek. This is when the base was built and King Salmon came into being. After the base was built in King Salmon, the first fighter planes were seen flying above Naknek.

Paul Chukan and many of his friends unloaded the base goods from the barges. The civilians were not allowed to go near any of the ammunition or weapons, only the military personnel were allowed to handle them. Paul remembers the planes coming back from the Aleutian Chain. The planes would usually come back full of holes; he sometimes couldn't believe that the pilots made it back alive and was grateful when it ended.

This was the beginning of King Salmon and the beginning of Naknek, too. Since then, they have expanded steadily. It brought Naknek up to date.

OLD, NEW, AND NOW SAVONOSKI

by: Teresa Hodgdon
revised by: Gayle Gebhart and Walter Hodgdon
contacts: Nina Harris and Vera and Trefon Angason, Sr.

Old Savonoski is near Katmai. They call it Old Savonoski because it is the original Savonoski. The Savonoski near South Naknek is the place where the people moved to when Mount Katmai erupted in 1912 and buried Old Savonoski.

During the summer of 1912, Mount Katmai erupted. Before it erupted, the banks nearest the volcano looked very red when the sun hit them at a certain angle. They looked as if they were on fire, but they weren't. This was caused by the heat of the volcano before it erupted. The creek water at that time was hot enough to take a bath in. In some places, the water was so hot that you had to dig a hole in the side of the bank to even soak in.

The volcano began to erupt in the evening. It was just like an earthquake. Then ashes began to fall. When the people went to bed that night, it was pitch black outside. When they got up the next morning, they had to light a lamp because it was still dark out from the falling ashes.

The ashes fell so thick that the people had to abandon Old Savonoski. Old Savonoski was beginning to get buried by the ashes. The people moved to New Savonoski near South Naknek. When a few of the village people went back to Old Savonoski, they couldn't find anything. All the trees, plants, houses, everything was buried. In some places the ashes were almost eight feet thick.

After the volcano died down and the ashes began to harden, people could sleep outside without a blanket because the ground gave off heat.

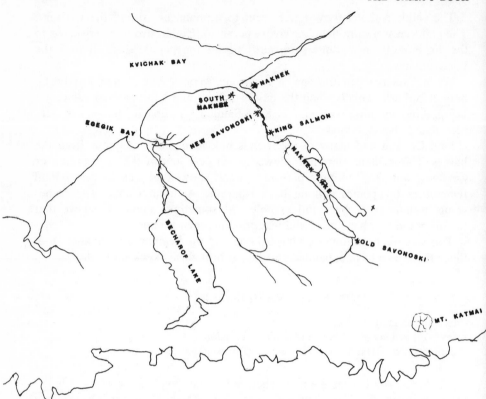

At New Savonoski, when all the housing was built, the people settled down to a new life. The country was always kept clean. They never threw garbage outside. They would dig a hole and bury the garbage in it.

The only type of transportation they had was a dog team. They used the dog team to go down to the store in South Naknek. They also used dog teams for hunting in winter.

The people would set out nets in the summer to catch fish for the winter. They stored the fish in dry sheds. A dry shed is a little house with a shelf about five feet off the ground. Before putting the fish on the shelf, they laid a bunch of leaves on it. This helped keep the fish clean. They could store about two hundred fish on the shelf. This is almost the same way they stored their meat. The only difference was that the meat was dried and then hung up. When they wanted meat for dinner, they would just go out to the shed, get a chunk of meat, and strip off the layer of dry meat. The inside was as fresh as could be.

The church at New Savonoski was built by a man named Nick Melgonak. He built it with one arm. He was out hunting at King Salmon Creek, and his gun was lying in the dogsled. When he reached for the gun to shoot at some

Old Savonoski years after Katmai erupted.

ptarmigan, it went off and shot his arm. He was taken to Kanakanak Hospital in Dillingham, but lost his arm.

One way of raising money for the church was giving a big dance. It was called a kusvik, and was held in a mud house, which was round on the outside and square inside. There were benches along all the walls of the mud house, and a 36-inch by 36-inch hole in the ceiling, where all the kids watched the dancers from. At these dances there were mainly three dancers, known as the directors. If they pointed at you and told you to go make them something, you had to do it. Every year the dance was held in a different place.

Savonoski today, on the winter road from South Naknek to Naknek. The Naknek River is in the background.

The people of New Savonoski were hit by the flu epidemic in 1919, seven years after the volcano erupted. This flu was all over the world, and they didn't have a cure for it. There were so many people sick and dying that the hospitals and schools were full. At Savonoski so many people died at one time that one big grave was dug for everyone; the people were too weak to dig single graves. At the Savonoski church there is a huge cross signifying where that grave is.

There was only one house in which no one caught the flu. This was Grandma Nick's house. She locked all the doors and windows, not letting a single person in or out. Before going to bed she lit some part of a fish and went around through all the rooms with it. She did this every night and every morning. It was as if the virus that caused this flu was afraid of the smell, because it never went to her house. It must have been some old Native medicine.

The people of New Savonoski began to move around 1954, mostly to South Naknek, which is about seven miles away.

There is now only one house left at New Savonoski. The owner is Mike McCarlo. He lived at Savonoski until 1979, and during the winters he used all the wood from the houses for firewood. His is the only one standing now.

None of the houses from the early 1900s are still up. They were all built near the bank and eroded away.

Everyone now lives in South Naknek. Everyone who survived, that is.

SLAVI

by: Teresa Johnson
revised by: Teresa Hodgdon and Cooky (Ruth) Alto
contact: Father Michael Oleska

I would like to thank Father Michael Oleska. All the information for this article has been provided by him. Father Michael is a priest in Dillingham. Besides having services in Dillingham, he also travels to the surrounding villages and holds services in them.

Slavi is one of the most important holidays of the Russian Orthodox Church. It starts on January 7 and lasts until all the houses have been visited. Everyone gets in on the celebrating, at least everyone in South Naknek, from the very old to the tiny kids.

Slavi has been around Alaska for 110 years or more. It consists of people singing, twirling stars, and feasting in every home. Slavi is also spelled Slaviq by some people.

The stars that are carried represent the star that the Wise Men followed to Bethlehem. The custom is for all the people to follow behind the star bearer(s), just as in the old days. The procession goes as follows: first, of course, are the star bearers; then comes the icon, which is carried house to house; and last of all are the singers.

The star used in the Slavi ceremony, held by Ted Angason.

John Wassillie and David Hodgdon spinning the ceremonial stars in the Russian Orthodox Church.

Slavi is about the same as caroling, with people going to all the houses singing songs and afterwards sitting around and visiting with the family. People also have food prepared for the Slaviers. At some houses there is a complete meal, but usually there are just desserts. That is the way it is in South Naknek, but up in the Kuskokwim area people prepare full meals at all the houses. (NOTE: Refer to the article on Slaviq which appears in the Yukon-Kuskokwim section of this book.) In the Kuskokwim area it usually takes two to three hours to slavi a house.

The koliaty, leader of the Slavi group, tells the Christmas story; and after it is sung, the singers start on the folk tunes. These are just happy-type songs; they differ in villages all over Alaska. The star bearers have parts from the Bible that they say after the koliaty has been sung. The parts lead the singers into the folk tunes. When all of the songs have been completed and the star bearers have finished their pieces, then it is time for relaxing and eating. After all the houses have been visited and the Christmas story has been spread for another year, Slavi is over.

"When all of the songs have been completed and the star bearers have finished their pieces, then it is time for relaxing and eating."

WEDDING: ORTHODOX STYLE

by: June Holstrom
revised by: Teresa Hodgdon and Cooky (Ruth) Alto
contact: Wassillie Epchook

A Russian Orthodox wedding in our area is a big affair. It is one of the few times of the year when the church is open, since we have no permanent priest. Like all weddings, it is a time to gather, see old friends, and enjoy the company of the comnunity.

When two people plan a wedding they have to tell their parents about the engagement and plan for their marriage according to church orders. The two people that plan to get married have to plan their wedding in Holy Matrimony.

Because of church law, the two people cannot get married on Saturday. Saturday is to prepare for cleaning of the heart for Jesus Christ and then the people have Holy Communion on Sunday. The reason for not getting married on Saturday is Jesus was born on Saturday. On Sunday, Jesus rose from the dead, thus the Holy Communion.

Before the wedding, the couple has to go to confession on Saturday night; Sunday morning they receive Communion. Then they get married during the week.

They can get married anytime of the year on Monday through Friday, but they cannot get married on Saturdays or Sundays. This symbolizes our purity and cleanliness of soul in the Russian Orthodox ceremony.

If possible, the people who get married should both belong to the Russian Orthodox faith. If the woman does not belong to the Russian Orthodox faith, and she wants to get married in our church, she can if her husband-to-be is Russian Orthodox. But the man has to go to confession and Holy Communion. The same holds true for a woman of Orthodox faith if her husband-to-be is not of the same faith.

The wedding starts when the bride walks into the church from outside. The groom is already in the church, as are the people that have come to the wedding. She walks in, then the groom takes her, and they stand on a rug facing the priest with their backs to the door and the friends and relatives surrounding them. The rug is in front of a little table. The rug is an emblem of happiness symbolizing a new path which they are entering in their lives.

Before the ceremony starts, the priest gives the bride and groom a lit candle; the priest also has one himself. Then the ceremony starts. The priest makes the sign of the cross, all the people make the sign of the cross, so do the bride and groom. The priest sings and the choir repeats after him. The priest sings the song "Lord Have Mercy" and the choir also sings the same song.

Carvel and Shirley
Zimin face the
priest at the start of
their Russian
Orthodox wedding.

"The priest sings,
and the choir
repeats after him."

The priest reads about the wedded life. Some of the parts are about the pair having children and about praying to God to give them a perfect and peaceful love. After this part the priest reads, then the choir sings "Lord Have Mercy" again; next he reads about Mary (the Mother of Jesus) with all the saints and then the choir sings "To Thee, O Lord." The priest says a prayer and the choir sings "Amen." It goes on like that for about twenty to twenty-five minutes.

At this point comes the crowning. The priest says another prayer, then the choir sings "Glory to Thee, O Lord, Glory to Thee." The priest gets the crowns and says, "O Lord, our God, crown them with glory and honor." The priest asks for the bride and groom to be blessed and then makes the sign of the cross with the crowns; he lets the bride and groom kiss the crowns, then he sets them above their heads. Here they are held by assistants, but in some ceremonies they are worn. After the crowning, nine verses are read from the Bible.

The crowns represent the honor and reward bestowed on the wedded couple and the purity of their lives. There is Jesus Christ upon the man's crown and the Mother of Jesus on the woman's. They are then blessed with icons.

The Epistle is read and after that the priest and choir sing "Crown of Pre-

"The crowns represent the honor and reward bestowed on the wedded couple and the purity of their lives."

cious Stones." This song is to ask the Lord to give the pair a good, clean life. The people sing it three times after the reader reads. He reads the Epistle from St. Paul to the Ephesians 5:20–33. After this, the priest reads; he prays for the Holy Spirit to come and witness the pair and give the spiritual bless-ing of Our Lord Jesus Christ.

Then comes the drinking of the wine. The priest reads again and then prays, makes the sign of the cross, and lets the groom drink some of the wine; the priest also gives some to the bride. They drink it until it's all gone. After the bride and groom drink the wine, the choir sings "Lord Have Mercy" and "To Thee, O Lord."

The wine issued is a sacrament in a marriage and it symbolizes what hap-pened in Canaan of Galilee which Our Lord blessed with His presence. There is water in the wine; it is served in the common cup of weal and woe and is given to both to drink.

After about fifteen minutes of readings, the priest, groom, bride, best man, and bridesmaid walk around the table with the Bible and a cross on it. They circle the table, then they go back to where they were standing, wait for

Traditional rice-throwing ends the ceremony.

about three seconds, go around again, and then go a third time. The circling symbolizes eternity and the Bible and cross signifies the oath forever; it is to preserve their marriage bond until death shall break it.

Finally, it comes to putting the rings on their fingers. The priest reads about the rings that they are going to put on. The priest lets the bride and groom repeat after him what he says as he reads from the Bible. After that, he tells them to slip their rings onto each other's fingers.

In the Bible, it says that a gold ring for the man symbolizes that he is greater in the family, and the silver ring for the woman symbolizes a substitution for her husband. In modern times, they may have any ring they desire.

The priest and choir sing "Lord Have Mercy" and then the groom kisses the bride. The priest dismisses the people.

After the dismissal, the priest congratulates the pair and tells the bride and groom to go up to the altar. The priest gives them a short lecture or piece of advice and wishes them good luck and good life. The people come back and congratulate the pair. Then the people go outside and make a path for the bride and groom to go through and, while they're walking through the path, the people throw rice.

It is not church law that you have to have a reception after the ceremony; the people that have just been married plan it themselves according to their desires.

THREE-WHEELERS

by: Rodney Alto and David Hodgdon
revised by: Doreen Williams and Mary Murray
contact: Dale Myers
drawings: Alec Peterson

In the early seventies a new mode of transportation arrived on the scene in the Bristol Bay area. Although not really new, the motorized three-wheeler changed the work and entertainment patterns of both adults and children. It has become almost an institution, taken for granted as cars are in the lower states. The only three-wheelers that are used at the present time in the Bristol Bay area are made by Honda.

Balloon tires are used on three-wheelers. The new tires have knobs but the old ones are slick. The best tires are the knobbys—they go better than slick tires in every different type of terrain except snow, because the knobs dig into the snow and bury themselves. The knobs can also be patched on the inside because of the split rim, whereas slick tires can only be patched on the outside.

A lot of people in the Bristol Bay area have three-wheelers. In South Naknek, a community of about 150 people, there are nearly forty three-wheelers; they outnumber the cars. A three-wheeler holds about 1.10 gallons of gas

Basic Honda
three-wheeler, an
institution in Alaska.
In some areas they
outnumber cars.

and usually you get about forty-five miles per tank. The ones in good condition have been known to get up to sixty miles per tank.

In the Bristol Bay area the three-wheeler is not only for just work, but also for fun and games. Some of the games people play are hide-and-seek, tag, follow-the-leader and many other games. The three-wheeler is basically for one person only, but many people ride with passengers. Another game that is played, in the winter, is to go down on a lake and bump into each other, seeing how far one can push the other around.

Tag is played using a rag. The person who is "it" takes a rag and throws it at another person while he is moving, and if the rag hits the person, he is "it." Follow-the-leader is played in the usual manner except the leader may go through a swamp, up a hill, over creeks, and through mud seeing how many players he can lose.

Three-wheelers are a lot of fun in the wintertime. They go extremely well if the snow isn't too deep. When summer arrives and things finally thaw out, many people use three-wheelers to cross creeks and lakes. A person of about 150 pounds will still be floating okay, if he has had the practice and has a good sense of balance. A three-wheeler propels itself but it goes very slowly, and you have to keep the spark plug out of the water.

During the last few years, people in the Bristol Bay area have been using three-wheelers a lot for hunting. They take the three-wheelers on long- and short-distance hunts across the tundra, down the beaches, or wherever there is game to be found. Often people use the three-wheeler for hunting about five miles or more out of town. Sometimes people take them down the beaches and hunt ducks and geese. Also, people tie the three-wheelers on the pontoons of airplanes and take them to more remote areas for long-distance

In the winter three-wheelers are used to pull loads over the frozen tundra. No other machine is as versatile in the Alaskan environment for year-round use.

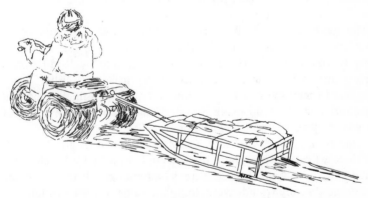

hunts. When people take the three-wheelers and tie them to the airplane pontoons, they leave them at the hunting camps for the season.

While the machines are there they use them for packing out caribou and moose meat. They pack out the meat by putting the meat into a cart towed by the three-wheeler; sometimes they put the meat into a basket that has been wired to the front of the three-wheeler. These three-wheelers can pack a lot of game such as caribou, moose, any game bird, and any hunting equipment used when the animal was caught. The maximum weight a three-wheeler can pack is about 220 pounds discounting the driver.

The local people in the Bristol Bay area also use the three-wheelers for

"Three-wheelers are a lot of fun in the wintertime." In Bristol Bay, the trails go for miles.

checking set nets, packing fish, and other summertime chores. The three-wheeler is sometimes used for pulling nets and moving buildings—jobs that were before reserved only for four-wheel drives.

The next section of this article contains two accounts of how three-wheelers are used by the locals of Bristol Bay in actual situations. The first story is told by David Hodgdon, and the second by Rodney Alto. "In the early winter when there's no snow or at least very little, we use three-wheelers to hunt caribou from South Naknek. No vehicle other than a four-wheel-drive truck could make it inland, and hiking and packing 200 to 300 pounds of meat is out of the question.

"One cool, crisp day in early October I decided to go caribou hunting on my three-wheeler. To prepare for the hunt, I packed a lunch and made sure I had extra gas. Also, I made sure I had enough oil in my engine. While I was doing this, my friends were doing the same to their machines.

"I started towards Diamond O, a cannery in South Naknek, to pick up my friends accompanying me on the hunt. In addition, a friend from town [Naknek] was going along. We all had the same vehicles and were set for a rough ride out. We traveled south, going inland from South Naknek over the frozen tundra. The three-wheelers bounced over the hillocks and into the hollows much like a wild horse. It takes a lot of skill and stamina to keep with it mile after mile. Every couple of miles we would stop to rest on a hill and scan the country for caribou.

"We averaged about twelve miles per hour and at noon we came up onto this one hill to see if there were any caribou around. About a mile away on a lake, there was a small herd.

The wrong way to put
a caribou on a
three-wheeler.

"When we finally reached the lake, we stopped and turned off our three-wheelers. All of us sneaked and walked our own way behind some trees to get closer. When we were about 150 to 200 yards away from the caribou, we all took positions to shoot. We each selected our own individual caribou that we wanted. Rodney shot first, then the rest of us shot, and all of us got one, which made four. After Rodney had our caribou skinned out, we put the caribou on the three-wheelers in a position that would be best.

"Dale found that if you put the legs over the seat so the legs are pointing back, they won't hook on the bumps as the bikes are traveling. Sitting on the caribou, we started our machines and headed back to South Naknek. Just before dark, Bruce and I made it back into town after a rough, bouncing ride over the snowless tundra."

"Usually in the summertime when the fishing season starts, I put a basket on the front of my three-wheeler. The basket is attached with wire and hooked onto the forks of the front wheel. The main reason I put the basket on my three-wheeler is so I can haul fish down the beach from our nets. I also use the basket for hauling groceries and other things in the summertime. When I use the three-wheeler for just playing around, the basket doesn't get in the way.

"When the tide is almost all the way out, I go to our nets with my three-wheeler. When I go up to the nets, I have to watch out for big rocks. A three-wheeler can't go over rocks or anything taller than 6 inches. When I

In the summer, three-wheelers are used to get to and from the beaches and to move salmon from the set net sites to the firmer sand, where the fish trucks are.

get to the nets I pick the fish that were caught; this is done at low tide. Only at high tide do I pick the nets with our skiff. After I pick all the fish out, I put them into the basket on the front of my three-wheeler. When all the weight of the fish is up on the front it's easier to drive, especially when I'm going fast. However, when I slow down it gets a little hard because of the weight of the fish on the front.

"On the way back down to town I have to climb a little hill. It's easy to climb with the weight because I don't have to lean forward. You have to lean forward when you go up hills, otherwise the front wheel will come up and it will go over backwards.

"When I get up the hill I have to go through part of town and then down to the beach again. When I get down to the beach with the fish, I put all of them into our skiff to be delivered to a scow in the river channel."

TOGIAK IN MAY

by: Rodney Alto and Dale Myers
contacts: Don Bill and Mike Hakala

The following article is written from a combination of research and interviews. Our main source was Mr. Don Bill, who has been working permanently for Fish and Game since 1974. He came to Bristol Bay in 1973, and worked three summers temporarily before that, so actually he has been here since 1970.

Don has a bachelor's degree in biology and conservation of fisheries and game. He works in the Commercial Fisheries Division of the department, in charge of managing commercial fish in the area, mostly salmon—and herring in Togiak. We asked Mr. Bill if he would tell us what he knew about the herring fishery and when it started in Togiak.

Herring is one of the most important food fish in the world and herring fishing in Bristol Bay is the number-two money-maker for fishermen in the

A "rag" of herring fills the back of a thirty-two-footer. Many fishermen want the law changed so they can use larger boats.

area (after salmon). The growing herring industry has changed the fishing industry here. Cannery workers and fishermen arrive months earlier to prepare their equipment; and many are seeking an extended limit on the lengths of their boats so that they can use the gill-netters in both the herring and salmon fisheries. A legal limit thirty-two-foot Bristol Bay boat is found to be too small to pack the tremendous loads that herring fishermen can catch.

The herring is a small fish averaging eleven inches in length. The average length herring found in Togiak is about ten inches long. Some of them get up to about thirteen inches. The size of the herring depends on the age. The older they are, the bigger they get. The fish is green-blue and blackish on the back, with silver on the sides, and white on the underside. When the herring are caught in a gill net, they turn on their sides and all the silver on their sides flashes.

Herring are peculiar in that their scales come off easily when they're caught. These in turn stick like glue to anything they touch: the boat, gear, and people. Herring eat crustaceans. The crustaceans are little animals without backbones and have an armor-like shell covering the body.

The fishing starts when the herring begin the annual spring migration from deep water to shallow water. The female herring lays 6,000 to 10,000 eggs, depending on the size of the herring. This is when the fishermen go after them. The eggs go to the bottom where they stick to seaweed, rocks, and other objects. It takes about two or three weeks for the eggs to hatch.

The majority of herring caught are made into meal, oil, and bait. A small percentage of the herring is used for people to eat. It is the eggs, however, that carry the most value and make the fishery so rich. The Japanese pay a premium price for just the right herring—ones that have a high egg to body weight ratio and are ripe and ready to spawn. Some loads that fishermen bring in may be worthless, others range upwards of $800 a ton, depending on the eggs contained and the going market price for them. There is no way of telling how your set will go until you pull in the net.

Herring fishing started commercially in about 1967 in the Bristol Bay area and it stayed about the same until 1975 as far as poundage is concerned. In 1967 the catch was 269,000 pounds. The low catch from then until 1976 was 55,000 pounds in 1971. In 1970 there were no commercial operations at all. In 1977 there was a lot more interest shown in the fishery; it jumped from 110,000 pounds in 1975 to over 5.5 million pounds in 1977. In 1978, it was up to 16 million pounds and in 1979 it was over 22 million pounds.

The recent interest is produced mainly by the price paid by the Japanese, who have been cut out of the harvest by the 200-mile limit (a federal law prohibiting foreign fishermen catches within 200 miles of the United States shoreline). They have been forced to buy the roe from American processors instead of catching the herring themselves.

In the last three years herring has really blossomed as a fishery in Togiak. The fish were always present in good numbers in that area; it was just the demand that caused the blossoming. With the interest in herring increasing, there has still been enough herring so far to meet the demands of the fishermen in what Fish and Game feels is a renewable harvest.

The only method that Fish and Game has at the present time for checking spawning population is aerial survey. Last year (1979) with over 10,000 metric tons harvested, there were still, according to the aerial survey, a lot of fish that spawned. The stocks at this time seem to be in real good shape according to Fish and Game biologist Don Bill. He explained, "The only migratory patterns we know about are some timing and distribution, and they are relatively unknown. We know that in this area the herring first hit the Bristol Bay area around Togiak and they gradually spawn a little bit later the further they go north."

The peak has been around the fifteenth or sixteenth of May in Togiak, Goodnews Bay, and Security Cove, just a little bit earlier than Norton Sound and a little later up the coast.

In 1979 the fish came in super early. They came in and peaked about the fifth of May, which is the earliest peak Fish and Game has on record. However, Fish and Game only has accurate records for about ten or twelve years. Hardly any of the processors were ready at this time because the season didn't actually open until May 1. Not very many of them were expecting the herring that early.

The herring winter and summer out in the Bering Sea. They come into shore to spawn and then return to sea. The only time the herring aren't out at sea is when they come in to spawn. The herring spawn every year once they're mature until they die of old age. Three years of age is probably the youngest they spawn. Most of the age classes in the Togiak area, for instance, are four- and five-year-olds and, after that, in lesser numbers of six-, seven-, and eight-year-olds. All of them are capable of spawning from three years on. Don Bill wasn't sure if any of the other foreign countries have tagged herring or if they tag them in Southeastern Alaska.

The Fish and Game gets the yearly estimate by aerial survey, plus by taking samples for age classes. They know, for example, that if in 1979 it was a strong four-year-old class in the commercial catch, then they can figure that in 1980 there will be a strong five-year-old class. Usually, if not many four-year-olds show up, then Fish and Game knows that there will be a weak run the next year. The same goes for all age classes. From the year before, Fish and Game takes the catch statistics and applies them to the next year to see what kind of run will be coming. At this point, Fish and Game doesn't know if the herring are like the salmon, coming back to the same spawning area.

"The first commercial operation for herring itself started in 1967 in Togiak. The roe on kelping started in 1968, a year later. I believe the first person over was Alphus Alford. He was the first buyer over there. It was for both herring and kelp. Last year's total catch for the Togiak area was 11,086 short tons, which is about 22,173,000 pounds. Of this about 6,390 short tons, which is about 58 percent or so, was taken by purse seining; the other 42 percent was taken by gillnetting," explained Don Bill.

"Last year a lot of the purse seiners in Togiak didn't do that well because of the type of weather they were having. Purse seiners cannot really fish in as bad weather as gill-netters. Even though they are out there, it is just too rough to purse. The gill-netters can come in where they usually fish, gillnetting closer to shore right before the herring spawn. The fish they take have a high percentage of roe; they usually get more money for their fish than the purse seiners.

"A lot depends on how the fish come in. With a purse seine you can purse them up and test them, let them go, and a large percentage are going to live. If the roe percent is not high enough the people are not going to buy them, so they let them go. Where as in a gill net, once you catch them they are dead. There are also problems with a purse seine, too. It does sometimes kill a lot of them. They suffocate if they purse up too much and test them."

The big question with a lot of people is, what is done with the herring after it's caught? "Most of them are processed right there in the Togiak area. In most cases, the fishermen deliver them to a scow. The scow takes them over to a processor boat. It has to be an American processor boat. Foreign vessels cannot process fish in the state unless they get a special exemption.

"The processing boat processes them and most of the processing done in this area is either by freezing or salting. They need 10 percent salt before it

Herring coming over the roller in a gill net.

is called a process. Then the Japanese or Korean, or whatever foreign vessel that they are going to be selling to, is sitting right next to the processor boat. It comes off the scow onto the processor, goes through the salting onto conveyer belts or tubes onto the Japanese or other foreign vessel. Then it's ready. As long as it is processed like that, then the foreign vessel can take it.

"We think the herring industry is looking real good for the Togiak area. They have good healthy stocks right now and we've got some pretty good regulations; we are learning more about the fishery every year and putting more regulations in when we need. Fish and Game is doing a lot of experimentation and scientific work, not only on the herring themselves, but also on the kelp and other grasses that they spawn on. They got a real good idea of the population right now if they can keep up on the age class and kind of keep control of the fishery, then it would look real good for the whole industry."

Although each herring fisherman gets prepared for the season in a different way, Mike Hakala told us how he goes about getting ready for herring. "Well, mainly I hang all my own gear and in the spring I have to get my boat ready. The main part is hanging the gear in my spare time in the winter and getting all my gear squared away so that it will be ready in the spring, anchors, buoys, and lines. It's about a twelve-hour run from Naknek to Klukuk Bay."

Once Mike's in Togiak, he finds out where his buyer is located and prepares to start drifting. Last year he fished a new area and fished there for

Suction hose being lowered into fish bin.

The last of a load of herring being sucked off the boat.

the whole season after trying several different areas. He tried several different spots in the same day, then, in the end, moved to a spot he fished two years ago.

"I take whatever food I need and as much fuel as I can handle. You can't carry enough fuel for the whole season, so you get as much as you can handle whenever you need more. You get it from the fish buyer."

The seiners, who run bigger operations, hire planes to spot the herring from the air as they school up. The planes fly around and when the spotter sights a school, he radios the seiner where to go, when to set, and when to close up the seine. The drift gill-netter sets his own nets and chooses his own areas in which to fish. But when you see fifteen airplanes circling in one spot, you get the idea quickly where the herring are located.

Once located in a good spot Mike explained, "Well, I just throw the anchor overboard, run ahead, and let it pull the net off the reel. I go downwind from where I throw out the anchor so the wind doesn't blow me on top of the net." When you pull the net back up with the reel, and as the herring come on board, you grab the web near the herring and give it a shake until the herring falls out.

Once the boat is filled the herring must be delivered to a processor. Mike explained, "The only way I delivered was by shoveling them out of the stern. The processors I delivered to didn't use any suction devices."

When the boat is loaded up and ready to deliver the herring, you either go to a major company that you fish salmon for or you might go to a cash buyer. A company that is a major fish buyer will have some shore-based facilities in the bay. They will store and repair your boat, buy other fish, but pay at a lower price. A lot of the cash buyers give the fishermen beer and food, some have showers. They pay a higher price than the old-time major canneries.

Actually, there are three ways to deliver herring to the processors. One is by shoveling, the other two are by wet and dry suction. Shoveling is when you get a regular snow shovel and shovel the herring into brailers. Brailers are big nets used by the processors to weigh the herring. The fisherman shovels the herring into the brailers, the processor picks up the herring and weighs them, then dumps them in a holding tank.

Dry suction works like a vacuum cleaner. It sucks all the herring up and into tubs that are up on the processor. The tubs are then weighed and the fish put into holding tanks. Wet suction is used just like dry suction, except water is hosed into the boats to make the fish move more easily, sliding to the suction hose.

Sometimes the weather really gets bad. "I find cover, throw the anchor out, and ride it out," Mike said. "It didn't cause any problems in delivering last year."

FLAT-BOTTOM SKIFFS AND DOUBLE-ENDERS

by: Artie Johnson, Jr., and Carl Zimin
contacts: John Lungren and Bob Hadfield

John Lungren related his experiences fishing in the bay to us. He's been fishing more than thirty years, but we focused on the days before you were allowed to have engines in the boats. Fishing has changed considerably since the days of sails.

"I was born here in Alaska. Most of the fishermen came up from the States on a steamship. There was Alaska Steamships coming up for some of the canneries. You could get passage [on them] and, then, the mail boat came in here, too. That was in the early forties. After '46 everything came up on the Alaska Steamships. The government had taken over all the cannery ships."

John explained that you didn't need to do exercises—to get ready was enough. "You had to rig all your boats up. You didn't have any kind of winches or anything back then to load your nets onto the boats. You had to do it all by hand or pack it by hand trucks. You had to work for your run money. Like, I generally was whipping and getting the boat ready for the season."

Once the season began that's when the work really started. "You had a roller that was in the stern of the sailboat; one pulled the lead line and one pulled the corkline. It was all by hand. There were a few gasoline-powered rollers in the later forties, oh, the early fifties, I guess. They had some, but the majority was all hand power.

"It was all linen nets, with cotton corklines. Generally you went through three nets a season. By the end of the season they were pretty rotten. Once or twice a week you had to bluestone them. You had to salt them down any-time you let them lay very long to keep them from rotting.

"You had a bucket and you had a wooden hand pump and a little bailer, too, that went in between the ribs," explained John while talking about keeping the boat afloat. In fishing, "You went with the current generally, unless there was a strong wind. You made one drift and very rarely you got up and made the second drift. When it was calm you had oars, fourteen-foot oars, to row."

In case of emergency, "There was no radio. The only way you got help was to put an oilskin up on an oar. If you were in shallow water, no one could come in and help you. If you were swamping, generally you should have tied your mast and boom across the boat to keep it from rolling over. But many of them didn't, and many of them drowned."

Monkey boats were tow boats used by the canneries. As John explained, "Monkey boats came in the late thirties; before about '39, nobody could tow

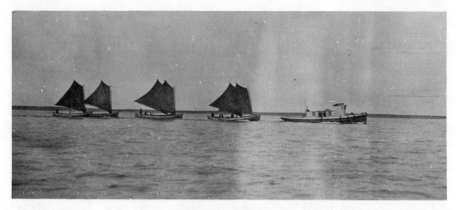

Sailboats being towed by a monkey boat.

a boat during the fishing season. You had to get to the scow on your own power by yourself. It was sort of a cannery ruling.

"In the fifties they started using power. We were allowed to use power for the first time in '51. They had power in 1912 but the canneries got a regulation passed so that there was no power until '51 in Bristol Bay. There had to be sails in the bay. Carlyle Packing Company up in Levelock had powerboats in 1912. Packers bought them out and there was no power until '51. The first sailboats had nine-horse outboards fastened onto a bracket on the side of the boat. Probably '54 was the last sailboat that I saw fishing."

Today we have a thirty-two-foot regulation for boats. "That originally came from old regulations, most of those boats were twenty-eight-footers. Probably APA had the best sailboats. They had carpenters over there. Nakeen and Libbey's had good sailboats. Packers and San Francisco outfits had clumsy boats; they didn't sail so good, but they packed more fish. They were clumsier to work. You could carry about 2,000 fish, and I've seen some as high as 3,000 fish. They were all brought up from the States.

"Originally the first sailboats were flat-bottom skiff-type boats. Then I think in 1912 they brought up the first round-bottom sailboat from the Columbia River. They were all brought up by the cannery ships on the decks." Once the boats were landed, they would be stored in warehouses each winter. They had steam winches to get them to the water and some of the canneries had slips and slid them into the water on high tides.

Sailing the boats took great skill and stamina. You worked around the clock for days with little protection from the elements. "We had a tent up on the front of the boat that we pitched. When you wanted to dry up, you pitched the tent and put some alcohol on the floor and it dried all the water up. You had a kerosene stove, what they call a Swede stove, on the boats for cooking and heat.

"Most of the time in the later years you fished from six Monday morning till six Wednesday night or six Wednesday morning. Then you went back

The fleet is in below
Diamond O Cannery,
South Naknek.

fishing from six Thursday night till six Saturday night. You had thirty-six
hours off on Sunday and twenty-four hours off on Wednesday. And during
the war years, you only got Sundays off. You had to bluestone your nets on
those closed periods."

The canneries paid only nine and one-half cents for a fish in 1934 and
John remembers that it was only ten years ago that they were being paid one
dollar a fish. All the companies paid exactly the same price for the fish, a tradition that is just now changing.

"Generally, the superintendent hired a captain of a boat and most of the
time allowed him to pick his partners. The superintendent had to approve
who was the partner." Each man received the same pay. And it was men in
those days, women weren't allowed. "You didn't have to pay anything for
the boats. You were an employee of the company. They even took out Social
Security."

Unions and strikes have become important as bargaining tools for higher
prices in the past few years. John told a little history on the subject. "Well,
the Alaska Fishermen's Union, which is still in existence today, started back
in 1909 or something like that. They were especially strong in the thirties
and forties. In '46 another union started in Dillingham. There were two of
them, one for Alaskans and one for outside fishermen. There were no independent fishermen. You had to join the union."

Unlike today where you have to travel across the bay to find a scow to
deliver your fish, scows for each cannery were anchored in many areas.
"Most of the companies had scows at the mouth of the Naknek River at Libbyville, Graveyard, Gravel Spit, and Johnson Hill." This was necessary because the boats were less mobile than they are today with engines. "If you
had a strong wind you could sail against the tide, but that wasn't too often
there.

"In the late forties, probably '46, they would come after you [if you
couldn't make it to the scow]. Before that they wouldn't come after you. You

A converted sailboat
delivers fish to tally
scow.

could be fifty feet behind the scow, and a tugboat alongside, and they
wouldn't come back and pick you up.

"At the time Alaska was a federal territory; you had the federal Bureau of
Fisheries and they had patrol boats out there. When you got caught, they
would pick you up and tow you in.

"The boundaries at the time were the mouth of the Naknek River and up
the Kvichak. It was above Diamond J at the time. If you were a Neknek
fisherman, you couldn't fish below Middle Bluff and if you were an Egegik
fisherman, you couldn't fish above Middle Bluff."

The worst part of the fishing in the sailing days was the loss of life. John
related, "Well, some years it's hard to say how many you lost. They lost a
lot of lives some years. There was seventeen or eighteen fishermen drowned
one year. Other years there was only two or three. A few fishermen drowned
during the season, and most of the time they were old-timers because they
took more chances on the flats. When they got on the flats, if they couldn't
get their centerboard down, they couldn't get off. Lucky if you could make it
[walk] to the beach."

Since Bob Hadfield's first days of fishing double-enders rigged for sail, he
has worked on a tally scow for Bumble Bee and presently owns Hadfield's
Bar. Bob was born in Seattle and came up to Bristol Bay in 1935 to fish.
The only means of transportation then was by cannery ship or by Alaska
Steamship Lines.

When Bob started, "No one fished independent, you strictly fished company. The company furnished the boats, gear, and stuff like that. All you

had to get was your oilskins, boots, and gloves." At that time there were only two men to a boat and they split the pay fifty-fifty.

"Back then you got four and a half cents a fish to split between you and your partner. Nowadays it's four dollars a fish—1942 and '43 were probably the best years. We had over 40,000 fish, and for a sailboat that's pretty good.

"It's much easier today. You have a cabin and a head and galley, not to forget the plower rollers and things. I would say it's much easier."

Contrasting today's comparative ease of fishing, Mr. Hadfield related, "You slept under the bow and it [a double-ender] had very little bow on it. It was decked back about four feet. When you took the mast down you could put up a little tent and you could crawl in there for a little bit of shelter. You also did your cooking under there. We cooked on what they call a Swede stove. It was a kerosene-burning stove. You primed them with alcohol. There was also a little locker on the bow to store food.

"After you had delivered your fish you could go in and have a bite to eat on the tally scow. The tally scow was a permanent scow anchored in the bay. Usually we had fish chowder or something like that. The canneries were pretty stingy with their food.

"You either hauled your net in over the side or you had a wooden roller that fitted on the side of the boat. At that time there were cotton nets, they didn't have nylon in those days.

"Most of the boats were made of Port Orford cedar. The boats were very much alike. They were called Columbia River double-enders and each company had a little bit different design in their boats. PAF boats and Squaw Creek boats sailed a little faster than the Packer boats. All the boats were brought up either by the company steamships or Alaska Lines. The pack [of salmon] was taken down the same way.

"After the powerboat was introduced, some men bought old sailboats and converted them. Also, the canneries converted some; but up until they got power, all the boats were company-owned."

In those days the territorial government regulated the length of the boats to about thirty feet in keel measurement. All the boats had pumps and Bob told us, "All we had was a bar with a plunger; you pushed and pulled and the water came out. Believe me it was hard." It was also hard not having an engine to push your boat around the bay. The canneries had what were called "monkey boats" that served to tow the sailboats around. A monkey boat was just a small boat with power in it that could tow you. If you had a load of fish it could tow you in case you had the tide going the wrong way. They could pick you up and tow you to the scow. If you missed the scow, you had to go up the river and wait till the tide turned. You always had men missing it. You had to be a pretty good sailor to make it.

"When you wanted a monkey boat and there was none in sight, you could tie an oilskin on the oar and raise it up and let it flap. They would see that flapping and come. The oars were big. Many times we had to row all the way

Power scow *Otter* tows twenty-six of Libby's Cannery's fishing boats to fishing grounds, 1946.

Fishermen picking salmon out of their nets at the Libbyville Cannery dock.

across the bay when we ran out of wind." Most of the boats held 2,900 to 3,000 fish on a calm day. You had to peugh all of them onto the scow by hand. If a storm came up and you had a load of fish, you just had to handle the boat yourself. One time my partner knocked himself out when the mast broke and hit him. I can remember one year especially that we lost somewhere around thirty-six people, that was a dirty year."

The territory regulated the fishing, but according to Bob, "They didn't enforce them [the laws]. The closest place they were was a little above PAF cannery. The boundaries were about the same place that they are today. One was at Naknek Point and at the time we could go way up to Sea Gull Island around Squaw Creek. We could come in front of Coffee Creek, but now they have that closed off."

The end of the sailing days came when the territory allowed the boats to have power. Everyone switched within a few years. It signaled the end to double-enders. Bob said, "Hungries burned many of theirs, just put them on the beach and burned them; but some companies converted them. Others just let them sit and rot."

SMOKED FISH

by: Al Ring, Dale Myers, and Gordon Grindle
revised by: Carla Wilson and Elaine Myers
contacts: Mary Lou Aspelund, Frank Hill, and Judy Fischer

Smoked salmon in Bristol Bay is very common and has been for many years. A lot of people like to eat it, but few people go through the process of making it anymore. Those that do make it for eating, and many older residents used to make it for their dogs as well. Although very few villages around here make it for their dogs, the villages up north still do because dog food is hard to get and very expensive.

The people of Bristol Bay make it during the summer and fall when the salmon are running. Some people, however, salt their fish and wait until fall when the bears are gone to smoke them. They smoke it throughout the winter for whenever they need it. Smokefish isn't very complicated to make—you just have to put in a lot of time and effort.

First of all, to make smokefish you have to have a smokehouse. Smokehouses vary in size and are made from almost anything. Frank Hill explained, "I think the best building should have lots of air and not really tight-fitting joints; you know there should be lots of air coming in on it so it dries." The average smokehouse is usually six to ten feet high and about eight to ten feet wide. Some of the smokehouses have a firepot inside, while others have the smoke piped in. You should have the smoke lower than the smokehouse when it is piped in because it will rise.

Inside the smokehouse are racks on which to hang the fish. They go across the length of the smokehouse and can be made of wood or pipe. You should keep the fish from touching when it is hanging so it doesn't stick together. The racks should be in two levels; one level is approximately four to five feet off the ground, and the other about three feet above that. Keep the racks level so that one doesn't touch the other and leave lots of air space between the racks so that the smoke and air will be able to move about freely.

Bugs and insects are often a problem so Frank Hill told us, "We try to continue to smoke in the house for one thing." The other way is to have the bottom tight to the ground and well vented, with a fine screen-like mosquito screen to keep the flies out.

Most people in the Bristol Bay area have a subsistence net in the summer. About ten fathoms long, the net is usually set when the fishermen are not out commercial fishing due to a closed period. "The way my family does it is we put the net out either for kings in June or reds in late June and July. Sometimes we share the work and responsibility of checking the net with other families, since you have to check the net twice a day, then pack the fish up the bank in gunnysacks to where you are going to clean the fish," explained Frank.

The place where most people clean the fish is usually just an old table or two oil drums with a piece of plywood for the top. Some of the things that should be handy when cleaning fish are a gut barrel for the guts and backbones; a barrel with fresh water to rinse the fish off; a barrel, some rock salt, and a hand-sized potato; and finally, a couple of sharp knives and a sharpening stone so you can cut the fish into straight strips.

When you're ready to clean the fish you fillet it so that the head is off and cut the backbone out by cutting along the rib cage. Try not to waste too much meat. At the tail cut the bone, but leave the two sides together. Cut slashes about one inch apart almost to the skin, so that the air and smoke will dry the fish faster. Then put the fillets in a brine solution.

To make a brine mix five gallons of water and about three pounds of rock salt until the hand-sized potato floats to the top of the brine. Judy Fischer uses one gallon of salt to every five gallons of water. She says that will help cut the slime. Gently stir the fish for a couple of minutes and leave in the brine for fifteen minutes to an hour, depending on your taste. Judy leaves her fish in the salt water for twenty minutes.

Kings are brined just about the same, but you cut them in one-inch strips and tie two together before putting them in the brine. Kings usually take a bit longer.

When hanging salmon outside to dry you can usually leave them a couple of days until you're ready to put them in the smokehouse. Judy Fischer does it this way: she hangs them on fish poles tail side up; if the weather is windy and sunny, you can leave them up for one day, turn them over to meat side out, and let them stay that way until they get a glaze on them, usually in another day.

Once the fish are brined and have been glazed by sitting outside, the salmon are ready to enter the smokehouse. Judy says when you think the glaze is deep enough (the glazed fish should have a very beautiful deep red shine), put them in the smokehouse to hang skin side out. For the wood, there are all different kinds to burn. For example, Frank Hill uses birch. "I don't know the reason, at least I think it's better. It has a better flavor. Some people use willow or alder; my family has always used birch. The fish doesn't get dark or strong-flavored." A lot of people around here use alder and a lot

Judy Fischer recommends hanging the salmon on fish poles tail side up until they're glazed (about two days), then moving them into the smokehouse.

use driftwood from the beach. Judy Fischer says, "Different people have different ways of smoking their fish; mine is alder. The reason for this is the pitch or the bark isn't as strong as willow or birch. Also, alder is more plentiful than the others, it grows back faster than the others too."

Once you have all your fish up on the racks, you start smoking it. You can either use a hot or cold smoke. The hot smoke cooks the fish, while the cold smoke slowly cures the fish. You have to be careful with a hot smoke not to burn the fish or cook it too much, or the meat will fall apart. A hot smoke is usually done with a fire in the smokehouse. The Hills use two big metal tubs, which were washing machine tubs. They are set into the ground with gravel all around. To control the fire, metal plates can be placed over the top to act as a damper.

A cold smoke can be done with a fire pit on the inside, but it is easier to have it piped in from the outside. You put a barrel outside the smokehouse and bring the smoke in at the bottom so that it will filter up through the fish. Most people here use fifty-five-gallon drums. You cut a hole in one end of the drum, then make a door for the front of it with a handle to open it. Make a hole big enough for a stovepipe to run to the base of the smokehouse. You will also need a damper on the barrel to control the heat of the fire. You don't want it hot enough to cook the fish. If you have a good fire pit and light it early in the morning, it should smolder the whole day. Then, let it go out in the early afternoon and during the evening, light it again and let it burn late at night. You can see why it takes a long time. You should have a screen over the bottom of the house so the flies and other bugs won't get to the fish and lay eggs.

For a cold smoke most people smoke their fish twelve to fifteen hours a day for two and a half to three weeks. Judy Fischer says, "The smoking process takes anywhere from eight days to two weeks [depending on the weather again]." When Judy thinks her fish are done, she takes them down and puts them in plastic bags and stores them in the deep freeze for the winter.

The final step is, of course, to eat the fish. It can be stored in the freezer if it is protected from drying out, or it can be canned. Many people leave it hanging in the smokehouse until it is needed and it usually lasts until spring. Sometimes it gets a little mold on it, but it can be scraped off. Good smoking!

Yukon-Kuskokwim Region

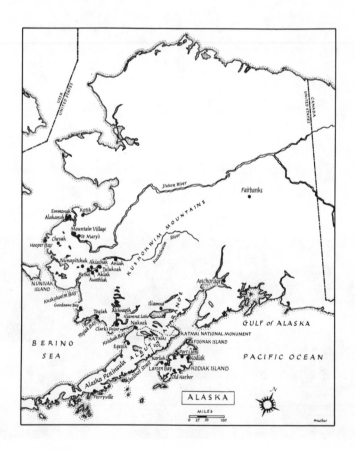

1. Introduction

THE YUKON-KUSKOKWIM REGION

by: Elena White with Gertrude Jacobs

The Yukon River starts way back in Canada and the Kuskokwim starts way back in the Alaska Range. These rivers flow through many small villages throughout the region.

On the tundra, land is flat and mushy. As winter approaches, the land hardens, and all the living plants are no longer growing. The white snow covers the area and the land is flatter than ever. But when the first goose honks, we know we have survived the winter, and all those worries and thoughts of starvation are over. Green grass can be seen, and trees, our small willows, get their leaves back.

For the people of this region, life depends on the surroundings. On the coast, seal hunting and ocean fishing are added to the tundra activities of berry-picking, hunting, and trapping. The short summers and long, windy winters are the same throughout the delta, yet each village has its own unique character.

A village consists of about 200 to 400 people. A bigger village might consist of around 500 people, but not more. Here in the village, activities are pretty scarce. On most days, meetings are held, and that's one activity that will probably never die. People live out their years just like any place else. For entertainment, most of the young people play basketball or otherwise go to the recreation building, which happens four days a week in my village.

There are food differences between the coastal and tundra villages. Usually people who live out on the coast eat out of the ocean and also eat ptarmigan, ocean birds that don't migrate, and many others that I don't know of. As for the people of the tundra, many wild animals are available during the winter. During the summer, some go down to fish camps and fish all summer so they can have fish available during the winter that is to come by again.

The people that live around this region are all Yup'ik Eskimos. Probably they are the original people of Alaska, as I have heard they lived in igloos and sod houses. I know they lived in sod houses because we have some old pictures of them. I think Eskimos have been here for thousands and thousands of years. From what I've heard they lived through much hardship. I also heard about the huge sickness that killed many. This happened after the white man came. They lived life as they always did; through hardship but surviving. Hunting and fishing were the means to survive. There are many spoken languages but there is one root, which is the Yup'ik language itself. The language changes slightly in every Eskimo village.

The culture is modernizing in so many different ways. It is helping in a lot of ways, and it's also hurting our elders in other ways. We have helpful things like clocks, watches, silverware, and, best of all, transportation. In so many ways, it's giving us more time to do what we want. The elders don't have to use oars to travel to a place thirty miles away. But, still, elders don't like some things. For instance, many of their kids love to go to parties, movies, and recreation halls. The elders don't like that idea, but what else can we do to entertain ourselves? The "why" of all this is because we, the Yup'ik Eskimos, started this relationship with the white men when they first came. If we didn't start welcoming them, it wouldn't have happened this way. Our culture can still be preserved by doing some of the things our way. Our language won't die if we keep it up. We have to do some of the things our elders did in order to keep the old ways.

The articles for this section were taken from *Kalikaq Yugnek, Tundra Marsh,* and *Kwikpagmiut.* Students carried out the project with the help of their teachers. The students taped while they interviewed, then went back and transcribed. After transcribing, translation was done. Sometimes problems came up during this process, as *Kalikaq Yugnek* adviser Dave Williams described:

> Our largest problem, then as well as now, has always been language. There were some strange interviews last year. I don't know how many times I sat at the kitchen table in some man's home, drinking tea, a tape recorder between us, bobbing my head, grinning like the proverbial village idiot, while the man I was "interviewing" recited his grocery list and the student with me sat in dazed wonderment that I would seek such information. Now we all know a little better. The students, many of them who were in the class last year, have the confidence to run interviews and I have the sense not to.

Through this project, we hope you can understand what our ancestors did for a living and why we keep the old ways alive.

NUNAPITCHUK

from *Kalikaq Yugnek,* by Elena White.

Nunapitchuk is a village of about 350 people located some thirty-one miles northwest of Bethel, Alaska. It is situated on the tundra amid

YUKON/KUSKOKWIM DELTA

Scammon Bay

Pilot Station

Kalskag

Bering Sea

Nunapitchuk

Bethel

Tununak

Toksook Bay

Mekoryuk

Chefornak

Nunivak Island

Kipnuk

Kongiganak

Kwigillingok

Kuskokwim Bay

Goodnews

numerous lakes and along the slow-moving Johnson River. The terrain is extremely flat and void of trees save for a few low willow bushes.

The people living in Nunapitchuk are all Yup'ik Eskimos with the exception of some of the teachers. The Yup'ik language is predominant in the home and everywhere except in the classrooms, where classes are conducted in English. Bilingual programs exist both on the elementary and secondary levels.

Nunapitchuk is a village founded by two people, my grandpa and his cousin. It started out on the southwest part of the village, which is the far end of the village now. There were a few people living on that part when it started out. But people came from other small villages to occupy this place. The other part of the village, which is called "Number Two," was mostly populated by people coming from "Nanvarnarrlak," which is four or five miles from Nunapitchuk.

There's a reason for calling this place Nunapitchuk. *Nunapicuaq* is how we say it in Yup'ik, and it means small land. The first land they settled was just a small piece of land and only a couple of houses were fit for it. It was just plain tundra and it wasn't suitable for housing because the land was mushy. The people who came from villages several miles away started build-

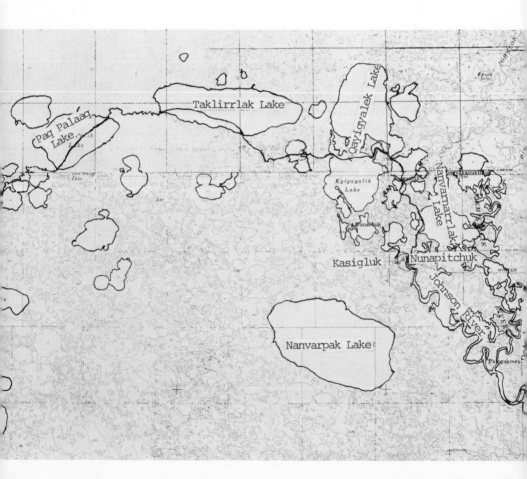

ing houses until the population reached about 450. About 100 people moved to a place called "Atmautluak" in the late sixties.

The people stayed in the village during the winter doing what was best for them, surviving through the winter by using the summer's catch. Frozen and smoked fish were their main foods and hunting activities provided furs for clothing and some cash income. When spring came they moved to spring camps. Spring was the best season of the year for them. Hunting muskrats, fishing for pike, and egg hunting were the main sports. When early summer came, it was time to move again to fish camp. They sold the muskrat skins and bought what was necessary. Fishing salmon and silver salmon came and everybody started fishing and soon started smoking the fish. In early fall, they moved back to Nunapitchuk. Some went to fall camps, probably to hunt for furs. Then they came back during early winter. That went on for years, but now it isn't done except by a few people.

The reasons why people stopped here rather than moving on I really don't know, but some people say school, which started in the year 1936, was one. Nunapitchuk has two schools and two school systems. The elementary school, K–9, is run by the Bureau of Indian Affairs and the secondary school, 10–12, is run by the Lower Kuskokwim School District.

2. How It Was

MARIE NICHOLS

from *Kalikaq Yugnek,* by Nick Nichols and Tina Pavilla.

Marie K. Nichols is seventy-five years of age. She was born near a lake called Pupiit, not very far from an abandoned village called Nunacuaq. She lived in Nunacuaq until everyone moved to Kasigluk, where she is living today. She always tells stories with her eyes closed.

"I realized that I was born at a time when my parents stayed near a lake called Pupiit. There's a small river near an abandoned village called Nunacuaq. Because all of my parents' children had died before me, the shaman told my mother to leave the village and go someplace where I could be raised. Then my parents moved not very far from the village, near the lake called Pupiit, which was my birthplace. One of the first things I started noticing were the two caches. My father trapped and did other things. There were no white men and the people didn't use any stoves. When they boiled blackfish or something of that kind in the winter, they cooked in the porch [entrance to the sod house]. Also, in the mud houses there were no camp stoves, but wood stoves were used for cooking and heating.

"When we stayed in the bush and did not have any pots for cooking food like ducks, we would build a fire and fry over the flames. My father and mother were old when I came to recognize them. Also when I first realized what I was doing, I thought people had only one child, just like I was the only one. But then I found out all my older brothers and sisters had died. When I got older my father made me a canoe, and to this day I am using one during the summers. Also, I had a bow and arrow and a spear. When I hunted I was told not to go very far. I also hunted for pike near the edge of the lakes in an area where there were a lot of weeds and plants. When I hunted for muskrats I would chase after them until they got tired of diving; then I would spear them. When strangers came around, I'd be scared because I did not meet people very often. When I went out to the bush, the sound of birds would sound so wonderful that I'd never get lonely or scared. Later on I noticed other kids had brothers and sisters, and I started to envy them. I would ask my mother why I did not have any brothers or sisters and she would tell me not to ask or talk about them.

"Just before fall the people fished. Dip nets weren't used yet, but the methods of using dip nets started during my lifetime. My father used to set two fish traps in a river near Nunacuaq. Fish was the main thing the people ate, but during my lifetime flour came around, and big crackers, which we didn't like very much.

"At this time there was no such place as Bethel, only the great-grand-parents of J. A. Nichols. There once was a village across from Bethel where the old airport is. Because the bank was eroding, the people moved, and these two people moved to where Bethel is and started the village. Men used to go to Bethel with skin boats, which had sails made out of grass or skins of pikes. After chipping and drying them out [these skins], the women would also make qaspeq or sails. People from a place called Cuukvagtuli would make their skin sails from lush skins. Also, using a certain kind of grass, women would weave and make rags to wipe with.

"I realized Russians were the first white men to come around. There was one old white man I used to see; he came during fall and built a small house with a store. This was the beginning of stores in the area. White thick cloth was the first to come around from this Russian man who had a store. I found out that the people nearly killed this man. I also found out Eskimos long ago would kill white men who came around because they believed they would make the Eskimos crazy.

"The way these Russians came was through Nome with dogsleds. In early spring we would go to spring camp; I would travel with snowshoes because there still would be a lot of snow. My parents didn't have very many dogs. On our way to spring camp we would camp. A long time ago, people used to pull roots, peel them, and use them to make traps for the ducks. For bait, decoys would be used. When the traps were checked, there would be some ducks. After checking the traps, we would tie a live bird for bait; this way we could catch more game.

"The people ate off the land where game was. Fish and ducks were eaten and their skins were used for parkas. Mink furs were used for pants and muskrat skins were used for underwear and also for coats. These are some goods the people used. People from all over traded for a blown-up sealskin filled with seal oil.

"The first school in Nunacuaq was in the early 1920s. The people did not know anything about churches. When priests came around, they preached in the qasegiq where most men stayed; we were amazed at them because they were new to us, and we didn't know anything about what they were doing.

"Girls were to get married to young men who were skilled and good hunters. When a young man was getting married to a young woman, the parents of that young man would give something of value like seal oil to the girl's parents so that they could come together; the ceremony of marriage didn't exist. Even if the couple did not like or love each other, the parents would have them get married. The young people did not do whatever they wanted to do. Only the parents made decisions for them until they lived on

"The girls got married in their early teens, and some very young men got married to old women. The older people did this because otherwise the young people might forget the ways to live off the land."

their own because they believed that otherwise the young people would turn out bad. The girls got married in their early teens, and some very young men got married to old women. The older people did this because otherwise the young people might forget the ways to live off the land.

"A married woman had been taught to breast-feed a son by sitting up and not lying down. And the woman feeding the child would not drink water even if she was thirsty. But if she was too thirsty she would take a feather, dip it in the water, and suck the feather for her thirst. This was done to the baby boy for a reason: boys who were babies were not to be breast-fed lying down; else the people believed they would be unlucky hunters. We were taught some methods or a tradition of making a mat for a baby. Toy objects such as moose, other animals, and people were placed on the mat for the baby to play with. One person would be in the middle of the qasegiq telling a story. Stories were told every night; they were very exciting.

"The time we went to Nunacuaq in the fall was the first time I saw a white man. Then there were the Moravian missionaries; the first were John Hinz [Qakineq], Ataniller, and Kilbuck. When the first missionaries preached, the people did not really care for their preaching; the preachers did almost anything the Eskimos did, like dancing and eating with them, and because the white men went along with how the Eskimos lived, the people got to like them. In fall the people did not dance, but feasted and ate instead. When visitors came around, the men would make masks and dance. In those days, the shamans would be the ones to make masks. And it is said that while one man was dancing he fell and blood flowed down from his mouth. When they danced they didn't fool around, but took it seriously.

"Everything we ate wasn't always boiled, and when flour was scarce, we would make Eskimo ice cream with just a little bit of flour and other ingredients. There wasn't any white sugar, only brown sugar. Most of the time we ate raw food and fish; even though they weren't really dried, we would eat them. When plants or berries were ready to be picked, we would pick them. And people would make some kind of waterproof bags, which they filled with berries or other food. These would be tied to a string and put in a lake for all summer, and when the lakes froze in winter, these bags would be taken out and used for winter food.

"The people used to meet in the qasegiq about three times a day, telling stories and other things. And in the evening when they were telling stories, one story would be so long they would hardly finish it. The longest story was the one about starvation; it was feared because it had happened. The starvation story was told more seriously than the others. When a person was hungry, he would not smile; and when a stranger or even a brother came along, he would not be welcomed during the time of starving. A muskrat would be chopped to pieces for use, and one dried fish would be eaten all day. Children would be asked to take a nap without drinking water, eating only after

"The longest story was the one about starvation; it was feared because it had happened. The starvation story was told more seriously than the others."

their nap. Water wasn't used for anything. Young men were mostly watched and taken care of.

"A long time ago, Eskimos used to fight between themselves, like the coast people against the island people, but they stopped after the end of starvation. There was a woman who ate a dead person from a grave. The way it happened was that the woman crawled near to the grave like it was some kind of animal. She had a bow and arrow with her. When she got close enough, she shot at the cross and hit it. After that she took the body out and brought it home because she had nothing to eat.

"Just before starvation there were two big wars. In the wars all the men were killed and young boys were hit against the poles. There was a lake which filled with dead children and older people, and the lake became reddish in color. An old lady pleaded with the warriors not to kill her grandchild, a boy; but the men killed the child, saying this child would fight against their people when he grew up. So they killed him and threw him in the lake. Then this lady, maybe because she was a shaman, looked for her grandchild. When she found him, she washed him up. She was wearing a sealskin parka. She said, 'Poor seal. Even though I pleaded, those warriors killed you. Don't you know what you're doing right now?' Then after swinging him, she threw him in the river. In a moment an enormous seal emerged; then it swam downriver snarling.

"The men who killed the child were going down the river killing people and soon they were at the sea. It was really calm. One of the men said, 'Look at that black line down there.' One of the men answered, 'When it's calm, the top of the water is usually dark.' But as it got closer and closer, the water got rough and it got windy, and on top of the waves was the big, snarling seal. It went toward the kayaks and sunk them, drowning the men in them; all except one man, who was left alive to tell what happened.

"In one area when men were being killed, there was a trap set up for the enemy. When all the enemy came into a certain river with kayaks, a man was hidden near the mouth of the river. When they got through, he made a coded call to another person further up the river. The river was surrounded by the others who were hidden. They attacked the men who were in the kayaks, killing all of them except one man. Then the man was placed in a canoe to be sent back to where he came from. His ears were cut off and part of his chin was sliced. They told him they did this because he might lie about what had happened. He was given a paddle and set free. This is how the enemy was tortured.

"They used to hear of a man out on the coast in Hooper Bay. It was in the spring that he was going down to the sea before the birds came. He went down to the sea ice for hunting, taking along his canoe and grass for his blanket. This was when they didn't have any clothing like they do nowadays. While he was down at the sea it was getting dark, so he put the braided grass beside him so he wouldn't face the cold wind. He sat and slept.

"In the morning when he got up, the sun had risen already. He heard a bird singing on the side of the braided grass. While the bird was singing, it was also talking to him. 'Netuvarama. When the wind is moving to the north, the birds and animals face the wind. That is when spring is here.' The bird sang once again. After a while the man ate, and then he stood and looked around him. There wasn't any island or tundra around him; he was on a piece of drifting ice somewhere at sea. He thought that the bird was singing because he was drifting away from the islands. He didn't know what he was going to do on the ice. Even though there were lots of animals to hunt, he didn't have a spear or harpoon to hunt with. All spring long the ice drifted at sea. He didn't have any more food to eat, and he started eating the kayak skin. [They used the skins of seals for kayaks.] The ice where he was sitting was getting small. It got smaller while he was sleeping.

"He woke up and looked around him. He was sitting beside land. There were mountains all around him. He stepped off the ice and walked on the land. While he was looking around, he saw a village; he was really glad to see houses. He was surrounded by tall grass, so he went closer to see what was in the village. He saw the women were qulugteq [all hunched over]. When he walked in the village, the men came. The wives and husbands weren't staying in the houses together; they were apart. The men stayed in one house and the women stayed in another house in the village.

"A man came with his wife. His wife was pregnant. The traveler asked why those women were qulugteq. They walked as if one side of their body was smaller than the other side. The villager said that when a woman was pregnant and had a baby, they cut her and then sewed up the incision where they took out the baby. That's why the women's sides were qulugteq. The more babies they had, the more qulugteq they became. There weren't any doctors or nurses a long time ago. So the older people helped the pregnant women have their babies.

"The people were from Asueryagmuit, and they called the place Tayaruq. The place had two names; Asueryak is an island somewhere up north. This traveler was called Teparlluar by the people from Asueryak because he crossed the sea.

"When evening came, one of the men from Asueryak took his knife and sharpened it. Teparlluar asked him why he always took the knife and sharpened it every night and why he didn't use it, even though it was sharpened. The man answered him that the knife was for his wife. When she was ready to have the baby, she would let him know. Then Teparlluar asked the husband to tell him when his wife was ready to have the baby, so he could let the woman have a baby like they did in his hometown.

"So when the wife was ready to have the baby, the man came and told him. And Teparlluar let the woman have the baby without the knife to cut her stomach. After she had the baby, he told her not to lift heavy things and to stay in bed until she got better. Now those people said that they had a good doctor. The people from Asueryak told everybody how nice a man he was to help the woman have a baby. From then on, the people didn't use a knife to make a woman have her baby.

"One day Teparlluar went out from the house to wash his Eskimo dancing hat. After he washed his hat, he hung it. The people from Asueryak told everybody that Teparlluar's hat had turned into a brand-new hat, maybe because these people had never washed their clothes. This man Teparlluar liked where he was staying, but he didn't know where his home was because he had been sleeping while he had been drifting.

"While he was sitting outside, some kids were playing, and he heard them saying that the people in Asueryaraq were going to kill him when spring was over. At night, he told one of the men where he was staying that he had heard the kids say that they were going to kill him when the spring was over. The man said that the kids weren't lying. Teparlluar said, 'How come you haven't told me?' Then a man made him a canoe and oar. The man tied his hand to the oar and took him to the river far away from the village. He told

Marie Nichols with her
completed grass basket.

him not to go during the day because the people would chase after him and kill him. The man told him to stay hidden in the tall grass until it got dark.

"The man was getting his things ready before he left at dark. While the man was waiting in the grass, there were canoes down the river looking for him. They were saying, 'Where is Teparlluar?' wondering where he was hiding. They were saying that they should have killed him before he got away. One of the men went toward him while he was hiding in the tall grass, but the man didn't see him. Teparlluar was waiting for dark to come, and when it got dark he went towards the village. When he went down to the sea, he got sleepy, but he never dropped his oar because it was tied to his arm.

"At his hometown, he had parents and a sister. At Askinarni one of the shaman asked him what he was up to, and he told him that he wanted to go home but he didn't know where his place was. He said that at Asueryak they named him Teparlluar and at his hometown they had called him the same thing. Then the shaman sent him back to his hometown just like that. He saw his parents and sister, and together they were happy."

RULES THAT ARE FADING AWAY

from *Kalikaq Yugnek,* and *Tundra Marsh.* Interview with Kenneth Peter by Sarah Phillip and Helen George; interview with Anna Gilman and Mary Chaliak by Hannah Andrew, Grace Tikiun, Sophia Brink, and Irene Sims.

In the old days when a girl had her first period, she had to follow certain rules. She had to stay in the house for ten days, and if she had to go out or stand up, she had to put on a belt first. The belt was made out of cloth, dried beaver's testicles, some tabacco ash (punk, a fungus that grows on some trees and is burned to ash and also used as a chewing tobacco flavoring), dried fish vertebrae, and a fish fin (tail) that's also been dried up. If a girl didn't wear a belt when she stood up, she would get tired easily when she grew older. Her legs would be weak if she didn't wear the belt when she was supposed to wear it. Also, some of the old women wore belts even though they were not having their periods. They wore the belt around the waist. This is still done by some of the older people. The belt is worn on the outside of the kaspeq or coat.

During a girl's first year of menstruating, she shouldn't go fishing. If a girl went fishing, even though she shouldn't have, the fish would turn red on the outside and die, and then there wouldn't be any more fish left. Also, she had to stay in the village for a year. She could not go to the riverbanks or go someplace in a boat; but if she had to go, she had to cover herself up with a blanket or something. If she wanted to pick berries, she had to take a hair from her head and tie two berries together before she began to pick berries.

During menstruation, a girl had to eat certain things. A girl had to eat cooked fish, but not the head. She had to eat only cooked food. "She should

Mary Chaliak.

never have eaten raw meat and sour berries for the sake of her teeth. Her teeth would rot before she died. Her teeth would loosen and fall out."

We were told that these rules were followed by the girls for one year starting with their period. After the year, they could go back to a more ordinary life. It was at this time, too, that the girls were available for marriage. (NOTE: A girl could prepare for marriage at an earlier age by learning the skills needed to be a good wife.)

The traditional way of choosing a wife or husband varied somewhat depending on the parents, the children, and the ages and talents of the children to be married. Sometimes the dealings were between parents only, with the children not having a choice in the matter; sometimes the children could choose a spouse if they chose wisely and sought the approval of the parents involved.

The woman should study the man's attributes. The man should not pick a girl by her looks. A woman is not to pick a man by his looks either. If a man picks a woman with the look of a flower, he might find out that she is not the one he thought she was. Some parents used to pick a girl for a wife for their son even though she was young (about the age of eight). The parents would take care of the girl until she had her period, and then they would let the man and woman get together. And sometimes they found out that it was a good union, and the two would be as man and wife.

The boys used to have a speaker who told them what to do. The speaker used to tell them what they should do when they grew up. These lessons were told so they wouldn't live a dumb and going-down-the-drain life. People might live a blind and invisible life. They were taught how to live by food and everything.

Both ladies and men were taught just the same way. The older people forced them to follow the rules. The men were always trying to provide. Same with the women. They would talk to them separately. One should not go from one house to another. If they did that, the people from the village would tell lies on them. The people that lived long ago seemed to know what they were doing.

For example, when a woman got pregnant, she couldn't get to a doctor, so the woman used to get the baby out of her stomach by herself. Some of the women had their babies outside by themselves, while others had their babies inside the sod house.

If the girl was going to have a baby, she had to take care of the baby. She was not to eat raw fish and oily foods; for in the old days girls didn't have milk that could be bought in stores, so the mother always fed the baby from her breast. The girl who had the baby had to take care of the baby so it would be healthy.

Some of the people who still believe in the old rules use them today. Old people today sometimes feel that the rules that they had are no longer useful because young people do not follow them anymore. Even though some people are keeping the rules today, it's important to have a written record of them because they are dying out fast.

Remembering the rules is your job. If people remember the rules and what their parents told them, they will live happily, they will have a job, and they will not have hard feelings about themselves.

Anna Gilman.

BIRTH, MARRIAGE, AND DEATH

from *Kalikaq Yugnek,* by Diane Trader.

This year I've been in the *Cultural Heritage* Magazine class and I've been working and finding out about birth, marriage, and death. I went out and talked to some people, including Minnie Carter and Lucy Beaver.

Birth

Minnie Carter was born on September 6, 1900, at Quinhagak. Minnie and Lucy didn't know how old they were, but a preacher told them their age just by looking at them. Lucy Beaver was born at Nunapitchuk and she is sixty years old. She said, "The women would deliver their own babies with no help. But sometimes some of them never had any babies. Some of them would have up to fourteen to fifteen kids. And when they had about that amount, the mother and father would take care of all of them, as much as they could, until they were old enough to go on their own. They would never get another family to take care of them."

Marriage

They never really got married in those days. Their parents would pick a husband for them, but it all depended on how the boys worked. They judged by the way they worked. Sometimes the boys would be surprised when they found out that they had a wife to take care of. They also didn't let a young man choose his own wife. And they never wore a ring like nowadays. It was because they had no copper, iron, or steel to make rings with.

Before the girls got too old, they'd let them get married. As for the boys, they'd wait until they were old enough. When a woman wanted to remarry, she could do it. But they never really got married in those days. The men would leave their wives when they thought there was something wrong between them. Sometimes they left when they couldn't get along. After all, they were not even married. Nobody would ever get married. They would just get a husband or a wife and go away for a new life.

Death

They buried their people by putting them in a little house that was made out of something like drift logs. It was on top of the ground. After they gathered the person's belongings, they would put them all around the grave.

When someone died, some people would come over and help out with the cleaning, hunting, and all the other chores.

When the men went hunting and didn't return, the wife would tell some-

Traditional
above-ground grave.

one to go and look for him, and the men just put their warmest clothes on and went to look for him. If the men didn't find him, the wife would be able to remarry. When there was a father but not a mother, the father got the job of taking care of the kids.

OLD-TIME MARRIAGE

Interview with Calvin Coolidge by Raymond Alexie.

"I am Calvin Coolidge, lay pastor of the Moravian church in Nunapit-chuk.

"A long time ago, when I was a boy growing up, I saw pastors. At that time, in winter, they went to villages by dogsleds to preach and they took care of how the people got married and baptized. If couples had offspring and didn't get married, another man or woman could get married with either one of them. At that time, there were few churches and some of the villages didn't have churches.

"I first saw a church at Nanvarnarrlak and that church had a lay pastor named Uyaquq. But he didn't let the couples get married by him, but by other higher preachers. I got married and my cousin's wife had passed away. We had a double marriage in the house. Reverend Harry Truedoll got us married. We were few. We had our witnesses and the reverend. Nowadays they get married by reverends and they invite a lot of people. In the old days they didn't invite a lot of people, but had only their witnesses. And the reverends were baptizing people, baptizing people at their homes when they didn't have churches. I know this from my days. We didn't feast after getting married like nowadays.

"Nowadays, the way of getting married is changing. Long ago, they didn't use wedding suits and gowns. We used our everyday clothes when we got married.

"There were other religions like Russian Orthodox. They didn't have a reverend or a pastor. But I saw a reverend from Kwigillingok named Ipcuk. He was the only pastor around here. I became a pastor in my young days after I got married. There weren't any health aides. When someone was sick, they came and got me at my house, even though it was midnight or early in the morning. I am happy about these health aides because they are taking our place by taking care of the sick."

THE WAYS OF THE PAST

from *Kalikaq Yugnek,* interview with Sophie Nick translated by Louisa Gilman.

"When I first became aware of people around me, I found out that they were poor, never receiving money from anyone. They always used to fish in summer or hunt game for their food. They hunted birds with traps. I used to go along on these bird hunts. The roots of trees were used for traps, and a female duck would be used for bait. After ducks had been skinned, we stuffed them with things and used them for bait to attract other birds. After a night we would go check it. Many birds would be caught; we would pluck out the feathers and sometimes hang them up like we do fish and dry them. We ate them in the winter.

"We had boots made out of skins of some animals. The kayaks were made out of some kinds of bark from trees. Men used to use the kayaks when going out on hunts or when fishing. Sometimes they'd be gone for days. They'd catch many animals, like muskrats. They hardly used guns when hunting, only bows and arrows or some other weapons. Very few men owned guns in those days. Many used handmade weapons when hunting. In the winter, we used to hunt ptarmigan; even women and girls used to hunt.

"I heard stories of men hunting caribou when there were plenty. When I started to watch what was going on, I saw only a few. For me there was plenty, but old people said there had been many more in the past.

"There used to be many old people. Hardly any died until they were real sick or too old. Whenever people would hear of a person's death, whether it was from sickness or a person was killed, we felt sad and thought about what effect it would have on the person's relatives. We mourned for the person, but mostly we felt sorry for the person's parents.

"In those days we knew nothing about kass'aqs [white people]. We only knew about a few. They never told us what to do, what to hunt or not to hunt. We did whatever we wanted to; everything belonged to us. We lived comfortably and there was nothing to worry us, not like these days.

"White people are taking over our land. They are making rules about the land, birds, and even sea mammals: what to do or when to hunt, when not to hunt. They even call off hunting until animals increase. Many things are getting dangerous.

"Parents these days always worry about their children. In my day people hardly ever used to worry about their children or relatives. Nowadays people hardly ever sleep, worrying about their children if they are anyplace; they have many sleepless nights.

"Maybe their lives go fast when they worry too much. Doctors tell me not to worry too much. They tell me to try and always be happy. I try. But there are too many things to make me worry. Ever since there has been liquor, people have hardly ever slept, worrying about people who drink. Most of the intoxicated people have accidents. I worry that some people I know might get hurt or badly injured. I get scared thinking my children and others might get hurt or involved in some accident. I can't even sleep at night, thinking about it. Some people kill other people. This is one thing many of us worry about. Maybe we get sick from worrying.

"When people were sick in the old days, we used to get medicines for them. We got medicines for the kids who had sores. We used kayaks to go to places where certain plants were plentiful. The plants we used to call 'starwastes' are getting scarce now. They were used for kids' sores. These days people go to hospitals whenever something's wrong with them or to the health aides. Whenever my kids had sores in their mouth, I burned the clam with the squirrel's tail until it got powdery. After this cooled, I let them chew some. They seemed to get better quickly. In my young days, whenever a girl had a sore in her mouth, a man or boy would let his nose bleed and let the blood drop into the girl's mouth. The blood was used for a medicine for the girl.

"People with TB were told not to keep still but to keep busy doing something. They would spit out blood. The medicine for them was tundra tea. The tundra tea [made from plants gathered on the tundra] was boiled and the people with TB were urged to drink a lot. Some got better after they had been worse.

"In March, people used to get ready for the spring camp. They packed food and anything they needed and took it to the place where they'd be camping. They brought their boats to use when summer came. They left home before the ice melted. The village would be deserted all summer starting in the spring. Many families would leave together. Some walked and some went in the dogsleds.

"In summer, we hunted eggs instead of staying in our spring camp. We filled many pots with eggs. These days people hardly hunt eggs. White people are taking over our land."

OLD-TIME MEDICINE

from *Kalikaq Yugnek,* interview with Maggie Hunt by Florence McIntyre and Marie Pavilla.

"A long time ago people used to make their own medication and used the medicine the best way they could.

"The people put ashes in small bags or containers and heated them next to a stove or even on a burner. When the ashes got hot enough, they used them for 'hot water bottles' for their aches and pains. Also, using some kinds of herbs which had leaves helped as medication for colds. [NOTE: What Maggie Hunt may have been referring to is the fireweed or the great willow herb.] The people used a dipper at all times for the amount of leaf juice they drank.

"One time I ran into a lady who had snow-blindness. The people used urine for medication in her eyes. What they did first was to leave the urine for a couple of days and then put some in her eyes, which made her eyes go back to normal.

"They also used beaver's testicles for cuts if people had cuts on their hands. They used to chew the glands of the beaver and place them on the cut. This is how they cleaned and healed the cut. When they had cuts, they used the glands.

"Some people still use herbs that grow on the tundra. They cook the herbs first, and then they take the herb juice and wash their bodies with it. If there is pain or even cuts and sores, they put herb juice on them, and that's how they are cured. The people also use some kind of oil that is fresh, like from a seal, whenever they have colds. They drink the seal oil that is not old for medication.

"These days some of the people are still using the old medications."

<<<<<

from *Kwikpagmiut,* by Robert Johnson.

This is a true story about a married couple who lived alone in a camp not far from Mountain Village. It happened a long time ago when this woman's husband was very ill and weak. He couldn't hunt or trap for food.

One day they were very low on food, so the woman decided to put ptarmigan snares out on the other side of the camp. The woman set out a couple of snares and then went back to cook what was left to feed her husband.

The next day came and the woman decided to check her ptarmigan snares. When she got there, she found out that she had caught two ptarmigan. She brought them home and cooked them. She would always let her husband have the breast because it had more meat than the back.

After a week went by, her husband was still feeling ill and weak. She said to herself, "Maybe I should try letting him eat the back of the ptarmigan." One week went by and something did happen. Her husband was gaining

A woman feeding her sick husband backs of the ptarmigans.

Robert Johnson

strength. She kept on feeding him the back of the ptarmigan and she ate the breast part.

Then one day her husband got out of bed and told her that he was strong enough to hunt for food. He put on his warm clothing and went out to hunt.

The woman had found out for herself that the back of a ptarmigan had more medicine than the breast, which had more meat. Even today, many older Eskimos eat the backs of the ptarmigan, for it is said that the oil in the fat of the back gives strength.

REMEMBERING THE SHAMEN

from *Kalikaq Yugnek,* interviews with Evan Chaliak, Andrew Tsikoyak, and Nastasia Keene by Joseph Nick, James Chaliak, and Mary Paul.

After transcribing and translating our taped interviews into English, we combined the information from our three contacts into a single article about shamen. We hope our translations are accurate. The statements made are based on observations of practices no longer occurring in our area. Because the topic is quite sensitive to many people, we have not used actual names of shamen or people affected by them.

Shamen had varied powers to do certain things. The major powerful thing they did was curing the sick and removing sicknesses or misfortunes from people. Many parents brought their children to the shamen. There was a belief that shamen removed misfortunes in one's future.

"The shamen were human beings, but they danced and danced and cast spells on people. They did this in the kashim. When they heard of sick people in another village, these shamen danced in the kashim and cast spells on these sick people. They wore a seal-gut parka when they were at work. In

Andrew Tsikoyak: "The shamen were human beings, but they danced and danced and cast spells on people."

doing this, they strengthened themselves and isolated the sickness from passing on to another person."

This dancing and casting spells in Yup'ik is tuunriq. The shamen also had powers to put bad luck on people they were jealous of or disliked. "Once I watched a little boy being tempted. I heard that his grandfather and a shaman were at war. The shaman was jealous of a new boat that belonged to the boy's dad. The shaman wanted to have his boat; and when the man said he wanted to keep it since it was his first own personal boat, the shaman told the man to keep it until it wore out. The man's son, henceforth, had bad dreams and nightmares. Many times he awoke and told his mother that a large white dog was after him. His grandmother applied holy water to him, and he settled down. This went on for a couple of days. One night, while the women were sewing, he awoke and said that a big man was trying to cover him with a boat. His grandmother saved him through holy water and prayer, and it went away."

People recalled that shamen had an ability to fly. One person that we interviewed said that they flew up to the heavens; and another person said that the range in which they flew was from the beds, at the end of the kashim, up to the kashim door. "A shaman flew in my sight when the village of Nanvarnarrlak was still existing. I was a member of his helpers. I used to watch him and run after him when he went out the door. I never caught up with him, even though he wore snowshoes. We never caught up with him. He just got further and further away from us and had a hard time taking off."

Shamen could cure the sick, and some people say they could fly.

Evan Chaliak

"There was this man who was a shaman from a village that doesn't exist anymore. He said he was going to boil in water. A bucket of hot water was put over a burning fire in a qasegiq and five large rocks were put in it. Two girls were standing by the door, holding sharp sticks. When the rocks burned, he went up and went into the bucket using his seal-gut raincoat. When he said 'Ready,' one of the girls went up; and when she touched the stick to the side of his neck, it went through his body smoothly and the tip of the stick touched the bottom of the bucket. The second girl went up and stuck the stick on the other side, and it, too, went through smoothly and touched the bottom of the bucket."

Due to the many modern things that were brought in and the changing civilization of this country, shamen are rarely thought of anymore in daily life. Their lives and acts are part of a fascinating past. This is a story about shamen by Billy Black, translated by Florence Nichols and Lou Mark.

"I have a story to tell about a man who used to be a shaman. A long time ago in the old village called Qingarmiut, there was a man called Taingussiq living there. The people were angry at him because they thought he was try-ing to kill some people in that village. They had just buried a dead body and they were gathered around the entrance of a sod house. The shaman was in that house taking care of a sick person. The person he was taking care of had been sick most of the winter.

"One of the men outside shouted to the shaman, 'Come out, come out if you're in there.' The shaman said that he was taking care of an unborn baby whom he named Ciqviilgnuq. Ciqviilgnuq's father had told him that people would be looking up to him with respect.

"While he was sitting in one side of the house, he asked the father to ask his wife if they had an extra baby wolf skin. They said, 'Yes, we have one that we skinned last fall.' Then the shaman said, 'If you are not using it, I'd like to use it.' They gave the skin to him. Receiving it, he asked them to slide it on his back so that it would fit and cover him. After he had put the wolf skin on, he asked the man to do him a favor. 'I am really going to miss and worry about my two sons. Would you please take care of them while I'm gone?'

"Before the shaman left, the wife asked him, 'How am I to survive when you're gone? You know that I have been sick most of the winter.' The shaman bent over her and told her to point to the spot where her stomach hurt most. Having located her pain, he started sucking on it. He was sucking and spitting the liquid stuff out of the woman's stomach. When he was alone, he got prepared to go. Before he went, he told the woman not to worry about anything and that she would be all right.

"The men who were waiting outside of the house were getting impatient and yelled for the shaman to come out of the house. The shaman then crawled to the door and paused for a while. When he touched the side of the door, he turned into a dog. The men who were waiting outside the door saw a dog going out of the shaman's house. The dog walked through the middle of the men and when he reached the end, he started running as fast as he could to the back of the house. There was a stream at the back of the house and he followed it. When the men called again to the shaman inside the house, the wife said he had already gone out. After that, they started suspecting that the dog was the shaman.

"When the men went to the back of the house, they saw the shaman's footprints. He had turned into a man. They went along the riverside where the shaman's tracks changed again. One foot was of a man and the other was of a wolf. Then when they went a little farther on, they became wolf tracks. They began to think it was a little difficult to catch him. They finally gave up and went home. The shaman, who was a wolf in the winter, was left alone in the woods.

"He traveled to many different places. As he was wandering, he saw a house and wanted to be around people once again. He saw two people who were spending their winter camping, catching blackfish for food. A woman and her grandson had seen the shaman coming slowly from some distance away. The shaman was still walking towards their house. It was getting dark when the woman instructed her grandson to paint their house with a rock and then put it on top of the entrance. [In those days, the Eskimos lived in houses partially under the ground.] When he was finished painting the house, he put the rock on top of the entrance. Then his grandmother gave him a piece of wild celery. Again, she told him to paint the house with it and put the celery where he had put the rock. The shaman was still coming slowly towards them.

"When he was finished, he went back into the house. This time his grandma gave him a beaver's scent gland. He went over the house as he did with the rock and the celery, and put it near them when it was finished. Having painted the house with all three objects, they went to bed after they had had their supper.

"Later that evening they heard the sound of footsteps coming toward them. When the shaman came up to the house, he stopped, then started walking around their house. They could hear him saying to himself, 'I thought I saw two people up here, and this place seemed like a house from further out.' As he was walking around the house, its figure was changing into a rock, celery, and a beaver's lodge. Whenever it turned into a rock or celery, the shaman had no way to enter. But when it turned into a beaver's lodge, he fell into its tunnel and from there he crawled into the woman's house.

"He told the woman about his trip and that he had seen her with her grandson while he was coming. He said, 'Since I had seen you by this house, I stopped and looked all around it instead of passing by. It was difficult to come in when it changed its shape into a rock and celery. As soon as it turned into a beaver's lodge, I fell into its tunnel and crawled in.' The woman then prepared him a place to sleep and some food to eat.

"After he had stayed with the woman for several days, he decided to go up to the Yukon. Before he left one morning, he told the boy to carve a piece of wood shaped like a blackfish. 'When you are finished with it, let your grandma take it to the water hole and drop it in,' the shaman called to the boy.

"The boy did as he was told. As soon as his grandma had dropped it in, it sank and disappeared. The next morning the boy went back to the water hole, and there he saw lots of blackfish swimming in and around the water hole.

"In gratitude, the shaman had given them enough fish to last all through the winter."

HEALTH

Interview with Nastasia Keene by Wilson Tikiun.

Years ago, before the Public Health Service set up clinics in each of the villages, Nastasia Keene of Nunapitchuk worked as a "nurse's aide" caring for sick people in her village. Now seventy-three years old, Nastasia still recalls health care in those days.

"I think Miss Hinman was my first teacher, or maybe somebody else was. Oh yeah, it was Miss Hinman who was my health aide teacher. She also was my boss.

"We used the thermometer to see how sick the children and adults were. When their temperature was around 102°, she used to let me give them shots. I never gave them pills; I only gave shots to the people who were sick and checked their temperatures.

"Even though it was cold or stormy, or even when the snow got soft and the trail got so soft that when you walked on it you fell, I worked every day. Even though I never got paid, I used to work. I didn't know they got paid

Nastasia Keene.

for working, but I didn't care because I was glad to help the sick people. It was the only way. By giving shots and taking temperatures—that was the only thing I did.

"One thing we knew was that when somebody got a high temperature, he got a seizure. After the seizure hit them, most of them died. The sickness made them die. That was what Miss Hinman told me. I can show you a picture of my teacher.

"The sicknesses were different. Some of the people were ill and some of them had colds—mostly the children. Adults didn't used to be happy about them. That was before we started using shots. The shots that we gave slowed down the death of the ill people.

"I don't know what kind of medicine they used to take before they had shots. I think they used to treat them as much as they could. When they got indigestion, they would rub seal oil on their stomachs. It usually helped most of the people. That is what the people who were taking care of sick people used to use. I didn't start by doing that; I started by giving shots to the sick people.

"I think there was less sickness in the old days because people were separated before they started to settle [permanent villages, most of which grew up around schools]. I think it was because there used to be a small amount of people in the village.

"When the people started having TB, we couldn't care for them. They told me that when they had TB, they would start coughing out blood. When they coughed out blood, we knew that those people had TB. I also gave shots to the people who got TB, but we separated the males and females. The doctor who came here showed us how to give shots to the people who had TB. Some people died, but most of them survived.

"When they started going to other places for treatment, fewer died and more people survived. They used to send them to different places like Mount

Edgecumbe, Anchorage, Seattle, Tacoma, Seward, and many other places. They said there were a lot of people going for operations for TB. Some of them died while going to those places, but a lot of them made it and came back.

"I don't know which teacher gave me a certificate when I quit working around 1960. I quit working when there was a trained nurse for this place. You can see my certificate if you like, but the words are hard to read. The nurse gave it to me to keep. She was trained in medical self-help training courses.

"I think I worked for about four winters."

FOODS WE USED TO EAT

by: Gertrude Jacobs and Elena White

We interviewed Nastasia Keene of Nunapitchuk to find out about foods that were eaten in this area in past years, especially those wild foods that were gathered.

Most berries that were picked were salmonberries, blackberries, blueberries, cranberries, and nagoonberries.

"Even though it was far, people would go berry-picking. Men and women went and spent the night. We would go upriver all the way from the Kuskokwim through the Johnson River. Sometimes we would reach the place 'Paingaq,' where I was born, located upriver from Atmautluak. We never seemed to be tired. Married couples worked hard and helped each other.

"When we got some berries, before we started seeing a lot of barrels, we would weave reeds to make a sack. We would tie a string to the bag, fasten it to a stick, and put the bag in the lake, completely immersed. Then, in winter when it froze, we'd take the berries out and see that they were as fresh as the ones in today's freezers. Very fresh, good, without water, staying just like when they were picked. That was when people cared for each other and respected each other's belongings, when they didn't steal.

"Greens and wild plants that were picked were cowslips, reeds, and mare's tails. These plants were most often picked. There's a certain kind of plant that's cooked called *kapukaraat;* you cook them until they're somewhat like spinach and then eat them with oil. The other plants that are picked in the spring are picked from along the lakeshores or the swamp. Some of these greens can be cooked before eating or they can just be eaten raw. Others that were picked were *anlleqs,* translated as 'mouse food.' You have to dig underground to get these, mostly where there are a lot of mice.

"The little mice's food in the tundra, the bottoms of reeds—in the fall we'd search for them, then after washing them, we'd clean them very well and cook them a little. Those were good, too—the bottoms of reeds, what the little mice gathered. Those were our foods, people's food. We would cut them and use them in ice cream [Eskimo ice cream made with fat].

"I used to watch people make ice cream. They used tallow and sometimes rabbit's kidney oil, the ones whose fur we'd use for parkas. Cook their kidneys in a skillet; when they turn to oil, combine it with the tallow and sometimes reindeer fat, but I didn't used to see lots of reindeer fat because they didn't used to hunt reindeer. But I'd see some. They used to use them.

"Also, we hunted eggs in the spring. There were different kinds of eggs that were hunted: swan eggs, crane eggs, goose eggs, and many others that I don't recall.

"Real foods and wild plants are all good: whitefish, dried whitefish, dried king salmon, and cooked fish from down there [the Kuskokwim]. All the same, they are good. And the heads, cut them and make stink heads out of them. Those we liked, and we'd eat lots of them.

"When we would go fishing, we didn't use to get good sleep because we wanted to take good care of the fish while we could, even if they were in very large quantities. When it turned winter, we quit doing that. We'd dip net and fish trap whitefish, pike fish, and lush fish."

Braiding herring with grass and hanging it to dry.

Traditional recipes from *Kalikaq Yugnek,* interview with Mary Abruska by Dora Williams and Louise Heckman.

"My name is Mary S. Abruska, and I'm originally from Russian Mission. However, I was raised in Kalskag. In these recipes, it must be remembered that Eskimos don't use measurements. They use a little bit of this and that. It is mostly to your taste. In the old days, we didn't have any spoons or measuring cups, and that is the reason there are no written measurements, at least until the kass'aqs came around.

Ptarmigan Soup

"First the man or boy must catch a ptarmigan while hunting. The girls tear or pluck the feathers off; if you're in a hurry, tearing is best. If it is a fat ptarmigan, you might want to save the fat; however, it will take longer to prepare it for cooking. Tear the skin off, starting from the neck and pulling it all the way down. Be sure to save and use the meat on the upper part of the wings.

"Cut up the ptarmigan just like you would a chicken. Take the intestines out, but save the gizzards, the heart, and the liver. You may want to drain the blood out. Put the ptarmigan in six quarts of water. Usually Eskimos wash it first; however, some don't wash the bird because they like the wild taste.

"Cook the bird for five to ten minutes in boiling water; then add one cup of rice and one cup of potatoes. Put in about one teaspoon of salt. If you add whole potatoes, use about three and be sure to peel them.

"Put flour in a bowl and add water until it is pasty but not too soft; then add the flour to the pot with the bird to make gravy. Let the pot simmer for about five minutes, and the ptarmigan is done.

Eskimo Ice Cream

"For a family of six, obtain a small king salmon, gut it, cut it up, and boil it. You don't have to add salt. Boil the fish for about fifteen minutes, starting with a fast boil but turning the heat down to a simmer toward the end of the time.

"Place the fish in a bowl of cold water. When the fish has cooled, take out its bones and squeeze out the water. Add two scoops of lard, mixing the lard and the fish together with your hands. Stir the fish and lard until the lard is fluffy, and then add another one and one-half scoops of lard. Continue mixing in lard until the fish is no longer sticky. If you feel that the mixture is too thick, add some of the water in which you boiled the fish to make it thinner.

"Add two cups of sugar and stir it in with your hands until you don't feel the grains of sugar anymore. Add as many kinds of berries as you would like to make the ice cream more tasty. Stir the whole mixture well.

Russian Pie

"They call it *piluguq;* it is better known as pillow.

"Make a piecrust out of four handfuls of flour, one tablespoon of baking powder, a teaspoon of salt, and two scoops of lard. Put all the ingredients together, using your hand to mash them into the lard.

"When the lard is like really small pebbles, use your hand or a fork to continue mixing it; then roll it out into a piecrust, adding about one or two teaspoons of water to make it smoother.

"Cut salt fish into three chunks and add it to about six cups of rice and water, letting it sit overnight. The next day, boil the rice and fish together.

"While the rice and fish are boiling, put the dough into an oblong pan, but make sure to cover the bottom and the sides with grease. Add the rice and fish with the rice on top. Cover the whole dish with the remaining dough and place in an oven at 350° for about forty-five minutes."

STARVATION WILL COME SOMEDAY

from *Kwikpagmiut,* by Emma Smith, Donna Smith, and Irene Smith.

Kirt Bell was born September 22, 1910, at the far end of the old village of Hooper Bay. Kirt now lives in the new village of Hooper Bay. He has four sons and four daughters. He works part time in the school as an instructor in cultural heritage. Sometimes Kirt is the main attraction at local activities. He is known as the best Eskimo singer and dancer in Hooper Bay.

Kirt remembers his mom breast-feeding him when he was very little. At that time he had no brothers or sisters. She always used to carry him on her back, bringing him downtown, and people said he was getting to know everything.

When Kirt was small, the people were starving and they didn't used to eat

The village of Hooper Bay on the Bering Sea coast between the Yukon and Kuskokwim rivers.

a lot of food. They got skinnier and skinnier. In those days, the people had no canned food, guns, or nets.

"The starvation will come someday to Hooper Bay. You'll soon remember the words the old have said. It's not always going to be like today. When people are hungry, they cannot laugh or be happy. They will be like this when their stomach is empty and their lips get black because of the hunger.

"I can remember my mother used to let me eat some of the bird parka. Also, she would take the furs and let me chew them when the dirt from my parka was gone. I would eat my parka when it was clean enough.

"During the starvation time, mukluk boots may help you through the day. First of all you boil them in the pot; then, you eat.

"If you have a kayak, you boil it and eat it with oil. But if you have an old one, don't cook or boil it because when you eat the kayak it will roll over in your stomach and kill you.

"You often see mice on the tundra. You laugh at them and kill them. If the starvation comes, you will even eat them. Mice are food. You put a mouse into boiling water until the fur comes off. Then you cook the mouse again in the boiling water [even if it's only one]. If you cook the mouse, the house will smell like food. It is okay if you eat the mouse."

Kirt remembers some foods like greens that are in the ponds. He remembers that the greens were near the end of the old village of Hooper Bay. Lots of women gathered like herds of reindeer to pick the greens in the water. They added oil to make them tasty to eat.

"Those things like berries were good to eat in summer: salmonberries, blackberries, cranberries, and alpine bearberries. If you combine mushrooms, moss, water, and berries, you can make Eskimo ice cream, which is called *akutaq*. But you have to stir constantly until it looks like shortening. You keep adding water, but not too much. When you finish making it, you put the berries into it. If you eat it too slow, it will turn into water.

Kirt Bell remembers when he used to round up the nets with other guys. In those days, the people didn't know very much about the nets that we have today. First they dried the sealskin. The men cut up the skin to make some flounder nets. Then the old women made the net longer. The salmon fishnet had the same mesh size as the flounder net. The men made smaller nets for needlefish.

"The people got skinny. Boys stopped working because of weakness. When people are starving, they won't be able to cheer themselves up. People won't be able to laugh or run like they used to."

Special thanks to Kirt Bell, who made this story possible.

SOD HOUSES WERE WARM

from *Tundra Marsh,* by Joseph Berlin, Jerry Sam Wassillie, John Wassillie, and James Chaliak.

We were curious about what it was like to live in sod houses. Being made out of mud, were they dirty? . . . did they leak? . . . were they hard to build? To answer these questions we talked with Allen Stone, Abraham Hawk, and Evan Wassilie, people who had built and lived in sod houses.

Allen Stone is an expert in building sod houses. He was born in 1918 in Rainy Creek, Alaska. He said Rainy Creek was in the mountains. Allen Stone lives in Nunapitchuk now, a village far from the mountains. He lives alone in his house. Besides building sod houses, he also knows how to build sleds. He has a dog team and uses it.

The sod house, once the home of every Eskimo family in this area, is now used as a temporary shelter for hunting, camping, or possibly while a person is waiting to complete his wooden house.

Abraham Hawk also lives alone. He is sixty-one years old. He remembers many of the good things about living in sod houses. Abraham is a bell ringer at the Russian Orthodox church.

Evan Wassilie was born around 1907. He lives in Nunapitchuk with his family. He has four daughters, two sons, and three sons-in-law. He has a dog team, but uses his snow machine most of the time. He also knows how to build sod houses.

We had three interviews but decided to combine them into one, picking out those things which each man told us about sod houses, putting these

Turn-of-the-century sod houses along the Kuskokwim River.

statements in the order in which they actually would happen if you were constructing a sod house.

"What part of the land is good to build a sod house on?"

"Eviineq [place where it is grassy and is higher than most of the ground —knoll]. It is better to build sod houses on knolls. If you build one on some other part of the land, the ground will get cracks in it."

"Do you dig into the ground?"

"Yes, dig into the ground. The floor may be four feet down. When the digging and putting posts and frames is done, grass is placed vertically and reinforced by overlapping it together."

"How do you start when you are going to build a sod house?"

"When I'm going to start, I cut the wood all in order. Then at last, I work on the small frames, all in order, too. After the frames are ready, I put the posts and frames in their places. After the frames and posts are ready, I drive them into the ground. I put on the end beams and put short reinforcements to help the posts stay still."

"Do you handle wood alone?"

"Yes, I handle wood alone, unless I cannot lift it. I use drift pine wood, but some people use thick pieces of wood if they have enough of them."

Traditional sod house frame.

Once the wooden frame of the house was completed, the next step was to cover the frame. Frames were covered with wood or willow branches if available. In more recent times, even flattened oil and gas drums were used to cover the sides and roof. Grass insulation was put on next and then covered with blocks of tundra.

"Do you use tundra that has twigs in it or without twigs?"

"The tundra without twigs. Use pure tundra."

"How do you cover the inside parts?"

"After I put the blocks on the outside, I put on another layer of blocks. Two layers of blocks are enough insulation, and you don't have to put any mud inside. We put soft mud on the top. I cut blocks into pieces and place them on top of the house. After that, I cover the pieces with smashed mud. At last I make it weatherproof."

"Do you put in windows?"

"I put in windows, but the windows are not put in horizontally. They are put directly facing the sun [to the south in this area]."

"What kind of windows do you make?"

"We use ordinary windows [four-pane glass], but some time ago we used plastic for windows. Most of the windows are put in diagonally." (Before plastic or glass was used, sealskins with their hair off, seal intestines, and pike skins sewn together were used for windows.)

"What happens to the plastic windows when the weather is stormy and cold in winter?"

"In winter, plastic windows would bust up, so seal guts were used to replace the plastic windows."

"If it drips, what is supposed to be done?"

"If it drips, cover the roof with permafrost, which becomes soft mud. When it is coated with that mud, it will stop dripping."

"Do sod houses have porches?"

"Yes, they do have porches. They need porches in the wintertime because people need to put their things in them. Porches are constructed as the houses are, but they are not insulated enough to keep the things warm. The porches are made to keep the snow out of the house."

"Do the doorways have covers?"

"Yes, we use wooden covers now. We used to cover them with blocks when we went out someplace. We covered them to keep the snow out while we were gone. The regular doors for everyday use were made from animal skins."

"Are the doorways little?"

"The doorways are not so little. We build them big enough so we can come in steadily with something that we are holding."

"Where do you put the door on?"

"I put the door in following the slanted side surface of the house."

"What do they have for the floors?"

"We spread arctic willows on the floor and spread grass all over the willow. At first, it is wet, but when it dries, it is as hard as cement."

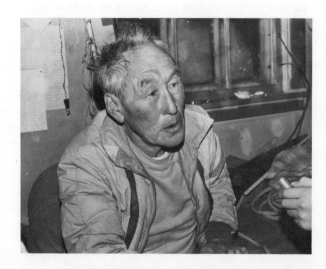

Allen Stone: "In winter, plastic windows would bust up, so seal guts were used to replace the plastic windows."

FIRE BATH

from *Kwikpagmiut.* By Oscar Johnson, Liana Baijot, and Dorothy Joe.
Translated by Evan Kokrine.

Rastus Jones is a sixty-eight-year-old man who was born and raised in
Hooper Bay, Alaska. He now lives in Mountain Village with his wife and
children in the housing development area. This is a true story about fire
baths in Hooper Bay—what they look like and how they are used.

"When making a fire bath house, a wide hole is dug in the ground and
logs are placed around the hole to make a dome-shaped wall. The logs are
then covered completely with mud except for a small opening, which is the
entrance. Inside, after the mud has dried, another small hole is dug for the
fire, and wooden benches are placed along the wall.

"Fire baths are large enough for four people at one time. A bath is usually
taken two times in one day. The fire is lit, and it heats the bath up. Everyone
has a basin filled with water for washing. After the fire dies down [about one
hour], the men wait for a while and then light the fire up again. After the
second fire has died down, the men leave and others come in their place.

"Since the heat becomes so intense inside the fire bath house, a wool hat is
worn to protect the hair and a special mouthpiece made out of wood is used
so the hot air won't burn or damage the lungs.

"Fire baths have been used for a long time, much longer than steam baths.
A fire bath is more favorable than a steam bath because a steam bath puts
out too much heat at one time. The heat from a fire bath grows gradually, so
it is more comfortable.

"Eskimos had a few laws for the fire bath house. Women were not allowed
inside the house, but if they were caught inside, they usually only got a
scolding. In the old days, people didn't break the law, so laws were not
needed.

Inside traditional fire bath house.

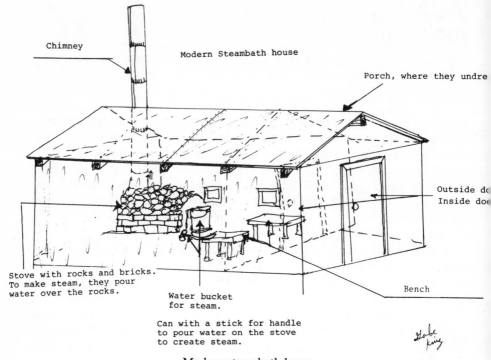

Chimney

Modern Steambath house

Porch, where they undre

Outside do
Inside doe

Stove with rocks and bricks.
To make steam, they pour
water over the rocks.

Water bucket
for steam.

Bench

Can with a stick for handle
to pour water on the stove
to create steam.

Modern steambath house.

"Up until recently, they never used to hold meetings in the fire bath house. Now, while the men are taking a fire bath, meetings are sometimes held. Once in a while they will have Eskimo dances and potlatches. Sometimes the men travel to different villages like Alakanuk and Emmonak to hold potlatches in their fire bath houses.

"To my understanding, taking a bath doesn't really have any meaning, but it is a place for the men to go when they are tired and having troubles, or just when they want to relax."

AK'ALLAAT AKLUT—CLOTHES WE USED TO WEAR

from *Kalikaq Yugnek,* interview with Marie Wassilie by Leonty Lupie and Fritz Beebe.

"When I was beginning to notice, they used to have matches same as what we have now. I didn't know they had [a time with] no matches. Our boots were made of bachelor seal [small ones] or sealskin, and we didn't wear socks. We put grass inside the fish skins for insulation. Then we put them on. They're really easy to put on. When I awoke in the morning, I just got up and put them on. My feet just touched the grass in my mukluks, with no socks to wear at that time.

"Clothes we were wearing usually were made by our parents, like parkas, pants, shirts, mukluks, and others. They were made of different animals, like rabbits, squirrels, minks, and all other animals, including fox. When they were all around, they weren't scarce. There weren't enough clothes to wear. I used to wear just one qaspeq. Lots of clothes weren't available.

"It used to get cold once in a while, and our windows were always covered with frost. When it melted, the snow fell from the window to the center of the floor. We used to have our windows up in the ceiling. We made our windows from seal intestine.

"When I noticed our night lamps, most of them used to be seal oil lamps. Some of us used oil lanterns. It looks like they made enough light. Only when we were working, like sewing something, did we use these lanterns. But there wasn't gas for them because there wasn't any Blazo around at that time; we just had to use those seal oil lamps. There weren't enough blankets to use. We just used our parkas for blankets.

"All women had long hair, and they never used to cut it. They used to tell us not to cut it and not to unbraid it. That is what our parents used to tell us. We used to wear our hair braided all the time; and when we put on our parkas we always put on our belts.

"Our homes never used to be warm. Our stoves were always turned off most of the time except in the mornings. We made hot water in our porch. And we always cooked in the porch, not inside. Our homes used to be made out of mud."

Interview with Nastasia Keene by Mary Paul, Anna Wassilie, and Gertrude Jacobs.

"From what I've seen, people didn't use to wear cloth material [clothes] or coats, but they wore parkas with nice fur that was just right for the weather. We didn't used to get cold 'cause we didn't used to travel to far places. Women used to go only on short trips. The old-time coats are better than the coats nowadays, and the boots are better than today's boots. The boots were made out of furs and sealskin. Sometimes we had *angyurak* that were made out of fish skin. People used to insulate the angyurak [fish skin boots] to make them warmer. Today only the elders like me use parkas and mukluks—not very many young people.

"I didn't catch the older women using old-time needles, when I was born they were using the kind we use today. I've seen people using caribou muscles [sinew] for thread for making mukluk soles or for making parkas. Only a few people used to wear clothes made out of fabric. But they weren't really without fabric.

"At night, they used to sew with a kerosene lamp on, and when they ran out of kerosene oil they would go to the stores. When people couldn't go to

Eskimo woman in traditional parka, with missionary child, Bethel area, early 1900s.

the stores [there weren't very many in the past], they would use seal oil for the lamps. But they weren't lit for a long time.

"Nowadays they use muskrat fur, moose fur, rabbit fur, and bird feathers. I never had a bird parka, but the bird parkas are warm. People would also use geese and all kinds of other birds for parkas. For mukluks, some used sealskin and the end parts of moose fur, and they also used fish skins. After they made the mukluks, they insulated them with a fur that was warm. Also, there were loon skins for sock insoles in the mukluks. The clothing was what our guardians had made for us. We didn't used to get cold.

"People had many kinds of mittens: rabbits and birds. They would pluck the loon and put the material outside the loon skin, but the men used warmer gloves than the women. Men also used seabird skins for gloves that had more fur. Even when they had enough clothes of any kind, they used to only use those that were warm.

"They used to wear socks when I was growing up, but they didn't have very many. I remember I used to have many socks that people had given me, and they gave them not only to me but to other people, too. We also used to have warm booties that were hand-made.

"People used to wear mukluks [boots] without socks, but some wore mukluks with grass inside for insulation. Insulation was used to keep from getting cold feet. They used to put it on top of the booties. All clothes were fur. I never used to see people wearing rubber boots or shoes. We used to stay in the wilderness during our lifetime. Also, I never used to see people wearing nowadays coats.

"I used to see women using scarves, but there weren't too many of them. I was born when all these modern clothes were starting to be; if you ask Mrs. Nichoale Berlin, she will answer you the same way I have. But there weren't many kass'aq clothes that were seen in those days. I'm also telling you [about] some of the old-time clothes that I haven't seen or grown up with.

"In those days, when we used to go back to the place where I was born, people were really friendly with each other. When an elderly man or woman was working, the young people wouldn't just ignore them. When I went with my mother to get ice from the river before she and I would reach the place where she got ice, one or two young boys would come running and take away the sled to get ice for her. When the sled was full of ice, he or they would bring the ice up to her house. The lady who was getting ice would just walk home.

"In those days, people were friendly and helping with each other. When a person who went to get some wood returned, one or two boys would come and take his dogs and tie them to their places. Then they would untie the rope from the sled and unload it. After they were done with that, the boys would take the wood and chop it up. The man would go into the house and eat while the boys were doing all the work for him. After the boys finished chopping the wood, they would bring the chopped wood into the house.

Sometimes the boys would get the job finished even before the man stopped eating. They were using love and kindness.

"I also told this part of the story when the high school students came and interviewed me before. I told it to them when we had nothing to say. Well, I have nothing else to say if you two have no questions to ask. But I told that little story when I thought of it. Since I like the story, I told it."

WHEN THE TIME OF HUNTING CAME

from *Kalikaq Yugnek,* interview with John Kassaiuli by Billy Tom.

John Kassaiuli is from the village of Newtok, Alaska. John is a happy, wise old man with an intelligent smile. Newtok is located on the coast of Southwestern Alaska, about 100 miles west of Bethel. The village population is about 300 people, including the students who are away going to high school and college. Newtok has a muddy area with wildlife such as geese, seals, and other land and sea mammals. Along the muddy side of the river there are boats, old and new. The newest kind of boats are the aluminum boats.

Newtok isn't only muddy. It has lots of grass and many berries to pick. Many women and girls pick salmonberries, blackberries, cranberries, and blueberries.

"When I was about your age, people never used to travel with dogsleds. When the men wanted to travel or go out hunting, they would wake up before the sunrise and start getting ready to travel. They walked long distances and stopped only when they reached their destination. When the night grew dark, they would set out a camp and rest until morning. They slept on the ground without tents. Some men would take along a sleeping bag.

"When the time of seal hunting came, two hunters would go out by sled until they reached their hunting spot. While traveling, the qaspeq [parka cover] of the hunter who was pushing the sled would trail on the ground. That's how they used to travel sometimes.

"When they started having dog teams, the way of traveling was a lot easier. Even the younger boys traveled by dog team. Some of them would travel to get willow trees. The younger boys would only take two dogs to pull the small sled.

"The hunter wouldn't stand around the village and not hunt when it was a good day. In the springtime we got more seal. The hunting was really good. Some of the men sat on the sled. When the traveling was slow and the evening came, the seal hunters would wait until morning and continue their journey.

"Whenever seal hunters came with more than one seal, the hunter would stop and take his bowl of food. He would share the food with us. He would give us a pinch of food. We would accept and eat. They always did this even with many travelers. Every younger person that met a traveler did the same thing. They were supposed to do this before the hunter got near the village. After we had the pinch of food, we would bring the seals to the house, taking two seals and leaving one seal on the sled.

"The lady would go outside with the serving spoon and fill the seal with snow. First, the lady filled the serving spoon with snow all the way to the top. Then she would shove it into the seal's mouth; then the leftover snow would be thrown out the door. They did this so that the seal's spirit would not be thirsty and the spirit could go back to the sea.

"When they caught a small seal, they would cut it up and cook it right away. When they were done cooking it, the lady would go out to get a bowl from each tent and fill it with seal meat. After they had been filled, the lady would take the bowls to the tents. After the people to whom the meat was brought had eaten the seal, the same lady would go out and gather the seal bones. After they did this for the whole winter, they would throw away the bones, which they had collected all winter. They took the bones to the lake and threw them away. This meant that they might have more seals in the following year."

HARDSHIP

from *Kalikaq Yugnek,* interview with George Beaver, translated by Nick Nichols and Joe Joseph.

"The very beginning of my hardship was when I was a little boy; that was when I got my kayak. At first when I watched my parents work, everything they did looked easy. I thought women never had any hardships. I think now of how women work and I find they work very hard each day. Long ago, they had to take care of their children and no man ever took care of a baby, for it was a woman's job. If the woman never did anything for her child, it would die—freeze to death or eat something that was poisonous. That was one of the hardships for women. They fed the baby, looked after him, and taught him to do things right as he grew up to be an adult.

"We never had stores, not like nowadays. We never saw any stores in those days. On cold days men used to hunt from early morning until sundown in order to keep the whole family alive, especially the kids.

"One early summer morning, Dad and I went out with our kayaks. The day was beautiful, the sun was out, and the weather was calm. Anyway, we traveled far by kayak. I really enjoyed it when we first started out, but as we went further and further, I got really tired, and I had to fight in order to keep up with him. The job was hard and never was done because we had to do it every day.

"I was getting close to marrying age and still every morning my dad would wake me up as usual. But it was getting harder and harder as I grew up. Well, one morning I had to go out and check my dad's traps because he told me to. There were fishing traps and all kinds of other traps. WELL! I wouldn't say 'no way,' so I got everything ready and started walking to the traps. I knew where they were. Long ago we never used to ask if we could use the dog team, for it wasn't right. So we used to walk for about twenty minutes.

"While we were gone out hunting game, the women were working hard back at the house or sod house. They had to take care of the baby. At night, if the baby woke up, the mother got up and took care of it. In those days, people never had a stove, or the stove would be out, and it was cold every night.

"Hardship was really there when I got married. Well, there were nine of us in the family and my dad had to take care of us. He gave us shelter and food. We got food by hunting because in those days, as I said before, we had no stores.

"One winter we were out of food and we were starving—all we had was a small piece of pancake. That was all we had for the whole day till the next morning. It was hard, no fun. Nobody could work hard. Little kids stayed put so they wouldn't get too hungry if they were around. My dad went out hunting every day but never got anything. Sometimes he'd get one or two ptarmigan. That was one of my dad's hardships. That was not the least of the hardships in a family, especially for the parents."

TRADITIONS

from *Kalikaq Yugnek,* interview with Mary Black, translated by Louisa Gilman.

"Old women used to have calendars made out of wood with sticks to keep track of the days. The piece of wood had holes in it for each day of the week. They knew when Sunday came. On Mondays they moved the stick back to the very first hole.

"The months they knew by counting from the night the new moon appeared. They knew when the months changed by some things like:

       January—Iralull'er—the bad month
       February—Kanruyauciq—frost month
       March—Kepnerciq—marking point from winter to spring
       April—Tengmiirvik—ducks fly back
       May—Kayangut Anutiit—birth of eggs
       June—Kaugun—hit king salmon on the head
       July—Ingun—ducks can't fly; molting of feathers
       August—Tengun—flying of ducks after molting
       September—Amirairvik—taking off fish skin boots
       October—Qaariitaarvik—month of Halloween
       November—Cauyarvik—month of drumming in Eskimo dance
       December—Uivik—beginning of circling the year

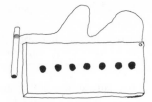

"Old women used to have calendars made out of wood with sticks to keep track of the days.

"They used to tell the time of the day using the sun. When the sun was high, we knew it was noon or about the middle of the day. When the sun got low, we also knew it was nearing nighttime.

"Boys were given advice about what to do when they were caught in a fog or storm before they left for their first hunt on the ocean. They never had compasses in those days. They said that the fog in the ocean is like a blizzard. People said this because nothing could be seen and there was no place to go without knowing where you were. But boys were told to check in which direction the small waves were headed. Those small waves always head toward land, not away from it. If a low tide came, the small waves will

"August—Tengun—flying of ducks after molting."

head away from the shore. Those ways were used like a compass in those days.

"There was also a rule to always help the orphans. By helping, the teen-agers would get respect and love from the orphans, old people, widow, or widower. Teen-agers would also be thought good by people they helped. That person who was helpful would have a good future and he or she would have many people's respect, and many things they wanted would be easy to get. That was the reward for being helpful to people.

"It was a rule to help poor men and women who had no one to take care of them or an orphan whose clothes were ragged and torn: give them something to eat, mend their torn clothes, or give your extra clothing to them. If a person never helped old men and women, his future life would get harder and harder for him. Things would be hard to get; also food would be hard to get. He'd get poorer and the young people he didn't help would grow. They wouldn't pity him or give him clothes or feed him. Young people never forget their past. That was why it was a rule to help the poor, orphans, and the sick. An orphan, when growing up, never would get physically or emotionally weak but would get stronger. People who never helped would not be helped when they needed food, clothing, or shelter. But if a person had helped someone, he'd do the same if the other person needed help in the future.

"These days I hear of predictions that people in these days will go back to living like the old days. The things that are plentiful now will get scarce. The clothing we wear will get harder to make. Also the food we eat will get harder to plant. It is also said to teen-agers by old people that even though we might not like a food, we should try to finish it.

"When Eisenhower was President, he told the people that when the big war comes, the food we eat and the clothing we wear will get scarce, and the plants we eat won't be able to grow again. Everything will get scarce."

JOAN HILL REMEMBERS

from *Kwikpagmiut.*

Joan Hill was born in the mountains seventeen miles west of Chevak near Cape Romanzoff. She is between seventy-five and eighty years old. Her family used to hunt there for food in the winter. This is about the Eskimo culture back in the old days. She says that life now compared to then is the same, but the mountains were fun.

"Long ago people lived in houses made out of logs, twigs, and sod grass. When they made a house, they had to dig a ditch. The ditch was about twenty-one feet by twenty-four feet. After digging the ditch they would put logs on the bottom of the ditch and then put logs on the sides. The last thing they did was to put the sod grass on top of the logs, or on the outside against the logs. The top was also covered. When the house was done, they would move in. The inside was very warm and in better condition than the houses that we live in now.

"Before modern clothes came along, they had clothes made out of bird skins and other furs from animals. They were warmer than the clothes we use now. The men would go hunting for different kinds of birds like geese, ducks, swans, and cranes. The bird skin was lighter than the skin of a sheep. One type of clothes that was made out of bird skin was the parka. The neck of the parka was made out of the swan's neck, and the head of the swan was made into a hood. When the parka was done, a woman would wear it as a coat.

"Before winter came, the people used to go out fishing. When they thought they had enough to last them the whole winter, the women would cut up the fish and hang them up to dry. They would hang them up where the dogs wouldn't reach the fish. When the fish dried up, they put it in the smoke-house and smoked it. They also dried seal meat and reindeer meat. But they weren't smoked.

"Long time ago my dad used to trade furs and get what we needed. There was no money a long time ago, so we just traded. The things my dad traded were mink, muskrat, and weasel furs. Also, a pail of berries was traded for something we wanted.

"We used to go berry-picking by walking. Mary Napoleon's uncle had a boat made out of sealskin, so we started using it and it was better than walking.

"The people didn't litter all over the village. They would gather all the trash into a bundle and throw it in one pile on the tundra. In the summertime, they would gather all the bones and put them in a sack so that they could dig a hole and throw them away. Or they would put them into a certain lake, buried in the bottom of the lake.

"Long ago, people did not know anything about dancing. Then after the shamen came, the people learned to dance. Eskimo dancing was fun, so the people started dancing.

"There were also games that the Eskimos played. Their favorite was playing tag. First they had to make a little house. After the house was done, they would start playing tag. They would play tag around the house that they had made. Whenever somebody was tagged, that person had to go into the house and stay still. There was one strict rule—you had to play around the house.

"The popular drink was Russian tea. That was long ago. In that time, flour was scarce; so was tea. They used to pack water from the pond because there was no well. The most liked was the water from the mountain stream. They liked it because it was cooler.

"Long ago the people never read newspapers or books. And they never wrote letters to relatives or got checks. There was no school around here and there were no whites. The things that we needed to learn were taught by parents."

THE FIRST KASS'AQS

from *Kalikaq Yugnek,* interview with Phillip Charlie by Carl Moses.

"One day I realized there was a sound not far from our place, the sound of machines. The sound was like pif-pif-ffffffffff. It came in and we could see the boat. The boat was white at that point and a fast one, too. In those days, we were scared of white people.

"Some other boys and I ran toward the right side of the riverbank, toward the red area. We hid under there. We stood there for a while. Nothing happened, so we went up the bank and went home carefully. One of them [with me] was Iingayuaq. The rest of them are all gone. We got to the place where there was a kashim and around it were lots of people. There was a boat that was covered with canvas. A small boat was tied to the white boat.

"When I went over to the kashim to check, there were two gentlemen. One had an eye covered on one side of his face. When he smiled, his teeth were white and shiny. The other man's eyes were wide open and there was no need of worrying about him. He had slippers that had elastic and had a buckle to fasten the hook. They sure had neat clothes.

"The same day they went to the kashim, and the man that smiled with his teeth shiny became known as Angyarrluk. The other man, who is still living, was Itkaq. In those days I never used to call them by their name. Itkaq, who is also known as Daniel Mann, had come to get a pet for his nephew.

"After the first kass'aqs came, I would hear a sound of machines when the weather was calm outside. I knew it was the Moravians' mission boat. Once in a great while, the kass'aqs arrived by a barge. Our kass'aq in those days used to do that. When we got to Qinarmiut, I saw a house for the first time. The house was very big, and it had a painted roof and no porch. I wondered who had built the big house. It was the first big house I had ever seen. I really wanted to check the big house, so I did. When I looked there was some plywood. I wondered who built that big house.

"In a few weeks or so, people said that the big house had some people in it. The people had arrived who were going to stay in the big house. They had with them the man known as Kumluilnguq or Matthew Phayele. He was one of my relatives. In those days I didn't know who he was. After that, people said that they had church over at the big house. I didn't know how they had church in those days, and I used to wonder how the people had church.

"Later I learned that the ship or boat had arrived with the bell for a big church. The ship's driver was Evon Petluska. Angutekayak from Napakiak is his father. Evon was the one that brought the bell.

"One day my auntie, who used to stay at our place all the time, took me along to go visit *apaq* [grandpa]. While we were staying there, the bell started ringing. I got ready and we decided to go to church. We went. It's not far from the place we used to stay.

"My auntie was holding my hand when we went in. When we went in, my eyes were hurting because of too much bright light. The whole house had bright lights to me. And it seemed like people's faces were white papers because they were pale. Way back inside were two bright lights known as light lamps.

"People who first stayed there are still living to this day and their parents are still living. Their Eskimo names are Tutmalria and Angciugun. Their younger brother, Petluska's partner, died.

"They had church, and they were singing 'Nanrakapiggluku Nanra.' I put that song into my heart and kept singing it. They also sang a song called 'Agyaq Tankigpalria,' and I liked it again and put it into my heart. When I went home, I sang it in our house. The first song went, 'Nanrakapiggluku, Nanrakapiggluku Nanra,' and the other one went, 'Agyaq Tankigpalria, Agyaq Tankigpalria.' That was the beginning of my life as a Christian."

FATHER FOX

from *Kwikpagmiut,* by Theresa Sheppard, Liana Baijot, and Mel Landlord.

Father Fox, who now resides in Anchorage, came back to Mountain Village to celebrate his Golden Jubilee. It was a festive and memorable occasion in which almost every villager took part. During his short stay, we asked to interview him about his various missions throughout Alaska. We think we've captured some of his thoughts which, when you read them, will send you back to a time that few remember.

"The first time I saw Mountain Village was in 1927 when the boat passed by here. I had come from the 'Lower Forty-eight,' and at the time it took me twenty-seven days from Seattle to the old St. Mary's Mission at Akuluraq. I came down the Yukon River by steamer as far as Holy Cross; then at Holy Cross I got on a small boat belonging to the St. Mary's Mission. It was just my luck that Brother Murphy, one of the brothers from St. Mary's, had come to Holy Cross to pick up the mission's yearly load of vegetables and potatoes from the garden. I got a ride down with him and landed in St. Mary's on August 27.

"After many years down on the flats, I was sent to Mountain Village, which became my headquarters. I was given Father Endal's job, which was taking care of this district. It ran from Mountain Village to a small village that lies between Marshall and Holy Cross. This small village had a little chapel where I went to say Mass about once a month. For the other villages, I would go up and down the district frequently, depending upon how often someone called when they got sick. I used to make the rounds with a small boat because there were not many planes available.

"I always had a boat of some kind. Once I had a houseboat that I traveled in. I had inherited it from Father Lonneux, who left it to me when he left St. Michael. After a couple of years of using the houseboat, I got a canoe for traveling. I never packed much because each station provided me with all the things that were needed, except for a few personal articles.

"In the beginning, when the priests first came down the Yukon, they saw white people only on the north side of the river. No whites went south of the Yukon because they were after something to make money, either timber, mines, or something like that. Strangely enough, all the towns of importance were north of the Yukon. Nome, Barrow, Kotzebue, and St. Michael were the main towns. If you looked to the left side, you'd see only the Natives hunting for meat and fur.

"That's the reason why when our Jesuit fathers came, they went south to the Eskimos. They figured, 'Well, for one thing, we won't have any competition with the Protestants because they went north.' There weren't any missionaries of any kind on the south side. Tununak was their first stop, but they didn't like it because the village was too hard a place to get to. So after about one and a half years, they moved to a new location, where they stayed from 1905 to 1949. In 1949, a boarding mission school was built, and in 1951 it was moved to where the present St. Mary's is now.

"I taught catechism classes at the mission, but when I traveled, it was closed except for services. In each village we had a man or woman who had the key for the church. Every evening they would open the church up for evening prayer. If I happened to be gone and a death or something occurred, word would be sent to me to come and take care of it. I never spent more than a week or ten days at any village. I was constantly traveling.

"In the year 1931, Father Menager became superior of the missions after a terrible plane accident which killed Father Delon, who had been the superior. Father Delon, Brother Feltes, Father Walsh, Ralph Wien, and some others had decided to go up and take a look around before they would leave Kotzebue for Fairbanks. While coming down to land after a few minutes of circling around, Ralph had overshot the field. So he circled again. For some unknown reason, the plane suddenly turned nose down and hit the ground at full speed. Everybody on board was killed. I was at Qissunaq when I heard about the accident. Anyway, I was sent to Hooper Bay, where I stayed for nineteen years, to take Father Menager's place.

"When I first came to Hooper Bay, some of the people had started moving because there wasn't going to be a mission church there. I wanted to have them go to where the present site of Chevak is, but at that time no one cared to go there because there was nothing there except tundra. So they started scattering in different directions toward Old Chevak, where there was hunting and fishing. After about two or three years, they started moving to where the present Chevak is now. George Sheppard had a store there, and that was the beginning of a new town.

"In 1946, I left Hooper Bay to come to Mountain Village. I was here steadily for ten years. In those ten years, I tended Mountain Village, Pilot Station, and Marshall. In 1957, I was assigned to Holy Cross, where I stayed for six years. Then I lived at the St. Mary's Mission for two years and taught there five days a week. The other two days a week I traveled to various other missions. After that, Mountain Village became my headquarters, and I stayed there for three more years.

"In 1968, I moved to Anchorage to become a chaplain in the Native Hospital. They needed somebody who was able to speak the language. In 1974, I was taken off the job for a while but was soon put back. So that's my present situation.

"Thinking back to my early years in Mountain Village, I remember how very poor the people were. They just had nothing. They lived from hand to mouth, same with most all the other villages. When they sat down to a meal, they didn't observe hours as we [non-Natives] do. When a person hungered, he'd just sit down anytime of the day to eat. There wasn't five cents in the whole village.

"For about my first eight to ten years in the area, nobody had any money; they just didn't need it. When they needed grub from the store, they would go see George Sheppard at Chevak with a couple of foxes, or whatever they caught, and they'd throw them on the counter there. Then they would begin looking on the shelves and tell George what they wanted in return for the fur. That was called bartering.

"There used to be some funny stories about it, like a fellow would come in the store, throw a red fox on the counter, and then buy himself a new gun and some ammunition, of course, and a few other things of that kind. Finally, the trader would say, 'Well, don't you think you have enough now for that red fox you have there?' And the fellow would say, 'But I have a fox, you know.' People had no idea of the value of money because they just didn't have it. In fact, the original collection on Sundays was not money but anything that they found useful for themselves, such as furs.

"The people didn't have any paying jobs then. All they did was to work for their living. They always had a lot of extra time.

"I would go around the village at six o'clock in the morning with a hand bell. I rang the bell in the tunnels (everyone lived in an underground sod igloo) and by the time I got back to the church, the whole congregation would be there.

"Maybe one reason why they responded so promptly was because they had no fire in their igloos, nothing except a little bowl full of seal oil. A piece of cloth was hung over the side of the bowl as a wick, and when lit, it gave all their light. There was always a black streak along the wall from the smoke going up. After people lived in a brand-new igloo for about a year, the ceiling would be pretty black. When I first crawled down an igloo, I'd sneeze from the air because of the lack of ventilation.

"The only heat they had for the first years I was there was their natural body heat. Then they started getting stoves. The first ones people had were homemade stoves that stood about three feet high. They were made out of a gallon gasoline can and smaller cans for a stove pipe. Then a couple of years after using this stove, they started getting camp stoves.

"The diet still stayed simple; there wasn't much to hunt besides fox and mink and other small animals. There weren't any bears or moose in the area. This was along the coast between the mouth of the Kuskokwim and the mouth of the Yukon River. That was the area where I worked for forty-one years.

"Traveling back and forth was always a long hard trip, especially in the winter. When my headquarters was in Mountain Village, it took me twenty-six days by dog team to travel from there to Bethel and back again. When I was in Hooper Bay, it was a good one-day haul to Nelson Island. I'd usually start about two o'clock in the morning and drive until I got there at six o'clock in the evening. On days when I traveled shorter distances and I had to pass Bethel, maybe I'd stop for the night at the main mission. In the morning, I'd say Mass and be off again.

"As a means of transportation for my traveling from one station to another, I rode along with George Sheppard, who owned some stores along my route. Whenever I needed a ride going toward the coast or coming back, I simply asked George and he would take not only me, but also my freight [if I had any], to wherever I was heading. He would also provide me with hot meals before I left or when I arrived at Chevak. And when it was getting too late to travel, he would let me stay overnight at his place. I would really like to express my gratitude to George Sheppard for his hospitality and kindness.

"That was the way we had to carry on for many years. It was our way of life. I think if I had to do it all over again, I would choose the same thing that I actually chose. I feel very happy over the work that God called me to."

YUUNGNAQSARAQ CIMIRTUQ (THE WAY OF LIFE IS CHANGING)

from *Kalikaq Yugnek,* interview with Theresa Tangak by Helen Chimigalria and John Henry.

"It wasn't like the way it is now. The people were really poor. It was sad to see people with no food and the people who had food had very little to share with them. They lacked food because they had no boats or engines like they have today. *Qayaq* [kayaks] were the only transportation other than walking that they had for getting around. During the winter, the men would use shovels to clear the snow from their doorways. They never let the snow build up even when the weather was bad.

"When it was time to move to a new camp, most of the poor people would have no place to stay, so they would make shelters in the snow by digging down into it, thus making walls. The summer was easier because it was warmer. The men and women worked very hard to get the things they needed. They never gave up on things that they attempted. When the winter was approaching, they would make mukluks out of sealskin. This skin would protect them from the wetness and cold.

"They would make waterproof mukluks and qaspeqs out of fish skins. They didn't have thread as we know it today, so they made thread from the sinew [connective muscle tissue] of such animals as birds, seals, moose, and many more. From my point of view, the people of today do pretty much as they please because they have more ways of doing things. Our mothers used to teach us how to sew mukluks, qaspeqs, mittens, and other clothing. They also taught us to cook foods like fish, birds, and seals. However, the young women today don't know how to cook some of these and some don't even know about them. The same goes for the young men.

"If they stopped the modern ways of living and had to return to past ways, the young men and women wouldn't know what to do. They haven't been taught; we older people could teach them, but they will not take the time to learn. It's true they have to go to school and work. If they have the time, they should use that time to learn the Eskimo culture."

3. Tales and Traditions

MIKELNGUQ QANLEK ANGTUAMEK (BABY WITH A BIG MOUTH)

from *Kalikaq Yugnek,* a story told by John Wassillie, Sr., of Nunapitchuk; transcribed and edited by Sophia Brink, Gertrude Jacobs, Raymond Alexie, and Anna Wassilie; introduction by Anna Wassilie; illustrated by James Chase, James Chaliak, Zechariah Chaliak, Jr., and Joseph Berlin.

Sophia, Gertrude, Raymond, and I (Anna) went to the house of John Wassillie, Sr., to try and find out about the old-time tales. When we got there, we asked him if he knew about any old tales. He said that he had forgotten the tales. His wife then mentioned a story about a baby with a big mouth. John then recalled that particular story. He began to tell us the story about the baby with a big mouth. . . .

<<<<

"Augkunek niitellruunga nunanek arnat iliit irniangyuinani, irniangelangermi irniangesciiganani, tuquaqluteng.

"Tamaani angalkut pilliniameng angalkut iliitnun, uingan taum', pilliniluku. Canek tua-i akiliqcarluku. Angalkuq tauna, yungyuglutek pilliniluku. Tua-i angalkum tauna arnaq pilliniluku, tamaa-i tuunritaqluku picsaqevkenani alaiqan kasngukevkenaku ilaminun talluqevkenaku tangercetaqluku pisqelluku.

"Pinariami qingalliniluni tauna arnaq. Irninariami irnilliniuq taukuk angayuqaagmi akiagni ikani irniami imkunek qerqullugnek, 'tamakut qerqulluut, nalluaci elpeci, can'get tupigluki plywood-aatun angtariluki, ketii una capkucillinia.

"Taum' arnam irniani tangercecunaku. Elliin taugaam tangvagaqluku. Qanerluni ciutegni ukuk tekillukek. Taum' cam nalluakun qerqulluut akuliitgun akulqucuggarkun tangvagqamiu tauna panini aamarciaqan, tuaten tangraqluku makua qanruluni wavet. Murilkarnauraagguq tuluryaarrlainarnek kegguterluni.

John Wassillie, Sr.

"I once heard about a woman living in a village who had babies that would die soon after birth. In those days, the shaman existed. The woman's husband told her to go to the shaman and to pay the shaman anything to get a baby.

"The woman followed her husband's orders and went to the shaman. The shaman spoke to the woman in a chant. While he danced for her, he told her not to be ashamed of her baby when it arrived and to show the baby to its relatives. As the days passed, the woman became pregnant.

"When it was time to give birth, she gave birth at the other side of the braided grass partition across from her parents. Then the lady put the partition over on the little baby's side. She wouldn't let anybody see the child, but she herself would watch the baby. It had a mouth up to its ears. The woman's mother would watch through the cracks of the braided grass while her daughter nursed the baby. She would see the baby's mouth up to its ears. As she watched the baby, she could see that it had very sharp teeth. The woman's parents told her not to be ashamed of the baby as a reminder of what the shaman had said when he cast a spell on her. Even though the shaman had told her not to be ashamed of the baby, she wouldn't let it be seen.

"Taum' angayuqaagken pilaryaaqelliniluku, kasngukevkenaku pisqellratun pilaasqelluku, taum tuunrikestelallran. Tua-i pingraagni kasngukluku tauna irniani tangaavkanrilkurrluku piaqluku. Tua-i tauna mikelnguq aurrsaurrluni waten, aurrsaurtengaarluni, unuut atam iliitni, camek tauna arnaq qiaryiggngalngurmek, uigarcami niicugniqalliniuq, qerqulluut amatiitnek qiaryiggluni, qiaryigtaqluni akma. Tuall' tauna arnaq picuqcaarluni atraqertelliniluni. Tamaaggun qerqulluut akuliitgun tangllinia ak'a tua-i caqutmi keggatii nanglliniluku, nerrlinikii aamaanek ayagluku aamallermini egmiutelliniluku.

"Egmian arnaq tauna pilugullraagni asarrlukek umciga'arrluni picuqcaarturluni anlliniluni. Uini qasgimi qavaan qarivkenani qasgimun agqerrluni, qasgimiut tupagqelliniluki, tauna panini irniaranun ak'a nangqatallininiluku. Nangkaku qaillun piciqa tayima. Allanun-llu egmirnayukluku.

"Imkut qasgimiut egmian up'ngartelliniluteng, qakemkut-llu nuliateng tupaqluki akluluteng ayalliniluteng. Ayiimeng uaqvaariikun pillilriit. Kuigkun allakun asgurluteng ayagluteng tan'germi avavet qemiurtellratnun.

"Tekiteqerluteng pilliut. Atam taum angutem nuussini, nuussirra'ani qaillun tayim' pitauralria, nem'ini tauni naparyam quliinun nalluyagutellinikii.

"Taukut-gguq uqilalingqertut nukalpiagnek. Tua-i taukuk pillinilukek tauna unicuminaku aqvasqelluku. Taukugnun apertuanqegcaarluku; itqagnek amiigem ukalirnerani naparyaq caavareskaku qulmun piluku, caavareskaku teguluku egmian utercesqellukek.

"Tua-i-llu taukuk nukalpiak qessavkenateg'am tumllermegteggun utqertellinilutek tayima. Kuiggaam painganun anngamek iralian napat akuliitgun ikavet nunat tangvalliniluki: piqanragnegun tauna mikelnguq, ika-i net qayutuurtelliniluki malruk wall' pingayuagni. Anlliuq aurrluni agaa-i, augmek tepervagluni. Tua-ill' ena tauna tekicamiu aurrluni egalrakun mayurluni tayima kanaqalliniluni.

"Tayima mulutacia qaill' utaqalliniluku, mulutacia tuaten cuqluku. Tayima muluuraqerluni, neriniarteqerlukek anlliniluni.

"Tuaten cali aurrluni tunglianun agaa-i mayuan, aipani pillinia: ika-i tekiteksaitellinia, cali tunglingqelliniuq malrugnek piyugnarquq. Egmian kana-

"The shaman spoke to
the woman in a chant."

"Soon the baby started crawling. One night the woman's mother heard
something like a crackling. It was coming from the other side of the partition
of the braided grass. She quietly got down and took a peek through the
cracks of the braided grass. The baby had already eaten his mother's chest,
starting from the breast. While she was breast-feeding him, he hadn't
stopped, but had kept on going.

"The woman's mother quickly put her old mukluks on, dressed warmly,
and quietly went out. Her husband was sleeping in the kashim. She hurried
over to the kashim and woke up the kashim dwellers and told them that her
daughter was being eaten by her baby and she was almost consumed. Who

"It had a mouth up to
its ears."

qautiini tauvet qeraqiluk. Yaatairrluku tauna kitu'urrluku itqercamek 'laa-turramun, aipani pillinia murilkesqelluku elliin paqcugluku qamna apertullra. Itrami egmian tauna tan'gercelengraan apertullra naparyaq yua-rluku pillinia pakma pakemna caqurrarluni apertullra. Egmian teguqerluku anqerrluni 'laaturramun, aipani pillinia, 'Tua-llu-qaa tayima cali piksaituq?' Tayimagguq cali piksaituq, murilkuryaaqaagguq.

"Kitak tua-i cali kanavet pikan, egmian kanaqaqan utereskiluk. Tauna kanaqaan tayima ayakallinilutek. Ayallinilutek tua-i tumllermegteggun aqva-qualutek ayagturalliniuk. Taukut kinguagni, ayakaniraqluteng, cirliqngelriit piluki. Tua-i ayainanratni angulliniluki taukuk. Tauna tua-i nuussiq tunllin-iluku.

"Tauna mikelnguq an'aqami qalrialuni pilallinilria, 'Aanaka ner'aqaa-lli,' tua-i qalarrluni tuaten 'Aanaka ner'aqaa-lli.'

"Tumai yaaqvaarnun maligqaarluki alqunarmek caqiqercesqelluki, tumait-llu amllerpek'naki pisqelluki. Tua-i-llu yaaqsigiiqaameng nutaan sagten-germeng ayagluteng.

"Taum mikelnguum taukut net nanglliamiki tumaitgun ayagyaaqelliniuq. Tua-illu tamakut tuncinraat nallarcamiki, taum'aanaka ner'aqalliillrem yinraat pivkenaki tuncinraat taugaam maligtelliniluki.

"Taukut yuut ayallret nallunrilkengameng tungiitnun nunanun tuavet ayal-liniluteng. Tua-i tekitelliniluteng.

"Qakuan, taukut ayagyuat uqilalriit paqnayugluteng kingunermeggnun utertelliniut, tuncinraat maliggluki. Tuntunek-gguq tua-i tamaani yaaq-sigiqerluteng tayim tuaken avtellratnek tekitaqluteng taklalrianek nerumaaq-luteng ilairumaaqluteng. Taum' pillikai, maligtelliniamiki tuntut. Taugken taum' kinguani tayima tauna qaillun qanrutkumangacuunani niitnauyuunani qaill'pillra. Qaillun taukut, nunanun allanruluteng pillilriit wall'u kinguner-meggnun utertellrullillriit."

‹‹‹‹‹

"The baby had already eaten his mother's chest."

knew what would happen next! Afraid that he might go on to another person, the kashim dwellers started to get ready and went to wake up their wives. They got ready and went away that night. When they left, they went further downriver from the village. They got to another river and followed it upriver.

"When they got to the hills, a man remembered he had forgotten his knife. It was his only knife. It was about four or five inches long and was kept on top of the post at his house. Those people had two young men who were fleet-footed. He told those young men to get his knife because he didn't want to leave it behind. He thoroughly explained to them the exact location where he had left it, which was at one side of the house. He told one of them to feel the post, to slide his hands up to the top and take the knife—then quickly return and give it to him.

"Those boys went back without hesitating along the trail they had followed. When they came to a bank of a river, they sat between the trees and

"They got ready and went away that night."

"They sat between the trees and watched the village across the river because the night was moony."

watched the village across the river because the night was moony. As they watched, the child had already gone through two or three houses. Then he went out crawling. Blood stains were around his lips. When he came to a house, he crawled up to the window and down into the house. They then watched the house and measured how long he was in the house. The child finally came out just when they were getting anxious. Again, he crawled into another house. Then one observer said to the other, 'He didn't get to it yet. The house has two houses next to it. When he goes into them, we should go across.'

"When it went in through the window of the next house, they ran across. They ran past the other houses, and went in the porch of the old man's house. One boy told his companion to keep an eye out for the child, and he would look for the knife that the old man had said would be there. He then went in. Even though it was dark, he searched where the man had said the knife would be. He felt a pole; then he reached up and felt for a cloth which was wrapped around the knife.

"When he had found it, he took it right away. He went out to the porch quickly and asked his friend if the child had come out yet. His friend said he had never come out, even though he was watching. Then the boy told him again, 'If he comes out and crawls into the next house, we should run back.'

"As the child came down the window, the two boys unwound the cloth wrapping and saw the little knife. Quickly, they rewrapped the knife and tied the cloth. The child was now in another house and was gone for a while. The two companions went running, using their same tracks, and they kept on going. The ones ahead of them had gone on only a little distance because they had to wait for the ones that were getting weak. While they were waiting, the two young men caught up with the group and handed the knife to its owner.

"They spread out and went in the direction of a village they knew."

"Meanwhile the child continued to crawl from house to house chanting, 'I ate my mother! I ate my mother!' After going through all the houses, the child tried to follow the tracks of the people. When the child saw reindeer tracks, he followed them instead of the humans' tracks.

"The people traveled, following reindeer tracks. After they went along the tracks, they were told to get into groups and suddenly turn away from the tracks, trying not to make many tracks of their own. They spread out far from the reindeer tracks. When they got far enough, they spread out and went in the direction of a village they knew.

"After the people had arrived in the other village, the fleet-footed young men went curiously back to the trail they had taken. As they followed the reindeer tracks, they came to some dead reindeer partly consumed. The runners assumed that the child was to blame for the reindeer's deaths.

"Nothing more has been heard or seen of this child who once ate his mother."

(Another related story tells a mother who has a nursing baby not to turn her back on the baby while sleeping. If the mother does this, the child may grow a big mouth and sharp teeth and consume the mother.)

"Nothing more has been heard or seen of this child who once ate his mother."

THE DOG THAT ATE THE GIRL TO SAVE HER

from *Kalikaq Yugnek,* story by Carl Flynn, translated by Cecilia Kasayak.

This story is by Carl Flynn of Tununak. He was born in Kvingartelleq in 1913 and has been living in Tununak as long as I have known him; he is planning to live in Tununak until he dies.

The story is mostly about a supernatural dog who has the power to save people's lives. It is an interesting Eskimo story, and I enjoyed listening to the story as I had never heard a story like it before.

"There once lived a man, wife, and young boy with his grandmother out on the tundra by the river. Down the river there was a village, not far from the place where they were staying. It took them only a day to get to the village by qayaq.

"One day in the summertime, when they got up, the boy's father had a headache. He soon died from the pain. The same thing happened to his mother, too. The grandmother couldn't do anything because she was old. She said to the boy, 'We are not going to stay with these two dead bodies, and I'm not going to be able to bury them because I'm weak. I'd bury them if I had someone to help me. Anyway, we'll go down to the village with your dad's small boat.'

"That evening she got ready to go. She packed food for the boy, and the next day they went downriver. She rowed the boat because the boy was too small to handle the oars. They left the bodies the way they were when they died. The only thing she did was close the window and the door so that some animals wouldn't come in and eat the bodies.

"While they were going downriver, it started raining, and the boy started crying when he got wet. He stopped crying when he was told to stop crying. They both got wet because they didn't have any raincoats. The boy stopped listening to his grandma and started crying again because he was getting soaking wet. The boat also had water in it, and they both were sitting in the water in the boat. Even Maurluq, the grandmother, started crying because of the cold weather. When she stopped crying, she looked at the boy. He was sleeping in the water.

"It was still raining when they got to the village. The village had a qasegiq in the middle of it. They stopped in the middle of the village by the qasegiq. After they got out of the boat, they turned it over and used it for shelter while they waited for the rain to stop. For a while the old lady closed her eyes. When she opened them again, she saw two feet. When she looked up, she saw a man holding a seal gut raincoat in his left hand. In his right hand he held an unfinished gut raincoat and a regular raincoat.

"He said, 'I went to check on you two, to see if you could save my daughter's life. I gave away everything to the angalkut for trying to save her life.

Ted Hootch

Qasegiq—traditional Yup'ik meetinghouse.

The only things left are these three raincoats. They're the only things left to give away.'

"The grandmother said, 'Give me the finished raincoats.' He gave her the raincoats, and she said, 'I wish the raincoats had been here with me when it was raining and the boy was crying. You can keep that unfinished raincoat. I wouldn't be able to use it. The only ones I'm going to use now are the finished ones.

" 'I want you to have the people go to the qasegiq. Tell them that there's going to be an Eskimo dance for your daughter. I want her to be in the middle of the qasegiq, lying on a grass mattress. You should put the other grass mattresses in the underground entrance, one on the ground and one to cover the door. Also, I don't want the girl wearing any clothing.'

"The man went to do what the old lady wanted him to do. As soon as he was gone, she stood up, holding on to her knees. She started walking up to the qasegiq. She stopped five times before she got to the door. The people in the qasegiq put the things in the order she wanted them to be in while she was walking up. When she went in, she saw that the things were already arranged the way she wanted them to be. She sat down for a while. She also saw the man's daughter on the grass mattress without her clothing. The girl didn't know there were so many people in the qasegiq. The only thing she knew was that she was in the qasegiq.

"Then the old lady said, 'I don't want you people to think that I'm doing all the things that are happening, because I'm not going to do the things with my spirit. Just think of it as if it's being done by you people who are caring for her. Someone or something is going to work on your daughter's body because she is dying, and the thing is going to give her life. I'm not going to stay to watch what's happening. I want you people to do what you want to do, sing or dance. Just do anything you want to do.' One of the guys asked her, 'Should we sing old or new songs?' The old lady replied, 'You may sing

any songs. I also want you people to be quiet when something happens while
I'm out.'

"After the old lady went out, they sang songs. Then something like white
smoke started coming in, and they got quiet just the way the old lady wanted
them to. The drummers put their drums on the floor and watched what was
about to come in. The thing had long ears with a little hair on them. When
the face showed, it was big and looked like a dog. When it got into the
qasegiq, it looked around and sat down on the floor.

"The thing had long ears
with a little hair on them.
When the face showed, it
was big and looked like a
dog."

"The people wanted to go out but had to stay in one place and watch what
the dog was going to do to the girl. The big dog bent his back and sat down.
When he got tired of sitting around, he walked over to the girl and smelled
her feet. The people in the qasegiq were just looking at the dog because they
had never seen one so big and ugly. At that time there were all kinds of
things that don't exist today.

"The big dog looked around the qasegiq. He looked worried. When he
went back to the girl, he started licking the girl's body. The girl didn't feel
anything at all even though the dog's tongue was rough. When the dog
finished licking the body, he sat down. Again the dog seemed worried. After
he had tilted the girl's feet, he opened his mouth to eat them and moved on
to the body. He ate faster when he got to the body. While he was eating her
feet, he raised his head up and listened to see if there was any noise in the
qasegiq.

"When he finished eating the girl, he cleaned the blood on the grass mattress and went out like lightning and thunder. After the dog went out, the
people inside the qasegiq were scared because they thought that the girl was
gone for sure. They started singing. Their songs were all mixed up. They
couldn't get together because they all had different songs due to the excitement in them.

"When they heard a voice from the underground entrance, they all stopped singing. The voice was from the old lady. She said, 'I would like two men to come out and get the girl because she is getting cold out here.'

"When the two men got to the entrance it was cold, and the girl was lying by the old lady on the grass mattress. The girl's body was not together. The body was on the grass mattress and the head, legs, and some of her ribs were on the ground. They put all the body parts on the grass mattress and took it inside. When they got into the qasegiq, they put the body parts together the way they were before the dog had started eating her. As soon as the body was together, the girl got up and she tried to cover herself. Then the old lady said, 'Give her back her clothing.' The people gave the clothing to the girl to put on. But she had a hard time, and they had to help her put it on.

"The people all went home. They were happy that the girl was not sick anymore. The old lady and boy went to the girl's house, helping her walk, and her parents went with them to their house. When they got to the house, the man said to the old lady, 'I would like you and your grandson to stay with us as long as you live. We will take good care of you two. We'll give you good clothing, food, and boats.' Then he said to his wife, 'Wife, I would like you to make beds for the two new family members that are going to live with us for the rest of their lives. Here we have a new son and grandmother.'

"The wife told the boy to come to her. The man said, 'We don't have anything more to give you two for saving our daughter. The only thing we can do is let you two live here, and my wife and I will take good care of you. That's the only way we can show you we're happy that you saved our daughter's life.'

"The wife made beds for the old lady and son out of deerskin. The family kept their promise to them by keeping the house clean and by providing food and clothing. When the old lady died, they buried her, and her grandson grew to be big and strong and lived happily ever after."

THE FOOLISH MAN

from *Kalikaq Yugnek,* interview with Mary Black, translated by Liz Jacobs.

"Once there was a young man and he lived alone in the forest. He used to go hunting every day. Whenever he went hunting he used to leave his lunch inside the cliff when he passed it. One day, after he went hunting, he went back to his place and went to bed. The next morning he got up early and went outside to check the weather. While he was outside he heard something and he listened again. It was a woman's voice. The voice was coming from the direction of the cliff where he used to leave his lunch.

"He hurriedly went to his house, packed his stuff, and started walking in the direction of the woman singing. He didn't use his kayak, but took off with his feet. The voice became louder when he got closer. He hid in the rocks and watched the young lady. The woman shut her eyes and slid down the cliff. Her voice became weaker, but it was still loud for him. She kept

sliding down and climbing back up. He walked to the cliff where she slid. The woman slid again and this time she bumped into him. But the lady didn't get frightened.

"The woman looked at him and told him, 'You used to bring me different kinds of delicious foods and I used to accept them all the time because I can't go hunting. I used to be real happy. But now I want you to let me know what my face looks like to you.' The man asked her to be his wife. The woman told him, 'After I get my sewing stuff inside the cliff, you must follow me.' They both began to climb the cliff. The woman climbed the cliff very fast. But the man was slow because the cliff was slippery. The woman helped the man on the cliff. The man saw many different doors. They went in and the lady served him Eskimo ice cream.

"They became man and wife. The man used to go hunting all the time and his wife used to take care of the animals. The woman used to work all the time making her husband parkas, mukluks, and other stuff he needed to go hunting with. During the summer she used to pick berries and fill all her barrels with different kinds of berries. Soon she had her baby and it was a boy. They were both happy with their son. After she had her baby, she no longer was lonely when her husband went hunting. Soon the baby grew.

"Fall came and her husband went hunting for moose. One day her husband didn't return from hunting. But the next day he returned. Again he left and was gone for a few days. Finally, when he came back, the wife checked his parka and mukluks but they were not torn. She found stitches on her husband's parka, but it wasn't her sewing. She didn't tell her husband. Again her husband left to go hunting. This time her husband didn't come home from hunting.

"The wife and her son stayed home alone for one year. Finally it was spring. The woman packed her stuff and her son's mukluks and parkas in a gunnysack. They brought lots of food for the journey. Early in the morning, they started on their journey. They traveled for days and days. The summer was over and they were still on their journey. By fall, they still were journeying.

"Finally they found a place and the woman saw human tracks. Someone had been walking in the forest. They stayed overnight where the tracks were. Before they went to bed, the woman put her son inside the warm parka and rested beside him. The woman fell asleep and she was sleeping well that night. The next morning she was tired of sleeping because she had overslept. She looked around right away, but she didn't see her son. She looked underneath her and saw her son. She got up right away, but her son had died already. She had closed her son's mouth by kneeling on him while she was sleeping and had killed him. She started to cry and dug a grave for him. She put her son inside the parka and put him safe in the grave, putting a stick on the grave. The long stick was her husband's harpoon.

"She left the grave late. By the time she started her journey it was getting dark. Finally she saw a village with its lights on; she saw a big house and it was a council house. She started walking by the village. There was a house but it was by the forest. She walked into the porch and a little dog was in the porch. The dog started barking at her. She heard a voice in the house and it was a woman's voice. The old woman told the young woman who lived with her to go and check the porch. The lady went out and when she opened the door, she said to her grandmother, 'It's a young woman and she's not from our village.'

"The grandmother told her to come in, that she might be in trouble or she might be a stranger. They let her in and told her to eat. But she answered, 'I already had my lunch before I started my journey.' The lady told the old woman that she had accidentally killed her son while they were sleeping not far from this village. 'We had our long journey looking for my son's father. Last fall he left for moose hunting. He didn't come back to us.'

"The old woman told her about a young man who used to come to their house and stay overnight with them. He had fallen in love with the young lady and they got married. 'I don't know where he came from.' The lady asked her, 'Where is he?' The old woman answered, 'He's in the mud house and they're having Eskimo dances. The mud house is full of people and they're performing.' The lady took out her beautiful parka made with different designs and she put it on. She told the old woman that she was going to the mud house to dance.

"She went to the mud house and entered. Her husband was playing the drums and singing. Everybody had finished dancing. But she yelled and told the people that she was going to dance and she would sing by herself. She started dancing and singing. In her song she sang that she was married to the man holding the drums sitting by the edge of the wall. 'After I had my baby boy he left us alone and I accidentally killed my son.' The man quit playing his drums and stared at his wife. Then the man went out ashamed. He wanted to go back to his first wife, but she wouldn't accept him. The man went back to his second wife.

"Even though he went hunting, he never used to catch animals; even if he put out his fishnets, he never used to catch any fish. Soon they both had starved and died. But his first wife married another man and they lived happily after her first husband died from hunger."

THE HORROR OF THE UNKNOWN

from *Kwikpagmuit,* by Ursula Beans.

Sometimes in Pilot Station when there's nothing to do during the evening, and my mom is not too busy, we ask her to tell stories about the old days—stories she heard from the older people. Most of the stories are short, and to make a short story long, this is what I wrote "about a man who never did cover his windows at night."

This story is about a young man who once lived away from the village. He'd come home every once in a while to the village for his needs, or when he felt like having company around him. He didn't have relatives living in the nearby village; he had few friends. He wasn't the type who made friends easily. He was so used to being alone and doing things by himself that he was bashful in meeting people.

One night he was home in his cabin. He didn't feel like going out visiting and, besides, he thought he'd get some things done. So he fed his dogs and chopped enough wood to last a day or so.

The night was cold, and the moon shone brightly on the white, snowy ground. The young man could see his dogs all cuddled up in their fur for warmth after having a big meal. He went back into the house and sat down to a snack of tea and bread.

He was sitting in front of the window. His dogs started whimpering like they did when they were frightened. He kept glancing out the window, not knowing what was happening. Suddenly, startled, he sat there frozen stiff, facing the window with his eyes and mouth wide open.

Some people said he had seen something horrible and frightening that scared him to death. And since then, people say you should always have your windows covered each night.

As I've heard it, this has happened more than once. Others have been found in different villages with the same frightened looks on their faces.

GHOSTS

from *Kalikaq Yugnek,* interview with Lucy Beaver, translated by Janet Kasayuli.

"My name is Lucy Beaver and I'm sixty-one years old. This month on October 10 it will be my birthday. I am from Nunapitchuk and now live here in Bethel; it's not too long that I have lived here. When we were young, they told us to never walk around at night. They always let us go to bed early because if someone walked around at night he would see a disembodied spirit or images of ghosts in front of the door. When they told us this, it would make us scared so that we never wanted to walk around at night. We were scared because something might happen to us. We used to believe what they told us without mistrusting them.

"In those times, when I asked my mom what that spirit or image of a ghost was, she would say that when a person walked around at night too much he would see a person standing out of the ground. And if he saw this, there was a rule that even though he was very scared, he should go over to the ghost and find his collar and try to touch his skin. That was the rule even though he was very scared. Then when he touched the ghost's skin, his hands would get cold immediately and that thing could not be held for a long time because it's very cold.

"After that happened, you were to try and touch the head of this thing with your hands; then slowly push down with all your might. That way the thing would go down. Then all of a sudden, the land would turn as the thing was pressed down. As it was pressed down, it would come up a little but yet go down as it was pushed; and then the world would turn even though it was very cold in the winter [when they spotted those kinds in the winter]. The world would turn them, and as it did you would use your hands and rub the image of a man's head, never looking at it until it really stopped the earth completely. What was that thing out of the ground? It was an image of a man who had been dead. That's what they used to tell us to believe when we were young."

◂◂◂◂◂

from *Kwikpagmiut,* interview with Alec Trader by Mary Augustine, Diane Trader, and Francis Peters.

"If a person sees a ghost standing in the air, he should try to walk in a different direction. If it doesn't work, if it keeps going in your way, try and touch his head. Push it down until it's all the way down to the floor of the house or land. If you don't do that, when he disappears you'll start vomiting green stuff and maybe die right there. Usually people from the dead appear to their relatives or maybe even to somebody else."

from *Kalikaq Yugnek,* interview with Anna Okitkun, translated by Cecelia Housler and Theresa Pitka.

"Here's a person who saw a ghost, but didn't do anything to make it go. One winter, Charlie went hunting with his dog team. As he was going along the trail, he met a man walking. The man told Charlie that his feet were freezing and asked for a pair of mukluks. This man had been dead for quite a while and Charlie had known him. Charlie looked around in his sled and found a pair of mukluks. He gave them to him. As he did that he thought, 'Am I crazy? This man has been dead.'

"Without knowing anything, he was asleep. Finally, he woke up. He looked around and he was on the river not far from the village. Charlie went back to the village and the people noticed that he looked different and started asking him questions. He didn't feel like talking at that moment, so he didn't answer them. Finally, he told them what had happened while he was hunting. He got sick a few days later. He started vomiting green stuff, but he got better afterwards.

"This happened again on his next hunting trip. It was different this time. He heard a crying sound and the same thing happened to him. He fell asleep without knowing it and woke up near the village. This time the villagers wiped him with fish. This was their custom to scare ghosts away. It never happened again to Charlie after that."

CINGSSIIKS

from *Kalikaq Yugnek,* interviews with Minnie Carter and Tom Nelson, translated by Theresa Pitka and Lovey Stephanoff; and Helen Chimegalria and Sophie Evan.

Cingssiiks are described as mysterious small magical people, like small elves. They are about a foot tall. They live mostly in the wilderness and hills, away from the villages. People are afraid of them because these little magical people used to steal their belongings. Some magical people are described as being attractive and others have animal looks. It is believed that when a person gets caught by these magical people, the time flies by without the person knowing it. For example, two hours may seem like two minutes and one year seem like one day. It is also believed that these magical people will grant you whatever you wish.

"A man from Eek was hunting moose up in the mountains. After hunting he went home. On his way he found a tiny sled fifteen inches long. He was planning to take the sled home, but decided to leave it alone. The next day, when he was back in Eek, he decided to go and get the sled. When he got to the place where the sled had been, the sled was gone and there were small tracks leading away from there.

"In one village there was a certain house where the magical people always went to play. One guy from the village who was always unlucky in hunting and fishing knew about the magical people. He planned to hide in the house and try to catch one of the magical people. He went into the house; soon the magical people came through the walls and began to play near him. They didn't come close to him, staying just out of reach. Then one of them came close enough and he grabbed him. The small magical person kept on struggling very hard to get away, but the man held on. Finally the magical person asked him what he wanted. The man told him that he was always unlucky in hunting and fishing. He let go of the magical person, and after that time he was lucky in hunting and fishing because the magical person gave him good luck.

"A long time ago, old people used to make their nets out of wood or willow trees because they didn't have any of the materials they use today. The men used to work on their nets all day and when evening came, they left the nets outside undone. When they would return to finish the nets, they would already be done. The nets or whatever they left undone would always be done inside out. This was believed to have been the work of the magical people."

"I noticed something different about the village; it seemed empty and the hills seemed to be really big. That evening we got some wood to use in the morning. When we finished, we went to bed.

"I woke during the night and I went outside. There was a light shining from the hills. Even the little pieces of wood on the ground made shadows. When I looked towards the hills, I saw faces of spirits along the top of the hill. The faces were shining extremely bright! I went into the house to tell everyone about it. 'Get up, get up! Quit sleeping! Look at the lights up in the hills!' Then we all went out to see. We started squinting our eyes and backed

"When we would watch the faces of the little magical people just for a while, the looks of them would make us feel dizzy and we would have to look away."

away from the bright light. The faces of the spirits were like electric lamps. Very bright! Some were on top of each other. Then suddenly the lights disappeared one by one. It was dark again. The lights that we saw on top of the hills were the lights of the magical people.

"I had seen them about three times before. Once I saw a woman with a cane. The cane was quite long. She was wearing a dress and a hat. I was heading towards her, but she started going over the hill before I got to her. When I got to the hill, she had disappeared. I looked around for her but I didn't find her. So I went on home.

"When we would watch the faces of the little magical people just for a while, the looks of them would make us feel dizzy and we would have to look away. We once thought they were the first white people around this area where we lived because of the clothes they wore, but now we realize that they are the little magical people that come from the wilderness."

LEGEND OF JOHN WOODS

from *Kalikaq Yugnek,* interview with Teresa Nanok, translated by Pat Nanok.

"It all began when there was a war between the Qissunaq people and the Yukon people. They used bow and arrows when they went to war.

"At that time in the village of Qissunaq, the men gathered together to get ready for war. They were inside the qasegiq [men's meetinghouse]. They asked one of the men if he was going with them. He answered back that he had no reason to fight with the other village.

"This man was sterile and he didn't have any children. Then the shaman said to him, 'If you go fight with the others, they will give you a child as a reward.' This made him very thankful. All winter long, the shamen of Qissunaq were performing the rites, trying to get a child for this man.

"Spring came, and the shamen would say that there was something in the north. It was in the summertime when the raid from Qissunaq came upon a woman and a child. The woman was a grandmother to this child. They asked her where she came from, and she said she came from around St. Michael. Her granddaughter's name was Caganaq, and her own name was Tayarin. They took them back to Qissunaq and gave them to the man who was sterile. They gave him this child as a reward for going to war.

"Soon the time came for Caganaq to get married. She had children, and one of these children was my father, John Woods. He remembered, as a little child, that the village had a fear of going to war. His mother used to tell her children that if the Yukoners should raid, they shouldn't take part in the fighting because they had relatives up at the Yukon.

"This man, John Woods [Alqalla Gnoraq], did not know fear, and he didn't like having company while at sea. He always went to sea alone. One time, the people of Qissunaq were pretty sick from some illness. John Woods was ill himself. He said he was going down to the sea to get well. It was like going to the clinic at the sea. The next day he came back. He wasn't even ill and he had brought a seal from the sea. So his wife cut up the seal he brought and took the blubber, cutting it to the size of a mouthful, and cooked it. After that, he delivered the blubber to the qasegiq, giving it to the men who were ill. That did the job of bringing them back to life.

"Once again he went out to sea to hunt seals in the month of March. All day long he was paddling in the sea. When the night came, he slept on an iceberg. The next day he caught a bearded seal. So he tied the seal to his kayak and paddled up to the same iceberg. He got up to the ice, holding the line which was attached to the seal. As soon as he stepped onto the ice, the seal struggled and let the kayak sail into the open sea. He took the pick to reach it but could only just scrape it. He didn't know what to do. The weather was cold and he could freeze. He managed to kill the seal with his pick.

"After he took the seal up to the ice, he took his clothes off. As he was taking his clothes off, he thought back to the time he used to swim in the river. He could always grasp the end of the kayak and jump right into it. He looked at the sea; it was cold. There was ice all around, thin ice. He took his pick and picked off the edge of the ice so he could lower himself into the water easily. As he went into the water feet first, his body was numb. His neck was like it was tied with some weaving grass [for making baskets]. He swam towards his kayak with his ice pick in his mouth. His kayak was already quite far away. I guess he swam about one mile.

"As he was swimming towards his kayak, he heard something. He found out it was his own voice, but he was too cold to notice. He also noticed he had lost his ice pick. The atmosphere around him was red like a medicine bottle. A male bearded seal came and splashed around him; finally the seal went away. As he was swimming through the icy water, he came upon a little ice which he thought would be a help to him when he caught up to his

"He swam towards his kayak with his ice pick in his mouth."

kayak. Again he went closer to his kayak. The ripple which was created by his body kept the kayak at bay.

"Finally he went around the kayak to the calm side of it. As he came to the calm side of the kayak, he tried to lift his arms out of the water into the hole of the kayak. But his arms were stiff in a bent position and wouldn't straighten up. He didn't know what to do, so he dove down and shook his legs. Somehow he managed to put his hands through the little hole on top of the kayak. He held onto it tight. He was weak and his body was freezing. He tightened his grip and tried to swim with the kayak as he had done in the summertime. This time he put the front of the kayak against his chest and, using the other arm, he swam on, even though he was going very slowly. Everything around him was real red as if he was in a medicine bottle.

"He knew he was in the process of freezing to death. As he was swimming along, he came to the little piece of ice which he had come to earlier. So he stopped and went from the front side of the kayak to the middle where he was going to get inside. He lifted himself with the support of the kayak and sat on the little piece of ice. As he sat on it, it was like sitting on a pillow. It was very comfortable because his body was too cold to notice the sharpness. Not just anybody could have made good use of this ice. So with the support of the ice, he pressed his hands around the ring of the kayak and was hanging inside it.

"After safely getting into it, he looked around and saw his ice pick in midair. He paddled over and just picked it up. Then he saw his clothes in midair, as if they weren't on the iceberg. He paddled to the iceberg where his clothes were. He got to the place and got out of his kayak, taking the kayak by the little hole. He pulled his kayak out of the sea. While pulling it out of the sea, he would sit back once in a while. He was like a little child pulling something to a certain place.

"He got it out of the sea and put his clothes on. He took his tobacco pouch and was going to chew, but he noticed he couldn't open his mouth. Following the saying, he took his water bag and urinated in it. He tried to drink it, but it seemed as if he was drinking through a straw.

"The atmosphere around him was still red. He put his head inside his parka to keep warm. Then he noticed he could still see the sky. So he put his head inside his parka again, but still he noticed that he was facing towards the sky. He just kept looking at the sky, and then he saw a parka made from swans coming down. It was all puffed up. The hood was up and the arms were reaching out, as if somebody was inside the parka and it was ready to be put on. It was so bright and pretty as it was coming down. The parka came down and landed next to him. Following the rule, he shoved it off without looking at it. After that it was gone, disappeared.

"So he went back to the position he had held earlier. Again he was facing the sky. Then out of the sky came a bearded seal gut raincoat. It was reaching out and all ready to be used. It just landed in front of him. Again he shoved it off. This man, John Woods, was a man who never forgot the rules, one who would swallow all the information and never forget it. If he had put on the parka and the raincoat, he could have frozen to death. He followed the rule and survived.

"Finally, as he was staying there, he saw an opening of sunshine way up in the sky. It came down very slowly and finally it hit the kayak. Now he noticed that the weather was real warm. So nothing was going to happen now. He got up, started cutting the seal, and went home. After that he still stuck to his routine.

"Years later, after he had children, he became blind and old. That's the story he used to tell us."

THE MAN WHO RAN AWAY

from *Kalikaq Yugnek,* interview with Esther Green, translated by Katie Green.

"This is a story about a relative of mine who is now living in Kwethluk. Well, the story begins this way: A man was married and he had two sons. For some reason he and his wife couldn't get along very well together. Then one day, some problem arose between this man and his wife. So his wife took a knife and said to her husband that she was going to kill herself and this made the man very scared. All he could think of was to run away from home. The minute he thought of that he went out of the house and he started running toward the wilderness, toward the hills. Then, all he had in his mind was, 'I know my wife killed herself already. What will happen to me if I go back and check on her? The whole community will blame her death on me. They'll think I killed her.' So he decided to keep on running and running.

"He didn't want to go back to his own village, so he stayed out in the wilderness. For many days, he stayed hidden under a stump of a tree and he was scared all the time. Men were looking for him. He could watch them, but they couldn't see him. And the way they talked and the way they looked around, it looked as if they were really looking for some kind of animal and this made him even more scared. Once those people started going home, only then would he go out and stretch around. He never even thought to eat. On the tenth day, he felt very light. On the tenth day when he looked at the mountains, the mountains between Bethel and Anchorage, he said to himself, 'Gee, I wonder how these mountains would look if I go nearer to them?'

"He just took two big steps to get to the mountains and he explored all around them, but he always had to go back to his one hiding place. Then one day, after he had gone all around the world, he went back to his hiding place. He was just sitting under the stump thinking to himself that maybe people would think that he was dead by now, that probably they wouldn't look for him anymore.

"So while he was thinking that, he heard something, kind of like thunder right above his head. And it seemed that it cracked and thunder came and then the stump opened. And the light came through the crack, bright lights shining in on him. And he heard a voice saying, 'What you are doing is wrong. You should go back to your family. Everybody is okay, but they are worried about you. You should go back. What you are doing right now isn't what humans are supposed to do, only the animals. You're not an animal, you're a human.'

"And the voice was telling him about how his place right then was in darkness, with no light. As soon as the thunder came back, it just shut the crack. All of a sudden he realized that he was in a really dark place under the ground and he felt scared. Before the thunder closed down, the voice that was speaking to him had said that if he did go back to the village, he should not go to any other houses except to the house that was on the very last row of houses in the village, where an old woman lived all by herself.

"After the crack shut, he felt afraid. It was like something opened his mind to the fact that he was really human, not an animal. He saw the entrance that he had used to go in and out through. That little hole was just small and he was wondering, 'How in the world did I used to go in and out and the hole seemed to be big all the time, bigger than my body.' But then, when he tried to go out, the hole was so small he had a hard time going out of it.

"Then finally he got outside and he looked at the place where he used to hide all the time. The hole was small; only a tiny animal could go in. He even had to break pieces of mud in order to go out. When he came back he did exactly what the voice had told him to do. He went to the very last house where the old lady lived. As soon as he walked in, the lady greeted him and she started talking to him, putting some sense in his head. And that was when he really realized who he was."

WATER CREATURE

from *Kalikaq Yugnek,* interview with Eva Black by Lucy Westcoast.

Eva Black, age sixty-nine, is a small lady about four feet tall with a medium build and gray hair. She was born in the winter at Hooper Bay, Alaska, which is located 100 miles northwest of Bethel. Eva has lived in Hooper Bay all her life. She never went to school when she was a kid because at that time there was no school. She knows a lot about the Yup'ik culture and told a story about "Capiliaq."

"This is a story about Capiliaq [warrior of long ago] who was hunting eggs behind the hills. He was getting eggs from a lake which had lily pads in the middle of it. After he took the eggs, he looked back where he had been wading through and he saw something huge! It looked like a monstrous bug with mouths on both ends of its body. He had learned to keep those creatures from harming him. He knew the admonition, 'Do not go around it, because it will eat you. Try to jump over it.'

"Using his long stick to hold down the creature, he vaulted over the monster. Capiliaq had to use all his strength to jump over it to get to the other side. After he got over it and quickly got out of the water, he looked at his thighs. They were cut and bleeding from jumping over the monster's rough-skinned body. If Capiliaq had gone around the creature, he would have been eaten. That is why people say that you are to try and jump over instead of going around it."

ESKIMO HUMPTY DUMPTY

from *Kalikaq Yugnek,* interview with Henry Teeluk by Sally Carter.

Before this story was told, Henry Teeluk told us that there are two different Humpty Dumptys. One he called the Eskimo Humpty Dumpty, and the other was the kass'aq Humpty Dumpty. This kass'aq Humpty Dumpty not only fell off the wall, he also fell apart and nobody could put him together again. This Eskimo Humpty Dumpty didn't fall—he hung on to a tree and he didn't break.

"Every village has grandchildren and they usually stay with their grandmas. Now at the end of the village lived two grandchildren. One of the grandchildren wasn't like a human. In the same village, there was a young man who had a daughter who wasn't married.

"Now, this grandson who wasn't like a human was all head—no legs, no arms, no stomach, no body, just all head like the Humpty Dumpty who sat on the wall. This grandson lived when a person stepped on him. In the morning he would start breathing. In summer, he heard young men about his own age having fun and hunting with qayaqs. He really wanted to go with them, but he couldn't because he was all head. No one heard his grandma scold the grandson and it was because he was all head.

"When winter came, he heard the young men had gone out hunting for moose and caught some. In his mind he admired the boys because he wasn't like them and if he were like those who moved around with arms, he would join them. In summer, he'd heard again the young men caught seals or any kind of sea animals.

"Every year his mind was always thinking of the young men, and he wanted to be like them. Then one day he had an idea. The head started to think of the young man's daughter. The young man's daughter was pretty. A lot of times men wanted to marry her, but she wouldn't marry them. Even if men from other places asked to marry her, she wouldn't marry them. Her father's mind was getting bad because his daughter kept refusing her suitors.

"Then one day the head's grandmother asked her grandson, 'Why don't you go see the young man's daughter?' The grandmother wanted the head grandson to ask the beautiful girl to marry him.

"One night when everybody was sleeping, he himself went to see her. Somehow he opened the door and went in. There he saw her in back of her parents, sleeping. He didn't really look at her that well, but he said, 'Wow, what a young woman she is!'

"He went not far from her face and laid down beside her. While he was lying down and before he fell asleep, the young woman woke up and saw him. She grabbed ahold of him, opened the door, and threw him out, but after she closed the door she didn't hear him land. She listened, waiting for a little while, and went back to sleep.

"Again he had come in and so she threw him back out again. Every time she threw him out, she would never hear him land. One time she stayed up longer and waited for him to come back. Then she started thinking, 'Maybe I killed him when I threw him out.' Then she decided to go back to sleep. But when she got up, there he was again. And again she grabbed him and threw him out. She threw him really hard that time, but still he didn't seem to land.

"He was gone for quite a while and she got worried about him. The head wouldn't come back in, so she decided to go back to sleep. While she was lying down, he came back and lay down beside her. This time she didn't pay any attention to him and said, 'You won't give up, will you? I'll just leave you alone.'

"They went to sleep and in the morning when the young woman's parents got up, they saw their daughter with the head. They thought that she got married to this head. The head stayed for a long time in their house. All summer and winter he could hear that they had been chasing seals and catching them.

"After a few years had passed, the head's wife said to him, 'Now sometimes in the early dawn before the people wake up or just when they're waking up, I wish I could have fresh seal for breakfast.'

"Just then the head said to her, 'Remember that time when I tried to sleep by you? You used to throw me hard without any feelings toward me. Okay, in the early morning before sunrise, take me and bring me out. When you take me, turn around once and throw me toward the sea the way you used to. After you throw me out, you can take your knife and sharpen it.'

"The next morning when his wife got up, she did what her husband told her to do. She took him out and, without looking back at him, she went back into the house.

"She looked for her knife and when she found it, she sharpened one side.

The woman throws the head into the sea.

When she finished sharpening it, she heard something land outside of the house. So she just put the knife on the floor and went out. When she went out, she saw two seals in front of the door, lying side by side. At the end of them was her husband. Before she had thrown him, she had given him a rope. Those two seals were tied to him. She went back in and sharpened the other side of her knife and went back out and cut up the seals. When she got through cutting the seals, she went around the village and gave some pieces to the people.

The head returns to
the woman's house,
with seals in tow.

"Whenever she wanted seals she would throw him out to sea. Then one day when she got tired of seals she said, 'I wish I could eat beluga whale in the morning instead of the same thing.'

"Then her husband said, 'Okay. Tomorrow why don't you tie me into a leather skin and throw me out to sea.' Then the following morning when she took him out, she turned around once and threw him. After that, she went back into the house.

"When she went back in, she sharpened her knife again really well, then started on the other side of her knife. She was about to finish when she heard a thud sound outside of her porch. She put down the knife and went out. She saw two large beluga whales lying on the ground. At the end of them was the head. After she cut them up, she let all the villagers eat those two beluga whales with them. Whenever she wanted fresh food from the sea, she would throw him to the sea.

"It was always like that. A year ended and another one. Then one day his wife said, 'I wish that tomorrow we could give the men who go to the steam bath some wood for their own.' The head man then said, 'That's simple. Why don't you throw me towards the east side in the morning.'

"The next day she went out with him and, as soon as she faced the river, she threw him towards the east. After she had thrown him, she went back into the house and just when she was about to sit down, she heard a thud outside. When she went outside, she saw two big logs and they looked really dry. Then those people who had not been able to find wood for steam baths took steam baths.

"Soon the wife of the head started loving the head because he was a good hunter. They stayed there for years and years.

"Then one day his wife said, 'Oh my, our mattress is losing its hair. I wish we could change it. Instead of moose hide next year, we should get a bear's hide.' The head said, 'Look, this is difficult for me.' The wife said, 'It's okay if it's difficult for you to catch a bear.' The head then said, 'You want it so much that even though it's difficult for me, I'll do it. Okay, like the way you usually throw me, why don't you throw me towards the mountains in the morning.'

"The next morning just as he told her to do it, she threw him towards the mountains along with the string for him. After she threw him, she waited quite a while. There wasn't a thud outside her house.

"Soon the daylight came and the people started waking up and running around. It was even getting dark and he was not back to the village from his hunting. The head's wife was lonely. Then her father asked her, 'How come he never came back?' The head's wife replied, 'Even though it was difficult for him to get a bear for our mattress, I let him go.' Her father then said, 'Okay, tomorrow when it's dawn, we will go towards the place where you threw him.'

"The young lady got ready for the trip. She got some food, too. And they started heading towards the mountains where she had thrown him. As they were going, they got to some small trees and looked around all over the place.

"While the head's wife was going along, she saw him hanging in one of the trees and right down below him were two bears. The string had gotten tangled in the trees and killed the head.

"The head's wife started crying very hard. Then her father wanted to take him down. The head's wife wanted him to stay where he was. She wanted her father to take the bears down. Her father climbed the tree and cut the string to get the bears down and when he did, the bears fell onto the ground.

"The head's wife told him to tie the head to the tree with the string and leave him. Just before she left him she told him this, 'Okay, you just stay there so the other people can see you.'

"Those willows, they call them Uqviguat. The willows have branches that are bunched up together shaped like an egg."

SLAVIQ (RUSSIAN ORTHODOX CHRISTMAS)

by: Gertrude Jacobs

It's almost time! Here I am, scrounging around the house looking for an empty plastic bag. Actually, I need more than one plastic bag, for I will not come home until they take a break. With Mother's stew brewing on the stove, the smell of meat fills the one-room house. "Eat," says Mother, "so you won't be hungry; it's cold out.

"Use your parka when you go, and don't forget the mittens I made to wear over your thin gloves. That way you'll keep warm. I will come and check on you when your father comes home. Stick close to the older ones so you won't get lost at night."

Mother's worries go on and on. The church bell rings and finally it is time. I get dressed in a hurry, not wanting to miss the first house. The young ones watch and ask if they can come. Mother says, "It is too cold." Kissing them good-bye and promising them a piece of candy when I get back, I take off!

Stepping out into the twilight, I take my first breath of cold air. Walking toward the Russian Orthodox church, I keep an eye out for my friends. Getting closer to the church, I can see people through the tiny frosted church windows.

I go into the church and smell the burning of incense. Candles are flickering on posts. After I find a place to stand, I listen to the service along with the little sound of crackling plastic bags. The church is full of people standing and sitting on the three available benches.

The service is going on with the choir singing and the reader reading in between. When the reader reads everyone is quiet. Anytime when the reader says, "Our Father," the people (Russian Orthodox) make a sign of the cross: forehead first, next breastbone, left shoulder, then right shoulder, with the thumb and first three fingers together. These have words to them: forehead—"In the name of the Father," breastbone—"and of the Son," left shoulder—"and of the Holy Spirit," right shoulder—"Amen."

Sometime during the service, the reader goes down from the right-hand stand, stands in front of the icon, makes the sign of the cross, kisses the icon, and makes the sign of the cross again. Then he goes back to the same stand. After him come the men from the same stand, and they do the same thing. Then come the singers, also from the same stand. They do the same thing. Then the singers from the left-hand stand come out, line up in front of the icon, make the sign of the cross, kiss the icon, and make the sign of the cross again. Then they go back to the same stand they came from. After them, the boys (also teens) on the right side line up and the girls (also teens) line up after them. When they are done, everyone else lines up. After they've done this, the service still goes on.

At the end of the service, they (singers and people) sing the slaviq songs, which are Russian Christmas carols, while the star spinning goes on and the candles burn on the flagholder. At the very end of the songs, everyone says, "Merry Christmas," and the service is over.

The two people holding the star and the flag lead the people out of the church to the first house by the church. Everyone is staying close behind. I'm somewhere in the middle, holding arms with a girl friend.

Everybody is entering the little mission house, which is tended by the Stalista, Abraham Hawk. People crowd in, and some stand outside because there is no room. Not really bothered by the cold outside, they listen to the

The star and flag lead the procession from house to house during Slaviq (Russian Orthodox Christmas).

"I can see people from other villages among the group, a couple of whom I know and have met recently."

slaviq songs being sung. At the end of the songs, everyone says, "Merry Christmas," and a sermon is given. After the sermon is over, candy is passed out. My friend and I are lucky enough to get inside the house, so we have our sacks out and wait for our share. There is always enough for everyone to get a piece. I can see people from other villages among the group, a couple of whom I know and have met recently.

Everything that needs to be done in the house is done. Again the two persons holding the star and the flag lead the way out of the house to the next house across the river. Putting our hoods and mittens on, we follow the group.

We reach the house of Herbert Brink, who is the First Reader of the Russian Orthodox church. Entering the house, I can already feel the warmth. Kettles are boiling on the stove and food is ready to be served after the service. With the candles lit and the star spinning, the singing is started. I'm standing in front with a bunch of other kids. The heat is getting too much for me, so I take my parka off. Songs are still being sung and kids are almost constantly being hushed. Some are uncomfortable due to body heat. But it doesn't stop the service. It still goes on.

When the songs are over, a sermon is said. Everyone is listening closely. We don't go just because of the gifts we are going to receive but also for the gifts we are going to receive spiritually. Older people say, "Real food is from God." After the sermon, food is being served. Older people and the singers are served first. Us kids will be served after them. I look around, wondering

"Eating here and there, we are listening to sermonists at almost every house."

if my mother came to check on me. No sign of her. Guess she'll be coming around later on.

It is time to go on to the next house. I'm all ready to follow along. Going back across the river, we go to the house of Elena Nick, wife of the late First Chief Nick O. Nick, Sr. The same thing happens: songs are sung, sermon is given, candy is passed out, food is served. There is always a different sermonist at every house. The next house is the house of Robert Nick. Robert is the First Chief. He is also the son of the late First Chief Nick O. Nick. Since it's close to our house, I run home with my friend to empty my sack. Mom is asking if I'm hungry or getting sleepy, and is wondering if I should call it quits for the night. Dad says, "Tomorrow's a schoolday." Still eager, I refuse. My friend is sitting and watching me, quietly telling me to speed up my business.

When I'm done doing my stuff, we go back out into the night. Holding hands, we walk off towards Robert Nick's house. When things are done there, the next house is Zachariah Chris's, the Second Reader of the church. After his house comes the house of Nickefer Chris, another Stalista of the church. When it's over, we go upriver to the end of the village to Golka Maxie's house; he is a member of the Russian Orthodox church. From his house we gradually come back towards the church. Eating here and there, we are listening to sermonists at almost every house. Somewhere in the middle I'm practically sleepwalking and yearning for my warm bed at home. Finally, I decide to call it quits. Broad daylight—I'm not afraid to walk home. Arriving at the house, I open the door, quietly walk in, and find my bed. I quickly undress and go to bed, thinking of the big day tomorrow until slaviq quits day after tomorrow.

4. How It's Done

DOG MUSHING

Peter Jacobs, Dog Musher

from *Kalikaq Yugnek,* by Connie James and Palassa Boots.

"Those people I caught up with used to travel by dog teams. They didn't used to have Ski-doos [snowmobiles] at that time. Some of them—my dad, you know, when he went out fishing—would go by pushing a sled or walking. No dogs, no Ski-doos. He'd arrive with a sled full of fish. When he finally arrived, we would, when we were small, eat them raw, his catches of fish; you know, those blackfish. We'd eat them raw because we didn't know what they were. They were food to us so we'd eat them.

"Then one time I decided to go out by dogs. When I did, they told me to use one dog and go. Holding the sled handle, I took off and then headed home really fast. I had a lot of fun. Then I went again, but the dog took me home because he was lazy, dragging me in the sled even though it was only one dog. I was a kid then.

"When I started handling three dogs, I'd use them to go hunting. My leader was a clever dog. Even when the weather was stormy, my leader would find our way home to my family. I really trusted and liked my leader. A few months later I had five more dogs. When I traveled I'd go further, and to me, I went fast because I wasn't using three dogs anymore.

"After a while, no, a couple of years later, I heard there was a dog race here in Bethel. I used to think when I was younger I'd join the race someday, and I did join. There were about 100 dogsleds, and we went way upriver, maybe about twenty-eight miles. Some would catch up with me but would never leave me too far behind. Even so, I tried. One time when I raced, I left people behind and won about $300 or something.

"Then I went to Anchorage for the dog race which Wien Air sponsored. Boy! There were lots of people, and it was kind of scary. Too many people. Anyway, while I was going, I was ahead and a little while later a dogsled caught up with me and passed me, although I was using seven dogs. I caught up with them even though they were using thirteen on up to eighteen dogs.

At one time I saw a sled ahead of me and I chased after him; when I caught up with him, I said, 'Hi,' and gave him a smile, but he didn't respond. He was a white man using thirteen dogs. I didn't know who he was. A little while later I caught up with another dogsled. After that I didn't catch up with anybody. You know, I was going on frozen tractor trails and one of my dogs tripped over the tractor trail bumps, so I didn't catch up with anybody else.

"When I left, I was number thirty, and when I reached the finishing line they informed me that I was going to be number eleven the next day. The next day I was using only five dogs. People were surprised because it was the first time they saw a guy using five dogs in a race. The race began, so I took off, trying my best to go fast. A little while later I saw a sled ahead of me so I chased it, catching up with it. He was using thirteen dogs, I was using only five, and I passed him. I kept going without passing anybody else. A helicopter was flying overhead, circling around me. Pretty soon I saw a sled ahead of me, and just before reaching the city, there was a hill. The hill was very steep and hard to climb. My dogs were really tired.

"Then when I reached the top, I saw the sled, so I chased it. Turning the corner, I saw lots of people. The people were cheering and proud to see me with five dogs."

Then Peter Jacobs showed us his trophies that he won during dog races. Two of the trophies were from Anchorage and the biggest was from Bethel.

"When we checked to see how smart our leaders were, my leader won that trophy. My leader was smarter than anyone else's. This trophy I won here in Bethel from Calista [a regional corporation for the Yukon-Kukokwim delta. Thirteen regional Native corporations were created through the Alaska Native Claims Settlement Act in 1971.]; it's the biggest one of all. This one here with five dogs I won in Anchorage."

"This one? Can I read it?"

It read: "To the first five-dog musher in the world, Peter Jacobs; Anchorage Electric Award."

<<<<

Training Dogs for Racing

from *Kalikaq Yugnek,* interview with Floyd Davidson by John Henry.

The wind was blowing, it was cloudy and the temperature was —20°. The races started in February, at the mouth of Brown's Slough on the Kuskokwim River. The Kuskokwim is about one-quarter mile wide. The racers race about twenty miles up the river and back. At the Bethel Fair, there were about thirty-two racers from different villages. The ice on the river was about four to six feet deep and there was about one foot of snow on the top of the ice, not quite enough for racing.

Bethel is on the north side of the Kuskokwim River. On the other side of

THE CAMA-I BOOK

the river there are a few fish camps and some old steamboats that have not been used for a long time. The trees are small pines and willow trees.

The racers took off at three-minute intervals, so that the dogs, sleds, and drivers wouldn't get tangled up. The teams that weren't taking off right away were waiting on the river. The racers started from the same place. When they started coming back, the racers were about five minutes behind each other—some as much as ten to twenty minutes behind.

I interviewed a white man from Aniak, and he had a good team of husky dogs. He spoke to us after the race about training dogs.

"I train my dogs three days out of four; run three, and lay them off one day, and then run three again. Sometimes it gets too warm, too slick, or the ice is bad and the dogs cut their feet up. Then I don't run them. But once they're in good shape, I only go about eight to ten miles a day.

"When I first started running my dogs, some of my team would fall from exhaustion. That's why I don't run them too far. I'd go two or three miles to start with, and sometimes I would go further, working up to eight or ten miles, which takes about half an hour. So I would work them out for anything from half an hour to an hour a day, depending on how far I went.

"Sometimes the dogs get tired and they fall. Right now they're kind of sore. I have run them every day for the last two weeks and they get sore, and they get tired, so they don't want to go. They just trot and walk.

"I have three lead dogs, and they're all different kinds of dogs. I would pick a different lead dog each day. Sometimes I would use a double lead and sometimes a single lead dog. The one that I'm using now for a lead dog is a male dog and he's about four-and-a-half years old. He's not the fastest one, but he sets the fastest pace, and he pulls as best he can. The other two are fast when they want to go fast, but they don't go as fast as the lead dog that I am using right now. He's the best leader I've got and he's the most reliable. That's why I picked him for the race because he would be the fastest for over twenty miles.

"The lead dogs don't tend to get tired. You make the lead dogs out of the best dogs you've got, the ones that want to pull the most and keep going when they're tired. I've got a couple of dogs who get tired easily, but the lead dogs are the ones that get tired the least. Any dog might get a little sick or not feel good. They might have got ahold of something that's not good for them. If they get sick, or if they get hurt, catch a cold, or something like that, they wouldn't run good.

"I have a fish wheel in the Kuskokwim River up in Aniak and I feed them cooked fish, mostly whitefish when I've got it. I feed them anything I can catch. I cook the fish and I put up quite a bit of dried fish, also I buy a lot of commercial dog food from Anchorage.

"That's the way I keep my dogs in good shape. I try to feed them the same thing all the time. I feed them fat in the winter. Right now I'm feeding them straight commercial dog food and Wesson Oil. I feed them just once a day. I water them twice a day. They get water when I feed them, and they get water two or three hours before I run them. The amount of food I give them depends on the dogs. Some dogs take more and some dogs take less."

Sled Building

from *Tundra Marsh,* interviews with Alexie Berlin and Carl White by James Chase, Mary Paul, Bertha Alexie, and Hannah Andrew.

Sleds have been used in this area for many years to transport people and supplies from one place to another with the aid of dogs, snow machines, and, in some cases, people as a source of power. We knew that not all sleds looked the same and that not all were used for the same purposes. We didn't know a lot about how the sleds are built, why some are different, and what changes have been made in sleds. We wanted to know.

The task at first seemed easy. Watch a sled builder, talk to him, and take pictures of him building a sled. It was harder than we thought. We had to translate a lot of words that are not used anymore, some terms were used that we didn't understand, and people were not always building sleds when we wanted to observe them. Things came up to either hurry the building along (therefore we missed some steps) or to slow it down (so we became somewhat discouraged). We didn't give up. We gathered as much information as we could from two good sled builders, Alexie Berlin and Carl White. We were able to photograph much of Alexie Berlin's sled as it was being built, and Carl was able to explain a lot about different kinds of sleds and how they are built. After several interviews with both of these men, we were able to get them together at the same time so that they could compare their ideas on sled building.

Carl White was born on February 28, 1919. He was born in Eek and moved here when he was around thirty-seven years old. He talked about different methods for building sleds. He builds many different kinds of sleds for people in the village and is a popular sled builder.

Alexie Berlin was born on November 23, 1936. He lives with his wife, Natalia Berlin, and their six kids. He said that he started building sleds before he got married. He made his first sled when he was about nineteen. He showed us how to make a sled and what kinds of tools we should use.

"Carl, what's the difference between Eek sleds and Nunapitchuk sleds— are they the same or different?"

"People's work is not the same. They work the best way they can. Some people's work isn't good because it is not completed."

"How?"

"Some people make sleds that are crooked, no good and easy to break because they are made without care. But when they are made with care, they last for a long time."

"Have you and Alexie worked together?"

"We haven't worked together, but one of us watches the other while he's working. This fall I came here a couple of times to watch him work on a sled, and his work wasn't like mine. Every man works differently from the others."

Alexie Berlin explained his method for constructing a hardwood sled.

"When I learned how to make sleds, I watched people make them or looked at sleds and tried to copy them; that is how I learned to make sleds, that is how I work . . . looking, watching, studying, then trying to copy the things that I observed in sled making. When I tried making my first sled, I wasn't good at it.

"It takes one to two weeks to make a sled. When the wood is ready, it takes less than a week to finish it. When starting to make the sled, rip cut the hardwood to make the parts. Most of the parts are about one inch thick. Let the wood dry for three days before bending it.

"Sometimes the runners break while being bent, so it is better to cook the runners and the ridge part of the sled for two hours. Bend the runners after they are cooked, putting the top rails and the slats into the bender at the same time.

Bending the runners.

"After the pieces are cut and the nails, slats, and runners are bent, the pieces are carefully planed and assembled. If you use screws to fasten the slats on, the screws will break, but if you use ordinary nails, they'll be stronger. You should use size four or six nails on each slat that you put on.

"If the runners have an extra layer on top of them, the sled will be stronger. Slant the vertical frames back and use the adjustable square to measure the angle. If you let the vertical frames bend at a ninety-degree angle, they will break easily. Put nylon rope in a crisscross manner between the vertical frames and at the back of the sled to help support it.

"The last step of sled construction is putting on the metal runners to help the sled slide more easily."

After the wood is bent, the
deck slabs (four-inch
hardwood) are nailed to
the sled.

The ridges are nailed down
to keep the sled's vertical
stands in place.

No matter how large the
sled, the supports are
always eighteen inches apart.

Fixing the holes for the
bolts with a bowie knife.

The correct way to bolt the sled.

Underside of nearly completed sled.

There is another kind of sled used mostly for freight and long-distance transportation of people. These sleds are called freight sleds and are mostly used by hitching to a sno-go. These sleds are easier to make and have less details than the hardwood sleds.

Carl White: "These freight sleds are easy to make—even a woman can make them. Cut the two by six as long as you want the sled to be; then use an ax to rough out the runners of the sled. Then use the plane to straighten the rough part of the runners. Put the crosspieces on. After that, you put the thick slats on. They are so easy that you can make them when you are going to go the next day and still get done before that."

Alexie Berlin: "Yes. If you're a girl, and you don't work on sleds, it's hard to understand them, but if you have an adult to advise you, you can understand things better. It's hard for young people to understand words or sayings. But when adults hear them, they will understand. Our elders will recognize the words and methods that we talk about."

"Looks like you two work the same way."

Carl White: "Yes, because my cousin here looks at my work. I started making sleds before Alexie. Also, these plywoods are stronger than the hardwood sleds, and the bridge of the sled doesn't touch the snow. Those plywood sleds are better."

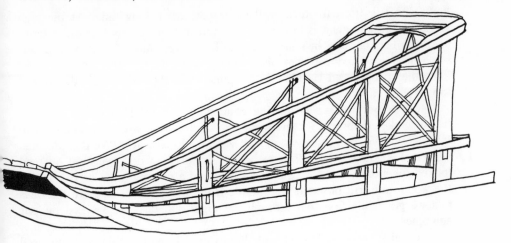

The finished sled.

HUNTING, TRAPPING, AND SKINNING

These stories were collected from several different sources to give a complete picture of hunting in this area.

Hunting

from *Kalikaq Yugnek,* interview with George Beaver by Steven Steven, with Chris Berezkin.

My ancestors used mostly wood for equipment—for fish traps, mink traps, and otter traps. In interviewing George Beaver, I learned that hunting was fun in the old days even without rifles and *sno-gos*. The people walked most of the time. They slept on the grass. It made me proud to be Yup'ik and happy for the old people. I was excited about the things they did and wanted to be like them. I wanted to be with them when they were hunting in order to learn all the skills they had and to turn the clock back for just a while.

Through this interview with George Beaver, a wonderful Yup'ik man from Bethel, I looked at something that is part of me. He spoke to Chris Berezkin and me about hunting in the old days.

"A person who doesn't work doesn't live the way he has to. It's true today, too. In the old days in this area, anybody who didn't try to make weapons for hunting was just like anybody who has nothing to do today. It's as though he were slow today. It's not easy to stop using hunting skills, so anybody who tries to learn them will have them for a long time. At the high school, when a student is not trying to learn in front of his friends, it looks like he is lazy because he's not trying to learn everything. In the past, a person who wasn't trying to get his weapons ready for hunting couldn't hunt like other people and couldn't catch game from the wilderness. He looked too lazy.

"Most of our work was making equipment and catching game. We first had to make equipment for the work on the river. We worked on equipment from wood. We didn't take wood as it was. We looked at it. We then decided what it was going to be. When we got ready for the wood, we went out and looked for more wood for equipment. We had a carving knife or two to cut the wood and drill bits that were made from hardwood. These are the ones that we got ready first. All through the night and day, we worked on our equipment.

"Breakable wood is braced with hardwood. Strips of the wood are used for holding things together. If you've seen a fish trap, the wood on top is in spiral strips. The third kind of wood is flexible tree roots. Unbreakable wood is like this. Wood that isn't mixed—it's used for wrapping around the wood which has to be braced. The third kind is like sinew. It's as strong as sinew. Another kind of wrapping wood is from the roots of an evergreen tree. It's stronger than any other kind of wrapping wood.

"Wrapping wood has a measurement, the space between your index finger and your thumb. On the third spread, cut the wood into long pieces. A fur-bearing trap has measurements, and the blackfish traps have other measurements.

"When we went to the wilderness, we tried to set the fish traps. When you see the wilderness or a river, it's hard to know how the fish trap is going to catch lots of fish if you don't know how to set it. We set the fish trap after we look over the river where it branches out. I took my children to the tundra and let them watch me set the fish trap. At first they didn't do it right, but as they went on, they learned by experience and became successful because I taught them. You go home and try doing it. Otherwise your work won't be done the right way and you won't learn the right way. I taught my children these methods, letting them do it by themselves, and usually they got better as they progressed. They know how to set fish traps because I used these methods. Even though I stay home, I can tell you what the wilderness is like."

George spoke of trapping mink. "Mink live in tunnels by rivers and lakes. You may not see the mink or see it dive. They get food from the bottom of the water. The mouth of the dam is dirty and frozen. Use an ice pick to take off the ice below it. If it's frozen, use a stick to find the hole where they go out of the den from the ground. Then make the hole bigger so that the trap will fit in. Set the trap where the side of the river is wide, and follow the same procedure in a pond. We set the trap where the mink won't go out through the top or bottom by digging in the ground and setting the trap at the mouth of the den.

"The mouth of the mink trap is the size of your fist. We don't know how to measure by feet and inches and we didn't used to measure the mouth of the trap any old way. But the entrance of the mink trap is the size of your fist. If the mink is in it, it won't go out.

"The mink trap is bigger and stronger than the fish traps. Minks are strong. After we made these fish traps and mink traps, we stood on them to see if they would break. I guess you've all seen evergreen tree roots. The evergreen stump's roots are the one we try to get for the traps because they aren't so thick.

"I don't sleep very much when I hunt. When I wake, I never stay still. I get up and try to do what I'm going to do. The people that hunt bear are more active than the bears. Rabbits and foxes can't be chased and caught easily. I have seen people follow a fox by foot. The people like that say when they catch up with the fox, they get it. They tell us to get up early in the morning before the sun rises like mink, otter, and foxes do.

"In the old days, we used to work one whole day preparing for a hunt. We used to hunt foxes apart from other game. We hunted them by walking all day until it was dark. It's hard work trying to catch a fox.

"We hunted the foxes in wilderness. We hunt the foxes in winter by watching their tracks, and if a fox is going to go far, the tracks will show it. Also, if the fox is going to stop, his tracks will show it. We know when the fox is going to stop and in what kind of shelter he is going to stay. Also, when we hunt rabbits, we look at their tracks. When a rabbit or a fox travels, it goes back and sniffs around its tracks. If it does that two times, it will stop there. Sometimes the animals go back a different way and stop there. Rabbits don't stop just anywhere. If there is snow, they dig down into it but leave their heads uncovered."

‹‹‹‹·

Hunting

from *Kalikaq Yugnek,* interview with George Beaver, translated by Amos Kaganak and George Smith.

"In the days of our great ancestors, things were very scarce. Things that are a comfort to us now were hard to find then. The men who hunted didn't hunt like us. They had their arms and legs for machines and weapons for hunting in the times animals were scarce. They used to have tools that weren't like ours, which are made out of metal. I don't quite remember how the weapons were in those days, but we used to listen to our parents when they told us stories about their parents and how they used to live. The way our ancestors used to live seems easy, but being without experience in living as they did, I know it was hard. They hunted and lived off many different animals such as moose or caribou, muskrats, foxes, beavers, and many types of birds. All these are very important to us, and we should not lose them or our weapons. But all these weapons and many other aspects of Native life are all disappearing and are not practiced as much as before. Some people cannot even go hunting without professional experienced hunters.

"If someone is hunting moose, there is a saying that he should not mess around with them. When people are hunting moose in the trees or bushes, sometimes they accidentally make noises which alarm the moose. When this happens, the moose makes noises. The hunter does the same thing after the moose. When a hunter wants to catch a moose real badly, he makes noises by hitting a log in a certain way.

"When a moose is angry or excited he hits his antlers on the willows around him. One day, in the evening, when someone was hunting moose, he sat still until suddenly out of the trees came a female moose that started to cross the meadow. While the female moose was crossing the meadow, a male moose was standing on the other side. This was the place where the male moose found a mate. When the male moose saw the female moose, he got happy and started to make noises and hit his antlers against the trees. Then the male feared nothing that approached. While the moose got friendly with the female moose, a brown bear suddenly stood on his two hind legs. The minute the male moose saw the bear, he charged a short distance and stopped to wait for the bear to charge.

"When the bear charged and leaped at the moose, the moose struck with his two hind legs; the bear flew, landing on the ground, and didn't move again. After the moose left, the man who was hunting that moose went over to the bear and found out that the moose had busted the bear's ribs, torn his stomach area, and left him flat dead on the ground. This was when the man found out that moose were very dangerous during the mating season."

There are two kinds of bears in this area, black bear and brown bear. Mr. George Beaver told us that once in the fall he was taking a trip for seven days in the hills. This one fall in the hills, a brown bear suddenly stood up ahead of him about twelve feet away. He said there is a saying that if a brown bear suddenly stands in front of someone, the person shouldn't move for any reason. He said that when the bear got close, he was breathing hard, and the steam from his mouth was bad for the face. If a person runs away from a standing bear the bear will definitely chase the person, so they should stand still until the bear goes away.

When a bear is angry with someone, he may charge or just leave. There is a saying that if a bear charges, the guy who is being charged shouldn't move but stay still until the bear leaps at him. The minute the bear leaps, the person should jump off the bear's right shoulder. If he tries to go through the bear's left shoulder, the bear has a chance to take ahold of him. There is a saying that if a bear leaps at you, that's the only time you should move.

One day, George Beaver's older brothers were going out to hunt bear. He

asked them if he could go with them. They said yes. While they were looking, one of them spotted a bear, so they all got down to the ground and
started to take off the clothing that could get caught on a stick or rock and
warn the bear. The other guy told him that if he missed the shot, the bear
would see where the bullet landed and start moving in the direction where
the bullet came from. George told the man to shoot because he was getting
scared. The other guy told him the bear's heartbeat hadn't yet been heard.
When they got real close to the bear, George told him again to shoot, but the
other guy told him that it wasn't time to shoot yet. When they got closer to
the bear, George was left behind, even though he was trying to stay with the
other guy. Finally, when he reached the leader, he swallowed some water
and found out that his mouth and throat were dry.

Right after George got there, the other guy stopped and told him, "I
thought you were always interested in hunting and never afraid of reindeer.
So right now you should be willing to catch this bear because it's our food."
So George was still following until the man stopped and told him to come by
him. After he went by him, the other guy showed him where to shoot the
bear. Above the bear's front legs, the heart could be seen by the fat that was
going in and out. When the first man aimed, George aimed with him. He was
waiting for the first man to shoot first, but George got impatient and pulled
the trigger. The bear fell to the ground. After George shot, he asked the
other guy if he had shot or not. The man replied that he had shot with him.
George didn't believe he had shot because he hadn't heard the second shot.

He Hunted with a Bow and Arrows

from *Tundra Marsh,* interview with Andrew Tsikoyak, translated by
Raymond Alexie, Peter Wassillie, Henry Tobeluk, and Moses Brink.
Reference: *Indian and Eskimo Artifacts of North America* by Charles Miles.

Andrew Tsikoyak was born seventy-four years ago in a place called Nanvarnarrlak. He lived there for twenty-five years. He used to hunt with bow
and arrows; and in wintertime, he longed for the birds to return in spring so
he could hunt again. He moved from Nanvarnarrlak to a place called
Kaluyaaq, where he lived for three winters. Then he came to Nunapitchuk
around 1928.

"They hunted with bow and arrows before guns, and they caught caribou.
But I didn't use bows and arrows to hunt caribou. We watched the people
who were making bows and we tried to make them just like the old men
made them.

"For the bows, they used to use dead pine trees, harder wood, or big
pieces of wood. Cut it with the adze [then you don't have to plane] and
carve it with an Eskimo knife until it's very smooth. Then you twist the animal's sinew to make the string for the bow."

We talked to two people about the size of the bows used in this area. They both agreed that the bows were about five or six feet long—they described the length by stretching out their arms and measuring from hand to hand. The bows were about two inches wide at the widest part. This was measured with the middle joint of the pointing finger.

According to Andrew, they used to bend the wood when they had their steam bath. "When we were young, we didn't bend the wood by ourselves. The men bent the wood that was supposed to be bent for bows and for some bowls."

Bows were made thicker and wider for those people who were stronger, much as modern bows have various degrees of force measured in pounds. To string the bow, they used animals' skins when they had no string, and they used to twirl skin around anything that needed to be fastened.

Evan Chaliak once told us about one type of bow that had a long string (made from skin or sinew). One end of the string was attached to the bow and the other end to the arrow. This set was used for fishing and hunting birds, making them easier to retrieve.

When Andrew spoke of hard and soft wood he was speaking of physical properties rather than the kind of wood, such as oak, walnut, etc. Most of the bows were made from whatever was available; however, Andrew spoke of using "Christmas trees" and the *inside* of the wood (where the wood is harder). Other people said that some wood is harder due to being in water or aged by the weather.

For arrows, people kept an eye out for nice straight pieces of wood—cigyak. There were several kinds of arrows that Andrew remembered and described to us. While he talked about them, he drew some pictures of the arrows and spears (which are closely related to the arrows).

"The nuusaarpak is an arrow with three points on the arrowhead, and the arrow with a two-pointed arrowhead is called akulmiqurataagnek. The one-pointed arrow is called nagiguyacuarngalnguut. They also had a harpoon with a small ivory tip—we call it pitegciraq kukgarangigarluteng. They used them when they hunted seal in summer. This is when they used to use them.

"For making the arrow, we didn't use hardwood, but instead we used the white soft wood because hardwood bends [i.e., warps]." Arrows were usually the distance from the underarm to the end of the person's finger in length.

"They made steel tips for some arrows; they cut the antlers and made nuusaarpaks. Some who had a little bit of ivory cut up some of their ivory and made tips for the arrows. When there was more steel, they made the arrow tips out of steel.

"People who had some birds from the ocean had uyalget feathers for their arrows, but we made them out of regular birds like cranes and ducks."

The spear and arrow thrower were also used in the area. We found out that Indians in Mexico and other locations also used similar devices. We found this out while trying to locate pictures of the throwers used in this area. The spear and arrow thrower helped the hunter by making the spear or arrow go farther and faster. The thrower is held in the hand by one end and a groove holds the arrow in place. When the hunter throws the arrow, it is as if his arm is longer than it actually is.

"They didn't make the thrower out of hardwood. They made the thrower from wide to narrower at the end. We could make two spear throwers from one piece of wood by splitting the wood lengthwise. The thrower is about the length of your forearm—maybe it's about a foot. They call it nuqaq—the thrower of the spear. You can use it with the nagiquyaq [the spear which has two points and is often thrown with the handle]. I'm talking about things as far back as I can remember."

<<<<

I Was Really Tired!

from *Kwikpagmiut,* interview with Gregory Joe, Sr., by Tony Sheppard, Eugene Landlord, Clarence Wilson, and Sinka Crane.

Gregory Joe, Sr., is a resident of Mountain Village. He has been living here almost all his life. He is fifty-six years old. His wife is Anna Rose, and they have ten children, six boys and four girls. Gregory Joe has been setting traps since he was thirteen years old. He was taught by his father and it took about one year to learn. During the first year his father used to accompany him; in the second year he went alone. Gregory described his experiences for us.

"I stayed about two weeks setting traps. Once a week I went to check my traps. I got lost one time when I was checking my traps. Because of a storm, I had to stay overnight. I had to go far away from town to set traps. When I had to camp overnight, I had to use a tent. There was no stove. At night I was always cold, and in the morning the food was frozen. I had to heat up the food so I could eat.

"I went trapping with someone who wanted to go with me. Sometimes I went with Willie Peterson. Willie set his traps where I set mine. Long ago when there were no snow machines, I had to use dog teams to set traps. It took about one day to get to where I had set my traps when I went with a dog team.

"Nowadays, when we have snow machines, we have lots of trouble. The problem can be the sparkplugs or something else in the snow machine. Even when it is cold out, I have to fix the parts. When I can't fix the snow machine parts, I have to walk home. It took me about seven hours to get home one time. I really got tired."

Gregory has been setting all kinds of traps. He sets traps for lynx, fox, and mink. He also sets snares for rabbits and beavers. Gregory sets fox traps on the north side of the trees, in a little narrow clearing or meadow. He puts the bait at the end of the short, narrow clearing and puts the traps in the mouth or middle of the clearing.

He also sets beaver snares. Before he sets the beaver snare, he puts together three pieces of wood: one about five feet long, another one about one-and-a-half feet long, and the last one about two feet long. He connects them until they form a right angle. At the base of the one-and-a-half-foot-long piece of wood, he puts the snares. The snare is about a foot up from the bottom.

He sets mink traps in a narrow stream. He faces the trap with the current. Then he puts branches on the sides of the trap so the animal won't go around the trap.

Setting a rabbit snare is very easy according to Gregory. First, he finds a rabbit trail that lots of rabbits have used. Then he takes a tree branch or willow and puts it above the trail. He secures his snare in the middle of the rabbit trail. He puts little willows or branches at the sides of the snare so the rabbit won't go around the snare.

When trapping season is over, he sells his furs to the local store. He keeps some of the furs for personal use. His wife makes parkas, mukluks (Eskimo boots), mittens, and slippers with the furs. The family also eats the meat of the rabbits, beavers, and some of the other animals he catches in his traps.

While trapping is not as vital a part of Eskimo life as it once was, many of the Eskimo men still set traps and snares. It is hard work to keep traplines, but the men seem to enjoy it.

‹‹‹‹‹

Beaver Trapping and Skinning

from *Kalikaq Yugnek,* interview with Wassillie Foster by Annie Carter.

This story took place at the village of Eek, Alaska, in the house of Wassillie Foster. In the house there were two kids and four adults present. When

A beaver house, covered with snow, is in the foreground. "They look like hills with twigs, wood, and dried grass." The trappers must dig through the snow to reach the ice.

Checking the beaver traps.

I was interviewing Wassillie Foster, I asked him questions about beaver hunting. Wassillie was cleaning a beaver skin, wiping the oil off the sides, telling about how they hunt beavers, trap, clean, cut beaver meat, cook and dry meat and skin, roll skins, tag and sell the beaver skin.

"Up and down the river, the ice is two inches thick. The hunters can find the beavers' house easily. They're easy to spot. They look like hills with twigs, wood, and dried grass. The beavers make so many dams that the streams are blocked and hardly any blackfish swim along the streams.

"In the beavers' house, there is usually a family of twelve beavers. Some of them weigh twenty pounds. Larger ones weigh as much as sixty pounds. The hunting season is open from February 1 to March 31.

"The size of the snares are number one x and number two x. Number one x is for shallow water. Number two x is for deeper water. When you set the snare, you leave about one inch from the bottom.

"The snare is about eight by ten, or ten by ten around. Put a strong twig on the side of the snare to keep it in place. Each snare has settings for size.

"When you check the traps, you'll find a beaver trapped in your beaver snare. When you catch the beaver, you try to choke it if it is still alive. Sometimes if a hunter doesn't know there's a beaver that is frozen on the ice, he will accidentally rip it up so its skin is ruined and the fur comes off. After catching a beaver, put the beaver on a sled, wrapping it in a sleeping bag and using foam rubber underneath. Then at the camp, take the guts out of the beaver to keep it from spoiling or freezing solid.

"Before cutting and skinning the beaver, you cut off the feet and tail so it

Setting several snares in a row
increases the chances of a catch.

Checking the snares. If snow has
filled the hole, the snares must be
dug out to be checked.

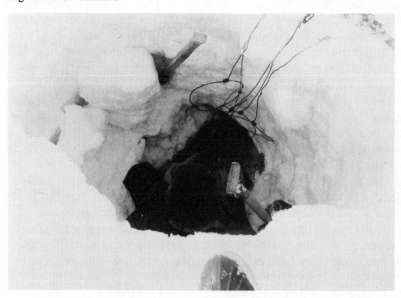

A beaver and an otter
caught on top of a
beaver house.

will be easy to skin. While skinning, try not to rip any of the skin. Also,
cook some beaver meat to eat, and put some meat into the freezer to cook
later on. Also, you can hang some on the racks to dry for a few days and
then cook it. The beaver meat tastes good after drying.

"Then make a round circle on plywood with a pencil so you will know
where you can put the nails. Then use a lot of nails to keep the beaver skin
stretched tight so that it will dry faster. While it's drying, you can wipe the
fat from the beaver skin. The beaver skin takes four to five days to dry.
Then you take the nails off and take the beaver skin from the drying mat.

"Before putting nails on the beaver skin, measure the diameter and the

"While skinning
[the beaver] try not
to rip any of the
skin."

width of the skin. Total the number of inches. If it adds up to sixty-eight inches, for example, it is called a super blanket. Roll the beaver skins that were dried with the fur on the inside instead of bending it like paper. The skins tear easily like paper.

"The beaver skins have to be tagged before April 15. Then take the beaver skins to the buyer. But the Fish and Game has made a limit not to sell over ten beaver skins. If the hunter oversells the beaver skins, they may have the Fish and Game looking for them."

‹‹‹‹‹

Fox Trapping

from *Kalikaq Yugnek,* interview with John Kassaiuli by Phillip Paniyak.

"When I used to go hunting, it would make the day longer. I used to go out a lot along the Ninglik Bay. It was during those days when we tried to make money off the tundra, like getting a fox and selling the fur. The fox got away and I tried shooting it, but the fox didn't fall. When I tracked the fox I saw a little blood on the tracks. So I tracked the fox because the tracks were visible.

"All day I walked tracking the fox and it made the day longer. Then I again saw it. It was evening. The fox went behind something. I ran, and when it appeared, I slowed down to a walk. Even if the fox saw me, I ran. Then he disappeared again. The fox appeared even closer. As I walked, the fox was sitting. As I walked and ran toward the fox, I got so close to the fox that I could see the ears. It was getting dark and I could see the darkness setting in. Even as the fox was watching, I ran toward it and followed it. Even though I could shoot it, I kept following without shooting.

"As it went down to the lake, it got into the middle and I walked toward it. The fox went down on its back and looked at me. I saw that it was getting dark, so I shot the fox. After shooting the fox, I brought it up to the land and skinned it right away. As I went home the night came. Even though I couldn't see anything I got home because I knew the way.

"I didn't lose any of the four foxes I trapped. The fourth one was a white fox. It had broken its leg off. I tracked it down and took it without further wounds. The fox had been caught in the trap, tried to set itself loose, and ended up having a leg cut off. That fox was the one that almost got away. The leg had healed.

"I don't think I'll do the trapping and things again; that's why I told them. When I did the last time, I was really tired. I was really tired."

‹‹‹‹‹

How to Skin a Fox

from *Kalikaq Yugnek,* by Paul James Paul.

To skin a fox you have to catch a fox. First of all, you look for a fox's den and see if the tracks are fresh. Then you put a trap in front of the fox's den. You have to do it carefully so that the fox will not notice it.

The white fox is a fox of the Arctic region, having fur that is white or light gray in winter and blue-gray in summertime.

To skin a fox, you have to start from the mouth and start cutting around the edge of the mouth until you have passed the eyes. Then stop. You have to have a knife or an uluaq to skin a fox.

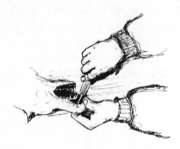

". . . start cutting around the edge of the mouth . . ."

". . . next you have to cut around each foot of the fox . . ."

". . . continue to skin from the face and keep pulling out . . ."

". . . at the end . . . you have to pull and skin at the same time."

Next you have to cut around each foot of the fox, leaving the palm out. After you have cut around the feet, continue to skin from the face and keep pulling out. Keep skinning the part that you can't pull off. Skin around the ears because they'll tear easily. Then keep pulling the fur out to the end of the tail. At the end, it'll be pretty hard to pull out the tail, so you have to pull and skin at the same time.

Root Snares

from *Kalikaq Yugnek,* by Paul Abraham and Dennis Jones.

We interviewed Joe Nichols, who is from Kasigluk, and he told us about how they used the roots of a willow tree for snares, nets, or for anything that we use string for today. The roots of willows are about four inches below the ground, and they are dug up when the ground is soft. Roots are sometimes long and they vary in length. The roots are then split according to the size you want. For instance, if the root is about one quarter of an inch thick, it is split into four parts, and if the root is about one eighth of an inch in diameter, it is split into two parts.

Before using the roots, soak them. This is done so that the root won't break when it is bent. Almost anything they used was soaked before it was used. The roots were stored in a damp place, not where it was hot or dry. The water in the roots will evaporate if they are kept in a hot or dry place.

When they used these roots as part of their weapons, they didn't put the

Root snares.

root on any old way, but in a certain way so it would not come apart easily. Whenever you have something, there is a right way to use it and a wrong way. For example, if you have a bird trap, you wouldn't set it under a small willow; it would get tangled if it trapped an unwanted animal.

Some women used these roots as thread before the reindeer came; then they started using reindeer sinew. Before they used the sinew, it was dried.

The nets that were made out of roots were usually four meshes deep and about four or five feet long, and they were used mostly for herring and kings (salmon). For an anchor they used anything heavy, but most of them were made out of bones. Joe Nichols never used this kind of net but he knows someone who has one.

⤙⤙⤙⤙

Skin Tanning

The procedures of skin tanning vary in the kind of skin used and in different geographical areas, but they are quite similar in many ways.

The following excerpt is from "Squirrel Tanning," *Kalikaq Yugnek,* by Lou Henry and another author whose name isn't mentioned. They interviewed Minnie Carter of Eek. In their interview, they were shown how to skin and tan squirrels. They pointed out that although animals are skinned differently, tanning is generally done this way.

"Before doing anything to the skins, you soak them in soapy, lukewarm water for at least two hours. For example, last night I put them in water before I went to bed. Then I got up at 2 A.M. and got them out of the water."

"Can you keep them in water overnight?"

"Yes."

"What is the purpose of the soap?"

"To clean the fur."

"Do you dry them?"

"You roll them up, starting at the tail, with the fur inside instead of out. This is done right after they are taken out of the water. This is to make the water soak through the skin well enough to remove tissue and fat easier."

One day later, with the fur inside and the skin outside, Minnie Carter gave us a very dull-edged uluaq (an Eskimo handmade cutting tool used in preparing food and in arts and crafts. A sketch of an uluaq is included in this article.) in order not to tear the skin. This is used to remove excess fat tissue. After the skin is completely dry and free of tissue, it should be ready for the next process. Before getting into the next part, though, sew all the holes or tears you may have made.

In the process of tanning you repeat oiling the skin and vigorously rubbing the skin together. You rub the skin and massage with oil. Then you hang it indoors. The old-timers used to use animal oil such as whitefish oil, moose oil, seal oil, and many others. Repeat the rubbing process over and over

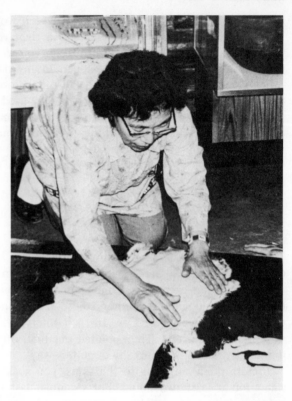

Laying out tanned skins to
be sewn.

until all of the tissues are gone and the skins are very soft and completely
dry.

"Do you have any other special equipment for tanning squirrels?"

"You could put the skins in salt water, too. Salt water can make them very
soft. This salt water is especially efficient for tough skins like beaver and
otter."

◄◄◄◄

Another method is to apply the water on the skin instead of soaking the
skin in water. There is a lot less of a chance of having the fur come off because of excess water. You just apply the water a little at a time with a rag
or by hand and put the skin in a moist place like the porch when you're not
working on it. If salt is to be used it could be just shaken over the skin
rather than adding it to the water.

When the skin starts to feel well soaked, the rubbing should be started. If
you feel or see excessive tissue on the skin, that can be removed with a
sharp-edged tool like the calugcissuun at this time. The calugcissuun is a tool
used by Yup'ik people strictly for tanning (removing excessive tissue). This
tool is pushed away from the user, with the filed side of the blade up.

SURVIVAL

Winter Survival

from *Kalikaq Yugnek*, interview with Grace White, translated by Emma Carter.

"I became aware of myself in Quinhagak and when I moved to Eek, the village was small and there were few houses. There were only two crosses and now there are many. There were no oilstoves, but they used wood stoves. At night, the fire was kept out even if they had babies in the house. In the morning, they started the wood stove. It was in the cold days. When they started having oilstoves, the people started to get cold easily.

"They only used dogsleds for travel and they traveled far. They didn't have any trouble trying to go home. Nowadays they use sno-gos and when the snow machine breaks down, they have to walk home.

"I've heard rules about when somebody goes out hunting. If he falls through thin ice and he has no warm clothes, he will have to take his clothes, wring them out, and put grass inside of his clothes.

"When my husband went out hunting, he fell into the thin ice. When he got out of the water, he wrung his clothes and put grass inside of his clothes and walked home. When he got here, all of his clothes were frozen. He didn't even get frostbite because of the grass.

"If somebody goes hunting and the weather gets stormy and he does not know where he is going and has a lot of dogs, he could get into the middle of them. He would not freeze because of the dogs' warmth.

"Also, if somebody goes out and the weather gets stormy all of a sudden, he has to stop, take a pole, and dig the snow to cover him. He would make room inside the snow and breathe through the hole made by his pole.

"The people used special kinds of clothes when they traveled. They used fish skins for mukluks. The women made soles out of dried fish skins for the mukluks. Cloth was scarce those days, so they used the pike fish skins for kaspeqs, and that kept them dry when it rained. They made mittens out of dog skins. They made fur hats out of squirrel skins.

"The people only traveled by sleds that they built themselves. Sometimes the person traveling would have one dog tied to the side of the sled to help pull the sled.

"The people made shelters out of woven grass tarps with a snow shovel for a post when they planned to spend the night on the tundra. The people never left the shovel and the ice pick behind when they went hunting, so if there was a blizzard, they could dig into the snow and stay there until the blizzard passed. The ice pick was used when they needed to check for thin ice."

<<<<

Frostbite

from *Kalikaq Yugnek,* interview with Charlie Pleasant, translated by Paul Mark.

"There were no schools long before I was born. The people used to teach their kids the way of survival, how to hunt on land or sea, so they would know what to do if stranded out on the tundra with no food or adequate clothing or if caught in a blizzard.

"A person who never goes on trips to the tundra with his parents won't know the tundra unless he likes to hunt excessively. He will begin to know how to hunt and recognize the landmarks and know how to stay alive on the tundra if he does these things.

"When caught in a blizzard, before you get wet or get cold, you should look for a snowdrift and if you find one, you should start digging a narrow hole in the snow and get into the hole you made. The most important tool you need to survive in that hole is your cane because without it, your supply of oxygen would run out and you'll die of exhaustion. What you do is to cover the hole you dug; then when the hole gets small, you enlarge the hole with your cane.

"If someday the ice under you collapses or you get wet while you're ice fishing, there are several things you have to know if you don't want to freeze or get frostbite. The main thing is, if there is grass around you, stuff the grass around your legs inside the pants; that way you will conserve much of your energy, which you will lose when you don't stuff the grass in your pants. If you don't do it early enough, your legs will turn stiff and you might freeze to death.

"Another thing I'm going to talk about is frostbite. There are lots of places on your body where you could have frostbite, but the places where we generally get frostbitten are the face, feet, part of our heels, and the hands.

"If you have just returned to your village from a long trip or any trip in the winter, you should always check to see if you have any frostbites.

"In the old days, when somebody had frostbite, they used to put the frost-bitten part of the body in ice cold water which had just been taken from the water hole, and let it stay until the person could feel the coldness of the water, which takes from one-half hour to about an hour. The main reason they used to do that is whenever we get frostbitten we don't feel anything; that's because the skin and the blood in the frostbitten part are below the body temperature. The other reason they put the frostbitten part in cold water is that the coldness of the water takes out the cold which is trapped in the body. But if you put the frostbitten hand or foot in warm water, the coldness inside your skin moves deeper below your skin. When it thaws out it could get infected. Then in some cases the doctors amputate.

"I tested that theory when I was young and it proved effective. After I fished, I went home. I put one frozen fish in the pan full of ice cold water and another on the table to thaw out. The one in the pan formed ice around it. That's because the coldness in it thawed out and ice collected around it, but the other fish on the table thawed out just a little bit. I cut the fish in the pan in half and the inside of it was thawed. Then I cut the other fish that was on the table and just the surface was thawed out.

"There's a story about a man who had his hands frostbitten. He didn't do anything about it and went inside his sod house. When he came in, he saw his wife preparing to make akutaq. The oil or grease his wife was stirring was warm and the woman was just going to cool it. He dipped his frozen hands into that oil. [In the old days that wasn't a wise thing to do.] As soon as his hands thawed he wiped them, but the cold inside his hands went in deeper and his hands puffed up and started to rot; then they got chopped. He lived through the summer, but later died in the fall. Long ago, and even now, you hear about people freezing to death. If a person is going to freeze to death, he doesn't feel anything; his body gets numb and he seems to get warmer. When he thinks he is starting to get warmer, he dies.

"Long ago, when the person was going to freeze, he would see an illusion of a person coming towards him with a bowl of steaming hot water. If he drank it, he would die. If that person didn't take a steam bath, he would also see an illusion of a person coming with a heavy fur parka. If he accepted that parka and put it on, as soon as he started feeling warmer he would die. That was what our parents used to tell us when I was young."

FISHING

Fishing Experience

from *Kalikaq Yugnek,* by Jimmy Paul.

I have been fishing with my dad for five years. We go fishing every summer. We bring our own clothes and food, Eskimo food such as dried fish and dried seal meat. We pay our own fare and rent a boat from a company. We also make a net for ourselves.

We fish at Ekuk, which is south of Dillingham, about four miles away. In May we fish king salmon, until the middle of June. Then we start to fish red salmon. Sometimes we almost sink our boat because we catch so many fish. We deliver fish to the scow, a boat delivering to cash buyers. We make a lot of money fishing.

‹‹‹‹

How to Set a Net Under the Ice

from *Kwikpagmiut,* by Joe Pete.

The way you put a net under the ice depends on how long your net is. For an average-sized net, you need three holes. Take a wooden pole about seven feet long, and measure on top of the ice with the seven-foot pole. The holes should be apart about three quarters the length of the pole. This will make it easier for you to set your net under the ice.

How to set a net under the ice.

After you've made the three large holes, tie a long rope to the end of the seven-foot pole, but not too tight; you will want to pull it up through another hole with a pole that has a hook on the end of it. Then you put your pole into the first hole and push it towards the middle hole. Let somebody else take the pole with a hook, put it through the middle hole and have him pull up the rope. Do this again on the middle hole and the third hole. When you're done, pull the net under the ice using the rope you have set.

After that's done, tie both ends of the net to two poles that are put horizontally over the hole and left in the ice as markers.

How to Check a Net

from *Kalikaq Yugnek,* interview with Albert Beans by Eliza Hooper and Henry Ayagalria.

The Eskimos don't fish with rods like the white man, but they use nets that are under the ice. They catch whitefish and pike, using jigs sometimes.

1. You have to have an ice pick in order to check your net.
2. Next you have to pick all around the ice where you put the wood until

it's open. There are two holes in the ice, fifteen to twenty feet apart.
The net is strung under the ice between the holes.

3. Next you pick around the ice at the other end; then tie a long rope
   onto the end of the net.
4. Then you can pull out the net where the wood was and take all the
   fish out of it.

◄◄◄◄◄

Fish Fence

from *Kalikaq Yugnek,* by Nick Jenkins.

A fish fence is a fence that is placed extending across a river. The job of
the fish fence is to block the fish from going downriver. A fish fence is usually made out of willow trees. Some of the trees have to be thick and tall.
Others have to be about two or less feet in diameter and about twenty-five or
fifty feet in length. The smallest trees would be about five or eight inches in
diameter and the length would have to be ten to twelve feet. Or you can
measure the depth of the river and make the layers smaller. Other smaller
trees with branches are needed for help in blocking the fish.

In order to get the fish out of the river, you have to use a dipper. The
dipper is made out of wood and net.

"The job of the fish fence is to block the fish from going downriver."

Working on the fish fence, which is usually made of willow trees.

The Eskimos start making the fish fence during the summer season. Then when fall comes, they start to fish. Some people start fishing before the river freezes up.

When the Eskimos prepare for the winter, they catch their fish by dipping. All you have to do is make a hole that looks like a dipper in the ice. They get all the men in the village together. Then they make a fish fence. They fish and fish until the ice gets too thick for them to fish. A fish fence such as this is tended by all the people in a village who care to use it.

FOOD

Food Preservation

from *Kalikaq Yugnek,* interview with Kirt Bell by Fred Polty.

When I got up in the morning, I was very excited for a good reason. It was the day that we were going on a field trip to Hooper Bay. As we flew through the air just outside of Hooper Bay, I saw a fantastic view of Cape Romanzoff, the flatlands, and the bay. As we descended into the village, I wondered what the experience would be.

As we taxied down the runway, I saw a collection of snow machines, and adjacent to them stood the smiling people of Hooper Bay. As we got out, we were greeted with friendly handshakes from those residents. After we rode into town, we were dropped off below the high school near the power plant with its huge silver oil tanks.

As Grant, Peter, and I walked through Hooper Bay, we met Kirt Bell, a short man, about five foot one or two, medium build, in his early sixties. He had a broad smile, showing a large quantity of wisdom and many years of experience.

"The homes in Hooper Bay were made of sod mud with frames of drift-wood. We put mud on the outside of the homes, and the windows were made out of seal gut. We had two qasegiq [fire bath houses]. One of them was still standing until a few years ago. It burned. Many years ago the men of the village slept in these two qasegiq. That is a tradition. When we stayed in the qasegiq, we did not have any mattresses. It was warm because we took a fire bath in the qasegiq and the floor was then compacted and closed in.

"It would be the men's job to begin making the fishnet, and they would make the fishnet in the qasegiq. They would use twelve mesh. The ones that were twelve mesh would be used for little rivers and creeks. Some of these would be used for little fish or would be made into dip nets. They were hardly ever used for king salmon, but were good with pikes. This is not a story I have made up, but it is what I have heard from my elders.

"They made nets out of string. They would also make fishnets out of seal-skin stripped in thin pieces, and some would be made to catch ugruuk [bearded seal] and spotted seal also. Even some would be made to catch the whales, beluga whales. We would make the fishnets in the qasegiqs, hanging them on end in a corner. The other end we would be working on from there.

"After you caught the fish, when you were taking care of the dogfish, silverfish, and sheefish, the insides of the guts of these fish [the eggs] would be set aside and partly dried. When they were partly dried, you put them inside a seal stomach and pressed so that there wouldn't be any air inside the seal stomach.

"The food had to be preserved. There are ways the people used to save foods. You took the fish eggs and bladder, boiling them together. When they had cooled down, you packaged them and put them in a hole you dug underneath your house. Then you covered it with soil and stepped on it until there was no more air in the hole. At the time of the year when people began running out of food, you could open whatever was put away underneath your house.

"As you opened the hole, the aroma of the food would be very inviting. After you took the food out of the little hole, you put it inside a bowl and filled it with water to soak it. After soaking it, you stirred it. You then put blackfish with this, and the women helped with this mixture. Your son was given a portion of this. A wife brought this to her husband in the qasegiq because that's where he stayed.

"Years ago, behind Hooper Bay, I found something which belonged to my mother's dad. He had buried some whale meat, skin, and blubber. He died before he had a chance to open the hole he had dug.

"The erosion by the river uncovered the food that my mother's dad had dug many years ago. As I was passing by this slough, I looked back and saw something white. So I stopped to take a closer look at it. I grabbed a piece of it and started chewing on it. It didn't taste like mud, but it had a taste of food. I can't say how many years that food was buried in the ground. That was how the older people used to preserve their food—underneath the ground. Walrus meat or walrus blubber was put underneath the ground and you kept stepping on the ground until there was no air left under the ground. It could be preserved for two or three years this way.

"If you kept for two or three years the food that you had preserved underneath your floor, it could sometimes save your life when you ran out of food. Even though the food was buried for that length of time, it would still be edible. Also, the fat of any living, moving animal or bird is nutritious."

Another source of food was birds. Kirt talked about this food that was preserved in an entirely different way.

"We took the sinews from the little birds, ducks, geese, seals, ugruuk, spotted seals, and we hung them to dry. The old ladies would twirl or twist the sinew. It was the women's job to stretch up and dry the sinew of these birds and animals.

"They used to make parkas out of ducks. You skinned a duck and dried it, then made a parka out of it. Sometimes when the weather was very bad and they ran out of food, the mother would cut off a piece of the parka and let the children chew on it. They would pluck off the feathers on the piece of skin and would chew it. In the first part of chewing on it, you would spit out the skins of the bird. Last year as I was sitting there, I looked up in my porch and saw the skins of two pintails, and I remembered the times that used to be many years ago when I'd get hungry and would munch on the bird skins."

<<<<

How to Dry Fish

from *Kwikpagmiut,* by Lala Charles.

Every summer, several families go out fish camping to fish and to store smoked fish. It is better to fish out at camps rather than in a village, but some people prefer fishing in villages. I like going out to camps.

The kind of fish that are caught in the Yukon are king salmon, salmon, and whitefish. Usually the best type of fish for dried, smoked fish is salmon. The king salmon are best for strips. They are preserved in a similar way, but they are soaked in salt water before they are smoked.

The area where our family fishes is on the lower Yukon River. Our fish camp is about five to seven miles west of Emmonak, which is near the Bering Sea.

A fish cache is needed to smoke the fish. Build it on the ground with drift-

Splitting and smoking
salmon.

Fish hung to dry, early 1900s.

wood. Build the walls of the cache out of wood. Sheet iron is good for the roof and plywood can be used also. A good fish cache should not have a crack where the smoke can escape. The size of the door should be like a regular door. The size of the cache depends on how much fish you want to smoke. Inside, on each wall, should be logs that are five feet off the ground, also in the middle. This is so you can lay fish racks on them when you are about to smoke fish. A large sheet iron wood-burning stove is placed in the middle of the room on the ground. Cache stoves are usually made out of empty tanks with large holes punched in them so that the smoke can come out. Flooring for the cache is unnecessary.

The fish are caught with nets placed in the water. This is mostly done by men. Take the fish out of the water; then place them on a butcher table to cut the heads off and to remove guts from the stomach. This leaves the fish without a head and with an open stomach which starts from the lower fish to the head end. Clean and wash the fish. Then the fish is ready to cut. This job is for women especially.

An uluaq is good for cutting the fish. Leave the fish lying on a clean butchering table. Then use the uluaq to cut the back of the fish, starting from the side of the tail, straight to the other end. Slide the uluaq over and back, cutting the meat until you have completely reached the other side of the fish. This piece should be at least one inch thick with the skin. Turn the fish to the opposite side, and again cut the back the same way as you did the first time.

After that is done, you have three pieces hanging from the tail. The piece in the middle is thrown away. Then, starting from the lower end, slide your uluaq up and down sideways, carefully, making sure you don't cut the skin when you do this. You should slide your uluaq slanted, not straight down, when you make the lines. Do this until you are about four inches from the tail. Do the other piece the same way.

Leave the fish hanging on fish racks. Then take them to the cache to have them smoked. Damp wood is good for dried fish. Smoke them until they are dry and almost crisp or until they are dried red-brown. It takes several weeks for the fish to dry.

Dried fish tastes sweet and like smoke. It's nice-tasting and chewy. Perfect for every meal.

Drying fish and smoking them in the cache.

Akutaq

by: Lala Charles

Akutaq is a dessert most people eat after and before meals. Akutaq is a mixture of shortening and many kinds of berries, or just one kind of berry. Akutaq is made in so many ways that I can't even name all of them. One of my favorites is one where you put wild spinach into the mixture of salmon-berries, shortening, Wesson Oil, and sugar.

Here is one way of making akutaq. I have used Elizabeth Joe's recipe.

INGREDIENTS

1 or 2 fish—depending on the size (3-pound average)

2 cups shortening

1 to 1½ cups sugar—sweeten to taste

½ cup seal oil—if available

3½ cups berries, fruit, or raisins— you may add more berries or less, this is up to the individual

Use whitefish, pike fish, silver salmon, sheefish, or dog salmon. Clean the fish. Cut the fish into small slices, about one inch. Boil the fish for about fifteen minutes and cool it for about fifteen minutes. Take the fish out of the water and put it in another pan to cool.

Take out all the bones and skin. Squeeze the fish, taking out all the liquid. Put it aside.

Mix the shortening, sugar, and seal oil in a pan until it is fluffy. If you don't have seal oil, you can use vegetable oil. Mix it with your hands. Add the fish. Mix it again. Add about 3½ cups berries, fruit, and raisins. Use salmonberries, blackberries, blueberries, cranberries, or fruit and raisins. If you wish to add more than one kind of berry, mix them into the mixture one kind at a time. You can freeze it if you wish.

Now it is ready to eat!

SKIN SEWING

Mukluks

from *Kwikpagmiut,* interview with Vivian Jimmy by Darlene Walters, Alice Kokrine, and Luci Ann Andrews.

Mukluks are handmade boots used during the winter. There are different sizes and different features. But usually everybody follows the main procedures and puts their own decorations on afterwards. Below is one method of making mukluks.

Vivian Jimmy is a resident of Mountain Village, living with her husband and eight kids. She was born in Sheldon Point. She is forty-eight years old. Her mother taught her how to make mukluks and she told us how mukluks are made.

"We got the calfskin from the store, but I skin the seal and take all the fat off. After that, I have to wash it really well; then dry the fur and stretch it to dry.

"Well, it's kind of hard work to make mukluks. Today, I was tanning this one sealskin. I have to cut it apart and sew the pieces together. This can't be done in one or two days. Soles are cut out from this tanned skin. The boot part is next. The trim is the last part we put on the mukluk. We use beaver and cloth. It's a lot of work to sew mukluks.

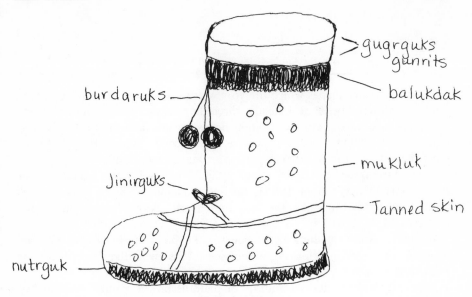

Traditional mukluk.

"First I make a pattern out of hard paper and use that pattern to cut the pieces of the mukluk out. Then I sew them together. I use dental floss to sew the pieces together. A lot of women now use dental floss to sew mukluks.

"I use grass to insulate the bottom. Sometimes insoles are used. My mom used to use socks made out of dried grass and these are called alliqsaqs. They keep your feet warm. Sometimes even rabbit skin was used inside the mukluk.

"People can make different kinds or styles of mukluks. In the old days, they used waterproof mukluks. They were made out of fish skins. The old people used to do that, but nowadays, I never see anyone wearing those fish skin mukluks.

"If you take care of mukluks, the way they should be, they can last for more than five years."

Taking care of mukluks is pretty important. Wearing mukluks in the rain will ruin them. If the soles soften and then dry up again, it will take a long time until they go back to their usual condition. Also, some people wear them without exchanging them. You have to exchange the sides maybe twice a week to prevent slanting. Also, try and hang them each time you take them off in a place where it's not too hot so they don't give off too much odor. At the end of the year, you might put them in a cool place. When the winter begins again, put new clumps of grass into the mukluks.

◄◄◄◄

Yo-yos

from *Kalikaq Yugnek,* by Annie Friendly and Lou Henry.

There are many shapes which the yo-yos are sewn into. The most common ones are mittens, bells, seal heads, three-dimensional leaves, and slippers. There are also hearts, mukluks, rabbit heads, drums, and mouse heads. The patterns are cut out of hard paper (not cardboard). The person cutting a pattern can trace it from another pattern or make one herself.

They started sewing yo-yos about 1954. When we were around six or seven years of age (about 1965), the most common patterns were mouse heads, seal heads, mukluks, the bell, and hearts. Around about that time, they cost $1.00 to $1.25.

We use sealskin, leather, and suede for the body of the yo-yo. For the handles, we use nylon twine. A piece of sealskin is cut in the shape of a rectangle or a trapezoid to keep the handles together.

After we trace the desired number of patterns on the tanned sealskin, we cut out the pattern pieces. We match the pieces into pairs according to color and texture, marking them with numbers on the backs. The numbers are to keep the pieces from getting mixed up. Afterwards we decorate them, sewing on beads in any pattern desired, or sewing on beads for eyes, nose, and mouth on animal heads. We may also sew on pieces of yarn.

After the beading, we sew the twine ends onto the inside of the cutout sealskin pattern. We sew close to the place where the twine will go out. The twine should be about two and a half to three feet long, with a knot on each end.

We stuff the yo-yo after sewing halfway; then when through stuffing, we sew closed the rest of the yo-yo. After finishing with the yo-yos, at each end of the handle we sew on the handle holders.

We try to have even stitches, not too large and not too small. If the stitches are too small, the yo-yo might fall apart; if the stitches are too large, they'll show.

You adjust the yo-yo so one end hangs longer than the other, about three inches. You hold the longer string while you twirl the shorter string. After a few seconds, you throw the string you're holding in the opposite direction of the one you had twirled. When you throw the other end, you twirl the two ends, with your hand making an up-and-down motion.

◄◄◄◄·

Making Dolls

from *Kalikaq Yugnek*, by Linda Moore and Sally Cleveland.

Eileen Jenkins of Nunapitchuk is a lady who is an expert in making wooden dolls. The dolls made by hand have come a long way, and probably every little girl had a doll of some kind.

The dolls can be any size you want. Driftwood is better to use than the other woods because it's easier to cut outlines, etc. Start off by making an outline about the way you want the pieces to be, how big and how wide. The driftwood is carved by following the outline.

After you outline, start chipping off the pieces. First carve the feet. They are about the length of your thumb (in the doll we watched being made). The legs are also carved, about five inches long. From the top of the legs to the top of the head is six inches long. The next thing is to carve the arms and hands, which are about four inches long in all. Overall, the doll is about twelve inches.

The face has to be carved neatly and carefully. The areas being carved on the face are the eyes, which have to be hollowed a bit; the nose, which has to be carved out about one-quarter inch at the bottom, or however you want

Classic wood and fur doll.

it to be; the mouth, however you want it to be; and the whole face has to be shaped.

When you have chipped the shoulders and the legs, you have to use an electric drill to drill through the shoulders and lower waist and also the upper parts of the arms and upper legs. Then you use something like a leather piece to tie a knot and put the parts together. Then the body is complete.

Making the doll parka is easier than making the bigger ones for people. This is not the way you make parkas for people, but only for dolls.

In order to make a small parka for your doll, you need materials like rabbit skins, needle, thread, and some other things like a calfskin, mink, or other furs for the trimmings.

Now to make your parka. This is for a doll which is about one foot tall. First, cut the body piece following the pattern. Make two body pieces about seven or eight inches long, depending on how big the body is. In this case, the width of the body is five or six inches.

The sleeves are about three or four inches long. The width of the sleeve is two and a half inches. Try to follow the pattern neatly and carefully.

The hood is about three and a half inches long and the width is four inches. Now, last but not least, the ruff. You can use any fur you like for the ruff.

Sew both sides together and also the shoulders.

Also, if the head part is too small for your doll's head, make a slit.

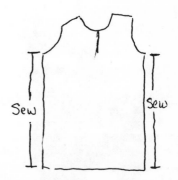

Sew both sides of the sleeve together and do the other sleeve like you did here.

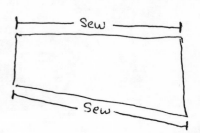

Sew the hood, and then if it's finished,
try to fit the hood to the body piece
where the hood is going to be.

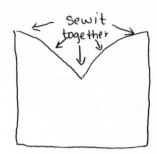

Make the ruff so it will fit the hood.

After you have sewn the parts, you are going to have to put the parts together to make a parka for your very own doll. First take the sleeve and sew
it to the body, where the sleeve is going to be. Next you take the hood and
try to attach it to the head part; if it doesn't fit, make a slit and then sew the
hood to the body. Last, the ruff has to be fitted to the hood.

HOW TO MAKE A BASKET

from *Kalikaq Yugnek,* interview with Lizzie Turchick by Emily Friendly.

I interviewed Lizzie Turchick from Chefornak to get information on many
things that would interest the young people of today. She said, "If I didn't
want the Eskimo culture to change, the Yup'ik language is the one that I
would keep." Another thing of interest to young people who want to keep
the Eskimo culture alive is the practice of Yup'ik skills. She said, "I started
the basket that I'm sewing now last week. Sewing a basket makes me sore
once in a while. They're never finished right away.

"To make a basket, you can start off with three to five pieces of grass.
This grass is like a green thin plant that grows in the water. Many people
pick these even though they're green. Then they dry the grass up and when it
turns white, they use it to make baskets. Some people pick grass when the
grass turns white.

Wrapping the strands.

"Wrap the three to five pieces of grass together using two pieces of grass that bind in a crisscross pattern. Also, as you bind them together, you make a spiral out of the bound group, sewing it together with needles in both wrapping strands so it doesn't fall apart.

"Before your grass wraps get thin, you add more grass a strand at a time. After you make the bottom how you want it, you turn the part you're sewing towards you or upwards and continue sewing it all around. If you want your basket to be small or short, you turn more of it towards you. You can shape your basket almost like a ball. When you finish off, you trim the ends of the grass, trying to even it up with the other strands of grass on the basket.

"When you start a cover, you go through the same steps as when you first started the basket. Then again you turn the wraps of the basket towards you, making a handle for the cover. You always add grass to keep your wraps even. Keep sewing around it. While you're sewing, you try the cover on to see if it fits your basket.

"I dye my grass with the store-bought dyes. We used to dye them with paper or anything that can release color. Then when it gets colorfast you boil it. Today, things are easier to get. Long ago, when we first began to sew, we used seal gut. To dye seal gut, we used cold water and kept dunking it in the dyed water. Then it easily colored.

"The prices for the baskets I sell aren't the same. Some baskets I send to a lady in Anchorage who likes my baskets and is glad when I send baskets to her. We used to use our baskets for putting our things away instead of selling them. When people first started buying baskets, we sold them much cheaper than we do now. Then we thought the money was enough. But now we sell them for over twenty dollars.

"Long ago when we never sewed, we used to braid grass. I learned how to braid grass together for socks, mats, grass curtains, anything. We used to use braided grass for mats and for insulation in mukluks. Also, we used to live in sod houses. Sometimes the whole floor of the house would be covered with grass that was braided. Those old houses, sod houses, were never cold. They were even warmer than the houses we live in now. Long ago, before we were born, the people never had stoves, so the women cooked in the porches. And when the weather was calm, they would make a window out of seal guts in the center of the sod house. We never had electric lights. We had seal oil for lights, using a piece of cloth for the wick."

PETER SMITH—MASK MAKER

from *Kalikaq Yugnek,* by Sally Bavilla.

Peter Smith is a mask maker, hunter, minister, and a father. He seems to be good at everything he does. As Peter Smith worked on masks, he talked to us about mask making and other things.

"I make about twenty-five masks in two months, March and April. Then I sell them for seven dollars apiece. It's lots of work and I give up—I quit working on masks, even if I hear of someone who wants one, and somehow the prices go up. In a Native store, they sell masks for fifteen dollars apiece. I find out what I'm making for them, and when I go down to the store, I sell them for thirty dollars apiece—more than fifteen dollars because the store man is selling them for that price.

"Now I will make some more and sell them at the same price. While I'm doing that at thirty dollars, they go up to one hundred dollars, and then everybody throughout Alaska will buy them. I've got lots of orders today from different places—Seattle, Anchorage, and Bethel.

"A while ago, I saw my mask some other place, maybe in an Anchorage store. The price was over two hundred dollars, and I recognized that I had made it."

"Somebody got it from you for one hundred dollars and sold it for two hundred?"

"Yes, I think so, because they like to get more money. That's why I like to teach the young people how to make things. Not only wooden masks, but

Wooden spiritmask in the style of Nunivak Island.

even things like spoons, kayaks, bowls, or the chewing tobacco box. Old-timers used to use tobacco boxes.

"My carvings have some ivory in them, you know. A long time ago, when I was seven years old, my dad let me study how to carve. He told me, 'Son, you are not a good hunter. Learn or work on any trade.' I understood my father. He wanted me to be a good carver, kayak maker, or builder of big sleds, big bowls, big dishes, something like that. He said that since I wasn't a good hunter, he would help me a lot on my handwork. Then he gave me a piece of ivory to make a toothpick, saying, 'Here, you make a toothpick today.' I asked my dad what it looked like. He said, 'A fish, something like a fish. Just smooth it and make a fish.'

"All day long I was filing. I gave it to my dad, and he looked at it, saying, 'Do this a little bit,' and I filed again. I didn't finish it that day, so I put it in my dad's tool box. The next day, I remembered what I'd been doing the day before, so I took it out and did it again. My filing was better than before. No more filing my fingernail. Then I sanded it. Sometimes when I sanded, I sanded my fingernail, too.

"Then I finished it, and he said to split it in the middle. So I split it in the middle with a hack saw, and I put a small piece of ivory inside. Then he said it was finished, it was okay, it was good. And from that day on, I knew how to make a toothpick.

"My dad carved a lot, too. Lots of ivory and lots of toothpicks, selling them at the same time. A man asked me how much I wanted to sell my toothpicks for, and I said fifty cents. I went down to the Coast Guard and showed my work to the sailors. They said, 'Give it to me; I'll buy it.' So I sold toothpicks for fifty cents, and I went home giving the money to my dad.

"My daddy smiled at me and said the Coast Guard would be gone soon, so I should sit down and make hearts. I sat down and made a heart, cutting the ivory to make a large heart. I said to him, 'How am I gonna finish it after I sand it?' He said to make a hole right here; he knew because he was an old man.

"When I went down to the Coast Guard and showed it to them, they said, 'Give it to me for fifty cents.' They gave me a nickel, and I said, 'That's not money.' They said, 'No, it's money. Five will make twenty-five cents.' So I answered, 'Okay, give it to me. Ten will make fifty cents.' And they didn't try to cheat me then. They laughed at me, and some of them [sailors] patted my back, some of them gave me neckties, and some of them gave me free shirts. They liked me very much, you know.

"That was at Nash Harbor. They don't have the Coast Guard there anymore. After they robbed lots from the village, the state told them never to land on Nunivak Island again. They robbed lots from the village, the sailors did, when there was nobody at the village. The captain didn't know it. They took anything: spears, ivory, hunting equipment, rifles. But my brother, he was lucky. He had a sealskin in his house and they didn't find it. He was lucky."

IVORY CARVING

How to Carve an Ivory Ring

from *Kalikaq Yugnek,* by Cliff Faircloth.

When you want to learn how to carve ivory, it is good if you have had experience with other types of art. It would be easier for you if sometime during your life you had picked up an old piece of wood or bone and started cutting on it with a knife. Knowing how to draw or paint will help you out if you want to draw pictures on the ivory. This will make your work more attractive. So it would be better if you have had past experience in wood carving, soapstone carving, or any other type of carving.

The first thing is to gather up all the ivory you think you want to carve. Just go out on the beach and pick up the ivory tusks that have been washed ashore. This will be quite simple if you are a Native and living in Alaska, but if you are in some other place you will probably have to pay for the ivory. Make sure that the ivory does not have any cracks in it before you start working on it. If you carve ivory with a lot of cracks, your finished product will probably break, and you will have done all this work for nothing.

To slice the ivory, place it on a table saw. Set the saw to about one quarter of an inch. Then cut the ivory. After you have sliced all the ivory that you need, place one slice into a table clamp with about three inches exposed.

Now you need a drill to make the hole to fit your finger. There are proper types of bits to use. You will need a keyhole bit. Get a bit that fits your finger.

When you have the drill and bit, you are ready to make the hole in the ivory. Drill into the face of the ivory. When the hole is drilled, put your finger into the hole to see if it fits. If it is too tight, shave out the inside of the hole with the drill until it fits about the way you want it to. Do not make it too loose because you still have to sand out the inside with sandpaper.

After the hole is to your liking, take a pencil and mark the thickness of the ring around the hole. Do not draw the line around it too close to the hole because the ring might break when you start cutting.

Now you need a coping saw. Take the coping saw and cut around your pencil mark. When the crude ring is cut out, you need files to get it smooth and into shape. One fine file will do for the outside and one fine rat-tail file for the inside.

Place the ring into the table clamp and start filing. Even if you work on it for an hour, file it down until it fits your finger comfortably.

Now, take a very fine piece of sandpaper and make the ring as smooth as possible. After sanding, you need to take Ajax powder and polish the ring.

Using Ajax cleans the ivory. Also, when you finish polishing, take Brasso and polish it again. This is the last coat. If you want to etch something into the ring, take a small hand drill with a point on the end of the bit. Then just carve the name or whatever onto the ring. Next take India ink and put some on a rag. Then wipe over your etching. The ink will go down into the grooves. This will make your etching visible. Now you have a finished product.

<<<<

Reflections on Ivory Carving

from *Kalikaq Yugnek,* interview with Homer Hunter, Sr., by Bernice Morgan.

Scammon Bay is located between Nelson Island and the southern mouth of the Yukon River. It is a village of about 200 people. Although the village appears modern, the people still live a subsistence lifestyle of hunting, fishing, and trapping to provide for most of their needs.

Homer Hunter, Sr., like many other Yup'iks, must earn some money to provide for supplemental food, electricity, clothing, and other necessities of modern living. To do this he carves ivory and is well known throughout Alaska for his expertise.

"Homer, have you lived at Scammon all your life?"

"No, I moved here twenty-three years ago. I was born at Hooper Bay; then I moved here. I've been living here ever since then."

"How did you get interested in ivory carving? Did your dad teach you how to carve? Did your parents have anything to do with your carving?"

"I got interested in carving because my dad was an ivory collector. In fact, he was a wooden mask carver. He made a collection of walrus bones and ivory, saving them until I was old enough to use them."

"How long did it take you to learn how to carve?"

"I started when I was twelve years old. I started out with Ivory soap when I was in the old Bethel hospital before it burned down. The nurses kept me supplied with soap and my doctor gave me his pocket knife. After I got discharged from the hospital, I came home and started with real ivory."

"What do you make besides rings?"

"In earlier years, I started with the real hard ones, the figures. I didn't do any etching. It was hard at first because I started carving those when I should have started with the easier ones and gone on to the harder ones. Right now I make watchbands, earrings, bracelets, and rings."

"How long does it take to make each item, or does it depend on the size?"

"It takes a lot of time; it isn't easy. It's tiresome because you do the same thing hour after hour. But I kept at it because one of these days my boys will carry on what I'm doing."

"Are any of your children carving now?"

"My fourteen-year-old son is carving right now. He takes real orders from boys and girls and from men and women alike."

"Before you make the figures on top of the rings, do you draw them first?"

"No, I usually don't do that. When I was in school, I drew a lot and now it seems simple to me. I can do the figures without drawing them first. I think I can do almost anything anyone wants me to."

"What do you enjoy carving the most?"

"I don't really have a favorite; I can do anything the people order."

"Where do you get the tools you carve with?"

"When I first started carving, I used the tools that my father passed on to me. Then I started making my own tools. Right now all the tools that I need for carving are available at any store."

"Is it easier now that they've got the tools you need in the stores?"

"Yes, it makes it easier and it's faster."

"Have you been able to do much carving this winter?"

"I haven't had time to do much carving because I've been working on my snow machine. I'm getting my snow machine and sled ready for winter. I don't have very much to show."

"So carving to you has become a hobby, something that you do in your spare time?"

"Yes, and it has helped to support me and my family. It's something I learned from my father, and I want to pass it on to my children."

"It must make you feel good to see that at least one of your sons is carrying on what you've been doing."

"Yes, it does."

"Do you have any particular feelings about ivory carving?"

"It's something that I want to see passed on to my children and grandchildren."

ESKIMO GAMES

from *Kalikaq Yugnek,* by Carolyn Moses.

The first Native Youth Olympics was held in the spring of 1973 at Bethel Regional High School. It was organized by the PE teachers, by Harold Sparck with the support of John Paul Jones, and by the principal of the school. They had gotten together and discussed this and made it part of the PE course for the students of BRHS. From then on, they have had this event every year with the help of other Native instructors to teach the selection of games and the original rules to the students. Now teaching of the games is an integral part of the Physical Education curriculum.

It takes a lot of hard work, self-sacrifice, and the help of everyone participating to make the games go. With these games, it is hoped that the people of Alaska will not forget the many traditional contests of their forefathers.

Leg Wrestling

Two contestants lie on a mat side by side and head to foot, locking arms at the elbows with the hands clasped across the torso. The contestants raise their inside leg and touch feet to the count of the referee. On the third elevation of the legs, the contestants link legs at the knee and try to push their opponent over. Whoever rolls his opponent over two out of three times is the winner. Or, if a competitor's foot is held three seconds, it is an automatic win to the other competitor. Contestants may not wear street shoes or boots, but must compete in soft mukluks, tennis shoes, or in stocking feet.

Seal Hop

There are several heats with six competitors in each heat, one judge per competitor. Each contestant must begin in what resembles a lowered push-up position. The upper arms must be even with the sides of his upper body. The hands must have the fingers curled underneath so that he is supported by the heel of the hand and the first knuckles. The contestant must remain in this position and hop across the floor on his hands and toes. The hop must be done by advancing the hands and the feet simultaneously and in parallel. The winner is the contestant who goes the furthest distance without stopping or touching the floor with any other part of his body except his hands and toes.

In a heat, all contestants begin at the same time upon a signal given by the official. Contestants may be disqualified for stopping and restarting, raising the upper body above the upper arms, touching the floor with knees or stomach, bending up at the hips, or for moving from the spot at which he/she stops before the judges have had a chance to measure the distance traveled by each contestant. Girls may do the seal hop with the arms extended and on the open hands but must adhere to all other rules for the seal hop. Boys must have arms even with the body, knuckles under.

Head Pull

Two contestants face each other in the middle of a ten-inch-diameter circle on hands and toes with no other part of the body touching the floor. A strap in the shape of a loop (one and one half to two inches in width and approximately seventy-two inches in circumference) is placed behind the heads of both contestants so that each contestant's head is inside the loop. At a given signal, the two contestants pull against each other in an attempt to pull the opponent out of the circle. Each opponent must pull backwards

Head pull.

in a steady manner. The loser is the contestant who is pulled forward until his hand touches the edge of the circle or who allows the strap to slip from behind his head.

Kneel Jump

Contestants kneel behind a line, sitting on their heels, with their toes pointed out behind them. The contestants then leap forward from the kneeling position, land on both feet simultaneously, and remain in that position without moving their feet or using their hands to retain balance. The winner will be the contestant to jump the furthest, and measurement will be from the heel closest to the line. The contestant must remain where he lands until the officials have had time to measure the length of the jump. Each contestant is allowed three jumps.

One Foot High Kick

Each contestant must kick a four-inch diameter object which is suspended a certain measured distance above the floor. The object must be kicked with one foot. The jump to kick the object may be started no further than ten feet from a point directly below the object. The contestant must jump from both feet simultaneously, kick the object with any part of one foot, and return to the floor, maintaining balance on only the kicking foot until the judges' decision on the kick. Falling or landing on both feet or the opposite foot after kicking nullifies that attempt. Each contestant is allowed three chances at each elevation of the object.

The kicking height is started at forty-six inches for girls and sixty-four inches for boys and raised in increments of four inches to seventy-six inches for boys and fifty-eight inches for girls; then in two-inch increases. After there are three contestants left, there are one-inch increases. The winner is the contestant who kicks the object at the highest elevation. In case of a tie, the winner is the one with the fewest number of misses. If a tie persists, the winner is the contestant whose misses occurred at the highest elevation.

Two Foot High Kick

Each contestant must kick a four-inch-diameter object which is suspended a certain measured distance above the floor. The object must be kicked with both feet or with one foot while both feet are parallel and touching. The jump to kick the object is started no further than ten feet from a point directly below the object. The contestant must jump from both feet simultaneously, kick the object in the manner stated above, and land on both feet simultaneously, maintaining his balance. Falling or landing with one foot first will nullify that attempt. Each contestant is allowed three tries at each elevation of the object. The kicking height begins at forty inches for both girls and boys and is raised in increments of two inches.

Two Foot High Kick.

After three finalists remain, there are one-inch increases. The winner is the contestant who kicks the object at the highest elevation. In case of a tie, the winner is the contestant with the fewest number of misses. If a tie persists, the winner is the contestant whose misses occurred at the highest elevation.

Stick Pull

Two contestants sit on the floor facing each other. The soles of one contestant's feet are placed against the soles of his opponent's. Both contestants must have their feet together with the knees bent at approximately a 90° angle. A stick twenty inches long and one and one half inches in circumference is placed over the toes of the two contestants, and both grip the stick with their hands (palms down). Once the pulling begins, the contestants may not change their grip or regrip the stick. One contestant starts out gripping and during each succeeding pull this arrangement is alternated. The starting grip is determined by a flip of a coin.

Each contestant tries to pull his opponent steadily toward him without jerking. Losers of a round are those contestants who allow themselves to be pulled over by their opponent or who release their grip on the stick with one or both hands, or who allow themselves to fall sideways. Winners are those contestants who pull their opponents as described above two out of three rounds of competition. Spotters are used if requested by both competitors and if judges agree.

Toe Kick

The contestants stand behind a starting line. Each contestant jumps forward and attempts to kick a rod (one inch in diameter and approximately twelve inches long) backward with his toes. The contestants may not touch the floor between the rod and the starting line. After the contestants have kicked the rod backward, they must land on both feet simultaneously at a point beyond the original position of the rod. The winner is determined by the longest distance jumped.

The competition begins with the rod thirty inches from the starting line for girls and forty-eight inches for boys and ends when all competitors have been allowed three attempts at kicking the rod. The rod is moved away from the starting line in increments of two inches after each round of competition has been completed. In case of a tie, the winner is the contestant with the smallest number of misses. If it's still a tie, the winner is the contestant whose misses occurred at the furthest distance.

Glossary

by: Anna Wassilie and Jerry Sam Wassillie of Nunapitchuk, and the *Elwani* staff

Akallaat aklut — Old clothes.

Akitnaq — An arrowpoint that slides on top of the water; it is used for killing small birds.

Akulmiqurataagnek — Two-pointed arrowhead.

Akutaq (also agutuk) — Eskimo ice cream.

Alliqsaq — Socks made out of dried grass.

Alotuk — Fried bread.

Angalkut — Shaman.

Anguyagcuun — A spear used long ago for killing large animals and people.

Angyurak — Fish skin boots.

Anlleqs — Bottoms of reeds used for food by mice and people.

Apaq — Grandfather.

Atauciqeraaq — One pointed arrow.

Badarka (also bidarki and bidarka) — An Aleut kayak covered with seal or sea lion skins. These were built in one-, two-, or three-man varieties. Also a gumboot.

Balukdak — Beaver.

Banya — A steam bath, usually a low room heated by a wood stove covered with stones. Water is heated in buckets placed on the stones. Called muckee in Bristol Bay.

Barabara — See "Barabra."

Barabra (also barabara) — An earth and timber dwelling built partially underground. Also a sod house.

Beach gang — The crew of a beach seine.

Beam — Breadth of a vessel.

Beam trawl — A towed net held open with a wood or metal beam.

Bidarka — See "Badarka."

Bidarki — See "Badarka."

Blackfish — A small fish netted in the winter and eaten with seal oil. Also a pilot whale.

Boom — The spar of a fishing vessel used for hoisting in conjunction with the winch.

Bridge — Control station of a vessel, usually enclosed.

Bridle — Any of a number of rope or cable Y's used for hauling or lifting.

Burdaruks — Decorations for mukluks.

Calugcissuun — Tool used by Yup'iks strictly for removing excessive tissue in tanning.

Chai — Russian-Native name for tea.

Cigyak — Straight pieces of wood used for arrows.

Cingssiiks — Tiny magical people.

Cod end — End of trawl where fish or shrimp collect.

Curuk — Baby doll.

Cuukvaqtuli — A place that used to be a village near the coast.

Devil dance — Traditional Native dance in celebration of the passing of the old year and the coming of the new.

Dory — A nearly double-ended flat-bottom boat with much flare and raking ends.

Ebb tide — State of falling tide.

Eviineq — A place where it is grassy and is higher than most of the ground. Also a knoll.

Fathom — Six feet or the measure of a man's outstretched arms.

Flying bridge — A steering station above the bridge, usually not enclosed.

Gill net — A set or drifting net which entangles fish's gills.

Gugrguks gunrits — Strips of leather.

Gumboots — Edible chitons, so named for their rubbery texture. Also bidarki for their fancied resemblance to a little boat.

Hold — Place where fish or cargo is held on vessel.

Jinirguks (also Cingirkaqs) — Laces or ties.

Kapukaraat — A wild plant cooked and eaten like spinach.

Kashim — Like a qasegiq, a gathering place for men. Also a bathhouse.

Kaspeq — A pullover top made of cotton or similar cloth and decorated with rickrack or trim.

Kass'aq — White man.

Kenriiruat — Old-fashioned supports for sleds.

Kikivik — Sewing handbag.

Kukgar — A harpoon point for hunting seals.

Kumlaka — Hooded sealskin parka.

Lead line — Leaded line or rope used to sink the web of a net.

Maklak — Bearded seal. Also "maklak" boots.

Muckee — Steambath.

Nagiquyacuarngalnguut — One-pointed spears.

Nagiquyaq — A spear which has two points and is thrown with the handle.

Nanvarnarrlak — Large lake near Nunapitchuk.

Nuiq — An arrow shot from a bow at birds.

Nunacuaq — An abandoned village.

Nuqaq — Spear thrower.

Nushnik — Outhouse or privy.

Nutrguk (also Naterkaq) — Sole.

Nuusaarpak — An arrow with three points.

Ohlock — The legendary hairy man of Kodiak and Afognak. Somewhat similar to the yeti, Sasquatch, or Big Foot.

Oil skins — Raincoat and pants. Also called rain gear.

Piluguq — Pillow.

Pirok — A salmon, rice, and turnip casserole. A traditional Native food.

Pitegciraq kukgarangigarluteng — Harpoon with a small ivory tip.

Power block — A huge hydraulically powered pulley for hauling purse seines.

Power roller — A hydraulically powered roller for retrieving nets.

Power scow — A large, bluff-bowed, wide-bodied, shallow draft vessel primarily used to carry fish or for crabbing.

Ptarmigan — A bird the size of a small chicken that is common to the tundra. It changes from brown to white as winter nears. Its meat is dark and is usually boiled.

Pupiit — A lake not very far from an abandoned village called Nunacuaq.

Purse seine — A long and deep net which when the ends are together may be pursed closed through the use of a line running through rings lashed to the lead line.

Pushki — Cow parsnip whose edible shoots are traditionally added to the diet in the spring. Can cause a nasty burn to sensitive flesh.

Qasegiq — Gathering place for men. Also a bathhouse.

Qaspeq — Parka cover.

Qayaq — A canoe. Kass'aqs spell it "kayak."

Rip tide — Where wind and tidal current oppose each other causing short, steep seas.

Russian Christmas — Christmas falls on January 7 by the Russian Orthodox calendar. New Year's is on January 14.

Schooner — Any fore and aft rigged sailing vessel whose masts are taller aft than forward.

Seiner — A vessel designed to fish a purse seine.

Setting — Getting gear overboard in an orderly fashion.

Single — A line running through a single pulley or block. No mechanical advantage.

Skiff — A small flat or V-bottom vessel, usually open.

Smokehouse — A small building where fish are hung for smoking.

Soundings — Mechanically or electronically measuring the depth of the water.

Sourdough — A type of dough where fermentation is used for leavening.

Splitting strap — A line or rope used to divide a bag of fish for easier hoisting.

Tally scow — A power scow which collects and tallies the fisherman's catch.

Teg'un — A harpoon point for hunting seals, used for taking the animals out of the water.

Trapline — The route that a trapper travels to set his traps.

Trawl — A towed sacklike net.

Tunnel stern — Where the bottom of a boat along the keel aft is concave to allow the vessel a shallower draft.

Tuquucissuun — A stabber to kill animals that are still alive when captured.

Tuunriq — Dancing and casting of spells by shamen.

Uluaq — Eskimo woman's knife.

Uyalget — A bird from the Bering Sea coast.

Waton — Russian-Native name for an edible mussel.

Web — The name for netting.

Weir — A fence across a stream to direct salmon so they may be counted for management purposes.

Wheel — Name for propeller of a vessel.

Whitefish — A large fish netted in the Yukon-Kuskokwim delta area for food.

Wings — The spread lateral edges of a trawl.

Yuungnaqsaraq cimirtuq — The way of life is changing.

List of Authors

Since 1974, junior high and high school students in eight communities in Southwestern Alaska have published a total of 4,000 pages in their publications *Kalikaq Yugnek, Kwikpagmiut, Tundra Marsh, Uutuqtwa,* and *Elwani.* Selecting 500 pages of that total was an arduous task. While every student could not have an entire article appear in *The Cama-i Book,* we feel each has contributed and ought to be recognized as authors.

KODIAK ISLAND

Trish Abston
Brenda Aga
Mario Agustin, Jr.
Yvonne Agustin
Nick Alpiak
Mark Alwert
D'Anne Amponin
Ed Amponin
Joann Amundsen
Laurie Amundsen
Sandy Amundsen
Bernice Anderson
Fred Antonson, Jr.
Joe Aramburo
Sherry Ardinger
Theresa Ardinger
Sheila Baglien
Craig Baker
David Baker
Teresa Barnes
Lucretia Beegle
Dan Benton
Diana Berestoff
Jeff Berg
Michelle Bergeron
Susan Berry
Don Biesen
Ken Bigelow
Cindy Blondin
Mimi Bonney

Liz Boucher
Steve Bradford
Fred Bradshaw
Lillian Bradshaw
Cliff Brandal
Tammy Branson
Thelma Brasie
Kris Brewster
Libby Brewster
Tissie Briggs
Susan Bruner
David Buettner
Doug Buettner
Kevin Bundy
Kyle Bundy
Bryon Burr
Naomi Burton
Darren Byler
Mike Cannon
Debbie Carlough
Theresa Carlough
Danny Carlson
Jean Carney
Todd Caroll
Fred Carver
Kathy Carver
Leonard Charliaga
Dave Chavez
Lori Chichenoff
Mike Chichenoff

Peter Chichenoff
Gerald Christensen
Ken Christensen
Wesley Christiansen
Andy Christofferson
Nova Chya
Scott Clark
Gerry Cobban
Steve Coleman
Paul Collar
Jeff Condon
Francis Costello
Pierre Costello
Richard Costello
Bernie Coury
Sue Covey
Dennis Cox
Deanne Craig
Tom Cubbege
Mike Curley
Jill Cuthbert
Diana Dahl
Greg Dahl
Walter Davis
Marlene Deater
Renee DeFrang
Gildo deGuzman
Eddie Delacruz
John Delgado
Jeff Delys

Paul Delys
Nick Demientieff
Peter Demientieff
Liz Denato
Joe Descloux
John DiBene
Cindy Dickey
Tony Dickey
Elaine Dinnocenzo
Linda Dinnocenzo
Kim Doctor
Linda Downs
Suzy Dyson
Tom Eggemeyer
Bob Ericson
Penni Erwin
Mary Eufemio
Minnie Eufemio
Debbie Evans
Dennis Evans
Brian Fairchild
Mitch Fairchild
Phil Ferris
Terri Fincher
Cheryl Fisk
Kelly Fitzgerald
Ernie Flanagan
Phyllis Flick
Fred Fogle
Bill Fox

Lori Francisco
Matt Freeman
Pam Frisbee
Dennis Frye
Scott Fuller
Laura Garcia
Amy Garoutte
Sherry Gibson
Ernest Gilbert
Lynn Gilliland
Anita Gilmore
Melchor Gloria
Brenda Gossage
Rhonda Gossage
Cindy Gowdy
Peyton Gray
Melissa Green
Mary Greene
Mike Greene
Bonnie Greenlee
Paul Greenlee
Eric Grosvold
Linda Gruel
Greg Guerra
Barb Gundrum
Tami Hajdu
Maria Haley
Jim Hansen
Kris Hansen
Lisa Harder
Peggy Hartman
Katie Heglin
Linda Heglin
Jim Hellemn
Larry Hellemn
Dennis Helms
Pam Helms
Jim Hicks
Ed Hochmuth
Joe Hochmuth
Shirley Hochmuth
Teresa Hochmuth
Toni Hoffat
Ken Hood
Susan Horn
Diane Houser
Marc Howard
Marci Howard
Renee Howell
Sean Huggins
Hugh Huleatt
Glenn Hunter
Jeff Hunter

Kelly Inga
Heidi Jacobson
Gwen Jarvela
Gordon Jensen
Joe Jensen
Suzanne Jensen
Dawn Jewett
Kim Jewett
Don Johnson
Heidi Johnson
Phil Johnson
Russ Johnson
Joe Katelnikoff
Robert Katelnikoff
Ron Kavanaugh
Laurel Kelly
Janeen Knight
Julie Koehnke
Laurie Koelin
Lana Kopun
Carol Kosbruk
Maria Kreta
Eva Kudrin
George Kudrin
John Lagasse
Phil Lagasse
Teresa Lagasse
Vivianne Lagasse
John Landers
Chris Langowski
Gene LeDoux
Jeff LeDoux
Shirley Lee
Buddy Leuder
Shawna Lindberg
Beth Lindsey
Rob Lindsey
Tracy Lockman
Rod Loewen
Patricia Logan
Sue Logan
Sonny Lohse
Charlie Lorenson
Gail Lowry
Jo Lowry
Sandy Lowry
Alvin Lucas
Janetta Lukin
Pam Luse
Agnes McCormick
John McCormick
Shelley McDaniel
Sandy McFarland

Kathleen McGlashan
Bronald McHenry
Jackie Madsen
Lee Mahle
Dennis Maloney
Peter Malutin
Buddy Martin
Karen Martin
Billy Mathis
Robbie Mathis
Debbie Maxwell
Mike Meehan
Lisa Mellon
Tommy Melovedoff
Cindy Merculief
Chris Metrokin
Heather Metrokin
Scott Metzbower
Tracey Metzbower
Bonnie Meunier
Yolanda Meyburg
John Miles
Mike Miles
Burt Miller
Michelle Milligan
Trish Milligan
Ward Milligan
Dan Moen
Toni Moffat
Kathy Monroe
Kim Montgomery
Lori Morton
Vince Mulcahy
Debbie Mullan
Diane Mullen
Ron Murray
Tony Murray
Alfred Naumoff
Eric Negus
Kirk Negus
Keith Nelson
Seldon Nelson
Kathy Nielsen
Tammi Nolan
Linda Nordgulen
Emil Norton
Kathy Noya
Jackie O'Donnoghue
Peter Olsen
Sandy Olson
Ila Omlid
Sherry Omlid
Val Osborn

Diane Oskolski
Tom Ossowski
Marie Oswalt
Jason Otto
Ilene Ourada
Ted Panamarioff
Laura Parish
Sandi Parnell
Pam Parsons
Anna Marie Pedersen
Eric Pedersen
Penny Pedersen
Susie Pedersen
Tona Perez
Gerald Pestrikoff
Geff Peterson
Jon Peterson
Kim Peterson
Roxana Pettet
Shannon Pettet
Verlin Pherson
Elizabeth Pohjola
Doug Powell
Patty Powell
Wanda Powell
Brian Pruitt
John Pruitt
Flay Putman
Ed Putnam
Scott Ranney
Billy Rastopsoff
Steve Reddy
Larry Redick
Tracey Reyes
Leah Rhoades
Vicki Rhoades
Ardina Rice
Robin Rickard
Sharon Rittenhouse
Rhonda Rodine
Clay Rounsaville
Donna Royal
Richard Rusher
Lloyd Russel
Chris Salazar
Barb Samson
Gwen Sargent
Wayne Sargent
Greg Saupe
Todd Schmidt
Robin Schwabe
Greg Shafer
Dennis Shangin

Lorraine Shangin
Lorreta Shangin
Dale Shuster
Laurie Simeonoff
Walter Simeonoff
Tina Simmons
Karen Sipple
Steve Sisler
Lars Skonberg
Theresa Skonberg
Esther Smiloff
Heidi Smith
Monya Smothers
Grant Stephens
Laurie Stephens
Terri Stokes
Alan Stover
Harold Strahle
Lynnette Strahle
Richard Strahle
Vicki Stratman
Donna Streeper
Brent Sugita
Cathy Sullivan
Brenda Suryan
John Swearingin
Cherie Swensen
Mike Tarr

Lynn Taylor
Marcie Taylor
Tina Terlaje
Dave Theideman
Leonard Thomas
Margo Thompson
Rick Thompson
Dave Thomson
Tim Titus
Cheryl Tobolic
Linda Tobolic
Dwayne Treat
Sandra Tussey
Leslie Van Zwaluwenburg
Amy Vogt
Thor Waage
Duchess Wallin
George Wallin
Kris Washburn
Kari Wasson
Rud Wasson
Richele Weaver
Mary Webber
Cindy Wheeler
Jim Whitlatch
Gina Williams
Kim Williams
Ernest Willie

Darryl Wilson
Gilbert Wilson
Janette Wilson
Jim Wilson
Marshall Wilson
Maryann Wilson
Mike Wilson
Ron Wilson
Shelli Winter
Caroline Wolkoff
Laura Wolkoff
Roy Wolkoff
Sharon Wolkoff
Shirley Wolkoff
Tom Wolkoff
Jeannie Woodruff
Mike Woodruff
Debbie Wurz
Elia Yagie
Billy York
Brenda Zeedar
Lisa Zimmerman

Teacher Advisor

David Kubiak

BRISTOL BAY REGION

Ronald Abalama
Sylvia Alford
Gerald Alto
Rodney Alto
Ruth Alto
Terri Alto
Valerie Alvarez
Amos Anderson
Bruce Anderson
Emily Anderson
Lorri Aspelund
North Aspelund
Shawn Aspelund
Matthew Bradford
Julie Caruso
Mel Coghill, Jr.
Sandra Coghill
Diana Cook
Roberta Deigh
Roxanne Deigh
Natalie Drew
Arthur Ernest

Gayle Gebhart
Gordon Grindle
Orville Groat
Mark Harrison
Bill Henriksen
Dennis Herrmann
Verna Herrmann
Carol Hester
David Hodgdon
Teresa Hodgdon
Walter Hodgdon
June Holstrom
Sheila Hutson
Alfred Ivanoff, Jr.
Artie Johnson, Jr.
Rosalie Johnson
Teresa Johnson
Charlotte Kie
Wanda Kie
Jodi King
Linda Lehman
Joe Lind

Laura Lind
Patrick Lind
Sheila Lind
Evelyn Mike
Janet Monsen
Dianne Moorcroft
Lori Murray
Mary Murray
Dale Myers
Elaine Myers
Pam Myers
Annette Nestegard
Marie Nestegard
Annie Newyaka
Kathy O'Hara
Tom O'Hara
Alec Peterson
Betty Mae Peterson
Kathy Peterson
Kathleen Pinette
Mike Pinette
Marlene Pope

Calvin Riddle
Al Ring
John Savo
Leslie Savo
Danny Seybert
Connie Spade
Sabrina Tibbetts
Terrel Tracy
Debbie Wassillie
Quentin White
Doreen Williams
Carla Wilson
Gloria Wilson
Julie Wilson
Jack Woods
Carl Zimin
Carvel Zimin
Randy Zimin

Teacher Advisors

Kurt Jaehning
Susan Tollefson

YUKON-KUSKOKWIM REGION

Fred Abraham
Margaret Abraham
Paul Abraham
Chet Adkins
Nancy Afcan
Doris Agayar
Mary Agayar
Paul Agnes
Bert Agwiak
Norman Agwiak
Betty Akerelrea
Clyde Aketachunak
Morris Akitalnok
David Albert
Bertha Alexie
Elena Alexie
Fritz Alexie
Nelson Alexie
Nick Alexie
Raymond Alexie
Steve Alexie
Ruth Aliralria
Sally Aliralria
Mary Aloysis
Donna Anaruk
Ina Anaver
Sam Anaver
Alice Andrew
Brian Andrew
Carl Andrew
Hannah Andrew
Joe Andrew
Josephine Andrew
Olga Andrew
Tim Andrew
Tommy Andrew
Josephine Andrews
Larry Andrews
Luci Andrews
Mary Andrews
Paul Andrews
Simon Andrews
Alice Andy
Mike Andy
Carrie Anvil
Ina Anvil
Alexie Askoak
Theresa Askoak
Nellie Attie
Mary Augustine

Henry Ayagalria
Laura Baijot
Lianna Baijot
Frank Bavilla
Sally Bavilla
Gerald Bean
Bruce Beans
Carol Beans
Doris Beans
Gladys Beans
Massa Beans
Norman Beans
Simon Beans
Ursula Beans
Carrie Beaver
Greta Beaver
Leo Beaver
Edna Beebe
Fritz Beebe
Francis Bell
John D. Bell
Joseph Berlin
James Billy
Heckman Bird
Lenora Bird
Lynn Bird
Larry Black
Olinka Bob
James Boguilikuk
Palassa Boots
Basil Borromeo
Moses Brink
Nora Brink
Sarah Brink
Sophia Brink
Jennifer Carl
John Carl
Ray Carl
Julie Carpenter
Annie Carter
Emma Carter
Nick Carter
Sally Carter
James Chaliak
Bessie Charles
David Charles
Lala Charles
Mary Charles
Bernice Charlie
Patrick Charlie

James Chase
Mildred Chase
Dorothy Chayalkun
John Chief
Arthur Chikigak
Boniface Chikigak
Martha Chikigak
Helen Chimegalrea
Paul Chimiugak
Yago Clark
Ham Cleveland
John Cleveland
Lucy Cleveland
Sally Cleveland
Sinka Crane
Sandy Curren
Cynthia David
Pam Demientieff
Sharon Dock
Linda Duny
Elizabeth Edwards
Ramona Edwards
Mary Egoak
Dan Ekamerak
Carrie Enoch
Jon Etter
Anna Evan
Joann Evan
Joseph Evan
Mary Evan
Nicholał Evan
Sophie Evan
Suzy Evan
Walter Evan
Darleen Evon
Cliff Faircloth
Ben Feenstra
David Fitka
Lena Fitka
Steve Fitka
Alberta Foss
Emma Foster
Carl Fox
Lucy Fox
Ralph Fox
Alice Francis
Diane Francis
Moses Fredrick
Ellen Friday
Annie Friendly

Emily Friendly
Michael Frye
Dan Galila
Annie George
Helen George
Larry George
Lucy George
Peter George
Stanley George
Louisa Gilman
Katie Green
Robert Greene
Stan Greene
Chris Gregory
Frank Gregory
Julia Gregory
Julie Gregory
Liz Gregory
Margaret Gregory
Matilda Gregory
Paul Gregory
Cora Hale
Terri Hale
Toni Hand
Marita Hanson
Martina Hanson
Albert Harry
Alma Harry
Carol Heckman
George Heckman
Louise Heckman
John Henry
Lou Henry
Ole Henry
Viola Hill
Murphy Hoelscher
Barbara Hoffman
Earlene Hoffman
Eliza Hooper
Nellie Hooper
Ernie Hootch
Gail Hootch
Herman Hootch
Joanne Hootch
Teddy Hootch
Wilma Hootch
Phillip Horn
Zena Hunt
John Hunter
Ole Hunter

Herman Immamuk
Anna Issac
Charlie Issac
Elsie Jack
Carol Jackson
Wally Jackson
Minnie Jacob
Oscar Jacob
Gertrude Jacobs
Liz Jacobs
Mary Jacobs
Charles James
Connie James
Eula James
Mary James
Anna Jenkins
Nick Jenkins
Bertha Jimmy
Delores Jimmy
Loretta Jimmy
Rachel Jimmy
Calvin Joe
Dorothy Joe
Elizabeth Joe
Francis Joe, Jr.
Yolanda Joe
Dorothy Johnson
Oscar Johnson
Robert Johnson
Roland Johnson
Dennis Jones
Dan Jorgensen
Chris Joseph
Fred Joseph
Joe Joseph
Minnie Joseph
Nita Joseph
Rose Joseph
Steve Jumbo
Amos Kaganak
Aaron Kameroff
Ellen Kameroff
Gretchen Kameroff
Leota Kameroff
Angela Kamkoff
David Kasaiuli
Elizabeth Kasaiuli
Cecilia Kasayak
David Kasayuli
Janet Kasayuli
Sam Kasayuli
McLaughlin Kashatok
Edna Kassock

Becky Katchak
John Kawagley
Susan Keene
Chris Kelly
Sally Kernak
Humphrey Keyes
Jack Kinegak
Gabe King
Carl Kiunya
Julie Kiunya
Alice Kokrine
Gabriel Kokrine
Xavier Kokrine
Rachel Kolerok
Shelly Kristovich
Joanne Kylook
Rita Kylook
Roberta Kylook
Benita Lake
Fred Lamont
Arlene Landlord
Eugene Landlord
Matilda Landlord
Balassa Larson
Huey Larson
John Larson
Nicholai Larson
Wanda Lawrence
Willie Lawrence
Margaret Lewis
Mary Lincoln
Lucy Lomack
Barnie Long
Jacob Long
Sarah Lott
Leonty Lupie
Florence McIntyre
Evelyn Maloy
Samson Mann
Louie Manutoli
Christopher Mark
Lou Mark
Paul Mark
Elena Martin
Lucy Martin
Nancy Martins
Evelyn Mathlaw
Ricky Mathlaw
Becky Maxie
Carl Maxie
Paul Maxie
Emma Michael
Alexie Mochin

Lena Mochin
Albert Moore
Esau Moore
Linda Moore
Bernice Morgan
Carl Moses
Carolyn Moses
Joe Moses, Jr.
Julia Moses
Richard Moses
Pat Murphy
Colleen Mute
Andrew Myers
Pauline Myers
Agatha Napoka
Becky Napoka
Hannah Napoka
Jacob Napoka
Olga Napoka
Agatha Napoleon
Becky Napoleon
Eva Nashonak
Curt Nelson
Doreen Nelson
Frank Nelson
Gordon Nelson
Walter Nelson
Chris Nevak
Mary Nevak
Carl Nicholai
Ella Nicholai
Esther Nichols
Florence Nichols
Nick Nichols
Balassa Nick
Joseph Nick
Susan Nick
Mollia Nicori
Marie Noah
Anna Nook
Harley Noratok
Helen O'Donnell
Sharon O'Donnell
Linda Oktoyak
Sally Olsen
Greg Olson
Ken O'Malley
Richard Otto
Phillip Paniyak
Robert Panruk
Charlie Past
Elma Patrick
Carolyn Patsy

Anna Paul
James Paul
Jenny Paul
Jimmy Paul
Laurita Paul
Mary Paul
Paul Paul
Paul James Paul
Ray Paul
Sara Paul
Olivia Paulson
Marie Pavilla
Tina Pavilla
Frank Pete
Gary Pete
Joe Pete
Xavier Pete
Chris Peter
Julius Peter
Martha Peter
Norman Peter
Phyllis Peter
Francis Peters
Emmon Peterson
Laura Peterson
Anna Phillip
Dorothy Phillip
Elevina Phillip
Esther Phillip
Joe Phillip
Martha Phillip
Sarah Phillip
Tootsie Phillip
Harvey Pitka
Lena Pitka
Theresa Pitka
Emma Pleasant
Ferdinand Pleasant
Fred Polty
Charlie Post
Rita Prunes
Willie Raphael
Charlie Redfox
Chris Redfox
John Redfox
Mike Riley
Lillian Rivers
Eleanor Roland
Bert Romer
Carla Romer
Ted Rose
Elia Sallaffie
Kevin Sam

Carol Sara
Martha Savage
Judy Seton
Donna Shantz
Sheri Shelp
Anthony Sheppard
Stanley Sheppard
Theresa Sheppard
Jewel Simon
Rose Simon
Irene Sims
Nellie Slats
Richard Slats
Howard Slwooko, Jr.
Clyde Smith
Donna Smith
Emily Smith
Emma Smith
George Smith
Irene Smith
John Smith
Johnny Smith
Polly Smith
Teddy Smith
Harry Stanislaus
Lovey Stephanoff
Olga Steven
Steven Steven
Willie Steven
Davis Stone
Ole Stone
Steve Stone
Susan Sundown
Fannie Temple
Pavilla Thomas
Bertha Tikiun
Grace Tikiun
Wilson Tikiun

Sophie Tinker
Henry Tobeluk
John Tobeluk, Jr.
Billy Tom
Suzanne Tom
Clara Tommy
Maggie Tommy
Aggie Trader
Diane Trader
Katherine Tulim
Dede Twitchell
Martha Tyson
Linda Ulak
Cheryl Underwood
Stanley Vaska
Mae Walker
Darlene Walters
Ernest Waskey
Olinka Wassalie
Alice Wassilie
Anna Wassilie
Jerry Sam Wassillie
John D. Wassillie
Koby Wassillie
Peter Wassillie
Helen Wasuli
Carol Watson
Jessie Westcoast
Lucy Westcoast
John Weston
Carl White, Jr.
Elena White
Clara Wilde
Albert Williams
Dora Williams
Helen Williams
Tina Williams
Albert Willie

Margaret Willie
Olga Willie
Charlotte Wilson
Clarence Wilson
Jim Wise
Jacinta Wiseman
Mary Woods

Teacher Advisors

Roger Adams
Mary Alexie
Peter Atchak
Patti Ayuluk
James Chaliak
Doug Glynn
Mary Gregory
Betsy Hart
Priscilla Hooper
Anne Lewis
William Mailer
Kirk Meade
Valorie Miller
Michael Murray
Alexander Nicori, Jr.
Pat Nysewander
Grant Shimanek
Rene Simao
Sue Strouse
Jacob Tobeluk
Deanna Tressler
Tony Umugak
Debra Vanasse
Sue Warren
Dave Williams
Jean Young